RIVIERA
A Novel About the
Cannes Film Festival

RIVIERA

A Novel About the
Cannes Film Festival

by
Robert Sydney Hopkins

WILLIAM MORROW AND COMPANY, INC.
New York *1980*

Library of Congress Cataloging in Publication Data

Hopkins, Robert S
    Riviera.

    I. Title.
PZ4.H7955Ri   [PS3558.0636]   813'.54   79-26825
ISBN 0-688-03618-X

Printed in the United States of America

First Edition

1 2 3 4 5 6 7 8 9 10

Book Design by Michael Mauceri

To Knox and Kitty for labor beyond the call of duty . . . and to Carla.

RIVIERA
A Novel About the Cannes Film Festival

≡ *Chapter 1*—Cannes, a Beginning

Madmen, charlatans, but damn few fools.

The thought was Brialt's as he stood near the old port watching the graceful *pointu* chug in one by one from the dark fishing grounds beyond the harbor entrance.

What truly drew these people here, the thousands who had already begun to flood the city?

The new breed who didn't understand the Festival as he did had their own sure explanation for all that was about to pass: money. Money brought the movie people to Cannes these two weeks each spring. And because they arrived, so came the others: the tourists and camp followers, the nomads, whores, and vendors. Without the buying and selling, they said, there would be no Festival. And with the precision of a calculator they would argue that a film winning the Palme d'Or was worth an extra million at the box office, or two or three.

Brialt smiled uncomfortably, for so much of it was true. As gravity was to the planets, money drove the Festival. Fortunes would be made these next fifteen days in Cannes. Careers would rise or fall behind the closed doors of deluxe hotel suites or on the sleek yachts already dotting the Mediterranean out beyond the treelined Croisette. These next score days this gentle city would be the Festival's witness, abused by wealth, unreasoned hope, chicanery, good luck and bad.

Brialt shook his head and turned to retrace his steps, wanting to reach the hotel before the girl awakened alone. He had had no better luck explaining the Festival to himself this year than in years past. Perhaps the Festival wasn't a single thing but something different to all who came here, a mirror reflecting what each brought with them in spirit.

His laughter came so sharply that a grizzled fisherman tending a net close by glanced up then away, dismissing him as an outsider. It is you, Brialt, likely to serve himself up as the fool these next two weeks. But the point is, he confessed, you are no longer sure about even that.

Exactly fifty-five hours earlier and seven thousand miles away, a metallic tan Rolls-Royce was seen turning at excessive speed from the Pacific Coast Highway onto Malibu Canyon Road.

The witness was an L.A. County sheriff named Farren, who had picked up the speeding car west of the old Rindge property near the Malibu pier. The single occupant of the car was a man. The license plate read PEDRO I.

He halfway expected the Rolls to slant left toward the gates at the entrance to the movie colony. Instead, it slowed enough to make a right turn onto Malibu Canyon Road, which wasn't such a good name because it didn't run along the canyon at all but snaked its way up the chaparral-covered mountainside. Farren flashed his reds, then hit the squealer. When PEDRO I didn't even blink, a hard, familiar feeling began to stir in the pit of Farren's stomach. He radioed his dispatcher for help.

On the long series of narrow switchback curves he tried several times to close on the Rolls, sensing the heavy, aggressive foot hard on the accelerator of the car in front of him.

As his report would later note, when he came out of the single two-lane tunnel at the nine-hundred-foot elevation mark, the Rolls was gone.

It was then he spotted a young, bearded man with a bright green rucksack standing near the low stone safety wall at the roadside. Part of the wall was gone, as if someone had punched out half a mouthful of teeth. Farren knew. Listen to your guts, he had been telling himself. He braked the car, made a grab for the fire extinguisher, and began to run.

The Rolls was there all right, like some crumpled candy wrapper below in the canyon bottom. The bearded young man swallowed heavily and gargled up a single decipherable sentence, which was, quote, it wasn't no accident.

The lone occupant of the automobile was pronounced DOA at St. John's Hospital in Santa Monica at 4:35 P.M. He was identified as Pedro Lehman, aged sixty-seven, of a Mapleton Drive address, Beverly Hills. The identification was confirmed by Harold J. Donnenfeld, attorney for the deceased.

Thirty minutes later County Sheriff Farren received some sage advice from his agitated watch commander. "You better have this one straight. Every detail. 'Cause you're about to get your face all over TV."

Siri heard the sound of the telephone far at the other end of the house.

She had been in the utility room, surveying the mound of purchases from her raid on Rodeo Drive, something she hadn't done in years. She was still uncomfortable in public and would have avoided the entire ordeal if less than forty-eight hours before Pedro hadn't taken her hands in his and, with mystifying solemnity, drawn her to sit next to him in this same room. "They're showing some of my films at Cannes this year. Some sort of tribute they give old horses before they shoot them."

"Nonsense, Pedro. You should have said something."

"I wanted it to be a surprise. The Festival people have invited us and are making a big to-do over the new film. We up to it?"

"Of course," she responded, reluctance running through her in a surge. Pedro had never looked more exhausted, so much his age.

"You'll love Cannes, Siri. The flowers, the air. God knows what you'll think of the people."

Something distant and uncertain was in his voice.

So she steeled herself for Beverly Hills with two very dry martinis and made the raid, working her way from Giorgio's to Gucci and choosing a pair of lightweight sports jackets for Pedro at Neiman's.

She had just unboxed the last gown when she looked up to find the birdlike figure of May Chan, watching her from the doorway. The Chans had been with Pedro since the first Mrs. Lehman. "The telephone is for you, missus," she said, nodding toward the extension phone in an airy way that had always struck Siri as so goddamned superior.

She picked up the phone to hear a familiar, resonant voice say, "It's Harold, Siri. . . ."

"Pedro's not back yet, Harold. The picture has been a goddamn trial, and he's still working for a final cut."

"Siri. . . ." Donnenfeld's voice caught, its tone triggering something shallow and dark in her mind. She had always known that one day she would receive a call like this. "Siri, there's been an accident."

She remembered little of what followed. Nothing of the drive to the hospital or of the young doctor's exact words that added up to Pedro dead. Only that it occurred to her maybe it was the trouble with the whole nasty town.

Where else, when a man was dead or dying, did they call his lawyer before they called his wife?

Teddy Kenrick nosed his bright red sports coupe into the right-hand bend onto Mulholland, tempted to ignore the too-insistent buzzing of the telephone near his right hand.

He answered it with a sharp "Kenrick," and heard Elsa say, "If you've something solid, grab on. Pedro Lehman's dead." Elsa had been with him long enough to know he wanted bad news straight and unadorned. "Larry Rentzler was visiting a friend at St. John's in Santa Monica when they brought him in."

"When?" Kenrick asked.

"Larry just called. An hour, outside."

"Anyone else involved?"

"If you mean Siri, no one. Not even another car."

"One man, one car, at four in the afternoon."

"I don't want to believe it," Elsa said.

"I'm on my way back to the studio," Kenrick said, putting the coupe into a tight U-turn. Already the sequence of what had to be done was ordering itself in his mind. "Find Rentzler and have him in my office soonest, along with whoever in publicity is handling the Lehman film. Then try Fiona MacCauley. Make a date with her to screen what we have on the final cut tomorrow morning. Early."

"Got it."

"Then call Aron Archer in New York, his home if you have to, and drop the bomb on him."

"What about Siri . . . Mrs. Lehman?"

He remembered the death of his wife, Anne, the shock and shadowy year that followed. The last thing that would have helped Siri was one more phrase of sorrow, especially from him. The mention of Kenrick's name in Siri's presence had more than once launched her off on one of her well-reported sieges of temper. "Offer her any assistance we can in the studio's name, and leave me out of it."

"And the Festival?"

"Where do we stand?"

"On a flight to Nice via Paris seventy-two hours from now with a reservation in Cannes at the Grand."

"I'll make it," Kenrick said. He damn well had to. "Better let the Festival people know about Lehman, the Festival director . . ."

"Brialt," Elsa provided. "First name Philippe."

". . . tell him we're still planning to show the new Lehman film." If we have a final cut, he added mentally. How many other ifs had Lehman's death added to Kenrick's list?

"It would have been something," he heard Elsa say, "seeing the two of them again in public."

At least half the equation was correct, but he spared Elsa the opinion. Lehman's last three pictures had taken a financial bath, and the studio's coproduction of his latest was hanging over Kenrick's head like the proverbial ax. Siri hadn't made a picture in nearly five years, but he could still have built a project around her in twenty minutes by telephone. "Yes, Elsa darling, it would have been grand."

Damn Lehman, Kenrick thought. He had died about a year too late.

Nicky Deane heard the good news on the massage table. An hour of racquetball with Beno the Pig had relieved a considerable hunger for combat that most people thought was purely physical. It had been a game intermittently roughhouse, with Deane tormenting Beno by dinks and careful lobs. Until Beno, in frustration, smashed his racquet to bits against the wall, and Nicky Deane walked from the court, smiling and a winner. Nicky Deane had the patience of time itself.

The girl they sent him was a blonde with hair trimmed closer than he had asked for. He took her chin in his hands, turning the face this way and that, judging her a good likeness, but nothing great. The girl resisted him, enough to show she didn't enjoy being handled like meat. He liked that. When she finally settled down to work, Nicky Deane shut his eyes, giving in to the hands moving over his body. "Anything special you want, you ask." Nicky told her to shut up because he didn't want that voice to ruin things. He closed his eyes again and tried to remember. Already the girl had worked her way down the ropy muscles of his shoulders, along his back, past the solid, thickening waist, to his buttocks.

She focused there now, tantalizing the sensitive regions with careful fingers. She had just begun to use her skillful hands in a more imaginative way when the cubicle door opened and Beno the Pig walked in, nude and sweating from their game. He carried a telephone.

"Get out, you schmuck," Nicky Deane growled. "Take a shower before you stink up the club."

"A real Nicky Gardenia," Beno said, bending to plug the phone jack into a wall fitting. A dark purplish bruise the exact size of a racquet ball marked the pale skin of his ample rump. He straightened, taking in the spectacle in progress with black button eyes. "You'll want this," he said, and held out the phone with a malicious grin.

Under Nicky Deane's returning gaze Beno's grin faded. He couldn't read Nicky very well because the eyes told you nothing. Like a street urchin's back in the old place, big and dark and too beautiful for a full-grown man. That was it: a woman's eyes, with long, thick lashes that fluttered when he talked. But behind them was something dead and cold.

Nicky snatched the phone from Beno's hand while the girl retreated to wait. She wore a nylon tank suit, and Nicky liked what he saw until the girl turned and he caught a smile at the corners of her mouth. She was laughing, teasing him. Later he'd see how much she'd laugh. His hands, too, knew a few tricks.

"Where you been hiding?" said the voice on the other end of the line. "I been having you paged."

"Trying to relax."

"I know how you people relax. I know that town."

Nicky Deane's eyes stayed on the girl, thought how it would be when he peeled off the tank suit, slowly, like a snake slipping out of its skin. "I'll send you a report. I'm busy, Meyer."

"So listen a minute. Like the good friend I am, I called to make sure you've covered your ass. Because some people we both know are going to be looking at you and me very close."

"Meyer, I like you. Somebody asks you the time and you tell them how to make a clock."

"Pedro Lehman's dead," he heard Meyer Tilman say. "Maybe you like that better."

Rod Donner felt the crunch of impact and saw the familiar black ball explode behind his eyes. He hit the ground hard, as a small, reasonable voice inside his head began to whisper a message he decided to pay attention to. Donner, the little voice said, you are much too old for this kind of fun.

And too damn fragile. Three concussions, a twice-separated right shoulder, and a pair of stiff football knees that would never permit him to spin lightly on the dance floor again. He was a living testament to his belief that the best thing to happen to a new generation of college fullbacks was the demise of the single-wing offense. If he had tried to explain it to any of the five great hulks of flesh looking down upon him, they would have figured him a contemporary of Rockne or Grange. Not quite.

"Hey, man, it's only a game," he heard someone say.

"Walk it off, Donner," came another voice.

Donner spit out a mixed mouthful of beach sand and blood and accepted the hand up from the immovable object he had just tried to pass through—a junior tackle from USC named Al Medwick.

What had begun as a friendly game of beach football evolved inevitably into a testing ground. "Your own worst enemy, Donner," Rayna had warned him. "That's going to be our problem at Cannes."

But he had been holding his own, despite twenty years and then some on any of the other players—until he caught a quick down-and-out and turned upfield to find the blur of Medwick closing in, low and full steam. The dip of a shoulder had been instinctive. And Medwick accepted the challenge.

"Take it easy on me, will you, Rod?" Medwick said, limping away. "I still got another year on scholarship."

Donner hurt, but seeing Medwick told him he had done

no worse than stay even. The thought lessened the pain.

He saw the report of Lehman's death on the six o'clock news. He snapped on the old black-and-white TV the landlord furnished with the room, still flushed from the four-mile run along the beach. No booze and a year of training, as hard as any year in his life, had pushed his weight down eight pounds below what it had been more than two decades past, when he had played for the Red Man at UCLA. Physically he felt as ready for Cannes as he could be.

At the mention of Lehman's name he sat forward. The newscaster's voice ran behind a zoom shot of a twisted automobile in a canyon bottom. There was an interview, of sorts, with a bearded, mildly hysterical young man clinging to a green rucksack while a microphone was thrust into his face by an insistent female reporter. "I just said he was looking for it, that's all," the young man said, trying to move away. You think a suicide? the reporter pursued. "Nobody drives like that unless they're looking for it."

Donner sat back, not sure he agreed. He had driven that road plenty, from the studios in the Valley over the Santa Monica Mountains to the Colony strung out along the beach at Malibu. A bad stretch, stoned, blind drunk, or a mixture of the two.

The TV report cut to a shot of Lehman's wife, Siri, unmistakable even with a scarf over her fine blond hair. The camera caught her leaving a hospital with a man at her elbow, ducking into a waiting car while police held back the crowd.

Donner recognized the tall, stooped figure of Hugh Remy, Lehman's longtime associate. Remy was a tough old crow who preferred to work quietly around the edges of a film and leave the spotlight to Lehman. As the minicam closed in on Siri, Remy angrily tried to cover the lens. A moment later the car was gone.

Donner had the distinction he still considered unfortunate of having played opposite Siri in her first screen role: two and a half minutes in a western made by her future husband, Pedro Lehman. One scene that demonstrated what Siri was about to become, a star, superstar, megastar, whatever superlative they tagged on these days. The scene had also shown a side of Donner he tried not to think about—an actor pressing forty with a range one character wide and a face that showed the considerable excesses of his life, including the three brawls he could remember. A face not easily forgotten, in any case.

There were still prints around of the film shown for laughs at those private screenings the people at the top of the industry took for a night on the town. Lehman had been too good then not to know exactly what he was doing, including the forty-five seconds of Siri added later—a sparkling monologue dropped in with crosscuts back to Donner looking stupefied and not very bright. Hell, maybe he hadn't been.

Because he watched the scene later with a half dozen drinks in him and went out looking for the villain, a scriptwriter named Hal Silver. He found, instead, his own agent, reasoned that he was part of the conspiracy, and punched him in the eye. Even drunk, Donner had known Kenrick was the wrong man to punch. He dropped Donner's contract like a hot stone, not that the drop was so far. Two years later Kenrick was running a studio and Donner hadn't worked a day since in the United States.

But he had worked, plenty, grabbing at straws. Twenty-four pictures in six years. Films in Italy, Spain, Yugoslavia, Germany, Australia, Ceylon, Singapore. Films indistinguishable in Donner's mind. Action-adventure epics on shoestring budgets for percentages you never saw and checks you would race to the bank to cash. Violence and blood, and casts that spoke their dialogue in whatever language they knew, with voices dubbed in later, all sounding out of a tin can. It had been Donner's route until the booze and too much weight had ended even that.

A different man now, he prayed so. Watching the car

21

holding Siri speed away through the crowds, he remembered all the things he hated. The photographers, the people sucking you dry. Yet here he was climbing back into the arena.

Donner rose and turned off the TV, telling himself, again, that he knew exactly why: nothing to do with Malibu real estate or shiny cars or all the other things he had surrounded himself with to make up for the real stuff that was missing.

He thought of the death of Pedro Lehman, figuring the grin that spread across his face must have looked borrowed from the devil. One less person to square with.

He dug out the expensive new suitcase and began to pack.

≡ *Chapter 3*—Cannes Minus One, France

Philippe Brialt snatched the yellow sheet of telex announcing the death of Pedro Lehman from his desk top and whirled to glare at the freshly painted salmon pink wall of his office in the Palais des Festivals.

Eight years as *délégué général* of the Cannes Film Festival should have given him a detachment from the crises that were the only sure thing he could expect in the fifteen days ahead. Yet it was the second time that day he had faced the announcement of a death. And despite the fact that, granted, it was death at long distance, a formless premonition of disaster had taken hold of him. He looked down to find the sheet of telex visibly shaking in his hand.

The face of that first anonymous dead man had greeted him from the back pages of the *Nice-Matin* he had bought that morning at a kiosk on the Croisette. Not an unpleasant face except for a gray, lifeless aura.

This unfortunate had been found on a vacant plot of land near Nice Airport, the cause of his demise unreported. Photos of such cases were published with disconcerting frequency in the local newspapers in hopes of finding a friend or relative who could make identification. But imagine the shock in turning a page in search of a football score and there be confronted with the half-open eyes and opaque retinas of someone you knew.

Brialt had closed the newspaper and walked hurriedly on, forcing his mind to other things.

Already along the palm-lined Croisette—the broad boulevard curving along Cannes's beachfront—there were signs that the International Festival du Film was indeed to begin in thirty-six hours, whether he and his people were ready or not. Workmen were busily planting bright flowers, while overhead, corps of electricians were mounting the lighted display panels that would soon advertise films brought to Cannes from around the world.

To his right the front of the stately old Carlton Hotel was already transformed into a gaudy façade of film advertisements, flashing lights, and cycloramas. A few days hence this still-tranquil promenade would have the look of a battlefield.

A block ahead the sight of the newly lettered "Festival du Film," high above the glass windows of the Festival Hall lobby, brought Brialt a stifled, resigned sigh. For the first time since he had directed the Festival he had no feeling at all about the two weeks that stretched before him, about nothing except Katherine.

And he hadn't the slightest guilt that the woman who had drawn his mind and body into realms long forgotten was not his wife. Indeed, not his wife, but a woman twenty-three years his junior, startlingly lovely, and, most unexpectedly, an American.

They had met six weeks before in the small restaurant he frequented near the permanent Festival offices in Paris. Within three hours they were in bed together in the small, cramped apartment she kept on the rue de Braque. Running his hand along the fine curve of her back, marveling at the fragrances of her youthful body, he knew better than to look too deeply into the mystery of sexual attraction. He wasn't a handsome man, he knew, although he had managed to postpone the anticipated sag of middle age thanks to a careful diet and a twice-weekly regimen of swimming and squash. That his male powers were intact and functioning, after so many dormant years, had been amply demonstrated by his response to the girl's seemingly insatiable desire. "You're a bull, Philippe, in gentleman's clothing. I sensed it the moment we met." And by all that was observable he might well have been.

They had taken the Blue Train down from Paris three days before, the heady fragrance of the Côte d'Azur only sharpening his appetites. A look, her most innocent touch could stir him instantly erect. He could now look back upon the years he'd wasted in airport lounges and musty screening rooms, tending to the endless, enervating tasks of Festival administration, with the horror of a man who finally knew what time was worth.

He was even considering a fresh attack on the novel begun years earlier while he was still a film critic. The novel he abandoned when he had taken the easier path of marriage to Monique and the series of deskbound positions that had earned him a comfortable living and the reputation among his peers as a sensible administrator. Thanks to Katherine, the words now seemed a death knell.

Thus, telling not even Katherine, the week previously he announced to a stunned Festival president his decision: This would be his last Festival.

"Don't be hasty," the president implored. "Think, Philippe. Take some time."

"I've already taken too much."

That morning he had recalled with some pleasure the president's ordinarily wooden expression finally registering shock when, ahead, he saw Claude Durand wave to him from the steps of the Festival Hall. A yellow sheet of telex flapped in one hand as though it were aflame. "From Los Angeles and signed Kenrick. I'm afraid our homage has become a requiem."

"Lehman?"

"Dead in an auto accident. You know how the Americans drive." Durand made a sharp, disgusted expellation of breath.

Muscular and thick-necked, Durand was a newspaperman by trade, seconded to the Festival each spring by the French

Press Association. His task was the Bureau des Comédiens, the Festival office mantled with the questionable honor of attending to the personalities and VIPs arriving daily like a changing tide. In the next weeks Durand would deal with stars who signed for meals, jewelry, and new automobiles in expectation that the Festival would find their presence worth every expense. He would face vendettas, professional and private, shoplifting, credit improprieties at the casinos, pretenders, illness, breakdown, and an occasional suicide or rape. To Durand the cable announcing the death of Pedro Lehman was nothing more than the premature arrival of business as usual.

"Damn," Brialt swore, trying to gauge how Lehman's death might damage the prestige of the Festival.

If this was to be his last, he didn't intend it to be a monument to his poor management. He spoke to Durand.

"Cable our Mr. Kenrick that we are continuing with the Lehman tribute as planned, including the final night's premiere. And, Durand, pray this isn't an omen."

Brialt later would reflect, how curious, at his mature stage in life, the extent to which he was capable of deceiving himself.

≡ *Chapter 4*—Cannes Minus One—California

Teddy Kenrick rose at the first boarding call for Air France Flight 061, Los Angeles to Paris direct, and beckoned across the passenger lounge to Aron Archer.

His elegantly tailored financial vice-president was, at that moment, wedged into a Formica-walled telephone cubicle, making his third call to the New York office since they had arrived at the airport. He forestalled Kenrick with a wave of his hand and spoke angrily into the mouthpiece.

Kenrick smelled trouble.

Archer had arrived two days before on the heels of Lehman's death, and for reasons of his own Kenrick met him at the airport. On the surface they were an unlikely pair of conspirators. Archer was the product of old Boston money, Harvard, and the upper echelons of corporate finance; Kenrick, a working-class suburb not ten miles away. His had been a scramble up through the agency business with a lateral jump, far up the ladder, to the studio. But these next two weeks at Cannes they were conspirators.

Greeting Archer at the airport, Kenrick wondered if Aron was up to what lay ahead. Too many Wall Street lunches and the self-imposed pressure were beginning to show. He was not yet forty, but Aron Archer's thinning blond hair was almost silver, the skin of his longish face the texture of pale wax. Shaking hands, Kenrick caught the distinct aroma of alcohol. "Where are we on the Lehman film?" Archer asked immediately. "If it's in trouble, so are you and I."

"Lehman always did have a nice sense of the dramatic."

"I was right then. Damn," Archer hissed under his breath. "It couldn't be a worse time."

Kenrick had answered the question about Lehman's film for himself earlier that morning. He had screened all the footage to date on Lehman's final cut with Fiona MacCauley, a matronly sixtyish woman who was as talented a film editor as there was in the business.

The slow shake of her head confirmed his own judgment. "The worst kind of film, Teddy. The toughest to come into late, just in case that's why I'm here. It's an almost-could-be."

The film had begun as a big, ambitious project, the kind Lehman had once handled with ironlike control. It was intended as a classical musical built on contemporary themes; publicity began an early puff campaign, mentioning *Showboat*, *West Side Story*, and *Saturday Night Fever* all in the same breath, and everyone crossed his fingers.

It had gone sour from the beginning: accidents on location, a mushrooming budget, the firings. But Lehman's company had raised half the financing, and Kenrick had reluctantly ridden it out, recognizing all the signs. That morning, as he and Fiona watched the story unroll, the cumulative effect was apparent to them both—the bad taste, the camera angles gone wrong, the errors of emphasis. And their star managed to look like a greasy kid with a crater in his chin instead of the dimple that had cost them a million and a half. Pieced together, it was a catastrophe. Either Lehman's talent was gone or he had purposely assembled the ultimate bad joke in film history. Kenrick had himself a *Cleopatra*. "So what do we do?" he asked Fiona.

Fiona MacCauley couldn't remember a time when she had seen Kenrick at a loss for a course of action. There were those among her colleagues who would have savored the moment. Kenrick didn't court popularity, yet she liked the man, appreciated his directness. The people who called him the Iceman were generally those who had promised Kenrick something, then failed to deliver. He was merciless with pretenders. But he also paid top dollar without quibble if he judged you were worth it and backed his confidence by taking advice. "Get some new positives, and start from scratch," she said. "And hope what Lehman threw out is better than this. How much time do I have?"

"We're screening it the final night at Cannes."

"Thanks a whole helluva lot."

Kenrick had briefly considered pulling it from the Festival. But any film withdrawn at Cannes incurred the wrath of the Festival committee and its *délégué général,* Philippe Brialt. Worse, there would be the inevitable rumors of forthcoming disaster, usually, as were most rumors at Cannes, absolutely true. And there was always Fiona MacCauley, who had saved more mediocre films than their directors would ever admit. Kenrick knew that if the first ten days of the Festival went according to plan, it wouldn't matter whether the film was a bust or not. By the time it was shown he would have made his play and won or lost. It wouldn't matter a damn, he told himself.

But the end of the Festival was two weeks away, and he saw no reason to admit how much trouble the Lehman film was in, even to Aron Archer.

Driving out of the airport two days before, he had walked a fine verbal line.

"The truth is we don't have a film yet, Aron. Lehman was trying for a final cut, and I've people on it flat out."

"No hunches?"

"Doubtless one of the great film experiences of our time."

Archer looked over to find Kenrick grinning. The trouble with Kenrick's smile was that it disguised more than it revealed. Four years ago he had been the youngest studio head in the business. His face was tanned and still boyish, one of those true children of California who would stay all trim and fit until he fell, smiling, into his coffin.

But to have called Kenrick's face open would have invited a dangerous misjudgment of the man. Kenrick wasn't open. He was closed tight, as self-contained and distant as anyone Archer had ever encountered, even more so since the death of his lovely wife some three years before.

Few people who knew Kenrick during those times noticed the well-concealed signs of pain, his pretense of trying to keep his work at the studio separate from the personal life that was dissolving around him. When the pretense did slip, those around him kept the secret, ignored the times when he would sit immobile at his desk, red-eyed and drained. So what if the man had found some solace outside himself, gambling, it was said? Who knew what else? Aron Archer understood what pressure unrelieved could do to a man. But in some perverse manner it eased his mind to witness that Kenrick, despite abundant industry opinion to the contrary, was human after all.

"I couldn't care less about Lehman's film as a film," Archer countered irritably. "It is a reflection of our credibility. If we're to make our move at Cannes, then we must leave no doubt in the right minds we're worth as much money on our own as we have been to the studio."

"Cold feet?"

Archer smiled, his pale blue eyes avoiding contact. "Actually, old chum, at this moment I could put a bullet into our corporate president and never think twice. A model boardroom assassin. He'll piece it together, you know. Stiner isn't as slow as he pretends."

Kenrick was sure of it. Parent company president Mal Stiner had come in, smiling, with the takeover of the studio four years before, a designate of the East Coast financier who had bailed the company out. The sour-faced chairman of the board had once called Stiner an ordinary, hirable, $300,000-a-year professional manager, meaning he could have bought a dozen Stiners from the pages of the *Wall Street Journal*.

Kenrick thought otherwise. Stiner learned fast, and his meddling always had its purpose. If there was a potential flaw in Stiner's judgment process, it was that he had let himself fall in love with the movie business.

"What Stiner does or doesn't do won't matter if we move fast enough at Cannes," Kenrick retorted. "Are you in or out, Aron? The moment of truth."

Kenrick had planted the idea months before, delicately, a what-if game of speculation. Later it became in earnest: the idea of breaking away to form their own studio. "What is a studio anyway?" he had argued then. "Sound stages? Real estate? Joe Kennedy said it years ago when he was running RKO. This is the only business in the world where the assets put on their hats at the end of the day and go home. A few key people make this place work. Why not do it for ourselves?" It sounded good. So good Kenrick was tempted to believe it. The planned breakaway at Cannes was only part of Kenrick's intention, the payoff something he shared with no one.

But over the past months Aron Archer had begun to see the breakaway idea, embellishing it here and there until he'd made it his own. But always he had withheld a final commitment, continuing to probe Kenrick's motives, looking for something beyond the obvious that Kenrick suspected he sensed but couldn't find.

With Kenrick's challenge two days before, Archer had sighed and leaned back in the car seat, forlornly regarding the crush of freeway traffic around them.

"Do you have any idea what my nut is these days? The high side of seventeen thousand a month. The apartment, the place on Fisher's Island."

"The boat, the three automobiles."

"Necessities, Theodore." Kenrick wondered if he believed it. "The problem is Myrna has no concept that I work for a living and that my earnings presently are finite. God, how that woman spends. I tell you this so you understand I'm throwing in with you not out of loyalty or affection. Money."

"A motive a man can trust. I take it you're in."

"Yes. Far above my head." Archer nodded once, firmly, reassuring himself, then said, "But you're the key. The one who'll attract the others. We'll need the right mix of talents in our trading basket and some deals put together in Cannes. Stars, a blockbuster project or two, an agreement with someone to distribute our films."

"But I can't squeeze the eagle."

"You mean money?"

"Damn right I mean money," Kenrick replied. "Because when the much talked-about bottom line is drawn, it will be some banker with his signature on a line of credit that launches us or not."

"But, dear friend," Archer said with some surprise, "nothing mysterious about that. Said banker will look at you and me and our track record. Examine what we intend to do, the deals we have on ice. Then he'll dig around on the street for ulterior motives, listen to every rumor anyone wishes to peddle, and consult his horoscope. If everything adds up consistent with risk and return on investment, we have our backing. If not. . . ." He shifted in his seat, uneasy with the implication. "Two weeks in Cannes, Theodore. You line up the people, and I'll find the money."

"How much do you figure we're worth?"

Archer had smiled then, Archer smelling a challenge not yet within his grasp. "A line of credit near a hundred million would be a fair bet."

Now, across the passenger lounge, Kenrick saw Archer hang up the phone and come toward him, worry ridging his high, aristocratic forehead. Together they moved off rapidly for the departure gate.

"Spill it, Aron. I've seen that look too many times."

"It's Stiner."

"Whose business is he meddling in now?"

"Ours. He's going ahead with the internal investigation of the studio." Archer looked at him blandly, something behind his eyes that may have been amusement. "It looks as if he has finally decided to chop off your head."

At the same moment Kenrick and Aron Archer were crossing the departure lounge, the actor Rod Donner, his craggy face set and unsmiling, hurried toward the hand baggage security check at the end of the international terminal. A noose had tightened around his throat the minute he stepped from the hired limousine. There had to be a first test, yet he hadn't thought it would face him so soon. Until now Rayna had arranged everything—the limo, the roll of French francs in his pocket, everything but climbing on the damn airplane. Donner hadn't boarded an aircraft sober in twenty years. Not fear of flying exactly. Airplanes meant airports, and airports meant the public, which he had never voluntarily faced before without liquid insulation.

The sweat was rolling down his stomach now, and he forced himself to walk on, slowing until one of the lines diminished at the security inspection. He had checked his single bag at the curb and now carried only a briefcase, heavy and reassuring in his hand. In it was his every tangible asset. One ticket, Los Angeles–Paris–Nice, first class, one way. Sixteen hundred dollars in traveler's checks, owed again to Rayna. And the script.

He put the briefcase on the black conveyor belt and watched it disappear. A second later a beep came from the entrails of the machine. A large, powerfully built black girl in a blue uniform pulled his briefcase from the conveyor belt and plunked it heavily onto an inspection table.

"Easy," Donner said softly.

"You got metal in there?"

"I don't remember," he said. His mind had gone blank.

"Let's open it up," the girl in uniform said, tapping the lock smartly. Donner felt a familiar anger. He hated to be pushed.

"You ever say please?" Donner softened it, he thought, with a smile.

The girl's eyes jumped from the smile toward a white-shirted policeman lounging behind a podium a few yards away. The policeman shuffled upright. Donner looked the other direction and took in a slow, controlled breath. He would never make it, not at Cannes. He couldn't get through a damn airport. Learn to walk away, Rayna would have told him, and just as clearly he could remember old Merle saying, "Give as good as you get, boy." It had never been Father or even Pop, but always Merle, giving him the benefit of his school of hard knocks. "Don't take no shit off people," Merle would have said.

Donner pulled in a breath and snapped open the briefcase.

The girl shuffled aside the magazines until she found the script. "That's it," she said, pointing to the thick metal clasp. She lifted out the script and riffled carelessly through the pages. "Paper," she said.

"Close enough," Donner replied lightly.

Her head cocked to one side, but before she could ask, "Say, haven't I seen . . ." he took back the script, closed the briefcase, and headed off down the corridor toward the boarding gates.

He could feel the policeman's eyes on him as he passed.

As Donner rushed to board Air France Flight 061, an ancient but immaculately tended Mercedes cabriolet was swinging onto the broad access road that led directly to L.A. International. In the passenger seat Siri Laurence sat with her hands folded in her lap, her apparent calm belying her inner turmoil. Large tinted glasses, the kind that were fashionable that year, covered her clear blue eyes and the dark smudges of fatigue beneath them that no amount of makeup could conceal.

Next to her, her dead husband's partner, Hugh Remy, gave her a quick glance of concern, then deftly maneuvered the car through the thick traffic. "Last chance to change your mind."

"I thought it was settled, Hugh. Honestly."

"It may have been decided. I'm not sure it's settled."

"Then drop me at the curb and go fishing."

"Look, I agreed to come along only because I can't say no to you any better than Pedro could."

"You're a liar of the first order, Hugh Remy." But she found herself smiling. He was a tall man, irascible and bone ugly, and during the past days the only solid, reassuring presence in her life. She wanted to tell him why she was going to Cannes, the truth. She was afraid if she told him everything, he would turn away, and she wasn't strong enough yet to be alone. She wasn't sure she had ever been.

The shock of the past days had knocked her off-balance. Pedro's death, that monstrous funeral that the industry considered a tribute but that had left her both sad and angry. In some perverse manner, it was the final blow, as delivered by the mellifluous voice of her husband's lawyer and reputed friend, that turned her back toward reality. Insolvent estate, Donnenfeld said, and she distinctly remembered her reply.

"Insolvent estate, my ass!" She turned angrily from the two men and began to pace. "How can anyone living in a house worth two and a half million dollars and papered with these," she said, flinging a gesture toward the Chagall on one wall of the den, "have nothing left but an insolvent estate?"

She stopped, fixing Donnenfeld with a firm gaze that made him shift uneasily. That goddamn magnificent voice and the guts of a jellyfish. The same voice she had listened to three days before telling her the life—protected and safe—she had traded a career to hold onto was about to tumble.

Near the wood-paneled bar Hugh Remy ducked his head, trying to reduce his considerable height. Siri walked past him, mixed a powerful scotch, took one good smell, and poured it down the drain.

"All right, Harold, gather up your courage, and tell me the financial mess I'm in."

"Now, Siri, I realize you're upset . . ."

"You're damn right I'm upset." The anger unleashed felt cleansing. She had spent half her life, it felt, suppressing entire sides of herself in deference to her screen image, that mask of cool beauty her late husband had skillfully sold the public.

". . . but you must understand," Donnenfeld was saying, "that both Hugh and I want you protected. It was the way Pedro wanted things. Although I know Pedro had no idea we'd be facing a situation that, well . . . is as unpleasant as this one has become."

"What's he talking about, Hugh? In words I can understand."

She instantly regretted her hardness. Remy had suffered through the past days with a grief nearly the match of her own. Pedro Lehman and Hugh Remy had been associated since the late 1940s, when Pedro formed his own production company at Paramount. He had plucked this shy, soft-spoken production manager from relative obscurity and offered him the chance to share in a career that was rising toward its peak. Like most of Pedro's choices, he had seen things in Remy that Hugh hadn't seen himself. And in the next years Lehman drew everything out of the younger man that he had the capacity to give.

She knew the exercise well.

Yet they were a marvelous complement. Pedro the lion, charging into projects, overpowering star and studio to get what he wanted, or beaten down in the try. While Hugh Remy trailed after him, collecting the promises, the lies given in all sincerity, the extravagant demands of talent and

36

their agents, the impracticalities inherent in all but the best scripts, and assembled them into budgets and production schedules that made films. Pedro was the dreamer; Hugh, the practical man. For Pedro the grand house in Beverly Hills was a necessity to match his ego; Remy retreated at every opportunity to a boat in the marina. Hugh Remy loved everything about the making of a film and hated everything else about Hollywood. Siri liked him because she trusted him and because they had both loved and needed Pedro Lehman.

Hugh Remy brushed an imaginary fleck of dust from the edge of the bar and spoke to the lawyer.

" 'Fess up, Donnenfeld."

"Somebody tell me," Siri implored. "Harold here has just announced in his magnificent voice that Pedro's estate is insolvent. I know what insolvent means. I also know the man I married four years ago was one of the most successful filmmakers this industry has ever seen. Which by this town's definition means one of the wealthiest."

"Unfortunately," Donnenfeld began, "situations of this kind happen more often than people realize. I know you and Pedro were close, Siri. I also know he made every effort to shield you. To save you any concern."

"What exactly happened?" she asked coldly.

When Donnenfeld remained silent, Hugh Remy spoke from the bar. "He'd been using his own money to finance the last three films. Three starters, no winners. We were lucky to get a release."

Siri sat for a moment, trying to comprehend.

"I thought he had a backer. Someone who believed in him."

"Himself," Donnenfeld admitted reluctantly. "He had me set up a DBA—a doing-business-as—and a separate bank account. He fed the bank account from his own funds and, when those were gone, loans from various sources."

"But why?" Siri asked.

Hugh Remy said, "So that no one would know the only

person who would back him these days was himself."

"Stupid," Siri whispered, angry at Pedro's inflated pride. It wasn't the money that wounded her, but the understanding of how much their four years of marriage had been a game of mutual deception. Pedro had lied about his deep financial trouble to shield her from the truth, doubtless to shield himself. Her lie to him had been one of omission, the true reason behind her decision never to make another film. A bargain to save her husband with a man whom she knew to be as pure an example of evil as there was on this earth.

"I told him to give it up," Remy said. "Everyone has to quit, sometime. Goldwyn, Selznick. The business changes. Or maybe the public changes. You can't keep making the same kind of film you did ten years ago, even five, and hope you'll get lucky. I told Pedro. But you know. . . ." His voice trailed off.

"What about the new film, the one he was taking to Cannes?" Siri's full attention was on Remy now.

"It will have to gross thirty, forty million to break even, I figure," Remy said, one large hand massaging his brows. "You know the odds on that. The best deal we could get from a studio was a coproduction, and if it hadn't been for Kenrick, we wouldn't have gotten that."

"Kenrick owed him," Siri said, biting off the words sharply.

"You can't blame Kenrick for Pedro's last three films."

"I don't. I blame him for turning his back on Pedro after Pedro put him where he is. I blame him for betrayal."

She saw something quiet behind Remy's eyes, a look that disconcerted her. Was it accusation? She took Remy's presence on the edges of her life for granted. Seldom did she consider how much he must have known about herself and Pedro, their life together, like some butler in a drawing-room comedy, privy to all, thought of as invisible because he was silent.

"In any case," Remy went on, "Pedro borrowed a final two and a half million dollars from a private source to come up with our part of the financing. The film is in debt up to its eyeballs."

Siri turned to face Donnenfeld. "And what about the houses, the paintings?"

Donnenfeld took a long, slow breath before he spoke. "Siri, I want you to know Pedro was acting against my strongest advice."

"Well, say it, goddammit. They're gone, too."

Donnenfeld's leonine head began to nod. "He'd already borrowed on the paintings; the people who backed Pedro wanted collateral, so he used the houses. When we've finished an audit and made our peace with them and the tax people, I am afraid the estate of Pedro Lehman will be declared insolvent. I wanted to prepare you."

"In words of one syllable, I'm broke."

"Yes," Donnenfeld said solemnly. "I'm afraid that's what it comes down to."

Was the final shock that same night really so unexpected?

Later, alone, she had mixed herself a drink and fallen into a shallow, dream-filled sleep.

It had taken several moments for the sound of the telephone to cut through to her consciousness, and she waited for one of the Chans to catch it. Then she realized her mistake. Not the house phone at all but the telephone in the cabinet on the bar, the private line, to which, she thought, only Pedro, Hugh Remy, and she had the number.

Something at the very base of her mind began to stir in warning.

She rose quickly and ran through to the bar. As she reached the telephone, understanding dawned upon her. No need to hurry. She knew the caller, with a certainty that sent a tremor through her entire body.

She picked up the telephone and held it close to her ear. Nothing. Not a word or sound.

"You sonuvabitch," she said quietly.

She heard the laughter then, malicious and confirming.

39

She could see the lips bending around the laugh, the mouth crowing victory, and with it the four years of peace with Pedro Lehman might never have existed.

The sound still in her ears, she slammed down the receiver as though by such a simple act she could be done with Nicky Deane.

As the Mercedes cabriolet reached the airline terminal, Hugh Remy beckoned a skycap and gave Siri a reassuring smile. She studied him, wondering if he could have accepted the reason she was going to Cannes without judgment. Quite simple, dear Hugh. I am running for my life.

≡ *Chapter 5*—In Transit

Aboard Air France Flight 061 the mood of the passengers was deceptively lighthearted. On that Monday, one day before the start of the Cannes Film Festival, the entire thirty-eight first-class accommodations were taken by movie people. Had the same passengers taken the flight three days earlier, the topic of conversation doubtless would have been the death of Pedro Lehman. But as Lehman himself had reminded almost everyone on board, at one time or another, Hollywood wasn't a town known for long memories. Today the conversation was overwhelmingly about the Festival and, by logical extension, a variety of subjects touching upon the dollar sign.

In seats 6E and 6F the operating head of Twentieth-Century-Fox sat quietly with his wife, mentally calculating the probable size of his bonus, pegged by a shrewdly worded employment contract to the studio's gross. The gross at that moment was going through the roof, thanks to a space epic that had already become the most successful film of all time. A million easy, he figured the bonus. Maybe two. He had had the great good fortune to say yes on that film, and if anything growing up in the business had taught him, it was how to protect oneself by saying no. He would say no a lot at Cannes. He was in that kind of mood.

Two seats behind the Fox executive sat the lumpish but ebullient new production chief for United Artists West Coast, as was his custom giving an opinion on the subject of each conversation within earshot. Since, like most studio executives, he was known to have the hearing of a professional spy as regards the conversations of others, his range was considerable. Superagent Freddie Harland, who had missed Flight 061 by precisely the same six and a half minutes it had taken him that morning to dispatch a quickie in the form of a cute blond never-would-be, was said to have the ability to carry on a conversation while overhearing two others, keeping all details separate and never missing a beat. That was talent.

Stopping to shake hands in the aisle, producers Paul Waxler and Edward S. Miles exchanged harmless lies about how could anyone vacation in Cannes when there was so much action going on in town, the implication being that Cannes was for laughs. But they knew. Cannes *was* action. Returning to Seat 13A, directly in front of an actor whose face Waxler remembered—a tough, creviced face he couldn't tie to a name—he extracted a list from his pocket of the items he was dealing in Cannes. Next to each item he penciled in the words "to buy" or "to sell." Halfway down the list he remembered the name that went with the face, Rod Donner, then promptly let it slip from his mind; Donner was no action at all.

Farther back in the aircraft, beyond the curtains separating first class from tourist, Leo Gold's thoughts were also of money—the forty bucks an hour he was saving by *not* flying first class. Leo Gold's wizened face crinkled with a smile as he savored it.

Not that his studio couldn't afford it. Not one of the Big Six maybe. More like the Big Twelve if there were such a thing, but the difference was the word "his." It was his studio, his and his family's and nobody else's, except for a slow-thinking son-in-law, whom the wife said he ought to start treating as family. He wouldn't have been comfortable spending forty dollars an hour in first class, money that didn't produce a thing. Did Leo Gold need a seat three inches wider? Not unless he gained a hundred pounds. More legroom or champagne, which he didn't drink at all? He'd sewn costumes for De Mille, earning *forty cents* an hour. Nobody left who remembered those times, and for that reason he found himself thinking about Pedro Lehman. Lehman would have remembered. Walsh, Mankiewicz hiding out in retirement, who else was left? His friends, they all were dropping like flies. Maybe he should have loosened up, spent money, but did a man change a lifetime of habits, start drinking and chasing floozies, because he sees the years of his life left on the fingers of two hands, one hand maybe? Not Leo Gold. He would spend plenty at Cannes, but when he did, he would get more for it than a padded cushion and cheap champagne.

The sure knowledge made Leo Gold content. The fact that Lehman was dead and he was alive should have made him feel even better, but it didn't.

In seats 1A and 1B, far forward, Teddy Kenrick and Aron Archer were reflecting upon the implications of their conversation earlier in the departure lounge: the items and people who would need to fall their way in Cannes before they could attract the line of credit to launch a breakaway studio; the damning blow a leak about the disastrous Lehman film would deal them. And capping it, parent company president Mal Stiner's intention to mount an internal investigation of the studio.

Kenrick had felt Stiner's enmity growing since the showdown they had had in New York months before on the Lehman film. Stiner had lobbied against it from the beginning.

"The three films he's done since *Lady Ice* haven't even made break-even," Stiner complained. He had posed himself in front of the broad expanse of window that looked out over Fifth Avenue and Central Park.

Kenrick thought he was well cast in his part. A big man, barrel-chested and athletic, his full head of hair worn longer now than when he'd taken the presidency four years before, but graying a little too perfectly at the temples. He wanted more control over running the studio so badly he could taste it.

Stabbing a finger toward Kenrick, he said, "You've a nine million budget, a shooting schedule out there in the boonies, and who says Lehman isn't senile or on the sauce?"

"I do. He's none of those, and you know it."

"But why take the gamble?"

"Because it's all a gamble. Production is my turf, Mal. Back off."

"But you report to me."

"If you want to try shooting me down over a movie that hasn't been made yet, by one of the greatest money-makers of all time, in the middle of the best year the studio has ever had, then you'd better have your suitcase packed yourself because you're gone. The board and stockholders will eat you alive."

Stiner glared at him. "Get out of here. Go back and work on your suntan."

What had made it more difficult was that Kenrick totally agreed with Stiner's logic. He had taken on the Lehman film because he had to, levered into it by an irresistible force that he hoped no one discovered, not until he found a way out.

But when the film went far over budget, he knew he had given Stiner an immediate powerful weapon to use against him. If the film were a success, everyone, including Mal Stiner, would take a piece of the credit. A disaster, and they would be calling it Kenrick's picture.

But Stiner was cunning enough to sense the distant flailings of someone in trouble and had now pressed his attack with the forthcoming internal investigation of the studio.

"The board won't go for it," Kenrick told Archer. "If for any reason the studio looks bad, the parent company sinks with it."

Archer countered firmly. "Stiner is claiming that his responsibility is not to the board, but to those gentle folk out there, the stockholders. He left for Cannes a day early with a corporate troubleshooter named Donald Eads. Just finished a long siege of mucking around in the internal affairs of RCA and top reputation as a snoop."

Stiner was to deliver the opening remarks at the studio's press luncheon at the Hôtel du Cap the tenth day of the Festival, a target date Kenrick had firmly in mind.

Kenrick frowned, trying to divine what Stiner was after, the exact way he would try to take Kenrick's head. "Stiner has to see that anything this Donald Eads turns up will be blown out of proportion by the press. Bad timing."

The town was still jumpy from the business at Columbia. Kenrick's counterpart had been recently caught with his hand in the till. When top management tried a cover-up, the Washington *Post* broke the story. The executive was indicted, the L.A. district attorney's office promised a wider investigation into film-industry wrongdoings, and the Justice Department jumped in with both feet. Its "Hollywood Task Force" was coming to town to investigate illegal business practices, a loose brief that included the relationship between Hollywood and organized crime.

There *were* connections, more than anyone spoke about. Mafia money backed a handful of name producers and underwrote the careers of several bankable stars. At least one board member of a Big Six studio also sat on the board of a record company whose connections with the mob was one of the town's worst-kept secrets.

One new example of fraud in the movie business would blow the town apart.

"Bad timing, or very good timing. It rather depends on Stiner's purpose, doesn't it?" Archer, with great control, raised a single eyebrow in suspicion. "Stiner claims his reason is to take a look at ourselves before the federal government does it for us. Reinforce the industry's wide propaganda that we're our own best police force."

"He's up to something," Kenrick said with certainty.

"But what?" Archer replied, mystified. "Look, in Cannes I'll get on the telephone, find out what's going around on the street. The trouble is Stiner has given this troubleshooter Eads all the tools, including the power to audit."

"And aimed him toward the Lehman film, no doubt."

A glance from Archer was confirmation enough. Damn, Kenrick thought. Had Stiner smelled that out, too?

Archer sighed. "You know it isn't the man with the gun we corporate types fear these days. It's the man with the audit."

Especially, Kenrick considered, when any outside audit of the Lehman film would show that one among them was a pretty good thief.

≡ *Chapter 6*—In Transit: Kenrick's Story

Lulled by the steady hum of jet engines, Kenrick tried to take advantage of the moment of calm between separate storms—the decisions of the past three days and the two-week street fight ahead at Cannes. He was ready, he supposed, for what his dead wife, Anne, would surely have identified as a patented Teddy Kenrick great leap.

Next to him Aron Archer fidgeted restlessly, called the stewardess, and ordered a drink. Below Archer's ordinarily controlled exterior something was cooking, and Kenrick made a mental note to find out what. Archer was key to his plans.

Together they had resurrected the studio. Four years before, they had come aboard a corporate *Titanic*, already hard upon the iceberg. The studio's only significant money-maker that year was Lehman's *Lady Ice*, the film that confirmed Siri Laurence as solid box office. Lehman owned a large piece of the film, but when the time came for distribution of profits, the former studio brass spent most of its creative energy devising ways to keep from paying off. With production down and $130,000 in debt they were using money due Lehman to get through the day. He was the wrong man to stiff.

It was common knowledge throughout the industry that a vengeful Pedro Lehman had gone East in search of money interested in buying into a studio in trouble at a cut-rate price. "I've seen this industry and everyone in it down a half dozen times," he once told Kenrick, "and it always climbs back up. Memories in this town are so goddamned short."

But he found one listener whose memory wasn't short, a financier named Robert J. Arthur. In the next few months Arthur and Company bought seven percent of the studio's parent company stock, while Arthur himself acquired an additional eight percent, enough for considerable leverage on the board of directors. Kenrick had never heard the name Arthur before, and little enough since. Aron Archer explained, "That's because Arthur is what Howard Hughes spent his whole life trying to become. An entrepreneur who can pull off the big ones from behind the scenes, safe and invisible. Sort of the Wall Street equivalent of levitation."

"Maybe I've been dealing too long with people who need media exposure worse than blood. What drives a Robert Arthur?"

"A kind of power you and I can only imagine," Archer said reverently.

With the takeover, an Arthur and Company appointee, Mal Stiner, was installed as parent company president, and ten days later Teddy Kenrick was lured from the top of what was then the most successful talent agency in the business, with a single mandate: Get the studio's filmmaking machinery back in motion. Stiner announced the appointment, but Pedro Lehman had engineered it.

Meanwhile, Stiner found Aron Archer in one of Boston's most influential banks, no coincidence that it was the studio's largest single creditor. A matter of buying out the enemy's general. Yet there was an element to it that even now Kenrick hadn't forgotten, given the nature of the battle that lay ahead at Cannes: Archer had come in as Stiner's man.

But the studio's climb into black had been his and Aron Archer's. If they broke out to form a new organization, any observer would know they were a nucleus to be reckoned with.

He was counting on it.

Within hours of Archer's committing himself to the breakaway two days before, Kenrick called his secretary, Elsa, into his office and told her what was likely to happen at Cannes.

Then he asked her to gather the file on the studio accountant who had been on the Lehman film, a longtime studio employee named Ray Tannis. "Save it for Rentzler."

"Teddy, is anyone else likely to be onto this breakaway of yours?"

"We'd better hope not."

Elsa looked vaguely troubled. "You had a phone call. Long distance. Chap named Galloway. Very English. I remembered the name. The *Financial Times* article Rentzler dug up on Robert Arthur was written by a Peter Galloway."

"What did this Galloway want?"

"An interview with you. When I said you weren't to be interviewed, he said he would find you in Cannes. Sounded positively threatening. And a little drunk."

Kenrick didn't like the ring of it. If it was the same Galloway, the man already knew too much: his interest in the financier Robert Arthur; Arthur's money behind the manipulations of the studio. He would need some journalistic bloodhound circling the edges at Cannes like a dose of the clap.

He thought a long moment before he spoke.

"Elsa, I want to hire someone for Cannes on a confidential basis. Someone who can make contacts, reach some people it might be better if I weren't seen with."

"The best at that sort of thing is a lady named Tate. Rayna Tate. PR, a one-woman office, and dynamite."

Kenrick had heard the name, but nothing else, all to the good. The best people in public relations drew little attention to themselves but had a finger everywhere in the business. The common belief was that eighty percent of the so-called hard news in the daily trade papers was planted. But at its heart it was a game of contacts, reaching people that mattered.

"Rayna Tate. See if the lady will talk."

Five minutes later his intercom buzzed, and Elsa said, "I

have her on the line. She says she's in the middle of something she can't break out of but said yes, she'll be in Cannes. She asked if you biked."

"Tell her I manage a run, most mornings. Santa Monica Pier to the Marina."

"She says she'll meet you."

"The pier—six A.M."

"She wonders if you could make it five-thirty."

"Well, now," Kenrick said, taking a second interest in this Rayna Tate. "Tell her I'll set an alarm."

"Done," Elsa said. "But you watch it, Mr. K. I said she's dynamite. I'm not so sure about scruples."

≡ *Chapter 7*—A Lady Named Tate

At precisely 5:15 A.M., two days before his departure for Cannes, Kenrick left his oceanfront apartment and began a slow, easy run south along the beach to keep his early-morning appointment with Rayna Tate.

The dull spring morning and leaden gray skies made him realize how much he was looking forward to a change, how stale he had become with the routines and rigorous work schedules he had loaded upon himself after his wife Anne's death.

Rayna Tate was waiting at the foot of the Santa Monica Pier.

He had anticipated someone sleek and polished in a color-matched training suit and fifty-dollar Nikes. At first glance he wasn't sure the creature *was* a woman. Her warm-up suit was Army-Navy Store flannel. The ski cap pulled over her ears revealed not so much as a strand of hair.

Without makeup her olive skin hinted at an ancestry he couldn't quite fix. Her almond-shaped eyes, steady on him as he approached, were soft, brown, and not particularly warm. At thirty feet she looked in her late teens, but closer, something confident in her eyes made him revise her age upward ten years, but no more.

"A morning for the dedicated," she said. "I thought you might have had second thoughts." The voice was extraordinary—a carefully modulated, highbred English. She added, "I don't usually bicycle so early, but I have an eleven o'clock flight for Paris."

"And from there to Cannes?"

"After a day or so." The spaces she left blank neatly and subtly conjured up the vision of a romantic liaison.

She brushed a line of perspiration from her upper lip. "Your direction or mine?"

"You're the one with the schedule," Kenrick said, aware he sounded defensive. So what if the lady had a lover in Paris or anywhere else?

Rayna Tate caught the interest in Kenrick's reply and gave him a smile of concealed pleasure. She was used to making quick assessments, lived her life by them, although she had made some colossal blunders. Her initial reading of Kenrick was nearly complete. A panther, some kind of cat. Kenrick the cat. Or maybe it should be Kat. A nasty way of labeling the people she dealt with. Donner the bull. Taya Linder the serpent, all smoothly muscled beneath her shiny exterior. But it was a useful device to keep her from taking them with the seriousness they usually took themselves.

Yes, a panther, restless but controlled. She tried to imagine what Kenrick was like in bed, step two in the game of instant appraisal, and found that she could visualize it very well. Interesting.

She let him settle into a pace that was comfortable, then pedaled along next to him.

"I'm surprised we've never met," Kenrick said.

"I doubt we move in the same circles, really." Not too close, Mr. Kat. "About the Festival. . . ."

A quick look from Kenrick, a flash of something before a smile made the corners of his eyes crinkle. He had caught the message all right. What an odd face, Rayna found herself thinking. Not one thing handsome about it, but . . . but what? Kenrick was younger than he photographed and nicely built. But uneasy when looked at, scrutinized too closely. Why, Mr. Kat?

"Ah, yes, the Festival," Kenrick said. "There will be people I need to contact in Cannes and not a lot of time. You know the Festival. . . ."

"Yes, I do, Mr. Kenrick. This will be my fourth."

"I think we could do without the mister."

Could we now? "Should I make it Teddy, as they do in the columns, or Kenrick, or do I have a choice?"

"Your choice," he said, but looked suddenly uncomfortable.

"Kenrick then. I like the sound. Ken-rick. Nice." My God, he's blushing. Back off, Rayna girl. "But how exactly can I help?" That's it. Humble bitch.

"I want to know where I can contact these people when I need to, what they're doing and with whom. Have some groundwork already laid. Is that within your reach?"

It came out sharply, and Kenrick caught himself. Those almond-shaped eyes had a steadiness he could have done without. He hadn't been prepared for contests of will or anything else, not at this hour. He was used to giving orders, not making requests.

"I'm afraid I already have a full basket at Cannes."

"Meaning what?" Kenrick asked.

She looked over, sharply. "Simply that I will be very busy. Things don't just happen at Cannes. If Holden or Montand walks across the terrace of the Carlton at five-thirty in the afternoon with photographers hanging about to get pictures, it happens because somebody made it happen."

"And you're the somebody."

"Wrong or right, it's an age of manipulation. All I'm saying is I have other clients at Cannes."

"What are they paying you?"

"This isn't a bidding session. If you're curious, at the Festival I bill out at five hundred a day plus expenses. If I am instrumental in making a deal come together, I expect four percent. The people I do things for think I'm worth it."

"And if I want all your time?"

"You couldn't have it. The Festival begins in forty-eight hours, and I'm committed."

"To whom?"

"That would be a breach of confidence."

Kenrick liked the way she handled herself. Direct, but with none of the shrill defiance of a person feeling threatened. He had intimidated bigger people with his directness.

"You think I'm too pushy?" he asked.

"You have the reputation," she answered. "You also have a reputation for winning more often than you lose. No, I don't find you too pushy."

"At Cannes I can't afford to waste any time."

"So I've noted," she said with a taunt in her voice. "Your studio has a competent public relations staff. Or is that a little too close to home for your purpose?"

When he let his silence provide an answer, she paused. "I know this isn't what you want to hear, but I meant it about the people I'm working for at Cannes. But maybe your needs can dovetail. I expect we're aiming for the same targets. Call them movers, moguls, elite, or whatever." She smiled. "People like yourself."

Kenrick didn't choose to bite on that one. "It's possible."

"I won't know until you tell me what you're after, and who."

"I'll tell you in Cannes," Kenrick replied.

The oval eyes narrowed, rebuking him mildly. "I do keep my mouth closed, you know."

"I've noticed. I'll know better exactly what's ahead two days from now."

"Then we'll meet in Cannes. How delightful."

It was after nine that same evening by the time Kenrick had finished his battle plan for the Festival.

He folded the long sheets of legal paper and placed them in a heavy manila envelope, a summation of eight months of blue printing begun the day he gave the go-ahead on the Lehman film. As an afterthought he dug out the *Financial Times* article by Peter Galloway, the one profiling the financier Robert Arthur, and added it to the folder. Ultimately his target in Cannes was Arthur.

In his seventies now, Arthur owed the beginning of his

business empire to the passage of the Eighteenth Amendment —Prohibition. His first millions came from importing quality scotch whiskey from Canada in an era better known for bathtub gin. From there he moved into the means for its distribution, trucking and shipping lines, always imposing barriers of secrecy between his enterprises and himself, mainly through the use of holding companies.

Kenrick had seen Arthur only once, and then by happenstance. He had been drinking a gin and tonic in the main bar of the L.A. Athletic Club after a hard game of handball when a porter asked the bartender for Robert Arthur. The bartender pointed across the pastel green lounge to a solitary man with a full head of startling white hair, sitting alone and silent in a straight-backed chair against one wall, hands folded in his lap. There were no other chairs nearby, nor could Kenrick see either a magazine or a drink within reach. The image was locked in Kenrick's mind, as was the sudden smile Arthur offered the porter when he bent forward to deliver whatever message he had brought, welcoming the intrusion.

Galloway's article focused on Arthur's methods, cleverly contrasting his entrance into the film industry with the two other barons who had bought in low, floated up on hype, and sold out very high indeed—Howard Hughes and Joe Kennedy, father of John F.

Again, Kenrick had the vague stirrings of uneasiness. If Galloway was in Cannes, he smelled something.

Kenrick stood to stretch the stiffness from his body, knowing the evening's work was not yet finished. The young lawyer Larry Rentzler was due any minute for a briefing on the special mission he was to undertake before he came on to Cannes. Rentzler's nervous enthusiasm would be a welcome change to his own ice-cold ponderings of the past hours.

Kenrick slid back the glass door to the balcony and took a deep, settling breath of salt air. His eyes followed the long curve of coastline to the south, a ribbon of lights that bent out to the Palos Verdes Peninsula, now lost in a wash of fog. A pair of tankers lighted like small cities, but separate and alone, stood off El Segundo. He turned his back on it, went inside, and mixed himself a strong whiskey.

At times like this the loneliness tried to close in again. That first year after Anne died, it had often driven him out onto the city's great safety valve—the freeways and wherever a night's wandering would take him. He could guess what Siri was going through in the wake of her husband's death. But a phone call would have been misinterpreted. By now Siri had had abundant offers of consolation, and he thought of Hugh Remy's acid comment about the town. Like the jungle it was, meat, dead or alive, never went long unattended.

Now the loneliness had become so much a part of his life he doubted he could muster the courage to open himself to another woman. With Anne's death something in him withered, and he found comfort only in the building of walls —of money, power, his schemes—beyond which he seldom strayed. Even given the chance, he didn't know if he would risk it. It was comfortable in there, inside that tight little world in his mind. Suddenly he found himself thinking about Rayna Tate, how easily she had controlled their encounter. A risk. He would have Elsa call her tomorrow, find someone else to do his legwork at Cannes. Thirty seconds later he knew he wouldn't.

When Rentzler arrived, Kenrick led him through to the bar and nodded for him to help himself. "What's up?"

Rentzler's admission into Kenrick's inner circle had come with the special investigation he had carried out eight months before.

The same day Kenrick approved the studio's coproduction of the Lehman film, he had asked Elsa for the confidential files on their entire legal staff.

Poring over his background, he thought he could detect the right mixture of intellect, hunger, and ambition—Harvard Law School, three years in the Justice Department, then a short sojourn with the Los Angeles city prosecutor's office before his move to the studio at a figure nearly double his salary with the city.

He had called Rentzler at home. "I'd like to talk, and it might be better at your place." He wasn't sure what a social anthropologist would have learned from a study of his own habitat, but he wanted another measure on Rentzler.

He heard Rentzler's faltering assent and five minutes later was driving east on Sunset Boulevard.

He seldom dwelled on the breadth of his power, which emanated not from him as a man but Kenrick the symbol, the top of this particular heap, a point he tried not to forget. He could change lives with a phone call all right, as good a definition of power as he needed. The irony was that circumstances and his own stupidity had conspired to give him so little power at that moment to control his own life. He hated to admit to the word "desperate."

Larry Rentzler opened the door to his apartment and stood blinking at Kenrick, as if truly hoping it would be someone else. He was Kenrick's height but thinner, with darkish hair already sprinkled with tufts of premature gray.

Behind Rentzler, a young man, fairer but about the same age, entered the room from the kitchen.

"My roommate, Tod," Rentzler said, an edge in his voice. "And yes, there is only one bedroom, and yes, there is only one bed. If that changes anything, so be it."

"You figure it should?"

"Just wanted it straight, that's all."

An hour and twenty minutes later he was riding down in the elevator. His request had been direct. "I want to find out who's backing Pedro Lehman. Where he's getting his money."

In his mind there had to be a connection between the pressure he had received to take on the Lehman film and the investors behind Lehman. That Rentzler's investigation would lead him to the idea of the apparent breakaway and one step beyond to Arthur, he had no way of anticipating then.

That night he was pleased with the questions Rentzler had asked, in amplification. And the ones he hadn't.

The report of Rentzler's investigation was delivered by hand two weeks later.

The report now locked in the desk in Kenrick's apartment was soiled from use, for in it was the foundation of all Kenrick was about to attempt. He doubted even Rentzler understood everything the investigation revealed.

"Subject," the report began, "Cinema Services, Incorporated, and the money behind it."

Spending several hours in various city and county offices, Rentzler had quickly discovered from the public record that Cinema Services was a DBA for Harold Donnenfeld, Lehman's lawyer, acting upon Lehman's instructions. "They set up a dummy company," Rentzler wrote, "to finance Lehman's films with money initially provided by Lehman himself." Rentzler added, "It is difficult to guess how much of his fortune went down the drain on the last three films. Millions. My guess is between six and ten."

But Rentzler kept digging.

"In light of this, the surprise is that Cinema Services (Pedro Lehman) was able to attract outside money for his latest film from a New Jersey-based corporation named Optimus Investments. To the tune of four and a half million dollars. With the introduction of Optimus into Lehman's financial picture the trouble begins. Particularly in the form of Optimus president, Meyer Tilman.

"Now there is nothing I learned from the phone calls I made to indicate that Optimus Investments is anything but what it claims to be: a small organization specializing in modest capital ventures. But being a Harvard Law School graduate, of my religious affiliation (and sexual preference), has given me access to places most mortals would not care to walk—i.e., half the legal staffs of the SEC and the Justice Department. Besides, there was something about the name Meyer Tilman that stuck in my cortical tissue.

"With a little snooping I found that Tilman had once been investigated by the Justice Department as a result of his sale of one-half of a casino and real estate company in the Bahamas called the Cayman Bay Development Corporation. This was before Optimus, when Tilman apparently was operating on his own. The other principal in Cayman Bay was an outfit called Playtime Associates, a company I'll come to in a moment.

"Together Tilman and Playtime bought Cayman Bay for two million dollars when it was little more than a couple of coral islets around a lagoon, with a shack and a pier. They put an additional two million into the building of a fishing club when, lo and behold, the Bahamian government issued them a casino license, and off they go. Suddenly a few million bucks of coral is now a marketable asset valued at around twenty million dollars. Don't ask how the Bahamian government, since deposed, just happened to grant the casino license in the first place. The Justice Department thought at the very least its investigation of Tilman would bring an indictment for tax fraud because it had a very good witness in the form of a Tilman associate named Marvin Jakes, who apparently wasn't getting his share of juice. But as the investigation was about to begin, Jakes was involved in a boating accident in Miami and lost at sea. Ahem! And with Jakes sinking beneath the briny, so did the probable indictment against Tilman.

"Anyway, a year after the casino was in operation, Tilman sold out his half of Cayman Bay to an Arizona real estate outfit called the Reynosa Corporation—for twelve million bucks!

"Now it so happens my friend at the time was the lawyer who ran the Tilman investigation. And though he is careful to preface his comments with the disclaimer 'that although

I can't prove it . . . ,' it was his opinion that Tilman and Jakes, RIP, were nothing more (or less) than a pair of high-level bagmen for the mob, given the task of moving money around. If so, it's likely the whole Cayman Bay scheme was a neat way to launder Mafia money and turn a profit at the same time. I remind you Tilman's capital gains from the Reynosa deal had honorable origins, were taxable and thus clean. With the money, Tilman formed Optimus and began legitimate *carefully chosen investments"*— it was Kenrick who had underlined the words, adding the note "The Lehman Film." "This is not an unusual evolution of mob-conducted business," Rentzler wrote. "The Bonnano family put profits from their legitimate business into *Deep Throat* and *Wet Rainbow,* and the porno film business has been run for decades on mob money. The Justice Department, however, has suspected for some time that the film industry has been set as a target for mob infiltration on a grander scale. But to hear Justice tell it, *every* industry is ripe for in-filtration on a grander scale. In any case I went back and had a look at Tilman's partner in the Cayman Bay venture— Playtime Associates.

"There is nothing secret about Playtime. It is a public company, and, as such, has filed a fat little document called a 10-K with the Securities and Exchange Commission, full of information about the people behind the people who run a company.

"According to Playtime's 10-K, the corporation is a hold-ing company of various leisure and recreational stocks. The largest single shareholder is Arthur and Company, the same Arthur and Company which presently owns seven percent of the parent company of *this studio.*

"Two months after Tilman sold his half of Cayman Bay, Playtime (Arthur) did the same. To Baguio Industries, a Philippine timber and mining company, for fifteen million dollars—a seven and a half times return on investment in two years. On a hunch I kept digging and found that Baguio is a wholly owned subsidiary of a Hong Kong holding company named Monarch, Ltd., of which one-third of the stock is owned by, yes, you guessed it, Arthur and Company. Arthur has a long history of buying into companies with short capital but in situations with long leverage—that is, a good deal of control over operations. And made a bundle doing it.

"The nearest reason I can figure why Cayman Bay was sold by one partly owned Arthur company to another partly owned Arthur company is that it was a slick way to remit large amounts of cash from the Philippines, all very legally. But by now, since both of the original principals, Meyer Tilman and Playtime (Arthur and Company), were out of Cayman Bay, I stopped chasing."

Here, months before, Kenrick had penciled something in the margin, a quote of financier Robert Arthur's from the Galloway article. It ended, "We negotiate every day with dealers, con men, shysters, and hustlers. It is not something we do unwillingly. It is called business, and it is the way fortunes are made in this country."

Kenrick's eyes again dropped to the page, scanning Rentzler's final discovery.

"I did find out one thing more about Cayman Bay, but I am not sure what importance it may have. The casino operations were leased to a Florida outfit called R and B Enterprises, incorporated under the laws of the State of Nevada and owned principally by—are you ready?—the Reynosa Corporation, the same people who bought Tilman's half of Cayman Bay. The man who actually ran the casino operations was one Nicholas Gardenia, and the Nevada Gaming Control Board advised me that he is honest, clean, and not known to have affiliations with unsavory people, etc. Which may tell us more about the gaming board investigations than about Nicky Deane, as he calls himself."

Kenrick could remember the anger that had run through him with this final revelation. Larry Rentzler had done his work better than he had any understanding.

Rentzler's conclusion read:

"It is not my nature to make unfounded implications. But one fact in the preceding investigation is clear: that Pedro Lehman, for whatever reason, accepted two and a half million dollars from a company that in all probability was financed by profits from a mob-related scam."

Facing Rentzler two nights before, a beer turning nervously in his slender fingers, Kenrick had given the young lawyer another special assignment. "You'll have a week, outside, to find out two things I need to know, then hightail it to Cannes."

Rentzler took a slow sip of beer, withholding his questions. Kenrick had to believe that everything Rentzler had dug out on his behalf was going in duplicate into a mental file. Rentzler's loyalty was as measured as Kenrick's trust and as yet untested. He was impatient, searching for some path of his own. But impatience made him efficient. And speed now was worth the risk.

"There's been some funny stuff on the Lehman film," Kenrick explained, "something I can't pin down. Money spent that didn't end up on the screen." Close enough, as far as it went.

"It should have been caught by the studio audit we run on each film."

"The accountant watchdogging Lehman's film was Ray Tannis. Elsa has his file. If there is a thief in the pack, Ray Tannis has to know."

"If he knows and kept his mouth shut, maybe it's Tannis. Or maybe Tannis and whoever signed the checks. You don't think Lehman himself?"

Kenrick considered it, staring out the window at the dark ocean. "Put a fear in Tannis, and see what falls out. I don't care how."

Rentzler was regarding his beer as though it had gone bad. "Something wrong?"

"Not a thing," Rentzler said. "This second item on Larry's little list?"

"The exact whereabouts of Robert Arthur."

When Rentzler had gone, Kenrick sat a moment. The dominoes were lined up, but miss one that had to fall at Cannes . . . and what? The end of a career, without doubt. Worth a killing to prevent? If someone judged enough was on the line, he shouldn't be surprised.

On the flight to Paris eleven rows behind Kenrick, the actor Rod Donner had another explanation for why he never liked flying sober. It was an unnatural act, compressing the human form into an airline seat designed for an everyman with legs six inches too short, feeding him reject cardboard, and advertising it all as fun. Friendly skies, up, up, and away. About like catching your skin in a zipper.

He was already on board when Kenrick and a well-tailored henchman took seats near the forward hatchway. They had never been close, he and Kenrick, as in close friends. Agent and actor, and all Donner had asked was that each know his job. He couldn't fault Kenrick on that score, but maybe if he had worked on the man's friendship, gotten drunk with him once or twice . . . old Merle's prescription for how to make yourself a friend.

As Kenrick came aboard, their glances touched the length of the aircraft, and Donner caught that funny, narrow smile. He couldn't recall ever seeing Kenrick laugh. He spent the next five minutes trying to decipher it.

Did the smile mean no hard feelings for that punch in the eye once upon a time? It was an industry where signs could be more killing than words. How much pressure in a handshake? Who kissed whom when they entered a party? Whole orders of power could be determined by watching elevator protocol or who was seated where in Ma Maison or the Bistro. A change in the location of a studio parking stall was grounds for a visit to your shrink or a celebration.

Maybe Kenrick *was* accessible. One look at a script was no big thing.

Sitting there, his stomach in a knot over what might or might not have been a forgiving smile, Donner swore angrily at himself. What in hell had he let himself in for?

The script in his briefcase had been sitting for almost a year in the office of a West Hollywood secretarial service he used as an accommodation address. A last slender connection with the town while his home changed from Poste Restante, Nice, to Rome's Via Margutta, to General Delivery, Sydney, and back again.

The script had been forwarded from Universal in a carton of fan mail dating from the syndication of a western TV series made twelve years before. Studios didn't read fan mail anymore. It was crudely sorted, forwarded, or burned. He had been lucky. A note with the script said, "You're perfect for this. I had you in mind." It was signed J. Shimkus.

If this J. Shimkus had glimpsed the man who lifted the script from its cardboard box, Donner guessed he would have enclosed return postage. He was in the States because he was out of places to run, forty pounds overweight, unemployable, and a borderline alcoholic.

He had taken the script without reading it and caught a Greyhound south, needing to put time and space between himself and the town. He finally opened it in an Oceanside motel room on a damp, foggy night almost eighteen months before. He could see now how close to the bottom he'd been. He was reared to be his own man, ornery old Merle teaching him to ride, hunt, fix junk cars, and lay concrete, showing him in every way he knew to be dependent on no one, a concept of what it was to be a man that Donner wasn't sure he would ever shake completely. A man can go it alone if he has to. Pride is something that makes you swagger when you ain't got a reason in the world. Donner had learned the swagger all right, but it hadn't done much for Merle when they put him on a kidney machine and kept him alive like a robot until the parts of him inside started giving up one by one and he died crying like a baby for someone to end it.

That night in Oceanside Donner's only friend was a certain Mr. Daniel's with a square black label. He was independent sure enough, a unit so solitary that no one else gave a damn whether he lived another day or pissed himself down the toilet. Rayna once was an exception, but their fiery parting in London had left no doubt how far they had moved away from each other. Along separate paths, she had said. And he agreed.

That night it was just Donner and this J. Shimkus and a small story about a father who sets out to vindicate the judgment of his dead son and retrieve honor for them both.

Ten pages in, Donner knew he was onto something, its visual images and crisp dialogue snapping in his mind. The next day he read it again with the harsh judgment of a hangover and knew what he was going to do, had to do. The first step was to find the author Shimkus.

A call to the Writers' Guild turned up nothing from its membership list, so he tried the return address on the note. It turned out to be a block of run-down apartments in Studio City, not ten minutes from Universal Studios.

No, he was told, Miss Shimkus hadn't lived there in more than a year. Miss Shimkus.

He tried to visualize the girl who had labored over the script. She had mastered a number of details about automobile racing and the Grand Prix circuit in particular, enough in any case to convince Donner. But where had the seed of the story come from, the relationship between the father and the dead son that was the heart of it? Writers had always been a mystery to Donner, how they found their ideas. Most didn't know themselves.

But the apartment manager had another address, left on the registration card the girl signed with the lease.

Donner traced it to a small house down near the L.A. harbor, by then having invested half of his two thousand dollars' life savings in a five-year-old Chevrolet. Los Angeles without an automobile was a one-legged man without a crutch.

It was a small board house in a neighborhood of tired automobiles and warped fences spray-canned with names like "Jaime de la Rana" and "Pepe of 203rd." The man who answered the door was probably sixty with a white stubble of beard, distant blue eyes, and the artificial glow Donner recognized all too well. He took a step back when the man spoke, trying to avoid the smell of alcohol lest it drive him off in search of the nearest bar. The smell could still recall a long line of drinking bouts and some good times back among the haze.

"I'm looking for Miss Shimkus."

"She don't live here. Hasn't in years."

Donner's eyes looked past the man, scanning the room for a photograph, something to flesh out the mental picture he had of the girl. Plenty of newspapers, a large color TV set, and no photos: the threadbare spareness of a man who lived alone and liked it. Crusty old Merle's kind of man, and Donner thought he could understand what might have sent the girl running.

"You her father?" Donner asked.

The old man looked at him, silent for so long Donner wasn't sure whether he had heard the question. "Was. She's dead. The people she ran with. Dope fiends. A man has to expect it."

Donner made one more visit a week later and found the old man and his living room unchanged, except for a visit that morning to the wine cellar. A bottle of white port was open on the TV set. That afternoon Donner bought the rights to the Shimkus script for five hundred dollars cash and a promise on a handshake of more if anything came of it. He had brought the money in ten-dollar bills, and the old man measured the thickness of the stack with his eyes the entire time they talked. In the end he signed a letter of agreement that had cost Donner another three hundred dollars to have drawn up by an attorney. Still, he left the house feeling he had mugged an old man and stolen his life savings.

The last thing he had asked was the girl's first name. The old man gave him an odd squint but said, "Judith." He added, "She wasn't much of a daughter," and shut the door.

The next day Donner started to work himself back in shape, planning what would need to be done. He was here now aboard an aircraft headed to Cannes for the two of them. A dead girl and himself, who had been close enough to dying to know what it was like.

One row in front of Donner, on the opposite side of the aircraft, Hugh Remy took a sip from his prelunch cocktail and wished he had ordered a double. Next to him Siri had retreated behind the impassive mask that revealed nothing, even to Remy, who by now should have known every tic.

She had appeared unruffled on their hasty transit through the airport, Remy praying that with speed they would make the passage with Siri unrecognized. Not quite. Jesus, the public, Remy thought. Out of their frying pan into a plane-load of producers.

If forty-eight hours before, anyone aboard had told Hugh Remy he would be on his way to the Festival, he would have called him a liar or a fool. After the days that ended with the lawyer Donnenfeld's breaking the bad news to Siri about Pedro's insolvent estate, he figured he had had enough contact with his fellowman to last a lifetime. He retreated to *The Pelican*, his boat in the marina, intending a long stay.

Later the same night Remy knew someone was aboard even before he heard the footsteps on the teak planking overhead.

Alice, his big Irish setter, who bedded beneath the hatch above the sail locker, began to whine in a way that warned of visitors. Finally, she let off a deep bark that said, "Be careful—there are two of us here not sure we want company."

He stepped into a tired pair of khakis and moved toward the aft companionway, hunching as he went through the cabin.

He ducked out on deck, ready to deliver his standard lecture on the bad manners of coming aboard a man's boat uninvited.

Siri was near the walkway, wide-eyed at his sudden appearance from below. Her hands were thrust deeply into the pockets of a pale blue trench coat.

"I know it's late, Hugh."

"Come on down. I'll make coffee."

He put the kettle on and mixed them both a drink. He shooed Alice out from underfoot and sat across from Siri, waiting her out. She had never been to the boat before, and her eyes had a worry in them he hadn't seen even in the days immediately following Pedro's death. Her face was gaunt from the weight she'd lost, and she hadn't bothered to make up the two dark semicircles beneath her eyes.

She was still the most striking female Hugh Remy had ever seen.

Not a big woman, although she looked tall and willowy on film. A trick of proportioning, he knew, and one part magic. The camera was a selective demon. It would take exception to one beautiful lady, finding every flaw, then smile upon the next—blue eyes became brighter, a profile unforgettable. Siri's beauty on and off the screen had always unnerved him, made him feel old and ugly and clumsy.

Watching that perfect face, recalling all that had gone into exploiting every quality, he sometimes found it difficult to imagine there had been a Siri Laurence before she had met Pedro Lehman. Even the story of their meeting had the sound of a Lehman press release rearranging the truth to fit something the public wanted.

Lehman claimed, even to Remy, that he had been walking the streets of New York one night unable to sleep—a habit strangely resembling a former friend, Carl Laemmle. As the story went, Lehman ducked into the last of an Off-Broadway show in the Village and found Siri in the cast. His eye for talent saw the possibilities, and the rest was history.

It made good copy despite the fact that Lehman hated New York and considered theater south of Forty-second Street strictly amateur dramatics. But Remy recalled the first day he brought her to the studio—a smallish, slender girl, poised even then, who couldn't keep her fine blond hair out of her face. He had seen Pedro's expression and known his vow to make her a star wasn't the usual gambit to fill a bed for a night. Remy prepared himself for a long ride.

It wasn't the first time a man with power in Hollywood had tried using it to build a star. Goldwyn had given his all to a Russian actress named Anna Sten; Columbia's Harry Cohn poured time and money into a feline blonde named Kim Novak. The elder Zanuck tried with a French *chanteuse* named Greco; Selznick, with Jennifer Jones. And back before the name Harlow meant anything there was an aging producer named Paul Bern who guided her career only to commit suicide two and a half months after they were married.

But Siri drew something special from people, and Lehman's handling of the girl showed a patience that wasn't his strong suit. Remy recalled the time clearly, for almost against his will he found himself helping shape a Siri Laurence the public would believe later had burst upon them full-blown: the elegant, beautiful blonde, with a smile, partly sensual, partly mocking, that said, "I'm my own woman; I do what I feel like, and when I do, you'll know it." It was a perfect mélange of Lombard and Grace Kelly, and in that style she became a star with *Isabella*, *Summer Season*, and the film that confirmed it, *Lady Ice*. Two months before *Lady Ice* was released Siri and Pedro Lehman were married. Less than six months later came her much publicized breakdown and Siri's decision to quit films.

Four years ago, to the month, Hugh Remy remembered.

That night on the boat she had asked to stay. "A little corner someplace, just for the night. I can't bear the house. You understand."

71

Her voice hitched, and he honest-to-God didn't know if he was watching Siri desperate or the skilled performance of a marvelous actress.

"Enough nooks and crannies in this old barge to bunk an army. But that isn't why you came out here."

Her look was quick before something closed off. "I used to be a pretty fair actress."

"I knew you when, remember?"

She smiled fleetingly and took the steaming mug of coffee he gave her in both hands.

"Hugh, I'm going to Cannes. I'd like you along."

"The hell you say. Fine. Go. But not with me dragging along. You know how I am with those things, the Awards, the Festival."

"The films of Pedro's they're showing. They're your films, too."

Not quite they're not. He had thought about that plenty: the difference between talent and the nerve to lay yourself on the line. Both seemed to have abandoned him.

"Siri, they'll treat you like a queen over there, and I think Pedro would have liked that. I'd cramp your style."

"I'm doing this for me, Hugh. I'm going back into films."

"I don't believe it."

"I need to get away from this whole damn town, maybe do a picture in Europe." Her pitch had risen, and he could sense the panic just below the surface.

"Hey, now. . . ."

"Hugh, there is something I've got to tell you. Because if I don't tell someone, I'll go crazier than I already am."

"I'll listen, you know that."

She began circling the narrow cabin, then talking compulsively about growing up, about following the hopeful trail to New York that so many thousands still tried each year. That any of them survived the ego-destroying exercise of becoming an actor or actress always seemed to Remy one of the greatest testaments to human endurance.

He wasn't sure where her rambling was taking them, only that she needed to unburden herself of something before it burst within her. "Four years of cattle calls and readings when you find sixty girls within an inch of your height and just as pretty. Four years of beating against it. Until. . . ."

She hung onto the word so long Remy finally said, "Until what?"

"I grabbed something to keep afloat."

"Siri, what are you telling me?"

"I'm telling you there was a man in my life when I met Pedro. Someone who wants back in. When I met Nicky Deane, I was a part-time clerk at Bloomie's. . . ."

The name had slipped so naturally from her lips it took a moment before Remy grasped it.

". . . a little gift at first. It didn't buy me, I told myself. . . ."

He could have stopped her then, told her his own experience with Nicky Deane. But he wasn't ready with the long explanation that would have needed to follow. Pedro's death was still too close in time and pain, and there was still a chance he would get out of the trouble he was in untouched.

He remained silent and let Siri tell her story. "An occasional dinner," she was saying, "then more than occasional, and things began to happen . . . calls to read, a small part. But some other things happened, too—things I didn't much like."

"Such as?" He wondered how much of the truth she would tell him.

"Phone calls. His calls. Sometimes to the theater or when I'd be visiting a friend. Even eating lunch in a restaurant. Nothing more than 'Hi.' Nicky was telling me that he knew where I was, always."

"So he was having his lady watched."

"I wasn't his lady. Not in my mind. But when I told him so, he just laughed. That was his first mistake." She reached over, took the bottle, and poured whiskey into her coffee.

"His second mistake was introducing me to Pedro Lehman."

Siri looked into her mug of coffee, frowning.

"I don't know how well they knew each other, or if at all. Did Pedro ever mention Nicky to you?"

"Never."

"Hell, I knew that Nicky was in something shady just from the places we went, the way people treated him, in restaurants, for example. He was born poor, I guess, one of those kinds of people that liked to impress you by dropping names you know, talking like they're old friends. I didn't believe it, not all of it, but I was fascinated. One night we were eating in a little restaurant on Forty-eighth Street, and he pointed across the room and said, 'That's Pedro Lehman.' I asked was he a friend."

"And Deane said yes?"

"He didn't say anything. He just grinned and walked across the room to where Pedro was sitting. A minute or so later they came back. Nicky introduced us and lied about my career. Pedro was a little embarrassed, I think, but very polite, sort of playing Nicky's game. He didn't stay long. But when he was gone, Nicky looked at me and said, 'I told you.'"

"Didn't you ever ask Pedro about it?"

"His name was never mentioned again," she replied. "Not after what happened next."

Remy had poured himself another whiskey and let her pick her own time to continue. Alice, the big red setter, wandered through the cabin, checking up on things, and retreated.

"I was doing a little show Off-Broadway, and the next night Pedro burst into the dressing room after the performance and said—not asked, mind you—said I was coming to Hollywood under personal contract to him to make movies. Boom, like that."

"I hope you told him to go to hell. The look on his face would have been worth it."

"I didn't have the chance to tell him anything. He followed me out of the theater, blustering away, the lightning practically flying out of his eyeballs. God, the vitality he had then."

She stopped abruptly, and Remy knew that Siri had experienced it even more than he: the sudden fade this last year; the draining away of Pedro's exuberance.

"Watching him talk that night as if I were the only actress he'd ever discovered, the only thing he intended to do with his life—he swept me away, Hugh."

"Don't apologize, lady. He was good at it."

"I guess I was ready to be swept. I didn't go home for two days, every second spent with Pedro. When I did, Nicky Deane was waiting at my apartment, inside."

"Nice fella."

"I was too angry to be scared. I said I wanted him out of my life, but he didn't move. He began talking like I wasn't there, and I began to see something crazy behind those silky good looks. Talking about Pedro and Hollywood, telling me the town was no good. . . ."

"He couldn't have been all that crazy."

"But don't you see, he knew. He'd known I was with Pedro. Wrapping himself around my life again. And the next second tears are rolling down his face, and he's talking about marrying me."

"Hadn't that occurred to you?"

"Never," she said, shaking her head. "How can one person feel so much and the other nothing at all? That was when I panicked. I went for the door and got the shock of my life."

"Pedro."

She nodded. "Coming up the steps with a cab waiting at the curb." Remy found himself smiling at the picture of it despite himself. "When he saw Nicky, he didn't even blink. He just took my arm and guided me to the taxi, as if Nicky Deane wasn't there. 'We have a reservation to L.A.,' he said. 'I'll have your things sent out.' "

"And Deane let it happen?"

"He couldn't move. Shock, I don't know. Only, as we were leaving, he said something through the taxi window. 'You'll come to me,' he said."

"A trumpeting male ego."

"He called tonight."

"But you can't twist around somebody's life if they don't want it to happen."

Maybe the lack of conviction in his voice was as apparent to Siri as himself. She was silent awhile, then said, "He can. That's why I want out, Hugh. Two weeks in Cannes, something will happen. Come with me."

"Siri . . ." he began, intending to repeat the same lame arguments. Already he could feel himself losing ground.

She interrupted him. "I need someone I can trust. I need you."

"That's not fair, goddammit!"

She rose then, knowing she had him, smiling in a happy way he hadn't seen in months. "Well, now that it's settled, you can show me to a bedchamber. A little frivolity chasing those pretty ladies I've heard flock to Cannes will do you good. Shake you out of this monastic existence of yours."

"Maybe I like this monastic existence of mine."

She looked at him inquiringly. "Because it's safe?"

"Something like that."

It hadn't always been safe. He could think of the hellish six years he had spent with Katia, trying to keep pace. The Whirlwind. Mexico's gift to half the hang-arounds on Sunset Boulevard. He hadn't noticed. She had had enough fire to burn them all out, and Remy, too. Then it turned inward, and one night she tried to cool it off with a walk in the ocean near Puerto Vallarta. The currents were powerful there. Maybe she had known.

Siri searched his face, started to say something, and changed her mind.

After he had settled her into a bunk forward, he poured

76

what was left of the whiskey bottle into his glass and went to bed.

Once in the middle of the night a noise on deck reached through the whiskey sleep. His dog bumping her way through the partially opened hatch.
But not quite.

He awakened early, knowing something wasn't right.
Life on a boat was filled with special sounds—the slap of rigging, the gurgle of water against the hull. Birds, bells, distant engines.
This sound was none of them. A deep thumping, coincident with the gentle roll of the boat. He couldn't place it. Then he did. Something was striking against the main mast, the metal tube conducting the sound into the depths of the boat, where the mast was stepped into the keel.
He heard Siri call out from the next cabin, "Helluva'n alarm you got there, fella."
But Hugh Remy was already moving toward the companionway.
In the pale light of dawn he hadn't been able to make out the reason for the sound. His eyes darted over the deck, mentally ticking through the checklist.
Then his eyes turned upward.
From the deck to the top of the mainmast was forty-one feet exactly. At that distance it looked like a red flag hanging in loose, draping folds. A flag waiting for the wind to blow before it would fill.
Vaguely he was aware of Siri, padding up the stairs to stand next to him, not even reaching his shoulder.
He heard her short, dry gasp when she too figured it out.
There was nothing to be done. He climbed onto the top of the cabin and unfastened the main halyard where it had been tied by someone who had never spent time on a boat.
Slowly, gently, as if it made a difference, he lowered

77

Alice's body down onto the deck and undid the line where it had been fastened tightly around the dog's broken neck.

Now, aboard Flight 061 to Paris, Hugh Remy was no longer thinking about Cannes or the Festival. He thought of what Nicky Deane had brought down upon all of them, Pedro, Siri, himself. His mind was filled with the good old-fashioned idea of revenge.

≡ *Chapter 10*—The Brothers Rampa

An hour south of Paris, Ms. Maxine Allston shut her *People* magazine and studied more closely the two men sharing the second-class train compartment.

She had been reading about the death of Pedro Lehman, a name she vaguely recalled and only then because he was married to Siri Laurence. It was hard to imagine being married to a man that much older, because she and Siri were the exact same age, both Libras, and now that she thought about it she seemed to remember an article she'd read in the *Enquirer* about a marriage agreement. Or something.

She had bought magazines like crazy because two weeks of traveling alone were wearing thin, despite the raunchy but thoroughly satisfying three-day screwing contest she had in Paris with a coarse Dutch youth eight years her junior. Already in the pages of her notebook it was called a "love affair," and her description of the boy neglected certain items of odor, dress, and eating habits that she had been willing to forgive given the essential. She had been reluctant to part with him to board still another train alone, but she was determined to see Cannes during the Festival. The word "glamour" stuck in her mind.

She jotted the word in her notebook, intending to deal with the image more clearly later. Since the university she considered herself something of a writer—poetry and short stories mainly, to date unpublished. Traveling filled her notebooks with sharp, witty observation, something teaching school in Principia, Illinois, failed to do.

The two men facing her in the compartment were an example.

Mentally she began to describe them, searching for key words to amplify later in the pages of her notebook.

Dusky complexions, possibly gypsy blood. French or Spanish and not at all well-to-do. The older of the two had carried aboard a plastic shopping bag, a *baguette* of bread, and a large bottle of *vin ordinaire*. He smelled of wine and garlic and had fallen asleep before the train left the Gare de Lyon.

It was the other one who attracted her. Brooding. The eyes of a sad priest. She liked the image. A sad priest whose eyes rested upon her with hidden desire. Younger than the other man by five or six years, but a resemblance. Brothers. She was sure of it.

The younger one wore denims and a jacket too heavy for the south of France this time of year and was, well . . . a bit scruffy. If he had taken better care of himself, tried a little harder, he would have been quite good-looking. As her mother repeatedly said, little things always made an impression.

She formed an opinion based on their clothing and the suitcase the young one had placed on the overhead rack. A large suitcase of heavy plastic, scarred from hard use and tied shut with a length of cord. She was willing to believe the suitcase contained everything they owned.

What brought them aboard this train heading south?

Maxine Allston let her mind wander.

Across from her Gaetan Rampa gazed without expression at the clean American face, radiating vitamins, soap and water, and good food. He had been with women like that occasionally, in Paris, ones he met on the streets. Ones on holiday wanting only one thing. As lovers he found American women unskilled but willing. Another time he might have anticipated what the ten-hour journey could bring. Time enough for a bottle of wine, the drawing of the curtains for an afternoon nap. What transpired would by necessity be quick and dangerous.

But that was the Gaetan Rampa of a year ago. Even his

brother, Maxim, had noticed his new sense of purpose, and the Lord knew Maxim was capable of noticing little enough.

And what had the woman observed? She had carefully studied them both, taking a particular interest in the suitcase.

The thought made Gaetan Rampa smile. Mistaking his intent, the woman returned it. Her teeth were too large but white and clean; a miracle to have teeth like that.

She wouldn't have found much to smile at in their suitcase, Gaetan Rampa thought. What would she have made of her two traveling companions had she seen the strange selection of items inside: the tuxedos, worn and smelling of tobacco as much a part of their fiber now as the filth of a dozen cities? Two tuxedos, soiled shirts, and a clean white envelope containing instructions the girl had typed in better French than Gaetan Rampa could write.

Yes, my warm, smiling chicken, what would you have thought if you'd seen the Browning pistol and the French-made hand grenade and guessed their intended purpose?

How then would you have enjoyed this ride through the French countryside?

Far to the south, Auguste Pascal watched the gray layer of clouds approaching from the sea, thinking the rain would be good for his plants.

He straightened, brushing damp earth from the knees of his worn trousers, knowing he must hurry, for he was late again. A sign, Pascal. One among many.

He had risen an hour early that morning to tend his budding garden, the flowers retarded this year by a merciless winter. He stopped for a moment now at the edge of the garden to gaze out toward the sea, a good ten miles distant. On a clear day one could see to the farthest cape of the Côte d'Azur just beyond St.-Tropez.

What the tourist thought of collectively as the French Riviera, or Côte d'Azur, Pascal saw as sixty miles of terrain not all of a piece. Each of the larger towns was distinct in his mind in form and spirit, sharing only the Mediterranean and the fact that they were French. Ste.-Maxime, St.-Raphaël, Cannes, Juan-les-pins, Antibes, Cagnes-sur-Mer, the only true city, Nice, then Villefranche, Beaulieu, and Menton, each as subtly different as the stones in a necklace of jade, although Pascal was less knowledgeable about jade necklaces than about the Côte d'Azur. He once gave his wife, Lucette, a jade brooch—how long ago?—eighteen years. Before he left for Oran during the civil war.

Even the mountain villages of the Côte, tucked away on the low front ranges of the Alps, were reluctant to be cast into a mold with the others, though most were dull, sleepy places of little interest to the tourist except in July and August, when no part of this fabled coast was left unexplored. In one such village Pascal had bought property with its garden and small house. He would be happy to retire here. It was all he could do these days to force himself to descend to the hurly-burly of those busy places by the sea, to Cannes most of all. But descend he must.

"Auguste!" he heard his wife call. But he had already begun walking back up the hill toward the house. "Hurry, Auguste. The car is here."

"I know, I'm late."

"They're waiting," she went on, beckoning him from the window of the small kitchen.

"Then give them coffee," Auguste Pascal said, appreciative of his wife's sunny disposition, which he had done little enough to encourage over the years. "Policemen always like coffee," he added.

Yes, Auguste Pascal sighed, descend he must.

Philippe Brialt looked from the window of his office on the third floor of the Festival Hall and swore at the layer of black cloud moving over the Palm Beach Casino.

A block away the smirk on the handsome face of the new James Bond, rotating on the jerry-built cyclorama on the roof of the Carlton dining room, seemed to be mocking him once every forty-five seconds. The hotel sold itself to the film industry these two weeks, every square foot of display space carrying a price tag. Brialt could just make out, beyond Mr. Bond, the inflatable plastic panther, bright pink, straddling the hotel entrance. Those who wished to enter were required to pass between the animal's outspread legs. How appropriate.

Brialt wondered why he continued to try at all, why he refused to give in. What difference would it make to the Festival with some other functionary behind his desk, equally adept at dialing a telephone and saying yes or no to choices any fool could decide between? Still, he found himself resisting. He would fight them all, dammit, this one last time—even if he didn't understand why—including the weather.

He was receiving weather reports every three hours now, for he knew from the bitter experience of the previous year's damp, dark proceedings that nothing killed the spirit of the Festival more surely than rain. That was all he would need. The opening ceremonies were in a scant six hours, and Brialt doubted they were going to make it.

As he hurried through the foyer of the Festival Hall, a team of workmen was still struggling with the new red carpeting. The buzz of a saw and incessant hammering came from the interior of a small prefabricated radio studio being constructed on the mezzanine, one of four that would provide live TV and radio coverage. Two dozen newly purchased potted palms were nowhere to be seen, and already he had needed to authorize additional expenditure to buy layers of asbestos fireproofing for the display booths on the fourth floor.

The Palais des Festivals was in truth a small, poorly equipped convention center which the Film Festival had outgrown. Even with the addition of the *nouveau palais*—the bland glass-and-aluminum office block adjoining the Festival Hall—his people were overflowing the facilities. The entire second floor of the *nouveau palais* was given over to the press. Passing through, he noticed that the bank of telex machines was still not functioning and that the room intended for press conferences looked incredibly small. "Three hundred people, maximum," Pouget, his head of press relations, said, spreading his hands helplessly.

"Talk with Allard about using the *grande salle* as a backup. There are times when it's free. This year we may need it."

A bit of good fortune that. The press conference for Coppola the ninth day of the Festival would draw a thousand reporters.

Already they had issued two thousand sets of press credentials. And worse to come. During the next forty-eight hours Pouget's office would be deluged with a crush of pretenders, journalists of dubious affiliation, and the honest but absent-minded, who would arrive having forgotten their press cards, jet-lagged and hung-over. The press section also administered its own post office, bank, typing room, and quick film-processing service for the protographers, who outnumbered the stars themselves.

As with most arrangements for the press, it was a short flight of stairs to the bar.

Brialt walked rapidly along the narrow hallway from the *nouveau palais* to the offices above the Festival Hall foyer, given over to Festival administration. It was an inflatable organization, dragged from a musty closet once a year and pumped up to full size with mercenaries. The surprise was it ran a Festival so well.

He was tempted to visit Protocol to see Katherine, but he doubted he could have carried off the employer-employee charade with conviction. The Protocol Office drew up the guest lists for the dinners he was expected to give nightly for a few select personalities in his suite at the Carlton. To his relief Katherine had fitted perfectly into Protocol. She spoke fluent French, and Brialt was pleased to discover that despite her abandon in private, she possessed a quick, orderly mind, certain to benefit them all in the chaos of the two weeks ahead.

Some of the memorable moments of the Festival could be expected during his dinners, a thought he would remember later with dread.

He continued on toward the large *salle* at the end of the hall which housed Claude Durand's *Bureau des Comédiens*.

Inside, the room had the look of a brokers office in a falling market. At six separate desks the telephones were ringing nonstop, the conversations taking place around him in at least three languages and at a volume intended to redress the inadequacies of the French telephone system.

He found Durand in front of a large chart pinned to a wall. On it were written the names of film stars, organized by date of arrival, with the departure date and hotel accommodations penciled next to each name.

In principle all were welcome at Cannes, although the Festival footed the expenses for only the officially invited and those participating in the films in competition. Durand more than anyone was aware of the gaps and deletions on the chart. Even in the last hours he was still trying to lure names known worldwide to the Festival. The more stars in attendance, the more action from the press, and that was the purpose of the exercise.

The French press was fond of believing that the Festival in former times had been a miraculous but accidental marriage of art and glamour. Not quite. From the beginning it was a carefully managed exercise in public relations, a Festival designed by the French government with the encouragement of a tourist-conscious city of Cannes as a glossy advertisement in self-promotion.

In their triumph the glamour had somehow slipped away. Increasingly, as the saying went, the business of the Film Festival was business. Who, after all, could expect old-fashioned glamour in an age of denim, rock music, and Italian kidnappers plying their trade like so many street merchants?

Still, they tried.

Durand tapped at the chart with his knuckle.

"Mastroianni and Dylan have canceled," he said in a tone signaling a personal affront. "But we have Liv Ullmann for the opening. Arrival this afternoon on SK Five-eighty-five."

Earlier Durand had been trying to lure either Kristofferson or Travolta, a younger, more electric element than the usual Festival standbys—Kirk Douglas, Curt Jurgens, Greg Peck—but he had been defeated by the telephone; he plain could not get through. He did find Jack Nicholson in London and got a maybe. "The only good thing that's happened this morning," he told Brialt, "is a cabled affirmative from Siri Laurence."

Durand found her a suite at the Majestic, a minor miracle. This narrow stretch of Mediterranean coastline was in the midst of an invasion that would fill every four-star-luxe hotel as far as Monte Carlo, thirty miles away.

Brialt left him and took the stairs up one flight, checking the time. In exactly twenty-three minutes he was meeting with the mayor of Cannes and the various heads of police responsible for the city's order these next two weeks. Chef de District Auguste Pascal would no doubt be punctual.

He moved rapidly along the hall, past the jury deliberation room, its long, oval table unattended for the moment.

In the past that room had become a caldron of hotly voiced contrary opinion. Maurois, Visconti, Fritz Lang, Tennessee Williams, Losey, Pagnol—they had all come to Cannes, and the chemistry of the juries was another of the Festival's unpredictables.

"We shall see," Brialt said softly. Last year's jury head died of a heart attack less than a week after the Festival's end. His debates with a voluble feminine American film critic were said to have aggravated his failing health.

In his office Brialt found a message. His wife, Monique, had telephoned, twice. He crumpled the note, promising himself he would take the time to call—but later.

He again made use of the stairs, irritated with himself for letting Monique's phone calls stir the first pangs of guilt. Dammit, he was seizing an opportunity that came to few people, the love and passion of a beautiful woman half his age. Perhaps it *was* love.

This time, as he crossed the Festival Hall foyer, he was struck by the change.

The new red carpeting was in place; the lobby, resplendent with flowers and palms. Inside the radio studio two men were testing the equipment, their lips forming test signals. But here the only sound was his own footsteps as he descended the broad staircase that led from the *grande salle* to the street.

He turned at the high glass doors and surveyed the lobby as it would not look again for two weeks, void of people and sound. There were plans for a new Festival Hall bigger, more impressive. Yet this aging lady would be hard to replace. Beyond the doors at the top of the stairs was the elegant *grande salle*, the theater where the nightly showing of films in competition, twenty-five this year, was the focal point of the Festival.

He had seen the elite of the film world gathered there. Had watched them disappointed, angered, elated, sometimes proud to be moved by several thousand feet of 35 mm celluloid. In this *grande salle* he had long ago fully understood why people in films—this business, this way of life—when touched by it found all others without spice or passion.

Brialt turned and went out onto the Croisette, late for his meeting with the mayor and police and not giving a damn.

≡ *Chapter 11*—Welcome to Paradise

Eighteen miles away the *festivaliers* were already pouring through Nice-Côte d'Azur airport.

The "Festival Crowd," as it was labeled with some disdain by the resident English-speaking population of the Côte, provided an exotic element to the springtime French Riviera. They arrived in Gucci shoes with Vuitton bags and dripping gold. In $150 jeans. In jumpsuits, or Savile Row tailoring, or peach-colored sports coats from Carroll and Company. More than a few brought deep, lacquered suntans rare on a coast not quite over winter. They arrived from Rome, Munich, Madras, Hong Kong, Tokyo, Toronto, New York, and Los Angeles, bleary-eyed, irritable, and speaking almost every language except French.

In a matter of hours, no more time than the turning of one day into the next, they hit Cannes like a human tidal wave and swept the city away.

Kenrick had seen it all before, but as he and Aron Archer debarked the connecting flight from Paris, he decided nothing really prepared you for Cannes. Except a month of sleep beforehand and the promise of a long vacation after.

They were met by the head of the studio's Paris office, an immaculately tailored Frenchman named Gérard, who had worked for the elder Zanuck when he tried to run Twentieth from a suite in the George V in Paris.

"Mr. Stiner would like you to call," Gérard said. "And I'm afraid you'll have to endure passport control." He gave a shrug meaning both items were beyond his power to manipulate.

Kenrick didn't mind. In Los Angeles, awaiting departure, he spotted Leo Gold. He wanted to make a tentative approach during the flight, where at least he would have the cricketlike Gold within the confines of an aircraft. Gold ran his own studio, the closest thing the industry had these days to an old-time mogul. He was on Kenrick's list as a possible distributor for the breakaway studio's films.

But on the transatlantic crossing Gold hadn't been in first class, and on the short flight from Paris to Nice there wasn't time.

Rayna Tate joined the same flight in Paris. Her traveling companion was a handsome, squarely built man with a Continental manner and a way of taking Rayna's presence for granted that hinted of intimacy. Rayna nodded once to Kenrick, her expression giving little away. By the time he had filed from the aircraft in Nice, Rayna, her companion, and Leo Gold were gone.

Kenrick shrugged and headed toward the long line waiting at passport control, taking in a deep breath of air with something in it he couldn't identify.

"Pine," a voice behind him said in a plum-in-the-mouth British accent, accompanied by the strong aroma of alcohol. "One of the three prominent fragrances of the Côte d'Azur. Pine, lavender, and the odor of petrol fumes."

The comment came from a thick-chested man in a shapeless tweed sports coat, with leather-patched elbows. Kenrick noted the three small colored bands worn on the lapel, decorations of some sort given by the French government for distinction in combat.

"Galloway's the name," the man said, staring myopically down at Kenrick. A thick pair of glasses magnified his eyes into large gray disks without focus.

"*Financial Times*," Kenrick said, leaving unmentioned that he knew damn well who Peter Galloway was from the article he had written about the financier Robert Arthur.

"Free-lance, these days," Galloway remarked without explanation. He fell in step with Kenrick, uninvited, and wiped the perspiration from his forehead with a well-used handkerchief.

"I've heard your studio is on the auction block," he offered casually. "Anything to it?"

Light enough to be a request for the time of day, but an iron fist wrapped in a velvet package.

"Is this on or off the record?"

"It's all on the record with me," Galloway replied. "What you say is what I write, and I spell correctly." He tried to smile, but it didn't take. Galloway's mouth puckered, froze, then relaxed as he gave up the attempt.

"*If* the studio were for sale," Kenrick replied, "it would be a remarkable value. We're finishing the best year in history, with some big films due for release."

Galloway grunted, knowing he was being fed predictable fodder. "So much for the frontal attack. I thought I noticed something out of the ordinary, that's all. A veritable squad of foot soldiers representing your studio at Cannes, including you and the parent company president, yet not even a film in competition. Odd."

Sid Mathan, the studio VP for acquisitions, was already in Cannes, as was Ernst Rucker, head of European distribution.

Kenrick was getting Galloway's style now, his way of coming back to the same concerns from a different angle. Behind the bluff, mumbling approach was a subtle interrogator. But what was he after?

Kenrick responded, staying on firm footing. "But we've the most important out-of-competition showing of the Festival. The final night."

"Ah, yes, the Lehman film. I hear it's in trouble."

"You heard wrong, Mr. Galloway."

The gray disks of eyes held him uncertainly. "I for one hope he pulled it off. I'd hate to think Lehman's last film was as bad as the three before it. He deserves a better monument." Galloway looked away myopically. "I wonder if the public understands what Lehman's death meant—the end of an epoch, absolute end. The last great filmmaker in the business since the silents. Gone. I don't mean the moguls—the Thalbergs and Siegels, the Warner Brothers. I mean filmmaker—Schary, Capra, Joe Mankiewicz, John Ford. Men who put their stamp on a film, and to hell with people who didn't agree with them. Now it's all run by accountants—and people like you."

Galloway made no attempt to soften his distaste. Kenrick liked him better for it. Galloway didn't give a damn either and felt no compulsion to mince his words, hoping for favor.

"You're a romantic, Galloway."

The reporter smiled, distantly. "Alas, it may be so."

"The business has changed. In the end the ones that lived long enough—those filmmakers you talk about—all made visits to the front office, and that included Lehman. Not one of them would have survived in the business the way it is today."

"I'm not sure they would want to," Galloway remarked. "Crumbled pyramids. That's what Selznick called Hollywood near his end."

"He saw it at the bottom. The film industry has never been fatter. The pyramids have been rebuilt, Galloway, bigger and better." He could hear too much hard sell in his own voice.

"Yes," Galloway said mildly. "Out of aluminum and tinted glass."

In the limo to Cannes, Kenrick found himself mentally replaying the conversation with Galloway, knowing in some way he'd come out second best. Why would his encounter with a seedy, myopic journalist have left him as unsettled as any interview with the press he had ever had?

Something about Galloway led him to one conclusion: Avoid the man. Galloway was dangerous.

* * *

"Dangerous and on target," Aron Archer said of Galloway exactly two hours later.

He held up his gin and tonic to the light, plucked out a shattered pip, and began pacing. Kenrick's hotel suite looked out across a broad palm-fringed garden at the Mediterranean, which was at that moment not azure blue, but copperish and threatening.

At Kenrick's retelling of Galloway's question about the studio's being on the auction block, a peculiar expression spread over Archer's face. He slipped off to the privacy of his own suite. An hour and three transatlantic phone calls later he returned, mixed himself a powerful drink, and delivered the news to Kenrick.

"I've found out what put the wind up Stiner. And this Galloway, too, apparently. Stiner flew to the Festival via London. Two days ago he had lunch with Clive Munson. Know the name?"

"Something about a try at buying the New York *Post*. Owns a London newspaper, something like that."

"And a chain in Australia. And two independent television stations, plus a book publisher. Self-made millionaire and self-proclaimed genius. Distasteful little man with a Cockney accent and lacquered fingernails. They lunched a long time at Munson's club."

"Which you read exactly how?"

"There's a rumor several parties are eyeing a buy of the studio. One of them is Clive Munson." In Kenrick's silence, Archer said, "It would explain the observable phenomena. Suppose Stiner's investigator, this Donald Eads, uncovers some rot, and Lord knows this is the movie business." Kenrick was thinking of the Lehman film, the likelihood that someone had skimmed money from the budget. "Our stock will drop like a roller coaster. Granted majority stockholder Robert Arthur stands to take the biggest pounding, but he is still only fifteen percent of the bundle. But a scare into the other stockholders, the ones with certificates in their mattresses, and they'll ruin whatever our profits look like."

"With Munson waiting to buy in cheap."

"Exactly." Archer finished his drink and made another.

Kenrick considered it a moment, then asked, "What sort of proposition would Munson have made to Stiner?"

"Just guessing, I'd say something to the effect that if Stiner does everything in his power to deflate the studio's reputation discreetly, he gets a special reward and not in heaven either."

"It would fit Stiner's shoving this investigation of the studio down everyone's throat."

Archer pointed a finger. "Make no mistake. If Stiner is out to drag the studio's reputation down, you're the target. Principle one, old chum: Find someone to blame. I'm afraid you're the man."

Kenrick rose and began changing his shirt. In fifteen minutes he was meeting his vice-president for acquisitions, Sid Mathan, in the bar. Mathan was a name on his list, one of the nuclei for the new studio.

"Then, Aron, we move before Stiner does."

≡ *Chapter 12*—Les Flics

At the exact moment Teddy Kenrick took the elevator down to meet his first target, Sid Mathan, Philippe Brialt was hurrying along a corridor in the city's Hôtel de Ville, girding himself for the encounter with the mayor and the police.

To each man waiting in the mayor's office that late afternoon the Festival presented a different problem.

For the mayor, a diminutive, balding man with a hooked nose and an excitable manner, the Festival was the prize convention of the year. "We have competition now," he lectured. "Montreux, Amsterdam—they all want conventions. It's good business."

The *festivaliers* would pour a quarter of a million dollars a day into the city's hotels and restaurants, and everyone had a piece of Festival action: travel agents, bill and poster printers, photocopiers and typists, rental agents, caterers, florists, hairdressers, yacht brokers, *parfumeurs. C'est fou,* the *Cannois* said, what was bought for whom during the Festival. But cash registers rang, everyone smiled, and no one smiled more than the mayor of Cannes.

To Police Commissaire Auguste Pascal the Festival was a two-week headache of car theft, petty crime, and responsibility. As *chef de district* he was ultimately on the block for the security of the Festival, a task he carried out each year with stubborn, plodding efficiency. As he addressed the gathering, it occurred to Brialt that Commissaire Pascal continued to be much in need of a decent tailor. His black suit was rumpled and too snugly fitted across his middle, the same suit that Brialt saw each year during Festival time, stored away no doubt in some musty closet to be withdrawn for this one occasion, wrinkles and all.

This year Pascal announced two additions to Festival security. "I've secured the services of a bomb disposal expert from the Corps Urbain in Nice."

So my nagging paid off, Brialt thought. The number of crank threats and bomb warnings increased each year, yet it would take only one who wasn't a crank.

"And we've decided to employ Charpentier's team on a twenty-four-hour basis." Pascal nodded toward a younger, athletic-looking policeman with a neatly trimmed coal-black beard. Charpentier, as it turned out, headed the SOS—the Section Opérationelle Spécialisé—a small elite action unit modeled after Scotland Yard's flying squad and the various U.S.-style SWAT teams. "What I need from you, Brialt, is a place to house them inside the Festival Hall out of the public eye. And perhaps a ready supply of coffee."

"You'll have it," Brialt promised, even if at that moment he couldn't imagine where.

Pascal went on to review the normal security arrangements inside the hall. Brialt could well believe that one of the more incongruous sights of the Festival was the drab locker room of the *commissariat central* an hour before the evening screening in the Palais: officers swapping their blue uniforms and boots for evening wear and Italian patent leather.

When Brialt mentioned to Katherine that one out of every four "ushers" inside the Festival Hall was a policeman, she had been surprised at the need for such security. "I think the spectacle of the Munich Olympics, the hostaging of Israeli athletes and the bloodshed, haunts even sleepy Pascal. An event like the Festival is fair game."

Thanks to a mixture of chance and careful management, films from neither Israel nor the Arab world were to be shown at Cannes that year.

The meeting ended with Pascal giving up the floor to Roger Haag, commandant of CRS 6, the unit of riot troops from the barracks at St.-Laurent-du-Var. Brialt found Haag, tall and erect, looking something like a young De Gaulle, a vaguely ominous presence.

For despite the magnificently turned-out Festival honor guard and the sharply dressed teams of CRS on each street corner, Brialt never forgot the stubby gray Saviem buses tucked on key side streets and behind the Festival hall itself. Inside were police in reserve with their racks of helmets, shields, and truncheons. The primary task of Haag's troops was crowd control, the surge expected to reach fifty thousand on the city's streets the first weekend of the Festival. If for whatever reason the crowds became unruly, Brialt knew that Haag would employ force in their management, without compromise.

Haag smartly tapped the map on one wall of the mayor's office and said, "This narrow rectangle holds most of the problems—the eight blocks between the hotels Martinez and Majestic with the Festival Hall in between. That's where my men are concentrated. If necessary, the area can be sealed off from the rest of the city in minutes."

"But can't we avoid giving Cannes the look of an armed camp?" the mayor pleaded.

And it was here an odd thing happened. Pascal was about to reply when Commandant Haag spoke instead, a veiled challenge passing between him and the *chef de district*. "One cannot expect the protection of the police without their presence," Haag said. "It is my belief that visible police are a greater deterrent to trouble than specialists hidden away in a back room."

Brialt would think little about the remark until later. Whatever jealousies and interior struggles may have strained the policeman inside the mayor's office, he knew to the public they would present a united front, come what may.

With the meeting ended, Brialt walked rapidly toward the Festival Hall. He would have time enough for a quick shower and a change into his tuxedo before his rendezvous with the minister of culture for their ritual entrance at the Festival opening.

As he moved through the slowly promenading crowd, Brialt didn't envy the police their job. He had seen too many festivals to sustain the romantic belief that the thousands of people pouring into the city were all fans hungry to glimpse the glamour of the film world—that mystical abstraction, the public. True, the spectacle drew tourists. But it was the other element he found disturbing.

Where did they come from, these cripples, beggars, vendors, prostitutes, gypsies, photographers with clicking Polaroids, these hordes of wanderers that descended upon Cannes each Festival? A few *performeurs des rues* were legitimate talents, but most were nothing more than beggars pegging a few pathetic notes on mandolin or guitar before holding out their hands.

As he approached the Festival Hall, a pair of street entertainers were already performing before the crowded outdoor tables of the Blue Bar.

At first glance they might have passed for any of his ushers, dressed as they were in black tuxedos. But a second inspection revealed the shiny, tired fabric, the darkish rings of perspiration and soil on collars and cuffs. The younger of the two had a brooding handsomeness one didn't expect to find passing a hat on the street. The second man was older, resembling the younger enough to be a brother, but with a face clearly showing the ravages of alcohol and whatever misfortunes life had dealt him.

Their act, performed in unison to music from a portable tape recorder, consisted of lighting a number of cigarettes in an elaborate, mock-debonaire manner to build curiosity. Then, one by one, they popped the lighted cigarettes into their mouths, chewed, and swallowed them. When they encored on razor blades, Brialt decided he had seen enough.

He pushed open the glass door to the Palais lobby and

caught sight of Katherine at the top of the stairs, watching the two performers.

"I thought you'd be waiting at the hotel," Brialt called out, and saw Katherine jump at the sound of his voice. Her smile came with difficulty.

"I thought I'd come down and hurry you along."

"I'll put you to work," Brialt said. "Unless you'd prefer to watch the show." He indicated the two men, who had begun again with the cigarettes.

"It's disgusting," she said. "Filthy and disgusting."

"No matter, darling," Brialt said, taking her arm and guiding her across the polished marble floor toward the stairs. "I'm sure they manage quite well."

In front of the Blue Bar, Gaetan Rampa's head turned, a cigarette frozen near his mouth. Ignoring his brother Maxim's whisper to stay in time with the music, Gaetan Rampa watched the man and woman inside the Festival Hall until they disappeared from view.

"Balls!" Donner said.

He surveyed the cut of his tuxedo and again tried to straighten the black tie that wouldn't square. He poured himself another glass of tonic water, thinking how much he would have liked the gin to go with it. He wanted a drink more than he could ever remember.

He gulped down the tonic and turned from the full-length mirror in his hotel room, trying to fight the panicky feeling that Rayna was about to dump him. Left to his own tactics in the delicate game of approaching people, he would no doubt take offense at something unintended, if his past history were any indicator, and blow the chance. He had been a long time coming to the discovery: You couldn't do it all yourself.

"I don't believe what I'm hearing," Rayna said when he had told her the same thing four months before, in her small, well-furnished office just above Sunset. They were standing closer than Donner intended. They had already made their appraisals of each other, and there was a moment when he thought they might end up in bed again before they talked much. But Rayna took a step away, saying, "Ah, ah," reading him and most likely herself. "If this is business, let's keep it that way." Once it had cooled he was glad they had.

He told her about the script.

"And you're off the sauce?" She was wary, and he didn't blame her.

"More than a year. From the time I found that story. Or it found me. I'm angry enough to make this crazy idea work."

"A little anger is a useful thing, Rod. Aimed in the right direction. Which usually comes back around to number one. Self-criticism hasn't been exactly your chosen instrument."

"Read the script," Donner said.

She called him at seven the next morning. Her choice of an early hour no doubt had a secondary purpose. There was a time when he hadn't functioned much before 11:00 A.M., even on the set, and then only with the aid of a couple of beers.

"It's all there," he heard her say. "Different levels, strong characterizations, all those catchwords you hear when someone is trying to sell something. Except this one really has them."

"And the character McCann?"

"It's you, you growly bastard." She paused. Donner understood it then, the item that remained after all the highs and lows and swings and changes they had been through together. They liked each other, and always had. "Rod, I can't promise you a thing. You have to understand that."

"Name the price."

"No . . . this one's on me. I'm not sure at the end of it, even if we get lucky, I won't still owe you."

"Stop," Donner said.

"We'll give it a try."

A try. Donner took in a deep breath to settle the tension and stepped out onto the balcony of his hotel room.

Below, the Croisette had come to life. Noisy traffic was backed around the crescent toward the Palm Beach Casino. A block in the other direction he could see the brightly lighted exterior of the Festival Hall. The crowds had begun to gather before noon in preparation for the opening gala that night. Several thousand people were there now, held in check by police barriers. Already a slow promenade moved along the sidewalks below, men in dinner jackets, women in long dresses, wending their way toward the hall. Soon the limos would begin arriving, playing their part in the obligatory opening of each night's spectacle—the grand entrance.

"But we go all the way, Donner. Or we don't play," Rayna had said. "My only condition."

He was pouring himself another tonic when the telephone rang.

He let it ring three times, picked it up, and grunted hello.

"Don't be cool with me," Rayna said.

"I have to try with someone. I wasn't fooling the room waiter."

"You ready?"

"As I'll ever be."

"The limo will be by at nine sharp. That will put you and the lady at the entrance to the Festival Hall about ten minutes before the opening ceremony. There's already a fat, curious crowd inside the hall and out. If you don't make the most sensational entrance of your life, I'll cut your heart out and eat it."

He could hear sounds in the background—traffic, voices, a waiter calling out a drink order. It would be the Bar Festival, the Blue or the Majestic.

"Brief me on the lady."

"Her name is Taya Linder. German with one good film behind her and some interesting ambitions. Calculating, hungry, and perfect. You'd better hang on."

"But a limo, for chrissakes. The Palais is only a block away."

"Listen, my thickheaded darling," Rayna said, her voice growing impatient, "I want an entrance. Because I want photographs. I want people to know you're here, looking better than you've ever looked. Then I can begin to work. *A poco a poco*, eh? This is my kind of business even if it isn't yours." There was a second's pause before Rayna said, "Donner, I'm coming up."

"Think I've got a pint under the pillow?"

"I'm not worried about booze. Not really. I want to see you, make sure it's right. Besides, an idea has come to mind, and I want to know what you think."

Twenty minutes later Donner heard two impatient raps on his hotel-room door. He let Rayna in, then took a step back.

She wore a long pale dress that accentuated her smooth olive skin. The neck scooped just low enough to remind Donner of the small, perfect breasts, the nipples incredibly sensitive. . . . He groaned, only half in jest.

"Save the performance for the people out front." She walked into the room, taking in every detail, then turned her attention on him, nodding after a professional appraisal. "You'll do."

"Performance, hell," Donner said. "Sometimes I look at you, all I think of are the things I've let blow out of my life—"

She cut in icily. "Then don't let this be one of them. I could use a drink."

"No booze. On the level."

She took a deep spasm of breath, and Donner could see she was keyed up and strung taut. How many other games was she juggling at Cannes? "About Taya," she said. "I might have been able to pair you with a bigger name—Paola Veran, for example."

"I could have suffered that."

"I even thought about trying for Siri."

Donner waved it away. "She'd have figured a way to make me look like a clod. Once was enough."

"I'm trying to get rid of that image everyone has of you. Big stud wrapped around a Latin lady, with a fat grin and a bottle of beer in your hand."

"Have mercy."

"I don't want people remembering that Rod Donner. Taya is a lady. By all appearances."

"Why not you?" Donner asked. "What the hell."

"Will you stop?" she said irritably. "I don't have time for this. And I don't mother people along anymore. Clear? If no one sees us so much as nodding to each other, I'll have an easier time of getting things done."

There was no real venom in it, and Donner grinned. She shook her head, exasperated at herself for not being able to stay angry with the man. "You're a pain where I sit."

"You came up here to remind me."

He caught the change in her expression. "Rod . . ." she began, "what if, somehow, we could get to Teddy Kenrick?"

Donner's laugh came quickly, a rough expulsion that very nearly spattered tonic water down his shirtfront. "And you wanted to be serious," he said. "Kenrick wouldn't touch anything I was involved in with gloves on."

"But it happens all the time. You said so yourself. People hate each other's guts one minute, and the next they're cutting a contract at the Polo Lounge all smiles and dollar signs. Look at Kenrick and Pedro Lehman. A year ago who would have figured Kenrick to go for another Lehman film, unless Siri was in it?"

"That was Kenrick and Lehman," Donner said somberly. He set the glass down carefully. "I was not only a bruise to Kenrick's ego, but somewhere during my foggy exit from Hollywood I punched him in the face."

"But what if I could get the door open again, get Kenrick to listen?"

"I hear a strange something in your voice. Don't tell me you and Kenrick—"

"Me and Kenrick nothing," she continued sharply. "This is business."

"Uh-huh."

"What I'm asking is if Kenrick were to go for you and the script—the whole package—would he be the right man?"

The whole package. Donner wasn't sure what the whole package would turn out to be. Whether, when it came down to the payoff, the hard time when the deal would be fleshed out, whether he would have the courage to play it all the way. Or whether he would fold to a compromise. His whole life, the pictures he had made, the women, had been a nice little amble following the path of least resistance.

Donner said, "Kenrick is solid gold. But you'd have an easier time running me for President."

"We'll see," Rayna said.

Rayna's planning proved on the mark in one respect: Taya Linder. Donner made the appraisal as he ducked into the back seat of the black Mercedes limo. Whatever Taya Linder might or might not have been, she was as stunning an accessory to Rayna's plan as Donner could have chosen.

The Festival had seen every swing in the concept of beauty. The era of big bosoms—Dors', Ekberg's, the Sylvas', Gina's, and Sophia's in their nubile heyday, before even the Italians made it fashionable to be sleek and underfed. Was it Loos who said it? On the Riviera one couldn't be too rich or too thin. When the other essential elements were lacking, nudity often served well enough. Skin always attracted the corps of greedy free-lance photographers hanging on the fringes at Cannes.

Donner didn't like photographers, and over the years he had made his position clearly known to three of them. He punched one in the Cathay Pacific men's room in Hong Kong's Kai Tak Airport, in the act of trying to snap off something in available light which would have recorded Donner in a most unflattering pose.

Later an androgynous Norwegian followed him around Ceylon for six weeks during a time when he was overweight and drinking heavily. That punch cost him twelve thousand dollars he didn't have in an out-of-court settlement; the photographer intelligently analyzed the situation and figured it was all he was likely to get.

The third photographer was a weasly Indian newspaper-man that he found on the balcony outside his hotel room on a beach north of Bombay. He removed a strip of film from the shaken man's camera that chronicled Donner's afternoon—the things that had transpired visibly between himself and a lovely twenty-year-old Anglo-Indian girl named Rayna Tate.

Here, in the limo, Taya Linder was her own definition of beauty, and it was quality. Wide-set green eyes in a perfect, squarish face that would print out a photographer's dream; a pouty mouth with lips colored bruised plum.

She let the fur coat slide from her shoulders, giving Donner a preview. A high-necked dress of some gauzy transparent material played on the imagination. Donner caught a whiff of strong cologne mixed with something else that, in combination, he couldn't quite place. He judged she was only a few inches shorter than he, with long, carefully tanned legs. She was returning the appraisal equally, judging him as a piece of hardware, a prop in her own game, which at that moment included an entrance into the Palais des Festivals, observed by people who mattered.

"You'll pardon me if I stare," Donner said.

She smiled, showing a line of perfect teeth. He hadn't expected anything else.

"Together we will do very well," she said.

Donner agreed, sure as hell. He placed it now, the aroma he couldn't identify. It was the good heady smell of fresh sperm.

Pressed close to a police barrier, Gaetan Rampa and his brother, Maxim, saw the arrival of Donner's limousine at the entrance to the Festival Hall. Of the three thousand people who witnessed the tall, broad-shouldered man with an elegant, willowy blonde pass through the high glass doors into what looked to be the interior of another world, none would find the impression more lasting than the brothers Rampa.

Earlier that evening Gaetan and Maxim had worked their way from the restaurants ringing the old port to the bars near the Festival Hall, timing their arrival for half an hour before the opening gala. There were things Gaetan Rampa was supposed to look for, and his eyes had been studying the men in tuxedos who, at first glance, appeared little different from him and Maxim. Well-dressed *prétentieux*, thieves of a different kind, and among them, the watchful ones who, even if he hadn't been warned, Gaetan Rampa's experience would have told him were police. He hadn't expected so many.

Next to him Maxim blissfully gazed at the steady arrival of limousines, humming with appreciation at the faces he recognized. Not a simpleton, Gaetan knew, but a child's spirit in the body of a broken man. Each morning now Maxim vomited blood with his coffee, and in the last year he had aged ten. Thank the filthy brothers Sallis for that; Gaetan Rampa prayed he had sent them both to hell.

Their act each night Maxim learned those last years with the Cirque Sallis, part sword swallowing, part rudimentary magic. It provided money enough to survive and a digestive system that each morning howled with displeasure. Long ago, before the accident, Maxim had worked the center ring with the troupe Spouggy, four men and a woman who some said were the greatest comic acrobats ever. There were the circuses Schumann and Hagenbeck, which Gaetan remembered when he traveled with Maxim as a child, the Super Circus Jumbo, the Circus Amar, finally the Sallis Brothers. It ended with the faulty air brake of a trailer truck and a shifting load that crushed Maxim's chest and left arm. Maxim fought back from the edge of a grave that should have claimed him, forcing himself to move again, learning with immense difficulty the routines of a clown. But it demanded too much from his body, and he accepted the lowest work of the midway. Anything, Maxim lectured him, to stay with the circus, to earn your own way.

Gaetan Rampa had been twelve when the Sallis brothers informed Maxim that he was no longer worth his money. Maxim was more than a brother—father, friend, teacher, confessor—but never again himself after their words. Later, when he had tried to hide his shame in a bottle, Gaetan Rampa watched and remembered. What did these film people with their make-believe know about things that were true, the anger a man could have? It had taken Gaetan Rampa three years to find the right time and place for the fire in a circus trailer that destroyed the bodies of the Sallis brothers, already dead by his hand inside. Ten years ago. Gaetan Rampa took nothing but pleasure in the memory, and in those times when living by his wits left him staring at the cold walls of this jail cell or that, he would warm himself over again with the memory of that fire.

Cannes was on a circuit that included Paris in the hard but lucrative winter months, then south to Cannes and back along the Riviera, reaching Biarritz and Deauville on the west coast during the peak of the season. They had done the city four times during the Festival. The idea had come to him long ago, watching these rich pretenders, and ripened with the headlines of the successes the Italians were having with such things. Those, and the daily reminder of coughing and blood that another such year or two, and Maxim would not see his fortieth birthday. All that had been needed was the intervention of a more orderly mind than either of them possessed—the girl, with hatreds every bit the equal of Gaetan Rampa's.

"Gaetan, look," Maxim whispered, his voice filled with awe.

The tall, broad-shouldered man with a hard, creviced face was stepping from a limousine beyond the police barrier.

With him was the most exquisite woman Gaetan Rampa had ever seen.

Maxim breathed a small sigh of desire as his eyes followed the movement of her slender hips, imagined the delicious pleasures her thighs might provide.

"You do your part," Gaetan Rampa said, "and you'll have a woman like that. Only money, Maxim, for those kind."

But he wasn't at all sure.

Teddy Kenrick arrived at the Festival Hall just in time to see Donner's magnificent entrance.

He had spent early evening waiting for the telephone to ring. A nine-hour time difference separated Cannes and Los Angeles, and he had put in the first of two calls a little before six that evening. Already his Paris manager, Gérard, had lavishly tipped the hotel telephone operators, but there was nothing else to do within Kenrick's power. During the Festival the competition for telecommunications was akin to a city under siege.

Finally, he reached Elsa and asked for Fiona MacCauley's progress on recutting the Lehman film.

"She won't say yet," Elsa replied, her voice coming through clearly. "She has two assistants in the cutting room with her, and they have a new set of positives on every foot of film Lehman shot."

"Give her forty-eight hours," Kenrick said. "Then have her call me direct. Stiner is sure to be on me because he smells trouble. When I lie to him, I at least want to know what the truth is."

"Has Siri made an appearance yet?"

"It's all a rumor, Elsa. I think she went to Mexico."

"You have no romance, Teddy Kenrick."

It took him another hour to reach Larry Rentzler, at his health club.

He heard the young lawyer's sharp voice saying, "Look, I *need* this or I'm going to start drinking. Trying to nail Ray Tannis about his audit of the Lehman film hasn't been easy. No show at the studio in three days, and when I go to his apartment, I find his wife. Only she's not his wife exactly, but soon to be his ex-wife, and she doesn't know where he is either. She said try their place out near Twenty-nine Palms, a trailer. Maybe it all fits. Maybe he's buckling under the pressure."

"And the whereabouts of Robert Arthur?"

"Teddy," he heard Rentzler moan.

"Use that gay Mafia you're always bragging about."

"I have people working, don't worry. I'll be on a plane to New York when I've seen Tannis, and to Cannes in two, three days outside."

Ten minutes later Kenrick entered the Festival Hall by one of the side doors and edged through the crowd to the rail of the mezzanine. He had no interest in the procession of well-photographed entrances transpiring below. His eyes roamed the crowd, seeking out targets, any one of a half dozen he could profitably talk with. Or be seen talking with.

What he counted upon was the accumulation of small details, gossip, the occasional bit of hard evidence that would, within ten days' time, plant the proper seeds of suspicion in one mind. Or was he guilty of what he suspected was the industry's special vanity, the believing in the extraordinary importance of one's self? The key figure, Robert Arthur, wasn't even at the Festival. Not yet. From where Kenrick stood he could see the lights scribing the outline of the Niarchos yacht anchored offshore and the smaller but still grand vessels that had arrived one by one during the past few days. That would be Arthur's choice. One of those or a villa in the peaceful hills behind the city. It was Arthur he had to smoke out, Arthur his ultimate target. And to do so meant walking a fine line between his apparent intentions and a finesse so skillful it all went without notice.

Below, near the high glassed entrance, Kenrick caught sight of Rayna Tate. Not quite the Rayna Tate of a few days before, clad then in a shapeless workout suit. A long white dress, backless, accented the olive gloss of her skin, her smooth back and delicate neck.

Kenrick turned his attention to the three men around her, trying to assess the relationship. The man to her right leaned close, a hand finding the small of her back, lingering a little too caressingly for an unintentional gesture. A pleasantry perhaps. Or an invitation.

Rayna laughed brightly but slipped from the hand as she turned and accepted a cigarette offered her by the man on the left.

Kenrick knew the whisperer. Dieter Furst, head of Germany's largest tax-shelter syndicate. The Germans were pouring money into Hollywood. Furst had just signed a twenty-million-dollar deal with one of the Big Six; Kenrick wondered exactly what they had given away to get their hands on the cash.

So, Rayna knew Furst.

The man who offered Rayna the cigarette was one of the Festival judges, an Italian director who for years had been trying to crack the American market, but without the right film.

The thickly built but powerfully attractive man across from her was her traveling companion on the plane from Paris.

Kenrick decided to find out what the hell that was all about and was headed toward the stairs when Donner made his entrance.

He saw Rayna lean close to Dieter Furst and say something.

But then Donner, his blonde, and the covey of photographers moving with them closed off Kenrick's view.

When he looked again, the group around Rayna had divided, like some cellular animal, each forming the nucleus of separate groups. Dieter Furst was now talking with Billy

Shinn, oldest son of one of the Shinn Brothers, who ran studios in Singapore. The Italian had joined the party entering the Festival Hall behind Donner—Festival director Philippe Brialt and, on either side, the French minister of culture and a Norwegian actress finishing a film in Canada with Newman.

Rayna and her handsome friend were nowhere in sight.

"Remind you of the good old days?" Leo Gold asked at his elbow. Kenrick turned to find a wizened, elfin face puckered up like a lemon. It was Gold's version of a friendly smile. Kenrick hadn't seen Leo since they had boarded the same aircraft in Los Angeles two days before. It was a break running into him, but the wrong place and time.

"My life with Donner was never the good old days, Leo."

"He looked terrific. He never looked that terrific when he worked for me. And that entrance. . . ."

"Maybe he fooled us both."

"I thought you discovered the guy," Gold said.

"A day for which I've paid dearly," Kenrick said. He had been a young, hungry agent then, drinking coffee one afternoon in the Formosa Café and dragging his feet on a scheduled meeting with a casting director named Dave Bruno. Bruno was under pressure to fill a small but highly visible part in a Duke Wayne western. "I want a new face, not some pretty boy from the Academy directory. And he's got to ride like a dream," Bruno wailed. Kenrick walked out the door to find Bruno's description in dirty overalls bouncing kegs of Eastside off a beer delivery truck. It had been that mystical juxtaposition of timing, the right part, and the right face that fueled the Hollywood myth. Kenrick's first words struck at the heart of the matter: "If you can stay on a horse, we're both going to make a lot of money." Chance. Donner could more than sit a horse. In the saddle he was as good as any wrangler, and a week later he was cast and under contract, wondering why everyone wasn't an actor. He had never polished what talent he had, relying on a confidence that came across on film and that tough-tender face. He was a small talent, but unique; if he had managed himself properly, he might have stayed more successful than not. Plenty of small talents had.

Kenrick never could understand exactly why Donner's confidence turned to carelessness and he became a brawler. Directors were his prime target. Kenrick's explanation was only a guess. Because it came easy, Donner never really thought the manufacture of make-believe on film was fitting work for a man—something as real as breaking a horse or wrestling kegs of beer.

Leo Gold's hawklike face drew back a couple of inches, sighting at Kenrick from a distance.

"You know your problem, Teddy. Your heart isn't in this." He made a sweeping wave of a small hand, around the foyer, beaming at the cut-glass chandeliers overhead. "You play a mean game, but what the hell else is this business to you?"

Given his intentions, he didn't think it the time to be fully honest with Leo Gold.

His decision to go after Gold was made the night he lined up the dominoes that had to fall during the Festival. Leo Gold had been coming to Cannes for twenty years and had a loyal stable of domestic and foreign exhibitors he didn't lie to. If Leo Gold announced that he had made a deal with a new studio to distribute its films, people would believe it.

Gold was saying, "I mean this is one of the last craft industries left on this earth."

"Leo, inside that nasty, calloused exterior of yours is a pussycat. You're the second idealist I've met today, which is pretty good for Cannes."

Leo Gold beamed at him. "I loved it down there tonight. Donner waltzing in like that. You don't think I don't know

113

his balls were shrunk up the size of chick-peas and his heart was pumping God knows what through his body. But he pulled it off, didn't he?"

"Yes, he did."

"You'd have thought he'd come here to collect the Palme d'Or, instead of getting off the canvas with more enemies than Hitler, every one of them looking to see him go right back down again."

"I'm rather expecting it myself," Kenrick said.

But Gold wasn't listening to him. "Beautiful." Leo Gold's hawklike expression took another couple of turns tighter. "You know I saw a film today—an action adventure pic with a lot of nobodies looking for a buyer. Except you know who had a feature?"

"Donner maybe. That's where he was last time I looked."

"Milland," Leo Gold said, as though it were very, very important. "I mean, I remember Milland back in nineteen-thirty-something, all sleek-haired and handsome, taking second billing to Lamour in a thing with a tiger called *The Jungle Princess*. And you know what the ad line was? Milland saying to Lamour, 'You savage untamed she-devil, I adore you.' And who says films haven't got any better? And there is Milland ten years or so later right at the top, an Oscar for *Weekend,* which was a runaway here in Cannes, the first Festival. And now where is Milland? Making B flicks in South Africa, Mexico, horror stuff, anything, and he's got to be seventy years old. But let me tell you, when he's on camera, you know you're watching a pro. And you, Teddy Kenrick, are going to tell me it's all for the money."

"It's been known to happen," Teddy Kenrick said.

"And it's been known to not happen," Leo Gold countered. "A guy like Milland is part of this business and knows it, even loves it maybe. If he stopped doing what he knows how to do, he'd be dead in a year. Lehman knew that, and I got to tell you I admired his courage."

"But you wouldn't touch his last three pictures either," Kenrick said. He was playing Gold's game. Leo liked an argument.

"That was business," Gold shot back. "I can't say I ever want Donner starring in one of my films again, but I liked what I saw down there, and I'd listen. This isn't a business; it's a way of life."

"It isn't a way of life," a plum-in-the-mouth British voice behind them said. "It's a racket."

Leo Gold spun around, ready to counterattack. Kenrick's look was more leisurely; he recognized the voice.

Behind them stood the journalist Peter Galloway, resplendent in a double-breasted tuxedo. The fabric and cut were excellent, but the item had seen better times. Galloway peered at them through thick lenses and tried his warming grin again. It faded as Leo Gold waded in.

"What do you know about it? I don't know you. If you were someone who knew something, I would."

When it became obvious that Galloway didn't intend moving, or couldn't, Kenrick made a brief introduction. He didn't want Galloway to trap Gold into a quote he would be sorry he said; Gold had that knack.

"Peter Galloway, Leo. Formerly of the *Financial Times*."

Galloway had planted himself in a stance just wide enough to support his size and condition. Kenrick could smell stale alcohol.

"I can understand the 'formerly,' " Gold said, sizing Galloway up. "You think this is a racket? So you get in it and see how well you do."

"*I* didn't say it was a racket," Galloway said, looking bewildered at the vehemence of Leo Gold's attack. "*Harry Cohn* said it was a racket. After all those years running Columbia I would have thought he knew what he meant."

"Cohn had a lot of bad habits," Leo Gold said. "One of them was saying stuff like that to people like you." He squinted at Kenrick, flicking his head toward Galloway. "Is this guy safe?"

"I don't think so."

Gold cocked his head up at Galloway. "I am not giving interviews. I am not to be recorded. What I got to say, I say like I do every year. At my press luncheon at the Eden Roc, and God damn the expense."

"And how does one get invited," Galloway inquired dryly, "to this luncheon?"

"That's your problem," Gold said. "Go back to work for the *Financial Times* maybe."

Kenrick put a hand on the small man's arm. "I want to talk, Leo. At your convenience."

Gold caught the tone and turned to say something, but Kenrick was already sliding away through the crowd. Gold had read it. The problem would be cornering Gold later, without a Galloway or anyone else around to bear witness.

Near the entrance to the *grande salle,* Kenrick picked out Freddie Harland and moved close enough to catch his eye. Without any apparent hesitation Harland executed a smooth shift in mid-speech and excused himself from the director and his wife he had been talking with. The director was not yet a Harland client, but the talk had an air.

"Terrific run of luck he's having," Harland said, telegraphing a warm smile across the foyer at the departing couple.

"Exploitable?"

"You bet," Harland said with a narrow wink. Six years ago they had been climbing neck and neck toward the top of the agency Harland now ran. He had since demonstrated an administrative skill that most people hated to admit, given his other excesses. He was known to prefer women, dope, and handmade cowboy boots in large quantities and in whatever order he came across them. He was usually seen in public with a pony-sized German shepherd, pure white, a blatant male totem named Cash. Harland was his own best advertisement and a generator of voluminous gossip. He had also managed Siri Laurence.

"Could you believe it?" Harland said. "Donner, for chrissakes, looking like he could play for the Rams. There must be a merciful God."

"Sign him up."

"After what you went through, no thanks. Midnight phone calls I can take. Broken bones I pass. But a nice little Festival, huh. Things shaping up?"

It was Kenrick's cue. "If you've talked with Siri."

"Don't I wish," Harland said quickly, but Kenrick saw he had marked it. "I'm not even sure she's here. An ex-agent is like an ex-husband—the last one to know."

"And you've heard nothing."

Harland inspected the sole of one polished alligator-skin boot. "Well, not nothing. Two days ago in L.A. I got a call from her, only I was unavailable for the moment. I mean if I'd known . . ."

"You would have rolled over and answered the phone."

". . . so I have two girls on the horn since then trying to get back to her. No luck."

"Does she want to work again?"

"Don't I wish," Harland cooed. "Four years I haven't heard a beep, and now she calls."

"Keep me in mind," Kenrick said, and started to turn away. Harland caught him by the elbow.

He could almost hear Freddie Harland's mental machinery begin to whirl. Hollywood was a town of lists—short lists, longer lists, preferred lists, shit lists. At best there were only a dozen names—with Eastwood, McQueen, and Redford at the top—around which you could build a film project with sure international appeal, directly translated to money up front. There were two women in that dozen, and Siri remained one of them.

Harland could visualize a project custom-built with his own clients—writer, director, a hatful of featured actors all given work by a man in Kenrick's position wanting Siri Laurence.

"The price would be high," Harland said. "Astronomical."

"Call me when she takes your phone calls."

"Very funny," Freddie Harland said.

≡ *Chapter 16—*Action

Rayna Tate saw Donner's entrance from the foyer of the Festival Hall.

She had been looking for Kenrick but hadn't seen him until she had already settled for her alternate choice, the German moneyman Dieter Furst. She steered Furst into conversation with Angelo Menotti, one of the judges, and Jean-Yves Climent, a young French director whom she had spent a day with in Paris. And a night. Both Menotti and Climent were clients, though neither knew it of the other.

When Donner and Taya stepped from the limo, Rayna felt the anxiety tighten in her stomach. She was never blasé about her people. But with Donner even the simplest introduction was a venture into the unpredictable; photographers were a catalyst of the worst kind.

Her glance left the two of them almost immediately, shifting toward the two dozen or so clustered on the stairs inside the Festival Hall. At Cannes they were like reef fish, moving in unison to this stimulus or that, quick to smell out action and equally adept at weeding out the uncommercial —the personalities in name only that weren't worth the film.

To her relief, as Donner and Taya entered through the parting glass doors, the cameras came up. The blink of strobe lights coincided with demands to look this way, just one more, as they climbed the stairs, while the silent ones who would pursue a subject into fiery hell to get one more shot pressed closer.

Donner knew how to milk it. Hand on Taya's elbow, he

guided her this way and that, his sense of playing to the camera showing them both to their best—moving, moving, giving the photographers new angles to shoot.

Rayna bent close to Dieter Furst, wanting to be heard. "Rod Donner," she said above the uproar. "Lord, what a face."

"Yes," Furst said, his voice flat and unrevealing. "But too old. Much too old," he said, balancing pluses and minuses.

Rayna seized on the doubt in his voice. "Come on, Dieter. There isn't a proven box-office draw under forty, and you know it. Maybe Donner is another late bloomer, like Bronson."

"Possible," Furst said, but Rayna knew that a concession was all she was likely to get. Dieter's feral gaze had settled on the near-transparent front of Taya Linder's gown. The gauzy substance was strained from beneath by two lovely mounds of flesh with nipples of stainless steel. Damn, Rayna thought, a trick she hadn't thought of. During those last seconds in the limo, Taya Linder's nipples had been pinched erect, a trick Rayna wouldn't put beyond Taya or Donner.

Next to her, Dieter Furst made a small sound of apppreciation. Observed and noted.

She found Teddy Kenrick in the balcony of the *grande salle,* halfway down the row of seats reserved for VIPs.

"I saw you working the mezzanine," Rayna said. "Very smooth." She meant it. Kenrick had an effortless way of controlling every situation, including their first meeting at the beach. She had reflected later upon it, noting that she had talked more than usual, a sign of her own unsureness. "I could learn things from you," she said, and was immediately sorry she had.

"And I from you," Kenrick said mildly.

So he had been watching from the balcony, her playing of Furst, Menotti, and Jean-Yves Climent.

Vulnerabilities, after all. And an interest that she hadn't

been willing before to consider. Alone, she would have to tote up how that might alter things—for and against—the way she handled Kenrick.

"Join me for the film," he said. "We can have that talk. I know what I'm after now. Or rather who."

She searched for a second level of the meaning behind the words, a playing with phrases. His mouth was a little too set for the contradictory flickers of humor that occasionally softened his eyes.

"I can't," Rayna said. "Too many things to do, dammit. Can we meet later?"

"Of course," Kenrick said lightly, his reserve squarely back in place.

"The municipal casino then. I'm dining with some people at the old port, and it's on the way back. Bad idea?"

"Not really."

"I sensed something. Poor tactics on my part, or did I pick the wrong place? I'd heard you once liked the atmosphere, casinos and all. Or is that only something everyone in the business talks about except you?"

"You don't give a person many places to hide," Kenrick said, a smile carving lines at the corners of his eyes. "Those casinos were the year my wife died. I gambled because it kept my mind off other things."

Rayna found his directness, when he chose to use it, unsteadying. She was used to dealing with people who would say anything except what they really felt. But with Kenrick she couldn't tell if it was true candor or a tactic completely under his control to open people up in return.

"Sorry, Kenrick," she said. "I dig in too hard for my own good sometimes. I hadn't made the connection in time between the two. Maybe I should have."

"Not many people did even then," Kenrick said. "And now it doesn't matter. The casino it is. Name the time."

"The stroke of midnight, naturally."

* * *

When Rayna was gone, Kenrick settled back into his seat. Her ability to conjure up delicately visions of clandestine rendezvous irritated him, and he was damned if he was going to waste any more thought wondering how Rayna Tate passed her time.

Before the lights dimmed, he took a moment to scan the house. Below, a stage covered with flowers and small palms sloped from the screen toward the first row of the audience. Three rows from the front Kenrick picked out the Stiner party: Ernst Rucker, the head of European distribution, and his French wife; Stiner's handsome daughter, Penny, and Penny's escort, a darkish young actor in the Pacino mode, whose name Kenrick couldn't remember. A sixth member of the party was a nondescript man, fiftyish and balding, whom he took to be Donald Eads, the corporate troubleshooter Stiner was bringing in to rummage through Kenrick's closet.

As if feeling his gaze, Stiner turned, found Kenrick, and gave him a shallow nod.

Kenrick returned it in kind. They would have their first joust tomorrow at the so-called strategy session in Stiner's bungalow at the Hôtel du Cap.

A moment after the film began Aron Archer dropped into the seat Rayna Tate had vacated. His long fingers massaged an imaginary patch of stubble on the point of his chin.

"Not like you," Kenrick said, "to go padding around under cover of darkness."

"Been doing a lot of things this week," Archer said, "that aren't like me. Besides, we're in trouble."

They stayed five minutes into the film, left via a fire exit, and found the nearest bar.

A few minutes before midnight Kenrick left Aron Archer and walked to the winter casino to meet Rayna Tate. Here and there a lighted bar still had its crowds dressed in evening clothes or denim, but the city was winding down.

What Aron Archer thought was trouble, Kenrick found something else again: a sign that word about the intended breakaway was spreading.

Over a drink Archer explained. "I've managed to put out feelers. Unfortunately we can't say to these people we want a hundred million dollars and not answer the question, to do what?"

"Who did you talk to?" Kenrick asked.

"The logical man, Novotny in Boston."

Any of the big banks or insurance companies could underwrite a hundred-million-dollar line of credit, given timing and the right approach. There were a handful of middlemen, experts at finding willing money, at a price, who were behind most of the big financial deals in the film business. Novotny was the best.

"Did he listen?" Kenrick asked.

"I'm not sure," Archer said, his forehead ridging in puzzlement. "At first there was nothing but the right vibrations. I explained that some of the most talented people in the industry—talented and profitable—were considering an association. And that if it came to pass, I would be part of it. I merely asked how such an undertaking might be viewed at the moment. And if viewed favorably, what it was worth."

"You put a hand in a man's pocket as softly as anyone I've ever seen."

"Teddy, I understand Novotny. I can tell when he purrs. He didn't have to stretch very far to attach your name to the deal. He was purring. He said he could probably put something together but would have to get back to me. When he did, the purr was gone. The operative word was no longer 'probably.' It had changed to 'possibly.'"

"'Possibly' defined exactly how?"

"That it would cost us an extra point."

"To Novotny?"

Archer nodded. "Call it a finder's fee."

"You call it a finder's fee," Kenrick said. "Any other business, people would call it something else."

"We don't like, we don't take," Archer said. "But what it means is that Novotny is going to sources beyond the ones he expected to guarantee the money. Because some of the people he talked with weren't interested."

Kenrick wondered if Novotny would have had the brass to approach Robert Arthur. Kenrick decided he would.

Archer said, "The next time we talk I must lay the program on his desk—who, when, and with what projects."

The *who* was proving the easiest part. To Aron Archer's name at the heart of the breakaway team Kenrick had added Sid Mathan. He had brought Mathan into the studio four years before to handle film pickups, the films made by independent producers with money from any place they could find it. Often they could be bought outright for a small percentage of their cost or, in the case of a particularly desperate producer, no more than the cost of prints and promotion, splitting profits fifty-fifty. There would be heavy dealing in pickups at Cannes.

But it was dangerous turf, the logic being that if a film didn't have the appeal to attract a major studio in the beginning, there must be something wrong with the project. To find the diamonds among the earthier substance, Kenrick raided his former agency for the most diligent pair of eyes he had ever come across, a former TV director named Sid

Mathan. It was a specialized kind of talent, and Mathan excelled.

Over champagne cocktails earlier that afternoon he had told Mathan squarely about the intended breakaway to form a new studio. "Aron is aboard, and Rentzler will be. We'd like you along, Sidney."

Mathan was quick to grasp Kenrick's levering point. In his current studio niche Mathan had topped out. But on the ground floor of a new organization with stock and a direct participation in profits his ceiling would be raised considerably. "And for doing exactly what you're doing now."

"In principle I say yes." A nervous hand smoothed several strands of limp blond hair over his bald spot. "If everything else comes together."

His hedge was predictable and anticipated. Kenrick dumped it squarely back in Mathan's lap.

"It's all up to you, Sidney," he said, stretching it a bit. "Right here in Cannes. We need a few films we can release the first months we're in business. If they're around, find them."

"They're around." Kenrick saw the mental wheels begin turning behind Mathan's eyes and knew he'd made the conquest. He had never expected anything else. On his list he judged Mathan the surest to make the jump.

Now, entering the winter casino, he was about to advance on another front—the subtle spreading of news about the intended breakaway through Rayna Tate.

At the cashier he arranged for a week's membership with the casino management and pushed through the curtained doors into the main salon. It was a large room with a high-domed ceiling, draped windows shutting off any view, in or out, and a half dozen smaller lounges off the main salon. The carpet was, as Donner might have described it, catshit yellow. Of the twelve tables, six were roulette.

As he looked for Rayna, it took a moment to adjust to the absence of canned music or the electrified lounge shows standard in Vegas; only the housemen at the roulette table calling out bets and the clack of ivory against wood. But for that it was the same: women with luminescent hair and bored expressions; men charting the action on small pieces of paper, looking in the pattern for an edge on chance. Rayna Tate was nowhere in sight.

He had just ordered a flute of champagne at the bar when, on the periphery of his vision, Nicky Deane stepped from a small shadowed room papered in red velvet to greet him with a crooked grin and upraised glass.

"Smart, Kenrick. Roulette is a sucker's game."

"They all are, I'm told," Kenrick said, but he could feel the coolness of his own glass against the sudden heat of his hand. Except for the tuxedo, Deane looked no different from the last time they had met, a year before. Thick black hair, those deceptively feminine eyes.

So Nicky Deane was in Cannes. The first and only question that made any difference to Kenrick was why. Was he the target?

"Doesn't stop people from playing, does it?" Deane said, stepping closer. Kenrick could smell a heavy cologne, scented gardenia. Kenrick said nothing. "I'm going to tell you a little secret. The thing that keeps all these places going— Vegas, the Caribbean, the Med. They'd get rich even if the odds on every game were dead even. You know why? Because a lot of people like losing. For different reasons. To show they got enough to lose. Or to impress someone. Some lose and call it fun. Others like it because it isn't fun." He stopped, punctuating the silence with a slow flutter of his eyelashes. "I never did figure out your reason."

Kenrick thought of those times now as an episode in the life of a man who no longer existed. In the year after his wife's death it had been only a matter of time, he supposed, before he found Vegas and the mind-numbing brand of action the city could provide. Five hours by divided highway, unimpeded by more than a stoplight or two. There were times when he would leave the studio, be at the tables by midnight, and be back at his desk pumped full of caffeine and adrenaline in time to deal over lunch the next day.

From the outset he was marked as a high roller: anything in the way of diversion comped and for the asking; lines of credit at three casinos, doubled the second month; then again. He had money and could think of no better way of spending it than trying to buy peace. He wondered if the sight of his blacks and pinks sliding across the table each night hadn't planted an idea in the mind of Nicky Deane. If Deane set him up, Kenrick made it easy, for reasons that he didn't understand until a psychiatrist named Myrna Javich led him to it. "Punishment" was the conclusion they'd come to together, "something to balance the fact that you had lived and your wife had died, in a slow graphic manner." Fourteen months, three remissions, and a final twelve days Kenrick remembered like no other time on earth.

Trying to figure out whether it had been he or others who helped him turn loser, he hired a former Las Vegas dealer named Edgar Moon, and one night he watched Moon deal him losing hands at will—one deck, two decks, from a shoe. To Moon it didn't matter. "Most casinos can lay their hands on a mechanic—a guy that can pack a deck or deal you seconds until your eyeballs get tired of trying to see it happen. Most of the time who needs one? The odds beat you if you sit there long enough. You can't win," Moon told him. "You can't even keep from losing."

With as much notoriety as a big winner, a heavy loser becomes known to a casino's management. Nicky Deane introduced himself to Kenrick the fourth straight night he had played and lost. "Anything I can do, ask for me personally. Ladies, anything."

"A bigger line of credit for openers."

"Why not?" Nicky Deane said.

He could recall every detail of the final night. Down seventy-four thousand dollars but still looking for ways to beat himself.

The office they invited him to four hours later was modern and air-conditioned, with curtains along one wall presumably covering windows. A large desk was lit from above, tiny pinpoints of light diffusing over the polished wood surface. A man Kenrick hadn't met before greeted him and his escort at the door. Nicky Deane sat on a sofa in one corner, not acknowledging Kenrick's entrance.

A third man in the room was standing. Dark suit, a string tie. Kenrick had seen him on the casino floor.

Judas in a string tie.

The man who had opened the door gestured to a soft chair and sat facing him across the desk. "I'm afraid we've a problem," he began. "I hope you will be cooperative."

He picked up the large brass key paperweight, cleared his throat, and looked across at Nicky Deane. It was Deane's play.

"The thing I can't understand," Nicky Deane said, "is how any guy in your position could do something so dumb."

He signaled the man with a string tie, who punched on a television set in one corner of the room like a Buddha. Kenrick saw himself across from a blackjack dealer, playing head to head.

Deane said, "We don't go to this trouble for everyone. We have Mr. Henderson here to thank for that." The man in the string tie massaged his upper lip uncomfortably. "Now Mr. Henderson is a shift boss, which means he knows every game out there like you know your pockets. He has a nose for things—about players. Feelings that nobody who hadn't lost his ass twice over in this town would understand."

Henderson winced but said nothing. The power was Deane's.

"But Hen doesn't gamble anymore, do you, Hen?"

"Two years August," the shift boss said. It was in his

voice: the certainty of an alcoholic who knows it's only a matter of weakness, circumstance, and time before he gives in.

"And it is Hen who starts asking questions when suddenly a client down seventy-four thou is now down only fifty-five and wanting to raise the limit. And it is Hen who looks at a couple of decks we change out of the shoe and begins to think maybe the surface of the face cards isn't as smooth as they ought to be."

Henderson bobbed his head.

"That's when they call me," Nicky Deane said. "Because they know you and me are friends. And I tell them it would be something to believe that anyone with your high reputation would be crimping face cards. I mean crimping face cards is one of the oldest scams on that table, not that we don't have people, smart people, dealers even, who try it every week. So I suggest we make a little home movie—a little videotape evidence that says you are innocent, but, oops—"

Deane pointed to the screen as the camera zoomed in on Kenrick's hands holding a pair of face cards. Framed perfectly, his fingernail scribed a small mark across one corner of the cards.

For several hours it had given him an edge in telling which down cards were face cards and whether to hit or stay against the dealer. He had pushed it too long. He had known it. Punishment.

"Now *that* puts me in an embarrassing position. Because a videotape is very good evidence in the Vegas courts these days, and what you just saw will put you in prison." He looked away again, a good job of acting, all in. "Why, when you've been having such a nice time here—when I would have arranged any pleasure?"

"Because I hate to lose."

"Well, you lost," Nicky Deane said, the pretense of friendship gone. "And I'm not sure what to do with a loser like you."

Deane delivered his instructions. Kenrick would be offered a room for the night, the usual comps if so desired. He was not to leave the room, and they would talk again.

Deane shook his head. "Crimping cards. Where does a guy like you learn a trick like that? I mean, you do it pretty good."

"A long time back. On tour in a Checker limo going to New York, playing cards with a saxophone player named Elvin Turner."

"You know what?" Deane said, the opening too tempting to resist. "He should have taught you to play saxophone."

Late the next afternoon Nicky Deane paid Kenrick a visit. Kenrick considered they might want more from him than money. It wouldn't have been lost on Nicky Deane that Kenrick had influence in a realm that attracted thugs of every cut, if only for its abundance of beautiful women. In his position, Kenrick could be useful, and it surprised him when Deane said, "You owe us seventy-four thousand bucks, by, let's say, the first of the month. And no casino in town wants to see you again. You got off lucky."

Kenrick heard something other than full accord. He was sure the decision hadn't been Deane's. For a reason that wasn't then clear, whoever Deane had talked with, someone higher in the chain of command, hadn't wanted Kenrick squeezed.

But it was Nicky Deane's last words that left him suspended anew.

"We'll talk again, you and me," he promised. "You see, I collect home movies."

That had been three years before. Not quite a year ago Nicky Deane had come for that talk, telling Kenrick to do everyone a favor. By opening the studio's door once again to Pedro Lehman.

While Deane possessed a videotape showing Teddy Kenrick was a thief, he could keep on collecting.

Nicky finished his champagne and and offered a smile

130

intended to allay Kenrick's suspicion. "Relax, Kenrick. I'm here on vacation. Maybe to invest in a film. It's such a nice, clean business."

When Nicky Deane left him, Kenrick walked into the small room from which Deane had emerged. It was empty, with walls of red velvet and high windows, heavily draped. Kenrick drew back the drapes, wondering what might have occupied Deane here. He could see nothing from the window except a small park next to the casino and, in the distance, the upper floors of the Hôtel Majestic.

"The idiot!" Hugh Remy said, pointing at the insectlike Citröen cutting into his lane of traffic. Their car was rented, and twice during the last frantic quarter hour as they skirted Paris on the *périphérique,* Remy had made the suggestion to Siri that maybe driving wasn't such a good idea after all and they could still catch a train.

"But you've been telling me how much you admire the individualism of the French," Siri observed, "their rudeness all a myth."

"I wasn't talking about French drivers. Besides, they're not rude. They're mindless."

Arriving that morning in Paris on the flight from Los Angeles, Siri suggested they go on to Cannes by automobile. "A slight case of nerves," she said. Remy was in no hurry to arrive in Cannes, by now full of the same people he avoided in Los Angeles, and he agreed.

At the Port d'Orléans exit he decided it was eat or be eaten and aggressively slanted the Renault toward the off-ramp to the tune of a bellicose honk from a *camion* behind them. "Feel better?" Siri remarked.

"Damn straight."

They had one fleeting glimpse of the Eiffel Tower in the distance, shrouded in low cloud, and twenty minutes later the city was behind them, a landscape on either side of rolling fields patched with forests green from spring rain.

Remy smiled, the feel of the land coming back to him, its look, the smells. When they made those last disastrous period films in England, he had several times escaped across the

Channel, gravitating to the stretch of Atlantic coast around St.-Laurent-du-Mer.

A few kilometers away were the sand dunes and beach once designated Omaha. A couple of lifetimes ago he had stumbled ashore there as a frightened combat photographer with the First Infantry. Five months later, a hollowed-out old man of twenty-three, he had had his first look at Paris. He had never been quite so sure of himself as then. People, places, they did change. Omaha was quiet these days with sheep grazing among the bunkers, the large cemeteries nearby well tended and silent. And you, Remy chum, what became of you?

Something inside always forced him to the heart of the action, toward the things that were sure to test a man. The war. The movie business. Even marrying Katia. But equally, some fault of courage kept him from plunging in all the way, making the final commitment of himself. Combat photographer, not combatant. Pedro Lehman's right hand, but never a try at directing on his own.

In her brassy style Katia once summed the fault in his life in a phrase: You had to be in it to win it. And Remy never quite had the courage.

Following the road and the red *Michelin* guide, they stopped the night at a mountain village west of the Rhône. Remy asked for separate accommodations and received, along with two rooms, one particularly curious sidelong glance from the desk clerk. "Sleep well, Siri girl. We'll get an early start."

"You, too."

But Remy didn't sleep well. He paced the noisy board floors until the early hours of the morning, turning it over in his mind. After lunch that day on the upper Loire and a second bottle of tooth-chilling wine, Siri finished her story about Nicky Deane, her confessional of sorts, begun the night aboard his boat. Her departure from New York, riding off into the sunset with Pedro hadn't been the end at all. After almost a year in Los Angeles Nicky Deane's game began again: the late-night phone calls, with silence when she answered. That business about a single gardenia left on the seat of her parked car or on her dressing table at the studio between takes.

"What was he trying to prove?" Remy wanted to draw all of it out, for his own sake as well as Siri's. Remy firmly believed that his former partner, Pedro Lehman, had taken his own life. Not many reasons would have been powerful enough to give Pedro no other choice, in his own thinking. A failing career, maybe. Siri, without any doubt in the world. And Nicky Deane around the edges, trying to drive in the spike.

"Nicky was telling me I couldn't escape. That's what I thought." She fell silent then, and Remy waited her out. "Then one day I get a photo of Pedro driving his car. Only there was a circle drawn around his head with an X in the middle of it like the cross hairs of someone aiming at him through a telescopic sight. That's when I knew I'd have to see Nicky and find out his price."

"You never said anything to Pedro."

"I couldn't forget the craziness I'd seen in Nicky's eyes. I was afraid."

She stared out across the countryside, but Remy wasn't certain she saw anything. "I had this hunch about one of the grips on my films. One day I told him I wanted to talk with Nicky Deane and watched him go bug-eyed."

"You figure he was the one doing Nicky's legwork with the flowers and photographs."

"It had to be someone close around. Two days later I received a note that said a room had been reserved for me at a motel in Palm Springs. That day I told Pedro a whopping lie, had the studio book a ticket home to Oklahoma, and drove instead out to the desert. I was trying to save my husband, Hugh, you must know that."

"Did Deane show?" Remy knew the answer.

"Yes," she said slowly. "He wanted me to leave Pedro and marry him. But when I said I planned to get married all right, but to Pedro, he put his fist through a closet door, and I thought he'd cracked. Then, all of a sudden, he became silent and gave me a choice."

"Choice?"

"He said if I ever made another film, Pedro would never live to see it. Clever, eh? Love or career, dumped right in my lap. What could I do? A week later I acted my way through a nervous breakdown and used it as an excuse to quit films."

"And that was all of it?"

"Yes, Hugh, that was all." She was looking away when she said it. After that Remy concentrated on his driving more than he needed to. He had given her the chance to tell him everything. And she didn't.

They reached Cannes late the first night of the Festival. Remy tried to get a room in the Majestic, where the suite had been reserved for Siri. The clerk looked at him as if he were mad.

"I'll scout something up."

"Come back, Hugh, later for a drink. Please." Siri had a helpless look that, in his recollection, had come from a scene in *Isabella*. She caught it, too, and laughed.

"Listen, you miserable wench," Remy said, "what you told me happened far away. You're in Cannes now, so live up to your press and stop looking over your shoulder."

"One drink. Champagne, to start things right."

After a moment Remy said, "I'll be in the bar," swearing under his breath. One of these days he'd have to learn the essential word: no.

When the bellman opened the door to a large, airy suite, Siri managed to cross the threshold, one step into the room, before she felt the walls around her begin a slow revolution.

"Are you all right, madame?"

"Yes, fine. A little fresh air."

The bellman opened the window to reveal a night-dark expanse of the Mediterranean.

The suite was filled with bouquets of roses and baskets heaped high with mounds of colorful fruit. On the dresser was a stack of welcoming telegrams and notes.

But it was none of these that loosed the wave of help-lessness that swept over her. It was beginning again, if it had ever truly stopped.

In the center of the room, on a low glass table near the bed, was a silver tray overflowing with pale yellowish gardenias.

☰ *Chapter 19*—Paper, Scissors, and Stone

"Kenrick, the breadth of your friendship astounds even me."

It had been a few seconds since Kenrick watched Nicky Deane make his somber exit from the main salon of the winter casino. Time enough to order a much-needed drink from the bar before the reporter Galloway's voice boomed its greeting.

"But suggest to the dear fellow he change fragrances. Leaves rather a trail after himself." Galloway's smile was bemused. His large pinkish hand encircled a slender flute of champagne.

"Not a friend, Galloway. Not even an old one."

"Another of your temporary alliances, no doubt."

The phrase brought Kenrick a smile. In the two years since the words "temporary alliance" had tumbled from his lips onto the pages of *Time,* it might well have become the guiding theme of his life. What were Rentzler, Aron Archer, Sid Mathan but alliances aimed at bringing each some individual goal? No friendships, only temporary alliances. It was a hell of a comment on the entire business if one chose to read it that way. It was clear from Galloway's tone he did and found the concept distasteful. Kenrick was instantly wary.

Galloway gestured around. "I enjoy gambling houses. Losing peels the veneer off the nicest people." He said something in quick, fluent French to the bartender and received coffee, cognac, and a greeting by name.

Galloway flushed, then shrugged it away.

"They know me around here, thanks to these"—he flicked the combat ribbons in his lapel—"and the bloody language. Can't say either was worth the trouble."

"The ribbons, French?"

"Came over with Squadron One in early 1940, when One and Seventy-three were flying Hawkers in France during the phony war." He saw Kenrick's look of question. "Before your time, but there was about six months after Hitler invaded Poland when not much happened. All the politicians sitting around, lining up their friends and figuring out who were enemies. I know something about temporary alliances, Kenrick. Never been a fan of so-called pragmatic politics. Suppose it's why I became a journalist. Unearth the silver-tongued devils, and put them in a bright light. These"—again he flicked the ribbons too carelessly—"were given in consolation when I fell out of the sky, several times. In '40, '43 again down here on the Côte, when we, ahem, liberated the place."

"Since when do they give medals for falling out of the sky?"

"I'd rather discuss this theory of yours," Galloway said firmly. He was through talking about himself.

"Your kind of temporary alliance and mine aren't quite the same," Kenrick said.

"You were referring to Hollywood today. . . ."

"Where every individual is a business. To put a film together—that is, find a writer, a director, and a couple of stars that count—means dealing with a number of separate companies, each with agents, lawyers, accountants, all battling for any advantage they can take. To get a film made and released means making a temporary alliance between people that very often hate each other's guts and at the very least want different things. It's a difficult job."

"And that has you fitting where? What is Teddy Kenrick's role in this new Hollywood?"

"A man in the middle," Kenrick said. "That's what I've

always been. Someone who brings the separate elements to-gether."

Galloway, sipping cognac, shut his eyes a moment in something very close to ecstasy. "The great problem of the times, dear lad. Too many men in the middle, and not enough of substance on either end. But I must say it's your moment in history. The epoch of the middleman, climbing upward and onward. And where does Teddy Kenrick jump next?"

"I hadn't given it a thought."

"Really?" Galloway said.

Rayna Tate's entrance was well timed, even if she was accompanied by her handsome Frenchman. She gave Kenrick a slender smile when she picked him out and crossed the main salon toward them.

"Kenrick, meet Jean-Yves Climent. He makes marvelous films."

Kenrick, reluctantly, introduced them to Galloway, who to his surprise, gave Rayna a deep, regal bow. "Indeed a pleasure, good lady."

Kenrick saw Rayna visibly stiffen, then turn from Galloway, speaking hurriedly. "Sorry we're late. Got stuck with some people impossible to get away from. The charming kind, who know everyone you know and have a story about them they simply must tell."

"I'll take that as a hint," the Frenchman Climent said, "and leave you people to talk."

"I didn't mean it as a hint to you," Rayna said. If it was a hint to Galloway, he took no notice. His eyes hadn't left Rayna since the moment she'd arrived.

"Really, I've something I must do," the Frenchman insisted, and extended his hand to Kenrick. "You'll be here the entire Festival?"

"Wouldn't miss a minute."

"Perhaps we'll meet again."

After he was gone, the uncomfortable silence finally penetrated Galloway's understanding. He downed his cognac, offered Rayna Tate a peculiar smile, and unsteadily tottered away. "We'll be in touch, Kenrick," he said. It had the sound of a threat.

"The bastard," Rayna said.

"He was charming, your Mr. Climent. And well briefed."

Her eyes snapped around, freezing with anger. "I meant Galloway. Their last weapon, his kind of worn-at-the-elbows upper crust. A bloody marvelous accent and three hundred years of inbred superiority to go with it."

"He's your countryman, not mine."

"But he's not, don't you see?"

"I think it's time for fresh air." He guided her out of the casino toward the oceanfront, the sharp chill of the evening, clean and bracing.

"You both missed it, you and Jean-Yves. I may be English to you, but Galloway knew the first sentence I managed to finish. Sliced, served, and placed geographically. He could have written a page of biography from my accent—and been very close to right."

She turned to look at him, the lights from the casino shadowing the hollows of her face. Kenrick was listening, but he had the sensation he was also standing apart, watching the two of them. From a distance it seemed almost certain that the boy, failing all else, would comfort the girl by taking her into his arms.

"I'm not English, you see. I'm Anglo-Indian. A minority, about like green-eyed Vietnamese. A hundred and fifty years of British administration, and all they managed to produce was a couple of hundred thousand crossbreeds, not much wanted by either nationality. Doesn't say much for the British sex drive, does it?"

"Hot climate and good manners." He could see it now. The soft dark eyes, the olive tint to her skin.

"Rupe being an exception," she said. "Old Rupe . . . my father. Sergeant Major Rupert Wolf Tate . . . oh, hell," she said, finding a smile in it somewhere. "It was a long time back, which is where we should leave it. I do until I meet a Galloway who can dredge it all up with just the right kind of silence. Come on, Kenrick, let's promenade. That's more of me than I want to talk about."

They crossed through a small park leading back to the Croisette. She was silent for a moment and in that time, quite naturally, took his arm.

"Suppose you tell me what I can help you with."

It was all dignified and businesslike, except they both were now more aware of touch than the words they were saying. Kenrick found that he had turned them in the general direction of his hotel. He hadn't let his instincts navigate his body in years.

Playing his part, he told her about the planned breakaway to form a new studio, taking the best talent from the present organization. It sounded neat and compact, and Kenrick could hear the conviction in his own voice, the first thing you learned in the business. Believe it yourself.

He gave in to the task and could feel Rayna's vicarious excitement, a technique perhaps of her own trade. She was quick to grasp Kenrick's concept of a studio that kept its overhead at rock bottom by leasing and renting, using other people's talents and facilities.

"The business about distribution," she questioned. "Farming that out. Is that why I saw you talking with Leo Gold in the Palais?"

"Unless I want to go for Warner's or Columbia. The problem is getting Gold to sit still long enough to hear my pitch, then making him see what a good idea it is in time enough to commit during the Festival. I'd like to use Gold's yes to raise money."

She gripped his arm tighter, the pressure working its way through his body to settle in his groin. "What if I could smooth the way to Gold?"

"How?"

"Simple barter. Leo wants something here at Cannes I may be able to deliver. In exchange he listens to you in the right time and the place to make your pitch."

"And what do I bring to this bartering table?" He didn't ask what Rayna had that Gold wanted.

"Money," Rayna said archly. "And something else that won't cost you much."

"She says."

"I'd like you to talk to Donner."

"That figures." He felt himself go cold, didn't know why. "Donner's entrance in the Festival Hall. I should have guessed."

"Sure I set it up, structured it, I like to think. The same way I'll structure the meeting between you and Leo Gold. I can't add the spark."

"What are Donner and I supposed to talk about, his left hook?" He realized he sounded juvenile and defensive.

"Business that might be good for you both," she persisted.

"Rayna," he said, untangling her arm from his own, "Donner looked like a new man in there tonight. But he's not a new man. He's an old face who has been on the fringes a long time, almost broken big, but didn't make it. I know one thing. No one at Cannes is looking to find Donner a project."

Her almond eyes narrowed, gauging how much to tell him. "What if he had a project? A good one. And it fitted him better than anything he'd ever done?"

"It would be like betting a weak pair in stud poker."

"Kenrick, a weak pair in stud will take many a pot. Or don't you play?"

Kenrick gave her a grudging nod. "What's it about?"

"I don't talk story very well. Auto racing based on something that really happened." She started to go on, then held herself back. "Enough."

"Okay, I'll talk to him."

She waited a second, then mentally told herself to hell with it and pushed all the way. "I want more than that. I want to set up a reading, for you and a few other people. Let Donner read some of the script."

"A script by whom?"

"A girl named Shimkus." She saw Kenrick frown. "All you have to do is listen. And try to forget some of the things Donner has done in the past. He's changed, Kenrick."

"Why are you pushing so hard on Donner?"

She took his arm again and guided them along the walk. It was several long seconds before she said, "Fair question. I guess it's my night in the barrel."

She looked amused at her own seriousness and for a moment let her eyes follow a white-hulled sailboat as it swung past the light at the harbor entrance. He could see her nostrils flaring slightly as she breathed, and he wondered if she felt the same stirring he did. Hell, a little lust beneath the palms never hurt anyone. Give in, Kenrick, but he knew he wouldn't.

"This is going to blow my cover, but before I reclaimed the name Tate, it was Donner. I still happen to care about the man. Not love, which wasn't part of the bargain. But I like him. And I owe him."

"Owe . . . bargain. You make everything sound like a Mexican market."

She turned, bridling at his remark. "I wouldn't have thought trade-offs were anything new to you. What words do you want to use?"

"I can't imagine the two of you together, that's all."

"In bed you mean?" Kenrick didn't answer. "Come off it, Kenrick. You look like a child who's had someone steal his sucker. Why not own up?"

"Own up to what? That I can't see you in a bargain with Donner?"

"That you don't like the idea of me and Donner making merry in the sack. All right, I'll take my chance because I don't think you will. At least I listen to my instincts, not that they don't get foxed now and again." She took a step closer. "Something has clicked between you and me. No labels, boxes, or names. But I'm going to play it straight with you

and let you shoulder the burden from there, good or bad."
She was looking up at him, mad enough to fight. "Tell me
I'm right, Kenrick. Risk yourself about half an inch."

Kenrick found himself searching for a hundred verbal
exits, the denial almost automatic. Saying no was the easiest
thing, but he didn't say no. He wasn't even sure he said yes.
For she was suddenly there pressed against him, her lips biting
at his until both of them knew that a quick grovel in the
shadow of a palm tree wasn't going to be enough for either
one of them.

"The good ones always happen fast," she said. "You know
that."

"I guess."

She could feel his body changing against her own and for
once felt part of it. "There are worse places to begin than in
bed. The Tahitians have a little saying I've always been
fond of. *Ai'ta pupa, ai'ta mai-tai.*"

"Does it mean anything?"

"No fuck—no good, approximately."

"I may need some time."

He did.

The ten minutes it took them to reach his hotel suite in
the Grand and Kenrick's bed.

"Your mouth," he was saying. "Use your mouth." But she
used more than her mouth. Her hands and tongue and saliva
and whatever it was beginning to flow from him by then,
everything sliding and her fingers moving over skin and
crevices, making little circles and pulling and biting because,
oh, yes, she was using her teeth, too, and she could do anything with him and it wouldn't hurt. She found she didn't
want to stop, even when he pulled her around, roughly, drawing her thighs toward him. And then it was *his* mouth that
found *her*, and they were together, needing nothing beyond
their own bodies to generate the heat. His tongue was moving around now, but with none of the calculation of those
bastards so thrilled with their own technique they don't even

feel it when the fire goes out and you don't give a damn whether they finish or not because they have the strange idea that it all starts and ends south of the navel.

They didn't come simultaneously, but one at a time, overlapping, although by then she could no longer tell where one body's feelings stopped and the other's began. She felt him begin to swell. In a clearer state of mind and with another man that might have been a warning, but she didn't care and held him even more tightly, and she guessed her hands were doing their share, too, because when he exploded, she didn't taste anything but good, already feeling the half ache, half heaven moving along her own thighs like current. When it focused and she was about to burst, she screamed instead and relaxed and let herself blow apart inside.

A little later she pulled herself around until she could look into his face. The acid test. A hard stare into your lover's eyes and pray he had the courage to look back, even if there was the funny smile that said, *I've been playing games.* In Kenrick's face was something she couldn't decipher, and the only word she could think of was "wonder."

"Where are you?" A dumb bed type of question, but she asked it anyway.

"Give me a minute, and I'll make up a lie."

"I can take the truth."

"Thinking about my wife."

"I should have given you the minute." She started to pull away, not sure whether she was angry at Kenrick's answer or because she had asked a silly question. He drew her more tightly to him. Oh, you could get answers here, sure enough. Usually to questions you hadn't asked. About wives who didn't screw and secretaries who did, but who didn't turn them on the way you did, dearie. About rotten kids, and where the men were going with their lives (always up); about their plans and schemes and places they intended to take you, be it over the face of the planet or into their particularly nifty inner space.

Worse were the ones who believed it, right then, with their whole being. Even though the being was full of dope or booze, and they would wake up cold-headed and look away because they didn't have it anymore and couldn't admit to you that they never did, except with a snootful. What a crock of euphoric junk she had heard from men whose ashes she had hauled. So she was good in bed. All it took was practice and a willing spirit. As long as she could get up and go home and at some point stand in the shower until it all washed away.

But she found she didn't mind it here, tucked up under Kenrick's arm, close like this with the musky sweat and the love smells coming from the two of them so thick they could have bottled it to turn on giant pandas.

But Kenrick said nothing, and suddenly she was afraid of the silence.

When he turned against her, she could feel him hard again, not asking to be favored by her mouth, but wanting her body and leaving Rayna in no doubt. Her last clear thought was they fitted well together, that was all, pure anatomy, although somewhere in their fierce coupling she realized her legs were bicycling the air to give him pleasure and the words coming from her mouth sounded stupid except that she felt them. At that point she began to wonder just who in hell was working on whom.

Much later still, too tired and spent to worry about anything, she said, "I wish I smoked. This is the time when people sit back and light up and talk about life and art."

In the dimness she could see his smile.

"I'll listen about Donner now if you want. He got us into this thing."

"I don't think he'd mind, not really." She was silent a moment before she said, "Do you know Bombay? I was born there."

She told him then about the city, with its great stretch of beach to the north called Juhu. About a Swedish lover

147

named Dirk and his promise to marry her. She hitched on the word "bargain" but went on to say that was what it was because more than anything she needed to be a missus-some-body-foreign so that she could get a passport out. "You see I hadn't a nationality really. The Indian government said I was British. And the British claimed I'd opted for Indian nationality with gobs of fine print to justify how right they were."

"I take it Mr. Dirk failed to deliver."

"In time-honored fashion he announced one day he was going home to wife and kiddies, previously unmentioned. He generously left the clothes he bought me and gave me a thousand dollars." Her mouth firmed tightly. "I give my time away these days if it pleases me, Kenrick. But I've never again sold it cheaply."

"When did this happen?"

"Six years ago. A month after Dirk walked out, Donner walked in. Or ran in, to be precise. I'd spent a lot of time that month walking the beach at Juhu. Standing there, when the wind is just right, you can smell the rest of the world out across the water—Africa, the Persian Gulf. I wasn't feeling sorry for myself. It was frustration. Knowing there was a world I was closer to in my mind than the country of my birth. I had this raw energy inside me ready to focus on something, and I'd wasted two years. Do you understand?"

"Perfectly." His face was in shadow now, his voice coming to her from out of the darkness.

"That day I was sitting on a sand dune like a zombie when far down the beach I saw this man running, running. Donner was carrying another fifteen stone on what he has now, and he was coming like a madman, that face of his all twisted in pain, fists doubled up as though he was ready to fight someone, something. I recognized the look with no trouble at all— the same kind of anger and frustration that was devouring me. I walked along the beach with him back to his hotel, knowing we'd end up in bed. Later there was some trouble with a photographer trying to take photos of us through the window, and I found out he was an actor."

"He hadn't said anything?"

"Not about that. I found Rod a place and moved in with him. He couldn't handle even the smallest thing himself, and his helplessness sort of tapped something inside me. A month later he said he'd marry me."

"Another bargain?"

"He thought he owed me, can you imagine, something I've never understood. He said the day we met I'd saved his life. Kept him from going over the edge."

She could see Kenrick now, a strange distant look in his eyes.

"What edge?" Rayna said. "Sure he drank too much and got randy with every woman around. I learned soon enough that his career was in a hole. But he was alive, healthy and seemed to be functioning. Can something be so wrong inside a person he can't keep going?"

"Yes," Kenrick said.

"But what happens when you go over? What form does this dreaded thing take? Suicide?"

"Of one kind or another."

"And you. You've been close to this edge?"

"I have indeed," he replied.

They were drinking *pastis*, the three of them, in a *brasserie* on the Boulevard Carnot. The film people never came here. Across the *rapide* from the Croisette it was a *quartier* of driving schools, laundries, and hardware stores. If people here spoke of the Festival, it was in tones reserved for distant events. The Festival might have been in Paris.

"But who?" the girl asked.

"I want Delon or Belmondo. Maybe Lino Ventura."

"They won't be at the Festival. Be practical."

"To see someone big like that when it isn't play." Gaetan Rampa spit. He could spit as well as Belmondo or Delon.

"Maybe Charles Bronson or that cowboy Clinton Eastwood."

"You're being a prick," the girl said.

"Or what's his name, Chuck Norris, or Bruce Lee."

"I don't think Bruce Lee," said Maxim.

The girl said, "Bruce Lee is dead."

"Dead?" So young? Maxim couldn't believe it.

"And a woman," Gaetan Rampa added. "I want a woman with them to watch how tough they are."

Maxim said, "What about the man we saw at the Palais?"

"Perhaps," Gaetan considered. "Yes. He is always very tough."

"Who?" the girl asked, growing impatient with his childishness.

"With the face, rough, you know. Blond, big."

"Donner?"

"That's it," Gaetan said. "Italian movies. Always brave . . . in films," he added.

"Listen," the girl said. "The idea is to take people known by the press. Pressure, so the money will come more easily. You understand?"

"Maybe James Bond. The first one."

"Sean Connery?"

"I can't say his name. Someone like that."

"Shit," the girl said in English.

"Someone like that," Gaetan Rampa insisted.

In the hour since Hugh Remy had put Siri into the hotel elevator, a second whiskey had diluted his alien feeling. A third was on the verge of making him downright chummy.

The bar of the Majestic at that late hour was more subdued than he had steeled himself to expect. He exchanged greetings with a handful of people he knew, including superagent Freddie Harland, who spied him from the door and homed in. The bar of the Majestic, the Blue, and the Carlton terrace were key watering holes during the Festival, and Remy guessed it was a checkpoint on Harland's nightly rounds. With him was his big dog, Cash.

"Hugh boy," Harland said, shaking his hand with a hearty, practiced grip. "Seeing you at the Festival, I don't know what else to expect. My condolences about Pedro. I really mean that."

"If thanks is the proper answer, thanks."

Obediently Cash hunkered down next to Harland's left boot, watching Remy with no particular interest. Remy wondered if a dog could be trained to smell out money. He was a big stud of an animal that led Harland to more ass than he deserved. Approaching single ladies, the dog was better than a pimp. What more casual entrée than a big, beautiful dog, inviting itself to be stroked, with master not far behind offering much the same proposition?

Whatever Harland's intention, Remy knew he wasn't the object. To Harland, he was a marker buoy that signaled the presence of Siri.

Remy could appreciate the agent's technique nonetheless.

While he delivered a glib patter of small talk, Harland's eyes took quick, darting side trips from Hugh Remy's face. God knew where Harland's mind was, but within ten seconds he cased the house, matched each face against his own private list, calculated there was nothing of value to be extracted, and eased out of their conversation.

But not before noting the waiter putting a full bottle of champagne in its ice bucket down next to Remy's table—Perrier-Jouet, Siri's favorite—and with it two glasses.

"Let me know what you're working on, Hugh. We should keep in touch, we really should."

"Sure thing," Remy said, knowing neither one gave the slightest damn.

Siri entered a quarter of an hour later. She hadn't dressed for show: a plain beige suit, her long blond hair tucked up under a floppy cap. A few heads turned, then moved closer together to whisper, but that was all.

"My suite looks like the mail room. I had no idea. . . ." She looked bewildered, but he could sense her pleasure. Yet a troubled something was behind her eyes. "Forty, fifty invitations, everything from boat rides and villa parties to a lovely note from the Grimaldis. Plus a gushy pageful from Freddie Harland naturally."

"He and his dog just sniffed their way through here."

"And an invitation to dine with the Festival director, Philippe Brialt."

"I didn't get any invitations." He filled her champagne glass and topped up his own.

"You wouldn't give a damn if you did, Hugh Remy." She raised her glass in a toast. "See, this isn't so painful."

Remy looked up in time to catch sight of Freddie Harland reentering the bar from the garden entrance. With him were two men Remy didn't know. They took a table across the room but with a clear line of sight.

"If I start looking like I'm enjoying myself, give me a hard kick," Remy said.

* * *

"Siri, dear Siri," Freddie Harland drawled. From the sound of it their meeting had been arranged in heaven.

"Freddie, my sweet," Siri chimed.

Harland avoided Hugh Remy's mocking smile and concentrated his full, sincere eye contact on Siri Laurence.

Remy had watched Harland pick his time, slither from his chair, and make the approach.

"You know how I felt about Pedro," Harland said, his small, hairy hands doing a dance of apology. "What can I say?"

"Of course. Thank you." There was an awkward second when it would have been appropriate to invite Harland to join them. Siri said nothing, smiling sweetly. Harland was quick to pick up the slack.

"I tried returning your call. For two days I had people trying to get back to you."

Siri looked into her glass of champagne. "Maybe there wasn't the urgency I felt at the time."

"Everyone at the Festival is talking. No, I mean it. There's a rumor you're coming back into films—back to us," Harland's emphasis was careful.

Hugh Remy knew sure as hell who had started the rumor.

Siri measured her answer before she spoke. "Let's just say it's possible and leave it there for now."

Harland held up a calming hand. "Siri, I know—at least I can imagine—the pressure you've been under." He bent forward, dropping his voice. "But I want you to understand, if you want to move, we can. Very, very fast."

The "we" was nicely played. Harland turned and cast a narrow glance toward the table he had just left. "Those people I'm with. The gentleman on the right is Dieter Furst —a very, very important German moneyman. Influential with the majors. The other man is an Italian director named Menotti. A genius—I mean, truly. Dino would just love to put something together, but Menotti's waiting for something . . . special. If you were to give me one blink, I could probably have a deal cut before we walk out of this bar. I mean it."

"But I've never heard of either your very big German moneyman or your genius Italian director. If you could make a deal tonight, think how much bigger one you might make tomorrow."

Remy was watching the Siri of old now. Buried inside the actress was a woman of shrewd instincts and a sharp mind for business. Or maybe the knack for survival.

"Not trying to push, Siri, merely mentioning the breadth of what is possible. Big things. Maybe you feel the need to write something after all you've been through, express yourself that way. You have a real story, Siri, your life. . . ."

Harland was light on his feet, able to shift stance in midstride to deliver a revised verbal package if he sensed hesitation in accepting his first pitch.

"My life?" Siri intoned, letting her eyes go wide. "I am only thirty-one years old."

"Swifty is camped at the Hôtel du Cap. If you want to talk—talk, mind you—it shall be done."

"Freddie. . . ."

Harland, knowing he'd stretched things to the limit, slipped in his final effort.

"One more name I'll leave you with," he said quickly. "Kenrick."

"I'm not sure I want to be left with Kenrick."

"I know you feud, Siri—"

"We do not feud," she corrected. "We do not speak. It is no secret about the way Kenrick and the studio once treated my husband. I do not like Teddy Kenrick. It is that simple."

"You don't even have to see him. All I am telling you is he wants to develop a Siri Laurence project. And like him or not, when Kenrick moves, he moves. Right, Hugh?"

Now, you bonzo, Remy thought, when you think I can drive home your case.

Remy nodded, grudgingly, then added his bottom-line assessment. "There are worse people to deal with than Kenrick."

"*Voilà*," Harland said, collecting his minor victory.

He picked the right moment to skip off; minutes later a second bottle of champagne was brought to their table.

Siri smiled at the waiter and asked that it be sent to her suite. "Come up, Hugh. Something I want to tell you, and not here."

"That wasn't the lot, was it?" Remy said. "The invitations, I mean. The things in your room."

She shook her head.

"Nicky Deane?"

"Yes, Nicky Deane," she said.

"I am going to see him, Hugh," she announced as soon as they entered the suite.

She opened the champagne and brought him a glass.

Even with the high window open, the room stank of gardenias.

Remy sipped at the champagne without tasting it. "I thought you'd spent a good part of your adult life running from this guy. Why the change?"

"Because I don't want to run anymore." She turned toward the window to look out toward the darkened sea. Remy wished he could have seen her face.

Remy put down his glass, crossed the room, and turned her gently toward him. "I'm going to tell you what I think, unsolicited. In my opinion, Nicky Deane is capable of nasty stuff. You forget I saw his warning hanging from the mast of my boat."

"What's the worst? Kill me? I'm the love of his life, Hugh." Her laugh was bitter, and she pulled away.

"So maybe if he can't have you," Remy argued, "he'll arrange it so no one else can. Some minds think that way."

"If that's what he wanted, why not before? I walked away from him in New York. He watched me marry Pedro Lehman. Look, I quit films because he had a hold over me—my fear he would hurt Pedro. Now there isn't any hold."

"If you say so."

She took an envelope from the bed and extracted a white card. "You don't invite someone to dinner at the best restaurant on the Riviera, with the intention of killing her. Except with calories."

"He's capable of anything," Remy said, holding his ground. "Things you haven't thought of."

Her expression became puzzled.

"Siri, I am going to ask you once—"

She cut him off coldly. "I'd rather you didn't. I am going to see Nicky Deane. I intend to listen to his offer because there'll be one." She turned then and gave him that impish smile, full of warmth by whatever artifice it was created. "And when I hear it, I am going to spit in his eye."

"*C'est fait,*" Durand said. "Finished."

"The police let her go?"

"At this moment she is in a plane over the Atlantic, feeling rotten, I guarantee."

Brialt sat down heavily behind his desk, heaving a sigh of relief to Claude Durand.

The headlines of the *Hollywood Reporter* that morning had run: "Cannes Fest Under Way with Much Pomp and Ceremony." The French press was calling it the most glamorous Festival in years, what with the unexpected appearances of the ex-heavyweight champion, still called *Le Plus Grand*, Siri Laurence, and an array of international stars who had arrived unannounced.

True, there had already been the usual measure of the bizarre: the python found in the men's room of the city's most elegant hotel; the mother of a twelve-year-old actress biting the waiter at the Carlton, for reasons undisclosed. By unspoken agreement the usual rash of auto thefts, accidents, and minor crimes that flourished in the city during the Festival had been played down in the press. Of course, Edy Williams had done her annual striptease for the cameras, this year on the roof of a car.

And then a well-known young actress picked 3:00 A.M. to go wandering along the rue d'Antibes, catatonic on drugs and wearing only the T-shirt she'd made famous.

Only Claude Durand's skillful intervention saved the young lady from the inside of a French jail and explosive headlines. Over the screaming protest of the producer who had flown her in for a reception, Durand escorted the dazed creature to the airport and personally cinched the seat belt beneath the bosom, known worldwide.

"Commandant Haag was there when Pascal decided to let her go. He thinks Pascal has gone soft, you could see it."

"Or become reasonable for a change. I don't like Haag."

"In his eyes the lady had offended the morals of France. If Haag had been in command, our young actress would have been on the guillotine."

"Fingers crossed, Durand."

"Fingers crossed."

The thought of the day ahead of him left Brialt paralyzed.

The heart of the Festival was the competition between twenty-five films from twelve countries for the Palme d'Or. But there were three lesser competitions designed to balance the criticism that the Festival had abandoned art for commerce. In total there would be fifty films shown in Cannes that day and each day of the Festival, including three separate screenings of the two films in the major competition.

The judges were meeting again after lunch, and by late afternoon Brialt would have a report from the president about the bickering, swings in opinion, and current favorite for the Palme d'Or. There were three separate press receptions he should attend and a TV spectacular direct from the gardens of the Majestic Hotel, on which he'd promised to appear. He had sent excuses and apologies to two beauty contests, one held by the Italians at the Sporting Club and the second on the Plage de Voilier sponsored by an independent film company. Both hoped their Miss Cannes Evening or Miss Cannes Beach would be striking enough to get coverage from the press. A spaghetti eating contest was taking place in Golfe Juan, for a purpose undetermined, and there were at least a dozen separate cocktail parties at which his appearance would lend legitimacy to whatever its sponsor was selling.

All this in addition to the film that evening in the Festival Hall, followed by his nightly invitation-only dinner in his suite at the Carlton. To do it all and survive, Brialt would have needed to be four people.

Worse, his wife, Monique, was arriving in Cannes.

"She's what!" Katherine exclaimed not one hour before.

"Arriving Tuesday. What was I to say? Don't come, you'll get in the way of my affair?"

"You could try."

"I did, darling, you must believe me."

Weeks before, he had invited Monique to join him for the Festival's closing gala. Each year he made the same invitation, and each year she declined. Until that morning, when he listened with a sinking feeling as she told him by telephone from Paris she'd changed her mind. "I'm catching the plane Tuesday. When the Festival ends, perhaps we can take a few days in Corsica." After a well-timed pause she said, "I'm sure you'll need a rest."

From the subcurrents in her voice Brialt detected everything she intended. Was her suspicion his imagination? Or a confirmation of that mysterious quality of Frenchwomen: a talent for perceiving, even at long distance, cheating on the part of their men.

Until then Brialt had included Katherine in his entertaining. The second night of the Festival she had volunteered for the dinner he was holding in his suite for the jury. With eight men and one woman it had been a perfect time and turned out so successfully he had decided to hell with people's suspicion and included her nightly from then on. She made a sparkling addition but once, in bed, confessed she found the dinners a crashing bore. "When you invite people who've spent a year together making a film, all you have is one big clique."

"Well, my wise darling, what do you suggest?"

"Some opposites," she replied, appearing to give it careful

thought. "People who would never invite each other to their own parties. Liven things up, Philippe. You're so stuffy, darling."

To Brialt it seemed such a harmless wickedness he couldn't help smiling in delight. "I've no objection to inviting opposites, as long as they are very important opposites."

"Stuffy, and a snob. It's really a pity I've fallen in so deep. Even when we're not together, I see you in front of me. But when it's over, this time together, I think I'll have something left, something no one can ever take away."

Brialt found it unthinkable to return again to his previous life with Monique, which, years ago, had slipped across the border from comfort to boredom. In dutiful feminine French manner his wife continued to make love well, but at a time and place of her own preference and almost always in the dark. With Katherine it was another act altogether, an ambush, day or night, and in any posture.

He thought of Monique's arrival, the lessening number of days he and Katherine would have together. Unless he chose not to accept its ending.

"Arrange anything you like," Brialt said, adding his own feelings with a courage he would have found unimaginable only weeks before. "As long as we're together, darling. I love you."

"I'll begin with the dinner for Siri Laurence. That'll be a dandy."

Like Brialt, Gaetan Rampa was having his problems.

Earlier he had been most worried about the means of transferring the money. "That's where they get caught," he told Maxim and the girl. "In the exchange." How it could be done was the girl's idea, who showed a surprising thoroughness in these things, even to the week's research in Geneva. The list of exactly *who*, he was assured, was taking shape. But *where!*

Even after he'd learned about the police on patrol inside the Festival Hall, he had made several cautious probes. There were parts of the hall accessible to anyone: the exhibitors' booths on the fourth floor; parts of the press hall; even the *grande salle*, during showings of little importance. But well-trained ushers controlled access to the suites of offices on the second, third, and fourth floors, where conceivably the right mix of hostages might gather. He thought of the jury room. But the concentration of police nearby would have left only a fool unfrightened, and Gaetan Rampa wasn't that. Conclusion: a place other than the Palais.

He considered taking a limousine and its passengers and with that in mind wandered into the garage of the Carlton filled with its Rollses and Mercedes-Benzes. He was immediately challenged by a ridiculous figure in a blue beach club T-shirt, armed, he was sure, with a toy pistol and meaningless badge.

If they had wanted a car, the guard would hardly have been a problem. But what then? In an automobile they would be vulnerable and without the line of communication they would need with the police.

Increasingly the one setting that provided every element became apparent to them all. With the decision made, Gaetan Rampa smiled. A block away he could see the bright blue sign of the Carlton Hotel.

"Where the hell is Kenrick?" Parent company president Mal Stiner cast a tight-lipped glance at the men nibbling the croissants he'd laid on for their breakfast meeting in his bungalow at the Hôtel du Cap.

It was 7:30 A.M., and Stiner had been up for an hour and a half, taking his ritual stroll in the pine-scented air of the hotel gardens. He knew Kenrick was an early riser; if he was last to arrive, there was a reason for it, and Stiner knew the reason. Kenrick had begun his game of nerves.

Stiner was about to telephone when his daughter, Penny, answered the knock on the bungalow door, to admit Kenrick. She mouthed a good-bye in her father's direction and discreetly made her exit. The men were sorry to see her go; she was a statuesque girl, with a chorus girl's figure and direct cat-green eyes.

"Burning both ends, eh, Teddy?" Stiner said with sudden joviality. He pumped Kenrick's hand with abundant energy. "Have yourself some coffee, and we'll get started. We've all got better things to do than sit around a hotel room."

Kenrick poured himself a coffee and decided to take it black. The night with Rayna had tested muscles in his body he didn't know existed, and he was acutely aware of certain sensitive regions between belt buckle and knees. The contrast between the warm bed he had left not an hour before and the gathering in Stiner's suite was enough to choke on.

Aron Archer raised a single eyebrow in acknowledgment, toying with a croissant he couldn't bear to taste; he wore a hangover like neon. Next to him Ernst Rucker stared out to sea, sucking on a pipe, lost in his own private world of release patterns and playdates. Sid Mathan stood, wolfing down a croissant as though he were being timed. In one sense he was. In the past three days Mathan had screened all or a part of twenty films, and he was worried how to cover the other three hundred-odd on the market that year at Cannes.

The sixth man in the room was the corporate trouble-shooter, Donald Eads.

Eads glanced at Kenrick over his coffee and looked away; the brief, initial appraisal of an adversary.

"Gentlemen, I want to introduce Don Eads," Stiner said. "And I want to tell you what he is about before you hear it from someone else."

Stiner explained his intention to have Eads undertake an in-house investigation of the business practices and procedures of the studio.

"Not that we expect to find anything wrong," Stiner said, pausing to look at each face for a measured second or two. "But the film industry is under attack. I want to hold our studio up as an industry model during a time when, frankly, the public is beginning to think we're a bunch of playboys and thieves. We don't want the Justice Department policing the movie business when we are perfectly capable of policing ourselves. Don's investigation will be a demonstration of that belief."

It had the rhythms of a political speech, and Kenrick bet at the studio luncheon six days hence, the gathered press would be treated to much the same pronouncement. Kenrick couldn't imagine anyone in the industry believing it. An investigation of the studio was a question of the way Kenrick ran things. If he was expected to react in a predictable manner, he decided not to disappoint anyone.

"Bullshit," he said, just loud enough. In one corner Archer shut his eyes and began to murmur a silent prayer. Eads took a careful sip of coffee, thus demonstrating his unflappability.

Stiner's complexion went deep red. "You damn well better have something more constructive to say."

His tone was angry enough to have been genuine.

Kenrick spoke. "We are about to announce the highest quarterly earnings in our history. We have as good a production schedule as there is in the industry. We are also trying to deal here at Cannes—with our foreign distributors, moneymen, you name it. Let the word leak out about some half-assed self-examination, we're going to look like a bunch of dummies. Mainly to people in the industry who know better than to invite trouble."

"To hell with them," Stiner said.

"And to hell with the stockholders? Come on, Mal. They're already nervous, given the current industry jitters. If I were them, I'd rather ask why a lot of the money that ought to be declared as dividends was going into pinball machines and Aspen real estate. Hell, we're a movie company."

"Diversification of the parent company is not your concern," Stiner roared.

"It is when that diversification is riding on the back of the studio. You announce anything you want, Mal. But start poking a finger too deep into things you don't know anything about, and you'll have to swallow what oozes out."

"I'll accept that responsibility."

"You won't have to accept it," Kenrick said, "because it will be in your lap."

In the taxi back to Cannes Sid Mathan rolled his eyes and asked, "What the hell was that all about? This business with Eads. Stiner must see he's forcing you into a fight. A fight or doing the exact thing you are—take your best people and leave him holding an empty shell."

"It doesn't matter what Stiner thinks. Just keep your eye on the ball, Sidney. We've got other things to worry about."

"I wasn't shaky when I was visualizing it all through a bottle of champagne. But last night I'm thinking about mortgage payments and college educations, all that middle-class *drek*. And I say, 'Sidney, maybe you don't have a right to be gambling like this.'"

"Then don't," Kenrick said. "Stay put, and maybe you'll pull a vice-presidency."

"Teddy, all I want is you to tell me what's happening."

"It's coming together," Kenrick said. "Fast."

He told Mathan about the additions he had made in the past forty-eight hours to the portfolio Archer would take to Novotny, the moneyman in Boston. It was a trading basket of goodies that would give any new studio a chance of surviving its first year, provided Kenrick could top it off with something extraordinary.

With that purpose in mind, he had spent the previous evening at a restaurant table with Paul Waxler, barely tasting the food that had earned it three *Michelin* stars. By the end of the dinner he and Waxler had hammered out a development deal that would be known to every other major studio before the Festival was over, if Kenrick knew Waxler. The meeting escaped no one's notice on the patio of L'Oasis and made the wag column in that morning's *Daily Variety*.

Waxler was just finishing a highly profitable association with Universal and had films in development with two other majors. They all were six-figure deals that provided Waxler a lavish personal life-style as the projects crept through the steps toward production. There were those who believed Waxler didn't give a damn whether his projects were filmed or not. He had worked the trick of making himself one of those half dozen big-name producers with whom major studios soothed the people to whom they owed money. Studio brass would point to the three films Waxler had made in the past ten years that were among the top hundred largest-grossing films of all time and forget the ones that he milked and let die in development. A Waxler film in the works was good for top management, even when the odds of seeing it before the cameras were longer than the Irish Sweepstakes.

Waxler had earned the highest accolade in the business: He was bankable.

Kenrick had told him he was looking for a big project, letting the producer read in all the implications he desired.

"I hear you're deep in red ink on the Lehman film," Waxler came back, testing the likely climate. "Worth the money no doubt."

"No doubt."

"Come on, Teddy, I didn't think you liked my kind of fun. Why the sudden warmth?"

"I am in the market for a big picture. I thought you were the man, Paul. If I was wrong. . . ." Kenrick shrugged, the gesture delivering the message.

"Not 'we,'" Waxler observed. "I did detect the first person singular, did I not?"

"The same first person singular willing to go very heavy in development—on the right project."

"What are you up to, Kenrick?"

"Now, Paul, you really don't expect me to spell it out. Not here. And not to you. With the kind of money that's behind it you shouldn't care because the checks will be good. And I don't even want you to send me a new car."

Waxler gave him a special smile, the one with six figures in it, and patted Kenrick's arm for all to see.

"We'll work something out."

"Something in writing," Kenrick said. "Something for Siri Laurence—within seventy-two hours."

"That's the catch. An idea for Siri."

"Not a catch, Paul. Your ticket to ride."

Four hours earlier he had ended a long afternoon meeting with Billy Shinn and his cousin O.K. He left their suite with an agreement in principle on a three-picture coproduction deal, the first film to star Siri Laurence. "Why not?" Billy Shinn said. "Anytime you come in with half the money and Siri's name on a dotted line, the old men are going to listen."

Billy eyed his cousin O.K., giving him a chance to question

the deal. Billy was the more conservative, favoring wire spectacles and business suits; O.K. went for flowered shirts, platformed soles, and, when he traveled outside Singapore, a lanky Scandinavian lady.

The old men Billy referred to were their respective fathers, the Shinn brothers. The organization was moving away from a heavy program of violence and kung-fu into films with a broader appeal. It was in their nature to understand that Kenrick might be manipulating a separate game of his own.

Billy shouted, "O.K., are you awake, or thinking about the usual thing? Kenrick is dealing."

"Sounds fine," O.K. said. "Everything does in Cannes until you take it home to live with."

Mathan himself had already contributed his share to the trading basket Archer would take to the moneyman, Novotny. Riding in the taxi back to Cannes, Kenrick told him so. A little of the worry went out of Sid Mathan's cramped expression, but not for long. For most people dealing at Cannes the films shown nightly in the *grande salle* of the Festival Hall—the formal competition—was a sideshow. For them, like Sid Mathan, the real action was a small, disordered office at the rear of the fourth floor of the Festival Hall—the operational center of the *Marché du Film*.

It was here that 840 hours of screening time were scheduled in four of the city's commercial theaters and the small, makeshift screening rooms in the Festival Hall itself to accommodate the hundreds of films in search of people who could distribute in foreign markets and blocks of territories from Iceland to Black Africa. Any manner of deal could and would be negotiated at Cannes, with any kind of buyer. The essential consideration was money.

There were still other independent filmmakers who would arrive with film or video cassettes in their suitcases and prowl the city looking for screening space. Even the city's two porno houses were booked solid, and by the fourth day of the Festival leaflets advertising screenings at this theater

167

or that littered hotel lobbies, the windshields of parked automobiles, and, prominently, gutters and waste cans.

From the films Mathan had seen to date, he had given Kenrick a short list of four, available for pickup and U.S. distribution. A handful of pickups would give any new organization pictures for immediate release.

"But we have to move," Mathan said, brushing the tired strands of hair across a shiny scalp. "The good stuff goes fast. The bad ones will be around next year this time still looking."

Kenrick told Mathan to go with all four. "Tell them we'll have letters of agreement out within forty-eight hours, and when Rentzler gets here, dump it in his lap."

"You don't want to talk terms?"

"You talk terms, Sid, argue terms. Start earning that impressive new salary of yours."

If there was any doubt about the formation of a new studio, the cold, hard print in the letters of agreement would end it.

"And, Sid, there's a French director named Climent. See if he is showing anything in Cannes and take a look."

Such a small request; it would come back to haunt him.

"To import, you mean? A film in French?"

"Have a look."

He was back at his hotel from the Stiner meeting a little before noon.

He declined the key to his suite but took the messages that had accumulated in his absence from the *concierge*.

Three calls each from Freddie Harland and Peter Galloway. One from Fiona MacCauley in Los Angeles, which meant something to report on the recut of the Lehman film. A telegram from Rentzler in New York that said he was catching the first available flight for Nice. Nothing about the accountant Ray Tannis or about Robert Arthur. Rentzler wouldn't have trusted the information to a telegram in any case.

The final message was from Rayna Tate, out of sight but not out of mind. He didn't know what hotel she was staying in or if there was a hotel. The single word "Working" was scrawled across the paper, with her initial, R.

He made one try at calling Leo Gold, then gave up, and left it to Rayna.

He didn't want to spook Leo Gold.

Through the high glass doors of the hotel entrance Siri watched the limousine turn into the drive.

In the security of a hotel suite her thinking had been a perfect model of logic. If she had been anxious about anything, it was simply to be done with Nicky Deane's game of shadow. "Meeting him is a bad idea," Remy persisted, his big bony hands working themselves in frustration. "Look, I'll tag along. A restaurant is a public place."

"Hugh, stop treating me like an eight-year-old."

But now in the limousine Nicky had sent for her she felt very much a child, alone and needing support. More than once Siri had reflected that her entire life she had moved from one crutch to another, always unwilling or unable to face things on her own. Desperate in New York, she found Nicky Deane, and the closed doors in her career opened. Pedro Lehman came into her life at the exact moment she fled Nicky Deane, stepping from one man to another without interim. Even now she found it difficult to separate her love for Pedro Lehman from the gratitude for all he had been—companion, manager, teacher—but more than anything the single person in her life that had given her talent a chance to flourish. But the talent was hers.

She had never admitted to a soul the resentment that had burned in her four long years at the bargain she had been forced to make with Nicky Deane. She had mortgaged a building career to keep her husband alive, not willingly, but from a sense of duty. She hadn't regretted it, but now the mortgage was canceled, and she was free. Yet already she was leaning on Hugh Remy for advice and friendship, for making decisions she was capable of. She didn't want to use Hugh. She wanted to face things on her own, control her own destiny. In a sense her decision this night to see Nicky Deane was an attempt to take that first solo step. She could do it.

The invitation promised dinner at a delightful restaurant she knew by reputation built in an old olive mill in a village near Cannes. By the time the driver wound through the twisting streets of the city she was lost, but she relaxed again when he found the highway north, toward their destination.

But several miles along, he made a sudden cutoff onto the *autoroute* and turned west, increasing speed.

"Where are you going?" she demanded immediately.

"*Je m'excuse*," he said. "No English." He was a young, seedy type with an expression that seemed pleased by her confusion. It was then the panic closed in, the fear she knew had been there all along, held in check by the deceptive logic of her own words, uttered in the safe presence of Hugh Remy. She wanted out of the car. She preferred to run than to be delivered to Nicky Deane like a parcel.

"Stop," she ordered. "You understand that. Here . . . goddammit! Now!"

The driver examined her in the rearview mirror, then pointed beyond the windshield at the divided highway, the narrow shoulders of the road. "No can," he said.

"No can, my ass," Siri said.

He shrugged but held the speed constant. In moments they had left all visible marks of civilization behind except for the highway and a scattering of other automobiles. On either side were thick forests, the trees blending together into a dark blanket with the approach of night. Ahead, rising sharply, was a tight knot of jagged mountains, the same ones she could see from the terrace of her hotel suite.

Unexpectedly the driver made another sharp turn, bringing them eventually onto the narrow road that skirted the coast.

She vowed not to be beaten by panic even before she began.

A man doesn't pursue a woman for years to take her into his arms and give her the kiss of death. That was the stuff of horror films and gothic romances.

Whatever was to come she was determined not to defeat herself.

Well into the mountains the driver turned off the winding coastal road onto a steep, narrow drive that took them upward and away from the coast. A moment later they passed a large sign carved in wood planking announcing a hotel just ahead and a few other things in French she had not understood; she thought the word *fermeture* meant closed. Yet the well-lighted old house in front of them was far from being closed. A magnificent place, built of stone and tile, peering out from a cliff edge more than a thousand feet above the Mediterranean.

The driver stopped the car at the front of a stone walkway that led up toward an imposing wooden door, crisscrossed with cast-iron strapping and rough black rivets. Through one of the broad windows she could see a man and a woman moving back and forth between a well-lighted kitchen and someplace out of sight, in the interior, the dining room no doubt. A comforting sight; but something lingering picked at her.

"*Bon soir, madame,*" the driver said, opening the car door.

She began up the stone pathway, then stopped. The limousine was retreating back down the steep drive. Off to her left, miles distant, was Cannes hidden beyond the mountains. All that could be seen from where she stood were a wide sweep of ocean and, far away, a blinking beacon light that might have been the end of the Cap d'Antibes.

Not the setting for a murder.

"Like hell," she said aloud.

She turned her back on the ocean and walked up the

path, recalling exactly what it was that disturbed her.

Hotels had customers, and customers would have come here by car. Yet not an automobile was in sight; the silence of the great house, unnatural in its completeness.

Above her, the great wood and iron door swung open to accept her entrance.

She was led through the house by a thick, somber-faced woman with coarse dark hair tied in a bun. She wore an apron over a black uniform. "He is waiting, madame," she whispered, her voice giving the words a mysterious significance. Black was the appropriate thing. Siri too had worn a black dress with long sleeves and a front that showed no skin below her neck.

From the kitchen came the aroma of fresh seafood and the various sounds of someone at work. If indeed the hotel was open, Nicky Deane had arranged to be the only guest.

What was once the high-ceilinged salon had become a dining room, with high arched windows and floors of pale marble tile. There were a half dozen tables, but only one was set for dinner. Near the windows stood Nicky Deane, wearing a tux and looking out at what could only have been a view of dark ocean.

He turned, eyes roaming over her body as though the tissue she wore were transparent.

The woman quickly lighted the candles on the table, opened a bottle of champagne, and slipped from the room.

"A little change of plans," he said, gesturing around vaguely. "What do you think?"

With his darkish, rough looks, Nicky Deane might have passed for a competent male companion, the kind of cultured hustler that prowled the grand hotels and casinos along the Mediterranean. Until he opened his mouth. When Nicky spoke, it was New York's East Village.

"Imaginative, in your usual way. All I want to know is why."

He offered her a smile and bade her to join him at the table. A half hour later she felt foolish for having been on the verge of hysterics less than an hour before. In her icy presence she watched Nicky Deane's self-assurance melt away. While they drank champagne and began with a platter of *écrevisses*, Nicky talked compulsively, scarcely looking at her, demanding nothing from her in the way of conversation. She remembered these rambling monologues, years ago, when they first met in New York. It occurred to her then that Nicky was using her to unburden himself of things that he could never tell other people, the people he was close to, if such existed. She had been mildly flattered but quickly became impatient and finally abusive. Once, when he telephoned and began that droning monologue, she put the receiver down and went to wash her hair. When she returned twenty minutes later, he was unaware she hadn't been listening.

". . . so here was this twenty-year-old kid making more money than he'd ever thought possible, with a half point in a Havana casino—pure gold—and a quarter of a million bucks in fifties and hundreds in a suitcase underneath the bed in his room, money that nobody knew about, not even the people he worked for because they would not have approved exactly, money he had skimmed off, a little here, a little there—and what happens?"

He gave up trying to separate the soft white meat of an *écrevisse* from its shell with a knife and fork and picked it up in his fingers.

". . . so, come this New Year's Eve, some smart-assed young lawyer stirring up a bunch of farmers out in the sticks makes his play. I'm talking about Castro. We all hear Batista's plane taking off, him getting out of the country, but nobody knows what is happening until the rioting starts. So this kid figures that everything is about to fall apart and that it might be the right time to be gone. Only he isn't about to leave with a quarter of a million bucks still under his bed.

But when he tries to make it back to his hotel, dressed in a monkey suit, like this"—he tugged at his satin lapels—"he knows that the odds on both getting the money and saving his skin are very long. Only one thing harder in his life he tells me later than walking away from all that money . . . you know what it was?"

The smile twisted on his face. She shook her head, for she already knew the answer, the point he was about to make.

"Watching a girl get into a taxi," Nicky Deane said, "with a guy she didn't have no business being with. And watching that taxi drive away, while he stood there doing nothing. This guy tells me he made up his mind about something both times. When you got a good thing, you hang on. You keep it close and don't let go."

"What do you want, Nicky?" Siri asked.

"Nothing any different. You to marry me. I've never asked anyone else."

She felt the impulse begin deep. She wanted to throw back her head and laugh. So simple, yet she had considered everything but the obvious, even after looking at this setting, hearing the woman who had led her in, that special, conspiratorial whisper. After all the anguish they had brought into each other's life, Nicky Deane was bestowing upon her the offer that miraculously was to make it all just and worthwhile.

"Then you're a poor, simple son of a bitch," she said.

"You got a mouth like a whore sometimes," Nicky Deane replied. "But you'll change."

"I'll never change," she said, standing. "It's been grand, Nicky. Old acquaintances and all that. Now, call the car. . . ."

"The car will be back at eight o'clock tomorrow morning. Later if I give them a call."

"You haven't been listening."

"I'm listening," Nicky Deane said, pushing back his chair.

"But a lot of times the things people say ain't what they really mean. . . ." He stood and smiled toward the stairway. "Come on up. You'll like the view."

"You're mad!"

"You and me in bed was always special. You told me so often enough."

"Oh, Christ. . . ."

"You liked it the last time, Mrs. Married Lady, in Palm Springs, remember? Or do you always say those things and look that way when you're screaming your head off to don't stop?"

"Okay, I was the idiot. I thought you were after a tumble in the hay, and when you got it, you'd go home."

"You're saying that now, but that's not the way it was. I got everything I wanted all right, and you liked it." He was looking at her, taking some special pleasure recalling that time she had lied to Pedro and met Nicky in Palm Springs.

It struck her then, the way he'd made her do things, the way he'd worked on her as if his cock were a weapon. Oh, God, had there been a camera?

"I bet your husband would have thought different about his wife if he'd got a look at you and me. You don't think I know when I tap one that hasn't been screwed right at home, maybe ever."

She whirled, sweeping the shell-laden plates from the table. She snatched up a champagne glass, aiming it at the broad plate glass window. Nicky Deane stepped forward and brushed the glass from her hand. It splintered into tiny shards on the tile floor. She expected someone to appear to see what happened. But no one came. They were alone.

She tried to twist from his grip, but he held her with ease. Close, she could smell the heavy fragrance of his cologne masking something strong and animal. It was true, she had liked their crude lovemaking; the thought had shamed her until this moment.

"So what do you figure a good screwing is worth?" she

176

said viciously. "What should a woman do for a few seconds of ecstasy?"

"What are you talking about?" Again she saw the sureness loosen, the confusion deep in his brown, feminine eyes.

"I mean you have to do something with the rest of your life. You can't spend twenty-four hours a day on your back, thinking about what tickles between your legs." She laughed, gaining strength from the sound. "I didn't realize it till now, but your getting through to me, your giving me pleasure I've never been proud of, made me realize just how little else about you I can stand."

He let her hands drop, bewildered. It was beyond him to reconcile the contradictions: that pleasure and self-contempt could exist side by side and that the self-contempt could be the more powerful.

He wandered away, visibly dazed, then with a quick explosion drove his fist into the wooden table, splintering one of the panels.

With no concession in her voice, Siri said, "Now will you call the car? Or do I have to hike back to Cannes?"

His head shook a denial, and she heard the stubborn turn in his voice. "Not let you go," he said, each word a separate resolution.

Alarm pounded through her. "Let me go? You never had me."

He spun toward her. "What does it take? Look at this." His arm flung out at the table, the room. To Nicky it represented something she couldn't quite comprehend, just as she herself had become. A world Nicky Deane wanted, a climb out of poverty? Was it that simple? "I roll as high as any of you film people. I buy film people. I owned your husband."

"Liar!"

"What do you know?"

She started for the door, wanting to shut out the insults, the preposterous things he was inventing.

His voice called after her, "You'll marry me. Because you're worth nothing unless I say otherwise. Zero."

"Whatever you say or believe, I liked myself around Pedro Lehman. Around you I smell."

"Don't," he said, raising a hand. It was an oddly toned request as though she were pushing him toward something he himself feared.

"Burn in hell if you don't like the sound of it," Siri shouted. "You have a hold on me that got you more than you deserved. But it's gone."

"You ask that long drink of water you're traveling with to tell you about Carole Wade. Then we'll talk." His voice caught, his features a dark mask. "I love you, you have to know."

"You're sick," she said, turning. "Or maybe just stupid."

Deane was still near the table when she opened the big wooden door and stepped out into the night.

She pulled it closed behind her as she heard his cry echoing from inside, a pained animal howl followed by the crash of broken glass as he vented his rage. Footsteps pounded toward the door in pursuit.

Siri ran.

Far below she could hear the ocean, its presence dominating the night. She fled into the darkness in the direction of the stone path that led to the drive, and it to the highway and safety.

Ahead, she saw a dark shape rise from the brush at the side of the path and move to intercept her, to prevent her escape.

She turned and saw Nicky Deane, stumbling down the stairs, the open door behind him. Hoarse sobs escaped his throat as he called after her into the darkness.

"Don't want to hurt you, Siri," he called, ". . . hurt you."

She was sure that was what he said, but already she was plunging through the rough brush away from the stone walkway, toward the sound of the sea. The spiny leaves tore at her face, began to pick and finally shred the fine material of her dress.

Behind her she could hear Nicky Deane calling her name, closer, then moving in the opposite direction.

Suddenly she was aware that she no longer was pushing through the thick brush. Her shoe crunched loose gravel, and she felt her footing give way. Her right shoe slipped into nothingness.

She looked down. Far below she could see the rocky edge of shoreline directly beneath her. The cliff edge. One giant step from where she stood would launch her into space, but oddly she felt no fear whatsoever. Below, the sea was calm, accepting, the sureness of death absolutely unrelated to the promise of peace it seemed to hold out.

She heard the sound as a powerful arm encircled her from behind.

"It's all right, Siri," Hugh Remy's voice came, soothing and calm. "You're safe," he said. "I've got you now."

"Help me, Hugh. Please help me."

In the darkness his face contorted with hard decision before he said, "I'll try."

"I knew it was wrong to follow you," Remy said. "But when I saw that limo swing onto the *autoroute* and turn on the steam, I knew I'd done something right for a change."

They sped back along the *bord de mer* toward Cannes in their rented Renault. Remy had already draped his jacket across her shoulders and insisted she take a shot from the bottle of cognac on the car seat.

"He's crazy, Hugh. I'm not sure what he'll do now." Remy could hear the helplessness. "Hugh, who was, or who is, Carole Wade?"

"Where did you get that name?"

"Nicky said to ask you about Carole Wade. Why?"

When Remy didn't answer her, Siri prompted, "If you don't tell me, I'll ask someone else."

"Carole Wade was an actress. For all I know she might be alive somewhere. Bright little thing and a fair comedienne. We used her in a couple of films seven, eight years ago. Not a great talent, but a nice girl."

"The kind that finally goes back to Texas saying, 'It's not worth the trouble.'"

"Something like that. Except about then Carole started running around with a character named Jackie Bolinas. Most people said Bolinas was a gangster—a mob messenger boy, mostly loan-sharking producers who needed quick money. But the story has it Jackie Bolinas began to like the film business. Especially when he falls in love with Carole Wade. Next thing we know he produces her next film. Not an unusual Hollywood story up to there. Man with money and actress girlfriend combine two loves, and thus another producer is born. It wasn't a bad film."

"I've never heard of either of them."

"Not quite the story's end," Remy said, slowing, trying to phrase what came next. "Well, I guess Bolinas's former employers didn't accept his resignation or his decision to pursue another career. You dance to the Mafia's tune, as the saying goes; you don't write your own. So one Sunday morning Jackie Bolinas and Carole Wade are found in a motel room on Ventura Boulevard, still in bed."

"They were killed."

"Bolinas was, sure as hell, a bullet where he thinks."

"And the girl?"

"Carole was right next to him. Only they hadn't shot her," Remy said. "Siri. . . ."

"Spit it out, Hugh."

"I guess . . . I guess someone figured she was the cause of it all, and that a bullet wouldn't have been payment enough. So someone had removed most of Carole Wade's face with a razor blade."

There are days on the Riviera you can never forget. Days when the winds that sometimes blow south along the valley of the Rhône sweep everything clean. Days when the sky and the sea are ragged panels of pure color, azure blue and deep green. On those days every line of building and earth is etched with a special fineness, and it is all you can manage, with the beauty of things, to remember your own name or what you intended to do with yourself beyond feel good. Even Kenrick found his fourth day in Cannes such a time— and allowed an hour to enjoy it.

Larry Rentzler caught up with him at a beach club far along the Croisette at a table alone, looking out across a small, crescent-shaped beach protected by an ancient quay of gray stone.

The sight made Rentzler pause. One didn't often catch Kenrick in a position to be observed. Rentzler's basic tool for analysis was a search for motive. As a skilled investigator, he was never comfortable until he tucked people into their motivational slots, as he thought of it. Find the precise nature of a man's need for money or position, and Rentzler would have a handle, if not for manipulation, at least for understanding.

Kenrick didn't have a slot. Not one that fitted without contradiction. Studio head on the climb? Cards and fast automobiles? Now this breakaway to build an empire? Something in Kenrick's manner when he spoke of the new studio didn't ring true to Rentzler. Especially when he added the investigatory work Kenrick had assigned him: finding the origin of the money behind Pedro Lehman, breaking the accountant Ray Tannis, and, finally, the seemingly unrelated search for the whereabouts of the financier Robert Arthur.

He remembered his encounter—as good a word as any— with Ray Tannis and felt angry at letting himself be used. For exactly what reason? To make Kenrick's ego trip a little easier?

Halfway across the terrace Kenrick sensed his approach, for he turned, giving him a piercing look of appraisal that would provide Kenrick with most of the answers before Rentzler had the chance. Rentzler admired Kenrick's talent; he wasn't yet sure about the man.

"You look like hell," Kenrick greeted him.

"I don't travel well. My brain ought to be about passing over the Azores." He ordered an orange juice, then changed his mind in favor of a beer.

"Don't look for help in this city," Kenrick said. Lines were in his face that hadn't been there a week ago. Maybe he was too hard on the man. There had to be things he cared about, and Rentzler made a mental note to keep digging. "Let's hear about Ray Tannis."

Rentzler took a slow sip of beer. "He cracked like an egg."

"That was the idea, Larry, even if you don't sound happy about it."

"He was easy. An emotional mess, old Raymond. Bad marriage, debts, boozy nerves, and a much, much overloaded conscience. Tannis doesn't have the mental equipment to be a good thief."

"He tell you all that?"

Rentzler looked away. On the beach a lovely bronzed girl turned from her tummy to sun the front half of her body. Her breasts in full display were young and pointy. Aware of more than one appreciative glance, the girl, in a gesture toward modesty, pulled the top half of her bikini from a wicker bag and, reclining gracefully, placed it over her eyes.

"He couldn't wait to tell me," Rentzler said. Kenrick

heard self-recrimination thick in his voice. "The Gestalt people call it closure, the need to get it out. All I did was push the button. Hit him with the item that we knew he was stealing from the Lehman film and that we're intending to prosecute. Then I held out the gentle hand of possible forgiveness. And when he began to crumble, I just took him in my arms and let him cry like a baby."

"What did Tannis admit?"

"About what you figured. Auditing the Lehman film, he was approached with a way to turn himself a quick bundle of cash."

Suspicion confirmed, but Kenrick wished he felt better for it. A film in production could be milked in a number of ways, but the location budget of a film was especially vulnerable because it dealt in cash. Hotels, local catering, transport, gasoline—the list was endless, and two films never the same.

If the man who signed the checks and a studio accountant were determined to steal from a film, they could find a way.

Kenrick might never have suspected the skimming of the Lehman film if his suspicions hadn't been alerted from another source. Nicky Deane had finally let the ax fall, suspended above Kenrick's head since that night three years before in Las Vegas.

"I'm in town," Deane's voice said on the telephone almost a year ago. "Let's talk."

They did. In the parking lot of a Thrifty Drugstore on the corner of La Brea and Fountain. Kenrick parked his bright red sports coupe next to Deane's boat-size Electra. It had Arizona plates. "You Hollywood types . . ." Deane began, looking at the sports coupe, the contempt in his voice poisonous. "I got something for you, playboy. An old friend of yours has an idea for a film. You and your studio might like this friend's idea very much."

"The friend being who, Joe Bonnano?"

"You should use those smart lines in your movies." He smiled, but the feminine brown eyes were mirthless. "I'm talking about Pedro Lehman. I want you to do everything in your power to consider this idea. I want Teddy Kenrick to be thought of as a bright guy. Not some thief who cheats at cards—and gets caught."

"So Lehman gets a film, you get whatever, and I get back the tape of me playing cards."

"Tape? What tape? I am asking you to consider an idea, friend to friend. A personal favor."

"I see."

"That's the way it is."

A week later he had given the go-ahead on the studio's coproduction on the new Lehman film and the day following hit upon the idea behind Larry Rentzler's subsequent investigation.

He was trying to determine the relationships of everyone involved. Between Deane and Meyer Tilman, the man whose company had lent Pedro Lehman his share of the film's financing. Rentzler discovered that both Deane and Tilman were involved in the Cayman Bay Development Company, the casino that Robert Arthur, among others, had invested in through a holding company.

But was Tilman Deane's front man? Or was it Deane who worked for Tilman, thus approaching Kenrick to take on the Lehman film to support Tilman's investment?

Or were Tilman and Deane reporting to someone higher in their organization, some gangster boss hidden far in the background?

It even occurred to Kenrick that Deane could have made a deal with Lehman independently. Forced him to steal from his own picture to pay off Deane for arranging both the Tilman loan and the studio deal with Kenrick.

And, finally, what was the tie, if any, between the people behind Tilman and Deane and the financier Robert Arthur?

He needed to understand the connections before he played his final card. They were beginning to surface. But when he had asked Rentzler to put the fear into Ray Tannis, he hadn't been sure what would turn up.

"So," Kenrick said in summation. "Lehman approaches Tannis at a time when he's down and vulnerable, and together they skim off how much?"

"Four hundred and twenty thousand bucks, of which Tannis got a third." Rentzler looked out across the water. "Only it wasn't Lehman who gave Tannis the idea. It was Hugh Remy."

They started back along the Croisette. The midday calm was nearly ended. In a brief midday truce the *Cannois* had retreated behind their shuttered windows while the Festival crowd sought outdoor cafés and corners of the sun. But now this mile of broad, tiled promenade was again coming to life —mothers with prams, strollers, police checking documents, artists, Senegalese trinket vendors and their gulu-gulu cry to attract attention. Here and there people clustered around a variety of attractions from a heat-prostrate tourist to a *performeur des rues*, this one moving in a precise mechanical circle like a large windup toy. Rentzler adjusted himself to the slow, weaving amble that made him feel like a fish swimming up a human stream to spawn.

Kenrick hadn't spoken since Rentzler dropped the bomb: the name Hugh Remy.

Finally, Kenrick said, "He could have been Pedro's bagman."

"Teddy, I can hear it in your voice. You don't believe it either. Tannis said he never saw anything to make him believe Lehman was in on it. Pedro was busy giving everyone grief over the stoppages and other problems." He squinted at Kenrick in the piercing sunlight. "You don't really think Lehman bled his own film for a couple hundred thousand bucks? Remy was always in Lehman's shadow. Maybe he saw Lehman was near the end and decided after all those years to skim a little cream."

Kenrick didn't believe it of Hugh Remy either. Yet Tannis

had put the finger on Remy. And mixed in it somehow was Nicky Deane.

At what level of power did Deane rest?

When the strategy began to take shape, he felt Larry Rentzler eyeing him curiously. Rentzler, like Donner, had never seen Kenrick laugh. Always the same narrow smile as though he had caught himself just in time.

"You scare me," Rentzler said.

"Let's hear about Arthur."

"Arthur. In my opinion there is no evidence the man exists. I spent six thousand dollars of your money in three days with the best private detectives in the country—guys with fingers in the FBI, you know, connections."

"They couldn't find him?"

"Maybe New York, they said. Or London. Or on the ranch out wherever it is. There is nothing to say he isn't dead lo these many years and a computer making the decisions. The way Arthur covers himself makes the late Mr. Hughes look like a media freak. Teddy, Arthur doesn't have to be someplace to make a thing happen."

"This isn't to make something happen. It's to keep something *from* happening. And if it will cost him through the nose if he doesn't, he'll show. Everything about the way he operates says so. But. . . ." Kenrick shrugged.

"So we keep trying."

"There's someone in Cannes who might know something. An Arthur watcher, who is very good." He was thinking of Galloway. "While I track him down, find Mathan. He has some letters of agreement for you. Have Sid leave a note in my box where he'll be about three hours from now."

"I need a vacation," Rentzler said dryly.

"Look around, Larry boy. You've got one."

☰ *Chapter 26*—Connection

Peter Galloway was enjoying himself immensely, drinking free champagne beneath the olive tree on the poolside terrace of the Hôtel Majestic. The champagne was being liberally poured by an organization called the Deauville Film Festival, for a purpose he had yet to uncover.

As far as he could tell, not a single soul among the fifty gathered under the olive tree had spoken a word about any film festival except the present one. He had, in fact, been listening to a piggy-faced young woman who wrote for one of the West Coast dailies tell him about her intention to cut Jane Fonda down to size at her press conference later that afternoon. "I saw her arrive this morning," said the young woman, whose name Galloway hadn't asked, "looking absolutely gorgeous and speaking marvelous French—she was married to Vadim, you know. I can't wait to see the leftist press rip into her. All her causes and earning that kind of money. . . ."

Galloway would have much preferred drinking champagne with Jane Fonda, causes and all.

"I'll get her," the woman vowed. "One slip, and I'll have it in caps all over Los Angeles."

"I'm sure," Galloway agreed amiably, leaning toward the barman for a refill.

When the champagne ran out, he ambled off· toward the Croisette.

He had just stepped off the curb, looking distrustfully lest some Frenchman *en voiture* choose that moment to exert his individuality by running a *feu rouge*. In time he realized his mistake.

He stepped back onto the curb as a bus from the opposite direction missed him by inches without the driver's bothering to sound his horn. Despite thirty years in various foreign climes, Galloway persisted in a habit conditioned by his youth and allegiance to Britain; when he crossed streets, he looked the wrong way. Even when his eyesight had been better, his instinct and reflexes reverted to cars with steering on the right and traffic that flowed on the left. The only two countries he found safe were Australia and Japan, neither to his liking. But Galloway had no favorites these days. Even England was no longer the England of a more rational time.

He stood on the curb a moment, wondering if, after all, the doctor might have been wrong. That his vision *was* becoming worse.

For many years he thought his deteriorating eyesight had been normal attrition owed to encroaching age and the great gobs of reading he did in poor light. When the print began to fade in the typewriter, he admitted it might be something serious, even cataracts. Correct, very nearly. Not cataracts, but glaucoma. Treatment arrested the disease, but the damage was done. He was very nearly a blind man, on top of which were the pains deep within his system and the bloody stools he endured each morning, his stomach and endocrine system taking their revenge for a lifetime of hard drinking.

Yet in an unexpected way his failing health focused his energy like nothing else in his life. Burning in him now with all the passion of a youthful reporter was a need to make some statement on it all. Galloway's theory of the universe, or *Why Everything Was Going Wrong*. He knew he was a bitter old man getting ready to die, but he was too stubborn to do so before he left something to a society he saw so little in these days to care about. "Bitter and full of contradictions . . . you old toad."

He waited until the traffic sounded distant enough in both directions for safety and then took his chance and crossed the street. Once he had engaged enemy aircraft one upon one and emerged victorious seven times. Now it was finding the courage to cross a bloody street.

"Galloway, you should break down and buy a dog. Swallow your pride, man."

He looked up to see Kenrick waiting on the curb, a figure in white sports shirt, pale slacks, and a blazer. Galloway's head moved this way and that. It was like looking at a target, the rings around the bull's-eye made of rainbows. But where the bull's-eye should be was no vision at all.

"I'll take a St. Bernard," Galloway said. "Fully equipped. No doubt you've a regimental tie somewhere to go with that outfit. Americans and their regimental ties. Appalling ignorance."

"Or not giving the slightest damn."

"Also typically American," Galloway said. At least Kenrick wasn't a man to hide behind pretension, and he liked that. He liked Kenrick even better when he suggested they split a bottle of champagne somewhere out of the sun.

"But why triangles?"

Kenrick had watched Galloway scribe the designs repeatedly on the back of a paper napkin. It had been a quarter of an hour since a waiter had taken their order for champagne; Galloway was drying out.

"Not triangles. Pyramids."

They were seated beneath the blue and white awning on a beach club terrace. Kenrick had intentionally avoided any place too intimate for fear Galloway might smell a trap. Beyond the white latticework divider next to them, a luncheon party of a hundred or so was in full flood. By a quick survey of faces, Kenrick could guess the nature of the affair.

As determined from speeches and bits of conversation, the purpose was the announcement to a select group of friends, that a film of undeniable stature was about to go into pro-

189

duction. What wasn't announced was that the project had bounced around for almost five years, never quite coming together because of a mammoth budget and some staggering production problems. Based on a fat, best-selling novel set in Asia and spanning sixty years, the action scenes demanded ships and thousands of extras, two of the most expensive items in modern filming. The project had been recently taken over by a French film producer, with the backing of the Shinn brothers.

Kenrick could see Billy Shinn and his cousin O.K. at widely separated tables, each with a well-known and solvent foreign distributor. The guests included an inordinate number of unattached ladies, attentive to the glasses of champagne. The ratio of freeloaders—about three to one—was no worse than usual for Cannes.

Kenrick guessed the Shinns were taking the same tack Levine had with *A Bridge Too Far*: preselling the film territory by territory, to foreign distributors willing to come in with large chunks of front money, thus making back the film's budget before the cameras rolled. For a number of gentlemen enjoying the lunch it would turn out to be anything but free.

Galloway cast the luncheon one dismissive glance, then went back to his pyramids. "One of history's first mathematical models, the pyramid."

"Models of what?" Kenrick was only partly listening. Across the restaurant he saw a face to which he was trying to connect a name. Maury Roman.

"Society," Galloway said. "Quite useful, really, in understanding our present state of corruption." His gray, disked eyes searched Kenrick's face. Galloway looked embarrassed at his own sincerity. "You see, I have this theory."

"You're in Cannes hunting heads, Galloway."

"Gathering evidence," he corrected. "I'd rather like it to disprove my hypothesis. Look. . . ." He took the napkin, folded it into a pyramid, and set it carefully on the table between them.

When the waiter arrived with the champagne, Galloway failed to notice, his fingers moving along the edges of the pyramid from tip to base.

"Let's call these two planes government and business—that is, so-called lawful society—and the third, this one, criminal society. You see at the base, the separate planes are all quite far apart. But"—using both index fingers, he traced along two edges of the pyramid to the top where his fingers touched —"the higher one moves up any given plane of society, the closer he comes to the other planes, until at the top they merge. Up here the difference between lawful society and criminal society, between legal and illegal, becomes indistinguishable. A milieu of total corruption where there are no judgmental standards, except one."

"Money?" Kenrick said.

Galloway beamed at him. "Of course, the danger with models is one tends to forget that people, not structures, are ultimately responsible for what happens in the real world. We tend to blame institutions for corruption—government, for example. Or the auto industry. Even all society itself. I don't go with that. Corruption is the result of willful choice on the part of men at a level high enough to count. That is, the people with real power and the intelligence to use that power for good or evil, but who abdicate their moral responsibility because at their level in the pyramid they find it financially costly. It's quite simple to distinguish wrong from right and act upon your perceptions when it doesn't cost you anything. But at the top of the pyramid—the point where capital moves freely between normal and criminal society—the amounts of money are extraordinary. One cannot afford to deal in good and evil, right and wrong. One instead substitutes the concept of mutual interest. And once that is done, the dividing line between illegal and legal, between one plane of society and another is no longer operable or necessary. At least to those people I've chosen to call men of bad intent."

"How does your theory fit in with what we're looking at now? With all this?"

"The Festival? It fits perfectly." He hastily drained his champagne and refilled the glass. "You see the film business is my example—my case study, if you will."

Kenrick didn't know whether he was being entertained by a master hustler of drinks or merely put on. Galloway looked away, struggling with a train of thought. At the party next to them the scenario was proceeding nicely. The French producer was introducing his English author, followed by his American director. Not the *intended* director. The director. By implication the potential investors were looking at a *fait accompli*, and if they wanted a piece of the action, they had better damn well get on the bandwagon. Behind the deal making at Cannes, fear of being left out was as strong a prod as wanting in.

"In your business," Galloway was saying, "one can actually observe the touching of the separate planes of the pyramid—government, business, criminal society. One need only have an interest in history and a good memory. For example . . ." Galloway named a studio that had gone under years before. "It was known to have connections with what we in the press call these days criminal elements. The studio was on a shoestring financially, vulnerable to the introduction of capital from interesting sources. See who ran the studio in those days and what they later became. More important, whom they relied upon to get there, particularly their banks. Fascinating history. The stuff doctoral dissertations ought to be written on if we're to understand what is happening around us. I'll give you another example."

Galloway named one of the Big Six studios. "Back in the thirties the studio was kept afloat through the Depression by the same bank that in one instance was the bank for the

Mafia. In Mexico I became acquainted with a well-known Mexican millionaire, who incidentally later married a movie goddess under contract to the same studio." He tilted his head to one side, pleased at the intricacies of his own theory, the neat interlocking of elements.

"The millionaire was the Mafia conduit into Mexico, investing its money in dog racing, amusement parks, using the bank to invest and remit laundered profits. A witty, charming old fellow, but a Mafia front, nonetheless. They don't all scowl like Brando, you know. Now if you look at the present outside board of directors of that same studio, you discover: One director sits on the board of a record company that is a known syndicate investment. Another board member was in the Kennedy administration, in a policy position dealing with Latin American affairs. And remember it was the Kennedy administration that made approaches to certain Mafia figures with contacts in Cuba to assassinate Castro. Certainly they would have needed to trade something in exchange, favors of one kind or another. You see at the top of the pyramid they all come together in a brotherhood of mutual interests. That's why I remembered your remark about temporary alliances. That's the mechanism behind my idea, that at the top mutual interest has substituted for absolute concepts of right and wrong."

"I've heard it before," Kenrick said. "Sixty families controlling half the wealth in America. Secret interlocking directorates of the banks and insurance companies. Military industrial conspiracies, Mafia-White House hot lines." Kenrick shook his head.

Galloway's smile was beatific, the gray eyes dancing in excitement. "But what if it's true? Not all of it. Say, one-tenth of one percent."

"It won't stand up in court. And no responsible editor would print it."

"Not without hard evidence. The model is only a working hypothesis, Kenrick, a device to help me fit together what I see. Your studio, for example. I suspect it's being used to achieve some nefarious and doubtless profitable purpose."

"I wouldn't know," Kenrick lied, "and wouldn't admit to it anyway."

"Possible," Galloway admitted, a clucking sound at the back of his throat, "but not probable. Although I've observed one corollary: People at various levels of the pyramid usually concern themselves with what is happening below them. They take for granted what goes on above. Does a director or an actor really care where the millions come from with which he is making a film? Or where the profits go once he had taken his bite? I do think you've looked up."

"Are you hunting my head, Galloway?"

"Not your head, dear man. I am out to save your soul. Our salvation is to replace the moral abdicators in the realm of power with men of good intention."

"You may be in the wrong town."

"I know they exist, although I don't know as I've ever met one. Not one with power. An inference something like the scientists discovering the planet Pluto. By observing the movement of the other planets, they deduced something must be affecting them from out there in the void. Men of good intention must exist, or the corruption would already be complete. Perhaps you'll be one of them."

"You're after Robert Arthur."

"Ah," Galloway breathed. "The dream of a poor dying man. Moral abdication without peer. Can you think of a more representative head to hunt?"

"Galloway, I have a deal for you."

"Yes," he said slowly, "I anticipated something."

"In exchange you get a story, one that involves Arthur. An exclusive as big as any this business has seen in years."

"You're offering me a temporary alliance."

"The only thing I want is your word you won't break the story until I say so."

He took a thoughtful sip from his glass. "Done."

Kenrick told him about the new breakaway organization he was forming.

"But what does that leave your studio?" Galloway's complexion had regained a rosy glow.

"Not a helluva lot," Kenrick said. "My question is: How will Arthur jump?"

"He won't let you get away with it. A shell of a studio would send his stock down like an elevator. He's spent four careful years building its climb. Never," Galloway said firmly.

You'd better be right, Kenrick prayed.

"The only thing my break hinges on is the final step—the promise of a line of credit."

Galloway's face flushed with anger. "You don't understand, do you? Still think my pyramid is hog swill. The people at the top, man, the ones you've gone to for money."

"You think through them, Arthur has learned what is happening?"

"It would explain everything."

Kenrick drew back, trying to judge if Galloway was rambling or drunk.

Behind his glasses Galloway's eyes were wild. "I couldn't understand it before, why he'd expose himself in such a situation."

"You mean Arthur?"

"Of course I mean Arthur," Galloway said. "He's in Cannes."

In the darkness Kenrick worked his way down the theater aisle until he found Sid Mathan near the front, intent on the screen. It was after six, and Kenrick was still weighing the mental jolt of less than an hour before, when Galloway told him Robert Arthur was in Cannes. "You saw Arthur?"

The excitable journalist waved the query away, qualifying himself. "Not Arthur really. He has three or four henchmen that do his bidding. Talking chiefs, you know, like the Samoans. Ran into one physically, coming out of the men's room at the Hôtel du Cap—a lawyer named Chastain. Arthur's nearby, believe it."

Now, forty minutes later and trying to bring the separate strands together, he had found Mathan. "This one has everything," Mathan said, nodding toward the screen. "Rape, incest, murder, and we're only twenty minutes in. I'm glad I finally saw a film in the Palais. I get tired of looking at movies down alleys."

"Sid, I was in a beach restaurant today and saw a face. You remember Maury Roman?"

"Sure, I know Roman. Used to make skin flicks, pretty good stuff. I thought about buying *Blips*, and trying to recut it into an R. But do away with all the frontal stuff and close-ups, you don't have zip. You know who did the camera work? Buddy Shane."

"If anyone ever figures how to get a camera inside, looking out, it will be Shane. But Shane would want to get right in there with it."

Mathan eyed him strangely. "You saw it?"

"No, I didn't see it."

"That shot, he has it. A fisheye lens looking out a long tube at this guy's approaching donger. Christ, it looks like the attack of a killer whale."

"But what's Roman doing in Cannes? I remember a thing in *Variety* about him as a witness in that Justice Department investigation of the guy with a chain of porno houses. The feds were trying to prove they were really owned by the Mafia."

"The Sahakian business. Roman did appear. Talked a lot and said exactly nothing. They tried to make Roman out as something more than an independent producer, a mob front like Sahakian."

"What came of it?"

"Zero. I'm not saying Roman is all soap and white linen, but he's not even making porno these days. In Cannes with a film in his suitcase and a two-picture schedule he's trying to sell. Exploitation stuff, but legit."

"If he's looking for financing, it doesn't sound like he has a hand on money, mob or otherwise. Sid, look at his film and set something up."

"You're kidding."

"Just playing the angles, Sidney."

It was late the next afternoon—the fifth day of the Festival —when Kenrick met Maury Roman. He had spent the morning convincing Ernst Rucker—the head of European distribution—to follow the lead of Mathan, Archer, and Larry Rentzler as the nucleus of a new studio. After a long private phone call, chewing the stem of a pipe gone out and cold, Rucker agreed, given one condition, a demand so obvious Kenrick damned himself for not thinking of it earlier. Rucker would run European distribution not from New York, but from Paris. Kenrick sensed the abundant power of persuasion the French Mrs. Rucker had on her husband's decision. Kenrick would have promised him anything.

A little before five Maury Roman edged into Kenrick's

197

hotel suite, expecting an ambush. His baby blue leisure suit had gone slack, giving it a borrowed look. Patches of gray stubble dotted a recently shaved chin. His hair was cut pixy-style, a shiny brown toupee, too young for the face it bordered.

"Sit down, Maury." Kenrick invited him toward the sofa. "Sid Mathan told me some interesting things about you. About this film of yours."

"Sidney and I go way back," Roman said. "Anything I can do for Sidney, I do." His voice had the manufactured confidence of noisy conversations in Schwab's and Nate and Al's, ones where everyone talks and nobody listens. Worry lines on Roman's face told a better story.

Still mystified at Kenrick's interest, Mathan had briefed him on Roman. For most of his career he had made porno films. But with the profits from a minor classic called *Blips*, he had edged into the bottom end of the legitimate business —exploitation films, full of chain saws and shotgun revenge. Scores of the type would be shown at Cannes in search of foreign markets, most so crudely violent that even Sid Mathan's ironclad sensibility wouldn't allow him to sit through a full screening.

The Maury Romans of the business lived in a different world from the Paul Waxlers and Pedro Lehmans. It was hard to calculate how many of their low-budget films ever saw even a single paid admission, let alone release by a major studio. Films with "stars" no one had heard of, stories indistinguishable from each other in their shoot-outs and *Bullitt*-like car chases. Mathan had viewed thousands and never bought one. From rejection to rejection the films trickled down through the levels of the business in search of an outlet until they reached bottom—the covey of barely legitimate distributors, with a theater or two in their pocket, who would deal a Maury Roman the final indignity: charge to watch his film, then sleep through the second reel. It was clutching at straws.

Often the less resilient of Roman's breed simply walked away, leaving the print of the film behind because it wasn't worth the expense to show anyone else. Six reels of corpse. In Hollywood there were rooms, closets, storage bins, and paper cartons filled with films that had come to the end. By Festival's finish hundreds would be left begging at Cannes.

Eyes flitting across the papers on Kenrick's desk—Roman read no doubt well upside down—he remarked on the weather, the crowds, and French food. "Me, I'm a homebody, you know. Malibu, the Springs." Kenrick gave him his minute to lie, then came to the point.

"Mathan says your film has possibilities."

For a moment Roman sat unbelieving, then sprang to life. "A good concept, good chemistry. And those kids, sweet kids —some real performances."

Mathan had capsulized *Candy Little Girl*, thusly: a troop of unusually mature Girl Scouts outing in a national park are pursued by a freak in a ski mask, who proceeds to molest and dismember the troop one by one with a chain saw. Eventually the survivors turn on their pursuer and, with cunning and the practical applications of their woodlore, impale him with the branch of a tree. "Formula stuff," Mathan said, "lots of blood bags. But on its level it works. The ad line says it all: 'Eighty-nine minutes of gut-crunching terror. Feel the pleasure of total revenge.' Teddy, its level isn't our level. Forget it." Kenrick had insisted: "I want to talk to Roman."

Roman started to go on about the film but caught himself. He'd talked himself out the door too many times and fell abruptly silent.

"What kind of deal you looking for?" Kenrick said.

He saw Roman hesitate, visibly regrouping his thinking. He had come here desperate, willing to take anything offered. Virtually to give his film away in the hope of having it picked up by one of the majors. Now, when he smelled it might actually happen, he was trying to guess how far he could push.

"Look, we made *Candy* for just under half a mil. You can check. . . ."

"I asked what you wanted."

"Well, now," Roman said, his thumb moving over the stubble on his chin, "we'd entertain a buy-out." When Kenrick said nothing, he said quickly, "Maybe a partnership, whatever works. The bottom line would have to be somewhere around half the negative cost. I figure two hundred fifty, say, two hundred thousand."

Kenrick took a slow tour of his suite. Roman fidgeted a cigarette out of his pocket and lighted it. He began tapping the matchbox, waiting for Kenrick's reaction.

"We'll think on it," Kenrick said. "Thank you, Maury."

Roman's eyes made a tight, nervous circle. "Hey, you guys are tough. Look, you pay for prints and advertising, you can have it. You can't help but turn a profit." Roman was on his feet now. "Kenrick, I have to admit something to you. I mean I have to be frank."

"I appreciate that, Maury."

"Other people are interested. Big people, a couple of producers, you know their names like Pepsi and Coke." The matchbox was dancing in Roman's fingers. "You want, I'll set you up a private screening. See it, you'll buy it."

"We'll let you know," Kenrick said. It was a cold dismissal, and Roman knew it. "Maury, thanks again."

Roman had no choice but to head for the door. Kenrick let him take a few steps before he spoke softly.

"Maury, one thing."

The reprieve galvanized Roman. "Anything. Look, we don't do this picture, maybe something else. Lots of ideas, I got."

Kenrick smiled. "I'd have to know something straight."

"Like I say, anything."

"You ever know a guy named Nicky Deane?"

Kenrick saw the wariness slide behind Roman's eyes like a filter. He sighed; he had expected it. Expected to get hit with something when you had made the mistake of letting yourself hope. Deep in his soul, Maury Roman was frightened and tired.

"Not really," he said, hoping Kenrick would accept it and let it drop. "I don't make those kind of films anymore. But hell, you know. A lot of legit people started with skin."

"What do you mean, not really?"

He looked at Kenrick, a hard, flashing glance that finally gave way to a smile. He dropped into a chair without being invited and stared at the carpet. When he spoke, the confidence was gone like air leaked from a balloon.

"You've never wasted time, have you, Kenrick? I mean everything you've done was aimed at taking you someplace you knew you wanted to go."

"I suppose it could look that way." It was a curious time and person to elicit an admission of doubt, but Roman wasn't listening.

"I'm not saying you got where you are by pure luck. But you're a lucky guy. Most of us don't have what you got. Here I am sixty years old, and I still wake up every morning wondering what I'm going to do when I grow up." He halted, his head shaking wistfully. "You know I used to produce TV shows. *Playhouse 90*, *Climax*, finally morning stuff for kids. Did you know?"

"No, I didn't."

"Thirty years ago, when TV was mostly live and better than it's ever been since. And me, what do I want to do? Make movies, that's all I could think about. Don't ask me how I got from kid-vid to porno and from there to here. I guess I got in the easy way, or so I thought, telling myself I'd straighten things out later. Then suddenly later is twenty years. You think I liked the junk I used to make? I mean some guys do. They like that life—I mean you never had to worry about getting laid. But, Jesus, if I never look to another cum shot or tripleheader again, it will be too soon." His face brightened, and he leaned toward Kenrick. "But

201

then, when I'm making *Blips*, I know, maybe, I have something different. The stirrup up and out with enough money to try something legit."

Roman's voice had altered completely. No longer was he the producer selling his illusion of success. He was a worn, aging man trying to convince himself the goal he spent his life chasing had been worth the time.

"The only problem was I run out of money before I get the bastard finished, about fifty thousand short. I'd already tapped my sources dry—the doctors, the dentists looking for tax shelters. But a guy I know says he has a contact who might be able to turn me on to some quick money. So I have dinner at a restaurant on Melrose with my friend and this contact."

"Nicky Deane?"

Roman's head bobbed, and Kenrick could see the rough part in the toupee, the coarse brown hair lacquered tightly in place. "He comes on very straight, no wanting to play with the broads, nothing. And he moves. A day later I meet with him and a man he says is an associate. A room in the Beverly Wilshire yet. We have lunch in the room, after which I am presented two things. A nice, neat stack of hundred-dollar bills. And an insurance policy on my life for a hundred thousand dollars. Very friendly. Little jokes, lots of smiles. Shylocks don't all run around in plaid suits with goons at their elbow, but I know. I sign the policy. They don't collect the fifty thousand plus interest, they arrange it so they collect on the policy. And that's how I got to know Mr. Nicky Deane."

"You have the impression Deane was in charge? That he was the boss. Or the other way around?"

"Who can say? The other guy signs the checks and is tipping the waiter. So I guess it was Deane playing Mr. Big. Who cares? The other guy was a businessman, I'll tell you. By the time I pay back the fifty it isn't fifty anymore, but a little over seventy. But I got *Blips* done, made my score, and I'm never going back to that if I have to sell shoes again. Hell, Waxler was a florist, you know that?"

"And I started booking bands."

Roman looked at him thoughtfully. "I guess it doesn't matter, does it? Once you get out of the mud."

"This businessman Deane introduced you to. He give you a name?"

"Sure he gave me a name," Roman said. "These people were very refined. His name was Meyer Tilman."

"We'll be in touch," Kenrick said, but he could tell Roman didn't believe it.

When Roman was gone, Kenrick discovered the modest tactical gambit Roman had made to convince Kenrick he was indeed facing formidable competition.

On the table, next to the chair Roman had vacated, Kenrick found the box of matches. The names on the cover were, in bold black letters, the producers Zanuck and Brown.

Donner's patience broke a little before ten the seventh night of the Festival.

Pacing the length of his hotel room, he had had it. He made a face at himself in the mirror, then scowled because it felt good for a change.

Since the opening gala he found it tougher each day to follow Rayna's game plan—seeing people he didn't like, saying things that caught in his mouth in their insincerity, and smiling. His face felt like a happy Greek mask.

"You promised, damn you!" she said when, earlier, he exploded.

"It's getting me nowhere."

"It's getting you exposure."

"One offer from an Italian director I've never heard of for a film that's still in his head. I've been there, thanks."

"We're laying a foundation, Rod. It's going fine."

"I don't see it."

"But other people do, and not only me. I bumped into Freddie Harland this morning, and that doesn't happen unless he wants to be bumped. He asked what you had going."

"I thought the arrangement between you and me was top secret."

"Freddie's mind is a waste bin full of other people's trash. He remembered we were married, and he recognized my style."

"What's his interest?"

Rayna took a moment to weigh it. "I think if we had

something ready to break, something big, Freddie might handle it. If the numbers were high enough, and if. . . ." She left whatever else she was thinking unsaid. "Let me work on it."

"I don't like Harland much."

"That's all right, darling, because he doesn't like you at all."

So he had gone ahead. Luncheon at the Eden Roc, again accompanied by Taya Linder, but this time with the German moneyman, Dieter Furst, in tow, a French director named Climent, and his lady, an Israeli actress named Pola something. By lunch's end Furst was cooing German intimacies to Taya beneath his breath, which Taya ate like candy. Donner couldn't have cared less because he had discovered a tall, handsome girl eating lunch across the restaurant with a slender dark-haired actor who looked like Pacino but wasn't. Donner stopped playing eyes when her date caught on.

No trouble here. No, sir. The Eden Roc was too visible an arena, strictly heavyweight. The pale green dining room on the edge of the sea was a peaceful retreat from the hurly-burly of Cannes five miles away. But the widely spaced tables produced plenty of action. Donner recognized two studio heads at separate tables, producers Kastner and Waxler, Swifty Lazar and his wife dining out on the terrace, and a few other faces he remembered but who wouldn't look at him. Exit, smiling.

The following day he made a brief passage through a reception at the Sporting Club given by the Australian Film Board. He was still smiling, for the camera this time, as a lovely receptionist pinned a small yellow kangaroo on his lapel while massaging his arm with breasts too firm to be true.

There had been three postscreening receptions and a hillside villa party; at each Donner was photographed embracing the right people. The photographers still got under his skin. "Stop fighting it," Rayna said, spreading out before him the dozen or so *Varieties, Reporters,* and *Film Weeklies* everyone began his day with in Cannes as in Hollywood. Each was opened to a photograph that included Donner. "Relax. Enjoy it."

But this night Donner couldn't relax. It was nearly ten, and he hadn't moved from his hotel room since one that afternoon, on orders. Rayna supposedly was closing on the people they both wanted for his reading of *Daylight* one day hence. But he had heard nothing. He felt as mean as nine snakes in a bag.

Got to get out. He shaved, went down the emergency stairs, and through a revolving door to a side street.

Not sure where he was headed, he turned away from the Croisette. A few minutes later found a long, curving street, and from the night sounds and the abundance of single ladies strolling with no place to go, experience told him he had found the high side of town.

He went past a club with an open front and a Brazilian name, its pitlike interior dotted with red, candlelit lamps. Temptation, that. He was pushing on when he heard his name called by a voice he would have recognized in a wind tunnel—a broncbuster's yell, giving each syllable of Donner's name a separate yowl.

Buddy Shane weaved out of the darkness, a white Cuban shirt unbuttoned to the heavy brass buckle hitched in his denims.

"Donner, old *compadre!* I heard you were around and looking good." Shane clipped him on the shoulder, then squeezed his right bicep. "Hey, you been working out. Come on in." He latched onto Donner's arm. "Some people inside I want you to meet. A few laughs, maybe."

Buddy Shane worked hard at giving the impression life was a twenty-four-hour party. He had been a cameraman on a pair of westerns Donner filmed in Mexico in the late sixties. When the cameras shut down, Shane had a nose for finding the best bar within a night's driving distance, best, by his definition, meaning women. He admitted to only two drives: never to pass a night without feminine company, and to win an Oscar. He had come close on both scores. Shane was a director of photography now with an Oscar nomination and a win only a matter of time and the right picture away. A year ago he had taken a crack at directing and turned out a neat little action-adventure pic again set in Mexico. Shane knew what he was, and Donner admired that; he and Shane had passed some good times together.

"Now you can't say no," Shane said. "Come on, it's been six, seven years. I been hearing rumors from you being dead to on the beach in Tahiti, sucking up rum."

"But you didn't believe them."

"Sure I believed them. Come on, hey, what the hell."

Shane's entourage had taken over a large booth at the back of the club. Always the entourage. But the way Shane hesitated, pointing to each in turn, Donner guessed the ladies were recent additions. "The guy with the hair transplant is Rich Landy. And that's Penny. . . ."

The pause, his finger aiming toward a large girl with dark shoulder-length hair. Donner saw amusement cross her cat-green eyes as she let Shane squirm. "Stiner," she finally said.

"Right. The guy with the nervous hands is Micky Goldsmith. He was about four when you and I started out." Shane gave Donner a nudge, then a rough hug. The one he'd called Rich, besides the transplant, had a mattress of chest hair, God's little joke. Micky looked like a Micky: compact, fair-haired, spring wire in every gesture. Donner didn't know either one, but he knew the type: behind-the-camera people, who, if they ran with Shane, were more talented than they looked; hanging loose and chasing tail came with the work. "Rich here did *Encounters*," said Shane, "and Micky is an all-purpose screw-up who's been stealing lenses from me. And this," he said, pointing to the girl next to Micky, "is Maxine. Maxine is a schoolteacher." The way he said "school" had about a dozen ohs in it, in a tone reserved for kings, popes, and presidents. "Tell us again where you're from, Max."

"Principia," she said, not quite making it without a giggle.

"There you go, Principia. Funniest city in America, right, Max? Can't say it with a straight face."

The schoolteacher was the riper of the two women. A nice, full chest near which hovered one of Micky Goldsmith's hands, draped carelessly across her shoulder.

But Donner found himself looking at the other girl and knew why: the same creature he had stared at a few days before across the dining room of the Eden Roc. She was holding his eyes with the same steadiness. When the contact became prolonged, Donner let his gaze fall away.

"What are you drinking?" Shane asked. "I ordered a bottle of scotch. I been drinking too much wine."

"A beer will do," Donner said.

"Since when?"

"Since I turned forty."

Shane shrugged and shouted to the waiter, uncaring that he was the loud American. Shane intended to be remembered one way or the other, and if demanding didn't do it, his large tip would. The second time he passed by, a place liked to see Buddy Shane. But Donner had observed his good spirits turn mean on a word, and together they had punched their way out of a bar in Durango, lucky to get away without being murdered.

"Hey, remember that bar in Durango," Shane began. "Man those Mexicans sure have a strange sense of humor. Can't take a joke, right, Donner?"

This side hadn't changed a bit. Later there would be Duke Wayne stories followed by Peckinpah stories. They would drink a lot, then they would drink too much, and Maxine the schoolteacher would love it, and maybe Penny what's-her-name would, too. Then they would head off to a discotheque, and somewhere about 4:00 A.M. they would pair off. Micky might yet get his hands up Maxine's sweater, or maybe it would be Buddy Shane, and they would hear all about it the next morning over coffee, and maybe fifty per cent of it would be in the direction of truth. Suddenly Donner didn't want it anymore. Not ever.

"Hey, Donner," Buddy Shane was saying, "tell them how Leone offered you the first *Dollar* western before he gave up and picked some bum named Eastwood."

You tell them, he almost said, but it would have come out wrong. He didn't want to fight Shane, not anybody. "Another time," Donner said, standing. "I'm a little rocky tonight. Sorry."

He nodded toward the others and started for the door. Behind him, Shane's voice rose in protest. "Hey . . . hey!" Donner walked into the night, his head pounding, feeling as if he had escaped the jaws of the monster.

"Teddy, it's Rayna. Wake you?"

"Not really," Kenrick said, stretching the truth. The first ring of the telephone had brought him out of shallow sleep. It was two-thirty in the morning.

"I thought I'd be back to you sooner, but. . . ."

"No explanation necessary," he said. Behind Rayna's voice he could hear soft music. If she was calling from a party, it was subdued. Or private.

"Can you take an address? Tomorrow about four," she said. "Expect Leo Gold."

"What did you tell him?"

"He told me. He said you're dealing a wide path through the Festival. He said he'd talk, but nothing more."

"Ornery bastard."

"You'll have a couple of hours together before the others arrive. Enough time?"

"If he's interested, plenty. If not, we'll need three minutes. What others?"

"For Donner's reading," Rayna said. "Kenrick, you're not the kind to back out on something?"

Something; everything.

"I said I'd listen."

"You're as ornery as Gold. I have to go." There was a silence, but she stayed on the line.

"What's wrong?" Kenrick asked.

"Nothing, really. Only that I find you on my mind when I ought to be thinking about other things. I hope it's not a symptom of anything serious. If anything goes wrong, I'll call," she added incongruously.

"What's likely to go wrong?" he asked, but this time the line was dead.

Kenrick shut out the light, trying to put Rayna out of his mind, her separate games, of which he was one. He wasn't in deep enough emotionally to be used, but she was battering at the gates. Was that her style, to set the emotional hook and work from there, as once it had been with Donner? Not a thought for the middle of the night.

He turned on the light again, reached for the telephone, and put through a call to Los Angeles. Ten minutes later he heard Fiona MacCauley's voice, sounding tired and strained. "We're ready to collapse," she said. "But I've a rough cut on Lehman's film. It makes sense, but not much."

"How much longer?"

"Another twenty, thirty hours to get the best we can out of it, then a rush to the lab and a courier to Nice. Teddy . . . we've done our best."

"Say it, Fiona."

"I'm not sure anyone's best would be good enough. Somewhere in the film he gave up. I can see him using all the tricks, the bits of business he always used, but his mind seems to wander, and so do the scenes. I can see why Bassy was fighting him."

Bassy had been the director of photography until Lehman fired him over "artistic disagreement."

"That film," Fiona MacCauley said, "is going to make Pedro Lehman look like such an ass. I hate to see it happen."

"To the lab and on a plane, Fiona. Then go home and drink up."

"I'm preparing for my first binge, thanks."

Nothing out of the ordinary, Rayna had said to Kenrick. *Like hell.*

She hung up the telephone, closing off his voice in midsentence. She felt stupid for telling him what she felt. And all the while he listened, smug, giving her nothing.

She vowed once never to let her business and personal lives mix. She had seen what an inability to separate the two had done to Donner. It was natural she supposed in a business where the mistakes ended up on a screen twelve feet tall and in color. But for her, the compartmentalizing was necessary for dealing with people; each was given a separate mental space, which she would visit in her own mind from time to time and, when appropriate, close off. The attraction to Kenrick, her inability to shut him out were inhibiting her freedom to act.

And already at Cannes things were beginning to slip out of her grasp. First, Kenrick, a man at least her match in calculation. Second, the conclusion she had to face, on the basis of a day of telephone calls and covering more ground on foot than she thought possible in a town the size of Cannes. Donner was missing. He had crumbled and fallen into the bottle again under pressure. Or reverted to habit, using the region south of his belt buckle in place of a brain.

She didn't care what had happened. She wanted to know where he was, and fast. His reading was tomorrow.

She made a special effort to put on her positive face, as she called it, and went back into the lounge, knowing there were still several mental compartments she would have to look into that night.

She had rented the same villa three years running at Cannes, at a cost the cautious girl she had once been would have recoiled from in shock. As with most things, she saw the villa as a tactical device, a way to help reach various ends. It overlooked Cannes from the hills close by, the glass windows above the small heated pool providing a stunning vista of sunsets and nights with the city spread out below. In one way the Festival was deadly, and it was her analysis of exactly why that had been the final point in favor of taking it.

The Festival was a mind bender, a drain upon human

energy almost beyond belief. No one could endure the fifteen-day span of the Festival without going blank from time to time, to surface realizing that three plates of olives and chips had disappeared in compulsive munching and that you couldn't remember the name of the person you were introduced to only seconds before. Time stood still or raced past crazily. Alcohol had no effect or instantly pickled the brain. Each day brought a wave of new people, new films, new gossip destroying the memory of the thing you never intended to forget. It was a case of overload. A few days at Cannes were enough to burn out the unprepared or unwary, and Rayna learned to deal with it by a retreat now and then, a quiet regrouping of mind and body, even if it meant entire days away and alone.

She quickly came to the conclusion that the Cannes syndrome struck everyone. She conceived of the villa as a refuge, close physically, but removed far enough mentally to restore frayed nerves and to give her carefully chosen guests a chance to emerge from behind the shields they took with them into battle along the Croisette. Visitors seldom numbered more than five or six. There was always music, champagne, and spare bathing costumes for all—and a pair of extra bedrooms. Most parties at Cannes were given to sell or promote. In the low-keyed gatherings at the villa, without any such purpose, by all appearances, she managed to arrange some extraordinarily fruitful liaisons.

Example: Dieter Furst and Taya Linder, in one corner, oblivious to the others. Earlier Jean-Yves Climent had availed himself of one of the bedrooms to take a brief rest with the Israeli actress he wanted for his next film and had later given Rayna a wink, signaling progress. On what she didn't ask. Nearby, Leo Gold had fallen asleep, after a long talk with Furst, sitting upright in a chair. She let him be.

As she watched, Dieter smoothed Taya's hand in a long caress. Not the greedy, furtive clutching of an aroused man suggesting their next step, but the secretive touch of two people already lovers. For slightly more than twenty-four hours, Rayna knew. Taya had called her late the previous afternoon. She had earlier lunched at the Eden Roc with Donner, Furst, Climent, and his lady, Pola, and found herself several hours later in Dieter's bed, exactly as she planned to be all along. "He's quite imaginative, really," Taya said, in a tone that signaled she had thoroughly enjoyed herself. At least with Taya there had been no scruples to overcome, as had been her own case. It had finally been put to Rayna three years before, by a British film impresario, who was willing and able to open doors at a level of the business she needed to reach. He asked only an occasional consideration, of a kind she totally understood. Yet she balked, until he forced her to a conclusion about herself and her ambitions. "Make up your mind, Rayna. You either want to climb up in the business, or you can walk out. If you want to climb, then you sleep with people. With some you'll like it better than you thought. With others you won't like it at all. But you'll do it." And so she had, as had they all. In their conversation an hour earlier Dieter Furst had approached Leo Gold with an initial feeler. The subject: the possibility of financing a film, near and dear to Leo's heart, but short of capital. The consideration: The female lead would go to Taya Linder. By such trade-offs were deals made, sex a currency as common as money.

Goddamn Donner, and Kenrick, too.

She found the bar and mixed herself a strong drink as an arm circled her from behind. She fought to keep herself from tightening against it, then relaxed and let her breast be discreetly fondled.

"Is it somebody's bedtime?" the voice whispered close to her ear.

Her reply came with great effort, but with all the charm she was capable of. "Soon, darling. Very soon."

Later, toward morning, she slipped from bed, careful not to disturb the noisy sleep of the man next to her.

She pulled on a kimono and, barefoot, walked out to the pool.

Beyond the hills the sky was changing with the palest wash of dawn, still an hour or two away. She let the kimono drop and stepped into the pool quietly. Even with Dirk and later with Donner she had accepted that sex was a powerful tool, only that; something she used, then as now, to gain something she valued more. Sometimes it was freely given. With certain kinds of men, skillfully withheld until a fraction short of the breaking point. She was still trying to understand the change in her feelings, her sudden reluctance. Earlier she had wanted to force the man away from her, cleanse herself in the pool to wash away the smell, the taste.

Not that their thrashing had been much different from the other ones like it, more than she could remember—the usual recipe of openers, followed by a quick mounting and emptying, to which she would respond with a feigned orgasm, barring the all-too-rare one hundred-proof variety. Tonight she hadn't bothered. She tried not to think about Kenrick.

Now, swimming in the cool water, she felt something in her life evolving quite beyond her control.

The opening of the sliding glass doors startled her. Freddie Harland stepped from the bedroom out onto the patio, naked and pale.

She spoke to him, unable to look at his body, the small penis and flaccid testicles beneath the soft pot of a stomach. "Go back to bed, Freddie. I'll be along."

"A bargain is a bargain, sweet."

"Absolutely, darling. Absolutely."

Donner bulled from the entrance of the nightclub, leaving Buddy Shane, his pals, and trouble behind he didn't need. He would find a taxi, skulk back to the hotel, and stay put. Rayna was right, not about everything, but about him: his own worst enemy.

The footsteps behind him caught up at the corner, the light fragrance of her cologne reaching him as she touched his arm. The girl from Buddy Shane's table was tall, nearly his height, with square shoulders and an open, healthy face, tanned and without makeup.

"Forget it," Donner said. "I'm not in the market."

"As the standard reply goes, I'm not selling. I've never seen anyone your size run so scared."

"I've been through too many nights that started just like the one back there."

"What are you afraid of, the booze or me?"

Donner stopped. "Listen. . . ."

"Penny," she provided. "We spent a lunch at the Eden Roc a day or so ago, staring at each other. Now tell me you don't remember."

"What are you, a collector?"

"A what?"

"You know, running around with a bagful of plaster of Paris."

"You mean a starfucker. That wouldn't quite fit now, would it?"

"Look, the business at the Eden Roc was nothing. I stare at girls all the time." Donner's eyes were searching around. On a busy corner of the Croisette he felt exposed; the two of them were beginning to draw curious looks.

"And they stare back?"

"All right, maybe you don't know the name, but this"—he pointed at his own face—"has been around a long time."

"I know you're Rod Donner, and I know when I saw the last movie you made in America, I was twelve years old."

"You're trouble."

"But I'm not twelve years old. Besides, you didn't answer my question. Me or the booze?"

"Both," Donner said. "You both scare hell out of me."

"Well then," she said, reaching for his arm. "At least we have it all out in the open."

Donner took a step back, out of reach. "No, we don't." She observed him levelly, making him feel stupid. He *was* scared.

"People said you were difficult." She had let a few seconds pass.

"Who? No, forget it."

"Buddy Shane, for one. He said you have a way of attracting trouble."

"Buddy Shane is right," Donner said. He began walking, the girl falling in beside him, matching his stride. "He also knows why I'm difficult. Because we've both taken too many orders from directors who say, 'Stand here, move like this.' Producers who don't read stories. Writers who can't write dialogue a human mouth can say. That's why I'm difficult," Donner said. Then, softening, he added, "People like me need a lot of help."

"Buddy Shane also said you're better than you give yourself credit for."

"Buddy Shane had a load on."

"What were you thinking out there that day at the Eden Roc?"

"Wondering what to have for lunch."

"Mitch sensed it. The boy I was with. Boyfriend, I guess one says." It sounded as if she were experimenting with the word. "He caught me looking and didn't like what he saw. But there isn't really much one can do about something like that, is there?"

Donner thought about asking the precise nature of "something like that" but didn't. Best left among the things he didn't know.

Somewhere ahead and to their right, the first strobe light went off, then a second dead ahead. Donner wasn't sure how many there were, four or five closing in, snapping off photos and dancing away in that backward skip a photographer learns before he can crawl. Blink, blink, shuffle, the pack moving away just beyond reach. Donner's first instinct was to put his head down and bull forward, punch off-tackle, and punish them with his shoulders and thighs the way the Red Man had taught him twenty years ago. He felt the anger rise at their intrusion and at that instant heard Penny call his name.

Miraculously she was there, beckoning near the open door of a taxi. When they were away, she said, "I'd hate to see you mad at someone. You should look at yourself."

"You saved everyone a lot of trouble."

"Then I expect a reward. I'm hungry, and I know just the place."

"Dear Lord," Donner whispered.

She directed the driver, in passable French, to a small *relais* midway between Cannes and Antibes, an old building set back off the highway. The entrance was sheltered by a trellis of vine leaves.

A small dining room on the ground floor was three-quarters full, and a sharp, tantalizing aroma of food greeted them at the door. Donner noted the keys hanging on the rack nearby, one each for the half dozen rooms on the upper floors.

A solidly built, unsmiling woman led them to a small table in a back corner. They squeezed into chairs at right angles, knees and legs touching. The girl looked at him peculiarly, but Donner felt the unremitting pressure of her legs. They ate their way through a feast of wurst and pickled meats brought with plates of sauerkraut, vegetables, and dark bread. The girl put away the food with unabashed appetite but drank nothing. Donner had a beer.

It was a small thing, her not drinking, but it eased his suspicions, and when she touched his leg beneath the table, he let it go, liked it, in fact. Later he felt her hand move higher on his thigh.

"Careful."

"No one can see anything. Oh, my God. . . ."

"What did you expect?"

"You're not wearing. . . ."

"You'd better slow down, or I'll knock over the table."

"I'm just playing." Her fingers had found the head of him, then slid along the smooth material of his trousers his entire length. "You don't like?"

Donner put down his fork. There were still three tables occupied in the dining room, apparently occupied with conversation and food.

"You know what you're getting into?" Donner asked.

"I see that scared look again. Yes, I know. It's going to be all right with you and me. Donner, touch me. Under the table. Here."

Her legs parted wide enough to admit his searching hand, let it move up the inside of her thigh. Her hand still touching had begun to pull at him, back and forth. At one of the other tables a matronly woman glanced in their direction, then down at her plate, stabbing into a great dark wurst with her fork.

"You think she notices?" the girl said.

"She will when I start to yell." Moving higher, Donner's hand found what he was looking for, about the size of a small, wet cherry.

"Ah, yes. You really know." She was beginning to move in her seat, but not away.

"Not about you I don't. It's brand-new."

"I've never heard that, ooh . . . before. Only . . . a thousand . . . times." She nudged his hand away and closed her thighs around it. "Maybe we should talk with the little lady about a room."

"Better if I sit a minute."

"I'll take care of everything," she said. "I've made a good start, don't you think?"

They barely reached the room and got the door closed behind them.

She turned to smother his mouth with hers, her hands locking around the back of his neck, pulling his head down. His hands slid down her skirt, then under, pulling it up, one hand going straight for the spot he wanted, had to have, would, at that moment, have killed for. She had about one second's doubt, but by then his fingers had found the swelling lips and went into the smooth between, seeking out that ripe little berry.

She was wet and downy and slick, and he heard her say, "you devil," as one of his hands began that clown's act of trying to undo his belt buckle one-handed. He would face the problem of getting the trousers down over the growing promontory when they came to it. But he needn't really have called for help because now there were three hands busy and loosening until he was hard and free, and already the two of them were breathing heavily, the sound like a broken accordion, bellows sucking wind through a dozen vents, but the only tone a hum that Donner realized was his own voice whispering a steady stream of border Mexican, about what he was going to do to her mother and to her sister and to her dog and her donkey, and everything he was going to do said *chinga*. He would have used hand-laundry Chinese if he thought it would have kept them moving. Screw the trousers, binding now around his ankles, or even trying to make the bed. Right here. Yes! Now? Yes!

When he slid into her, standing, she made a sound like

unh, and she came the first time about twenty seconds later but didn't make a sound except for a grunt with a lot of spit in it because she had sunk her teeth into his right shoulder. The next orgasm rolled out layered upon the first, as already she had swung her legs up and around him, pulling him into her in rhythm with his every thrust. He had been with ladies who came fast, and others only after labor that should have gone with breaking rocks. It was a small source of pride that he stayed in there, so to speak, that he didn't hit and run, leaving the other half of the team up there, hung-out and spread-eagled, while he upped and went home. Service by any definition. But this one wasn't to be worried over. Fend for yourself, Donner, you've a fight on your hands. A big girl, strong in body and will. *Chinga.*

"You *chinga* yourself, you motherfucker."

Chinga. Fuck me. *Chinga.* Fuck me. And off they went. Donner never remembered losing it faster or better since old Merle had fixed him up with one of the ladies on his route. The Wednesday lady it was, figuring it the right time for that pubescent kid of his to get his cherry picked, though not technically since he had gone off about six inches short of target between a pair of pale, mottled thighs and later had to listen to old Merle laugh himself into a hernia when he found out. The girl felt him explode all right, but that didn't seem to matter because she just gripped him tighter with those muscular legs and began rolling her pelvis backward and forward until his cock, giving up inside her, began sliding across those beautiful little parts, and instead of the sensation's becoming hurtful, he felt himself turn hard again, and they were away.

Except this time they made it to the floor. And Donner, not really giving it much thought, wondered if their room was above the dining room because, if so, there was a chandelier jumping over someone's *quiche* and there wasn't any nightclub up here, friends. *Chinga.* Yes. Not again. Yes, yes.

"I've got to have a rest."

"Not yet."

By the time they made it to the bed Donner was ready to employ it for its fundamental purpose. Some of the heat had gone out of Penny's eyes, but her skin glowed as if she were being heated from within. "Maybe we should have shaken hands," she said later through a drowsy sleep. "Seems we've tried everything else."

"We could talk."

"I think I'll undress first."

Later he told her stories, a few unsavory episodes that had amused him but never thought would interest anyone else, until then. She roared with delight, a good, open laugh that several times provoked someone in the next room to hammer on the wall. Everyone should laugh like that.

Somewhere toward dawn, feeling his eyes roll inward with the final, powerful spasms the girl had drawn from him, he thought it might after all be love. But in the thin silence of early morning they both knew they had exhausted it; no place to go they hadn't been, a night open and complete and impossible to match. "Let's just leave it," the girl said. Donner, smiling at her wiseness, agreed.

They took a taxi home, the girl giving the driver the address of the Hôtel du Cap.

"Whoever keeps you," Donner remarked, "does it in style."

"You really don't know, do you?"

"I missed the last name, if that's what you mean. I figure it's a little late to ask."

"My father keeps me. And keeps me."

"Any complications about arriving with the sun?"

"There shouldn't be," she said, but it came slowly.

At the hotel gate she said, "Have the taxi stop here. The walk will do me good."

"Nonsense," Donner said, and pointed the driver toward the low buildings off through the pines. Mistake number one. What was there inside that made him push things?

The taxi stopped in the gravel drive. The girl was bending with a good-bye kiss when she whispered the word "damn."

Donner saw the young actor walking toward the taxi, looking as intense as Pacino. Black suede jacket, tailored denims. The times like it flashed through his mind. A man with a camera, a spiv with a shiv. Or some guy stepping from a doorway with a bigger claim on the lady in question, in his own mind, than in the lady's.

Without hurry, Penny kissed him lightly on the cheek. "Never a night like it, Donner. Never. Maybe. . . ."

Donner told her to shush. She nodded and stepped from the taxi. "Better go. Before there's a scene."

Donner ran it through in his mind: slamming the taxi door. Riding off comfortably as Penny turned to face what's-his-name. He could visualize it clearly and knew he was kidding himself.

"I'll stick around—a minute or two."

Donner made his second mistake when he climbed out onto the gravel drive.

The young actor stopped ten feet from the two of them, his breath condensing in the cool morning air. Up close Donner could see the resemblance to Pacino hadn't been left to chance. The emphasis on black, the styling of the hair. He couldn't really call the actor young. Mid-thirties, training like a jockey to keep lithe and looking hungry. Donner waited.

"The best you could do, Pen?" The actor flicked his head toward Donner.

Next he'll call me a has-been or never-was or some such salvage-my-*huevos* crap. Donner could tell by Penny's expression, Mitch or Mike was talking himself right out of her life.

She started past him, saying, "Just forget it," or something that began such, but she never finished the sentence.

The third mistake wasn't Donner's. The young actor's fist lashed out, catching Penny on the side of the face, snapping her jaw shut in mid-word. She didn't even see it, sinking like a folding chair in collapse. But by then Donner was on him.

His left came up from the waist, in close, a light punch with the purpose of landing first. Donner's single fighting tactic: Be first and hope you're still around to be second. He considered later the left had likely given the kid a new slant on a career. Donner felt his knuckles crunch through the fine bridge of a nose. His second punch was a straight hard right. It connected with his weight behind it, breaking away a set of expensive caps and spraying Donner's shirtfront with flecks of blood and tooth enamel. That was all. A matter of about a second and a half and the kid could relax because he sure didn't look like Pacino anymore.

Donner thought about hitting him again, and would have if he hadn't looked up at the taxi's engine gunning, the driver making it a well-timed exit. He never did figure out where the policemen came from.

The lobby? Patrolling the grounds? They were almost on him, two, in blue uniforms and white hats. One had a short black billy; the other was fumbling for his pistol.

Penny shouted it was all right, but who knew what it looked like, who had assaulted whom?

Donner did the smart thing. He straightened and raised his hands over his head.

He could see the curtains going back from hotel room windows, a man in a morning coat with his face pressed against a lobby window next to a bellman. The cop with the billy stopped a couple of feet from Donner, while his partner circled to the side. Penny tried to get up, and when she began to slip down, Donner reached for her, pulling her to him.

"All right? No double images?"

"No. Okay. Really."

It was possible that what came next was all a misunderstanding. His concern for Penny, their exchange taken by

224

the cops for something else—a whispered escape plan. Donner didn't know.

All he felt was the billy, jabbing him hard in the back. Once the billy jabbed, the cop's sweet way of telling him to get a move on. Twice, and Donner told him not to do that.

When the cop tried it again, Donner's quick left caught him in the Adam's apple. He never did get a chance to throw the right. It was on its way when back behind the eyes Donner saw the star burst, not black, but bright yellow. After that not another thing.

For Kenrick things were moving fast, but in the wrong direction. With the sound of Freddie Harland's machine-gun voice loud in the telephone at his ear he remembered an old, black talent booker named Ben Barney telling him something years before. "You can have everything going for you," Barney had rasped, "but there are times when you gotta have luck. And any gambler will tell you one thing about luck. Good or bad, it eventually turns around."

Now, with six days left in the Festival, it had gone bad.

"No deal," he heard Harland say. "Siri doesn't want to hear. She'd rather make a film in Botswana than for you, Teddy boy."

In Kenrick's pocket was a copy of a five-page film idea delivered the day before by messenger from Paul Waxler. From anyone else it would never have seen the light of day— a mélange of master scenes from Siri's former movies with a story line about a career girl scratching her way to the top of the Paris fashion scene. In quality it was a 5.5, maybe a 6. With Waxler's name attached, it became a property. With Siri above the title, it was bankable.

Kenrick twisted around in the phone booth and cast a glance toward Aron Archer at the bar. "I've talked with Novotny twice," Archer had just informed him. It was a little before eleven in the morning, and Archer was sipping Pernod. "I explained what's come together. Novotny wants it to go as much as we do, but we need the big one, something to give him that his people can't say no to."

Now, as a result of his talk with Harland, the Waxler notion for Siri was so much worthless paper.

He argued back, "She'd be dealing with Waxler, not me. He'd give her anything she asked for. Hell, have Remy direct."

"Teddy, it's a dead item. Besides, I've advised her to forget a comeback."

"I must have the wrong number."

"I mean it," Harland said. "Siri hasn't done a film in almost five years. Fifty percent of the box office are kids under twenty. How many are going to shell out their hard-earned bucks to see some thirty-one-year-old broad their parents thought was great?"

"Tell that to Dunaway or Jackie Bisset. What happened to you between now and the last time we talked?"

"What do you mean?"

"She dropped you, or I don't know what. But that speech you made is Freddie Harland trying to give himself a reason for not sounding stupid."

"Go to hell, you bum," Harland said. Kenrick heard the receiver slam down with venom.

Freddie Harland turned from the telephone, cold sweat on his forehead. In times of stress, he told himself, take care of number one. Behind double-locked hotel room doors, he worked the fine powder into thin ridges on the mirror of the small, antique compact he carried habitually in his breast pocket. He had scored the dope off an actor dumb enough to bring it into the country, and he was wondering where to find more. Christ, he needed something.

He waited a moment until things began to look clear, very sharp, in fact, then went to the tray left by room service. On it was a bottle of cognac and a plate for ground meat for Cash. "Here, dog. Come and *manger*."

He heard the German shepherd stir in the other room. Eat, sleep, and crap, I swear. Harland looked at the red meat and felt the gorge rise in the back of his throat.

He had found the bloody skull of a small animal, a sheep's

head, he guessed, stuck on the shower nozzle when he pulled back the curtain that morning, straight from the mildly entertaining evening he had passed with Rayna Tate. He knew half a dozen jerks who were great practical jokers, and hell, they all had seen *The Godfather*. But still, the small head with its skin removed, those bright, bulbous eyes and feline teeth, made him want to throw up. Mornings were tough enough.

Ten minutes later he had taken a phone call, a man's voice, that didn't sound like any of the practical jokers he knew. It was a long, convoluted conversation, with things hinted at, but never quite said. The guy could have been an agent with all his concern for Siri's fragile health, his stated affection for dogs. Harland finally got the point: Drop Siri or lose his best friend, four legged or otherwise.

Cash was going for the tray of meat when it struck him. "Oh, my God," Harland yelped, and made a grab for the dog's collar. The dog jackknifed, trying to bite his hand while Harland pulled him away from the food. "Shut up, you mutt." He locked the dog in the bathroom, listening to him begin a howl that must have been heard on the Croisette. He lifted the plate of meat to his nose. It smelled fresh, but what did he know? He dumped the meat in the plastic bag from one of his laundered shirts and put it in his briefcase.

He let the dog out of the toilet. "Listen to me, will you?" The animal bared his teeth. Teeth! Harland took a shot of cognac in a gulp. "You're lucky," Harland told him. "Dogs don't worry because they're too goddamned dumb. It takes someone smart to worry."

The dog was looking at him, a great pink tongue leaving a track of saliva across the carpet as he began a search for lunch. "Just let me worry," Harland said, calling after him. "You're lucky you got me for a friend."

"I'm telling you, they're gone." Larry Rentzler turned to

recross Kenrick's hotel suite, giving him a shrug of frustration. "Look, I'm a lawyer, not a private detective."

"You're doing fine," Kenrick said, trying to steady him down.

"I only know that Siri checked out of the Majestic a little before noon. Remy was staying at a hotel on the rue d'Antibes and same story. Maybe they went home."

"Not a day before the Lehman tribute."

Rentzler brightened. "There's your answer. When they show for the first screening, corner Remy then."

"I haven't a day to waste." It was a problem of access to Siri and leverage. Harland had dealt himself out, and the chance of Kenrick's approaching Siri directly was zero. But Rentzler had provided him a very long lever on Hugh: his part in skimming $430,000 from the budget of Lehman's film.

"I thought you didn't believe Remy was a thief?" Rentzler questioned.

"I don't believe he approached Ray Tannis without a good reason. Besides, so far it's only Tannis's word."

"What reason?"

"I don't know and don't care. But I'll promise Remy he is headed for jail unless he can convince Siri to commit to Waxler's project. Let her back out later, but I need Siri's name up front."

"You'd tack up Remy?"

"With the longest nails I can find."

Rentzler stopped pacing. He didn't like Kenrick much right then.

"We assume they're still in Cannes or close by," Kenrick said, knowing it was more hope than logic. "Go back to square one, the hotels they just left. Phone calls, anything."

"Nobody's going to talk to me."

"Spend some money. Take Gérard along. He'll know how."

"Okay," Rentzler said, bristling reluctance. "Okay," he said again, shutting the hotel door behind him, not at all gently.

Two hours later he was back. "We have something, but I'm not sure what. Gérard had a talk with the desk clerk at Remy's hotel that cost you five hundred francs. This morning Remy made three telephone calls. One to the U.S., a number I recognized."

"Ray Tannis?"

Rentzler confirmed it. "Doesn't help Remy's case, does it? The other two were local. One was a bar in Antibes, a wrong number maybe."

"Maybe."

"The other was an old hotel in Juan-les-Pins, a place called the Résidence Fleurie."

Kenrick took a taxi along the *bord de mer* eastward to Juan-les-Pins. Time was against him now. In three hours he was to meet Leo Gold, followed by the Donner reading he had promised Rayna he would attend. Gold and Siri were the final names on his list, but like objects one reaches for in a dream, they danced just beyond his grasp.

The Résidence Fleurie was an old hotel with streaks of rust on its chipped, white walls, set in the pines from which Juan-les-Pins drew its name. Why had Remy and Siri forsaken Cannes for this remote spot, if in fact they had?

He told the driver to halt some distance away and had already paid him off when he saw Remy come down the hotel steps. He crossed to a blue Renault and a moment later, unnoticing, sped past Kenrick in the opposite direction. Kenrick pointed after the car and held up a hundred-franc note. "Okay," the driver said, pocketing the bill and swearing something down his shirtfront.

Five minutes later, far ahead, Remy's car slid into a parking spot near some old fortifications along the Antibes oceanfront. When Remy set out on foot, Kenrick followed.

By the time they reached the narrow streets of the old city Kenrick began to sense something purposeful in Remy's intent. He dropped back then, waiting to see what came next.

Perhaps only a drink, for when they reached the open city market beneath a roof of warped corrugated iron, Remy entered a bar at the far side. One of the telephone calls Remy had placed that morning was to a bar in Antibes.

Through the window, Kenrick saw Remy join a man sitting alone at a table. His drooping mustache, cap, and a bulky blue duffel coat gave him the look of a seaman. They didn't shake hands.

Kenrick recrossed the square, bought a Paris *Herald Tribune*, and stuck his face in the newspaper to wait.

The conversation in the bar lasted less than ten minutes. From a distance, Kenrick wasn't sure the man with the mustache said a word. Finally, he rose, drained his glass, and walked from the bar without looking at Remy.

For a moment Hugh Remy sat motionless; then he signaled for another drink.

Kenrick folded his newspaper and crossed the square. It wasn't the right place for what he was going to do. He doubted there was one.

The bar was narrow and long with round scarred tables lining one wall and a counter topped in marble-textured plastic along the other. At the back, four men were playing cards, under the watchful eye of the bartender.

When Kenrick entered, Remy fixed him in the mirror at the end of the room but showed no recognition even as he lowered himself into the same chair vacated by the man with the mustache. Remy took a sip from his drink, a careful raising of his hand that needed concentration. Remy had been drinking plenty.

"We'd better talk, Hugh."

Remy continued to look into his glass. "You ever sail, Kenrick?" Something inside Hugh Remy was about to bubble forth, whatever Kenrick might have wanted to discuss. Kenrick took in a breath, thinking of the time slipping by, and gave him a cue to bring it on.

"No, Remy, I've never sailed."

"Every second you're out there you deal with forces outside yourself—wind, currents, the way a particular craft will take to them. I didn't say fight because you can't fight the wind or the sea. Use them against each other maybe, but never fight. The man at the tiller knows that, knows he's the only person he can look to. Pray if you want, but God isn't any more forgiving on the ocean than anywhere else." He brought the glass level with his eyes and judged the color. "But back on land we start looking to everyone for help but ourselves."

"You came here looking for help?"

"I came here looking for a man to break fingers or a head." He tacked on, significantly, "Or worse."

He broke into a sudden grin that took a dozen years off his age. "I must have given everyone a few laughs. A guy like me, and a foreigner to boot, looking to buy muscle. Back there in Cannes, we think it's Palm Springs with a beach. But six blocks off the Croisette it's a world where you and I mean nothing, Kenrick. The *Unione Corse* is the power here. Not a village on the Côte without its connections right up to the caids and Mr. Bigs in Marseilles or Grenoble or Bastia, safe and protected, because they have their hands in the police, politics, everything." It was Galloway's pyramid again, the various planes of society, law and outlaw, merging somewhere just out of sight. Kenrick didn't believe it, not all of it. But at that moment Hugh Remy did.

Remy said, "Everyone here pays the *pizzo*, the tribute, the license to go about your business. The grocer, the woman who checks your coat at the casino, the guy who runs this bar." Remy tossed a thumb toward the table of men playing cards. "They all pay. But they know, too, if they can raise the money, they can buy an import license, an extra telephone line—or justice. I'll give that to these people. They're not waiting, believing the police will solve their problems for them or save their families. Themselves, Kenrick."

"Where'd you get this about the *Unione Corse*?"

"Some rummy Englishman who works the boats in Cannes. Cost me a couple of hundred francs for the information and the name of a man, a head breaker."

"The guy with the mustache?"

Remy made a quick jerk with his chin that Kenrick took for a yes. "No interest. Not for an outsider. So I was a fool," Remy said. "Not the first time. But if I don't do something, I'm going to lose."

Kenrick took a chance, but not so big a one. "To Nicky Deane?"

Remy merely nodded, giving him a distant smile. "If it were only me . . . but when you see it happen to someone else."

"Pedro?"

"I meant Siri."

"Siri!" He'd never considered that Siri might be part of the equation that included Nicky Deane.

"Kenrick, I've never been desperate before. In trouble, but never helpless." His huge fist pounded the table in frustration, bringing an uninviting glance from the men at the back of the room. The realization was so self-evident, Kenrick would have wagered on it, was about to.

Hugh Remy was in love with Siri Laurence.

"Come on, Hugh," he said, taking Remy's glass. "Let's get away from these smiling faces."

They bought coffee at an outdoor stall and stood behind the high jetty wall out of the wind.

"What's Deane after?"

Remy told him about Deane's pursuit of Siri years before in New York and the later harassment when she had fled to Hollywood with Pedro. "Trying to wrap himself around her life, to leave her no other choice but him. When she married Pedro, Deane went for them both."

"You figure Deane put a scare into Freddie Harland?"

"Harland would be a piece of cake. Pedro was going to quit, you know. Then he found the musical, bigger than anything he should have tried."

"That never stopped him before."

Remy shook his head, remembering. "We had a helluva row. I'd never talked to him hard like that. Hell, I loved the old bastard. A great career, I said. He had Siri. Stop while there was cash in the bank. In the end he agreed, relieved to be done with it. He knew he was tired."

Kenrick saw accusal in Remy's eyes. "And then two things happened. A backer comes in with money, provided Pedro stake everything he has left for collateral. And you and your studio offer him a deal. All of a sudden the old rooster is puffing himself out again, ready for another try. Unless I'm wrong, you and I both know how it turned out."

"A bad film," Kenrick confirmed. "Only three people know how bad. You, me, and Fiona MacCauley."

"Pedro knew. Hell, we were lucky to get a film at all. At least I gave him the chance to pull it off. You think I regret what I did, you're wrong."

"You mean the money you and Tannis skimmed off the film?"

"Sure I mean the money." Remy's eyes glittered with anger. "When you walked into that bar, I knew. Tannis cabled, said your snooper had been around."

"But why skim the film? It never did sit right with me."

"Because I was paying, Kenrick. Drivers, caterers, talent. I told you how Deane worked, around the edges, trying everything to bring the film down. Bust Pedro to nothing, take his pride, his last penny, and, when he had all that, his trust in Siri. But he didn't make it," Remy said, a triumph in his voice. "No, sir."

"Bring the film down?" The disbelief in his voice brought Remy forward, his gaze intense.

"First time it happened we're on location ten, maybe twelve days. The novelty is gone, and it's beginning to grind. So one day the chow wagon doesn't show. You know that's where a crew on location lives, and now I have union stewards on my back reading me rules. So I drive thirty miles to see the guy who doesn't show up, and he says his truck has flat tires and someone put lye in the stroganoff, you name it. All right, I know someone—Deane—has got to him, scared him or bought him off. So I say how much is it going to cost me to have him chance it, get on the job again —a little cash bonus, me to him. And he says five thousand bucks. So I pay because every day the camera doesn't turn is costing me five times that much."

Remy ran a palm over his windblown hair. The back was shaggy, and Kenrick realized he trimmed it himself.

"So I get that fixed," Remy said, "and the lens locker disappears. We airfreight in a spare set, and suddenly Ronnie Mauer says he has a pulled muscle and can't dance when he's got three days left on camera. And that costs me the Winnebago he was using for a dressing room. It was Deane buying, threatening, picking away."

Kenrick nodded. "I get the drift."

"The money had to come from somewhere. It was a battle, Kenrick, between me and him. It still is."

"Does Siri know what Deane was trying with Pedro?"

"There's a lot Siri doesn't know," Remy said, suddenly guarded. "Pedro is dead. Let it be."

"But why would Deane want to bust a production he helped finance?"

Remy shielded his eyes from the sun, taking a clearer look at Kenrick. "Finance? I don't follow."

"Rentzler found out the people who loaned Lehman his money and Nicky Deane go way back. Here in Cannes I cross-checked it with a guy named Roman, who once borrowed cash from the same people. The introduction was arranged by Nicky Deane."

Remy thought a long moment. "Nothing to lose, maybe. They had the house and paintings as collateral against the loan. If the film went under, they still collect, and Pedro has nothing. It fits."

But Kenrick was thinking how much the studio stood to lose with a film put in trouble by the scheming of Nicky Deane. There was a weapon for Kenrick somewhere, hidden in the past, in the connections between Deane and the loan man Tilman and whoever was back farther still, the link with Robert Arthur.

"Maybe there's a way to break Nicky Deane's head."

"My problem, now," Remy said. His large hands were hanging loose at his sides.

"Listen to me, Hugh. Deane blackmailed me into ramming the Lehman film through the studio. He has a videotape of me marking a deck of playing cards in a blackjack game a long time back. Dumb, but there were reasons that made perfect sense at the time."

The admission brought a wry laugh from Remy. "They always do, Kenrick. Welcome to the club."

"But I'm bringing something together that may also get Nicky Deane off your back because he is linked with the people involved."

"Keep talking," Remy said, but he was wary.

"I need you to convince Siri to take the Waxler film. I need it in the next twenty-four hours, so the news will leak."

"I don't get the connection with Deane."

"But I do."

"So I do your bidding, and you score."

Kenrick met his eyes directly. "Either that or write out a check for four hundred and thirty thousand bucks."

Remy offered him a nasty smile. "That's the boy I know." But he looked troubled a moment later. "I'm not sure I have the influence. Siri isn't listening to me." It was a painful admission.

"Try, Remy."

"If Deane learns you're giving her something to grab onto, he'll be around. You thought about that?"

"I hadn't."

"You'd better," Remy said.

It was nearly four, the afternoon of the Festival's eighth day, before Kenrick left Hugh Remy and took a cab to the address Rayna had given him the previous night by telephone.

The narrow road wound into the hills behind Cannes, past widely spaced villas hidden beyond heavy foliage and thick walls. Down below, in the city, the Festival had moved into its second act. New film posters lined the Croisette, and the sensations of the first week were pushed aside by new faces, their antics and quotable quotes splashed across the media. It was a point in time when all who had lasted since the opening prayed for a second wind and plowed ahead to sell whatever it was they had brought here, for in one fashion or another, they were all selling something: a film, a territory, or merely the illusion of success.

He was let into the villa by a white-jacketed servant and led through to the pool. Another servant was busily arranging a buffet, and to one side were two large ice tubs filled with champagne.

Leo Gold was motionless on a lounge at poolside, the loose folds of white skin beneath his chin giving him the look of a reptile expiring in the sun.

Neither Rayna nor Donner was to be seen.

"You're late," Gold said without opening his eyes.

"Yes, Leo, I'm late."

The meeting with Gold went as well as he could expect. Rayna had been correct; Gold knew of Kenrick's intended breakaway from the studio. "A secret like that keeps maybe an hour and five minutes," Gold said.

Kenrick told him, in outline, of their plans, emphasizing the new organization's intention to stay lean. "We want someone else to handle the mechanics of distribution, advertising, promotion. You, Leo."

In half an hour Kenrick went over it in as much detail as he could without bringing in a team of legal and financial advisers. He didn't expect a yes or no on the spot from Gold and wasn't surprised when Gold said, "I'll think on it," and nothing else to indicate how long this process of gestation might take. Gold's big promotion luncheon was two days away, the time when Gold revealed his plans for the coming year to distributors and the press. Kenrick hoped he would want to fly the deal in front of them.

Kenrick left him, found the telephone, and called Aron Archer. It was just after five, and Kenrick's call caught up with him in the hotel bar.

"Will he go?" Archer asked, clearly apprehensive.

"Trying to predict Leo is like trying to guess which way a cricket will jump."

"But when will he decide?"

"I don't know," Kenrick said. He heard Archer groan, rung off, and turned to find himself facing Rayna Tate.

"Remember me?" she asked lightly.

"I remember."

She had badly needed a moment alone to compose herself, and the last person she wanted to catch her off-balance was Kenrick. She might have told him of the frantic day's search to find Donner. The bars, hospitals, finally Cook's and American Express, in case he had panicked and bought a ticket out. In desperation she sought out the Festival director, Philippe Brialt, and told him the truth. "Donner's gone. I don't care why, but I must find him."

Brialt called in a colleague, a solidly built man named Durand, who didn't consider Donner's disappearance in the slightest out of the ordinary. "Let's see what we can do." An hour later he telephoned with the news. "He's in jail.

239

Assaulting a police officer. Perhaps other charges. Grave, but negotiable."

She had prepared herself for worse, and it wasn't the first time she had bailed Donner out of jail. Exactly twenty minutes before Donner's reading was to begin, they were riding up the long hill toward the villa in a taxi. Donner looked as if he had tangled with a bear and was still mad enough to go another round. She didn't want to burden Kenrick with any of it, and thus, avoiding the question in his eyes, she asked him how things had gone with Leo Gold.

"It was what they call in government a fruitful exchange. He'll come around." But his confident smile was forced and unconvincing, if not downright false.

She studied him intently, then said, "What are you up to, Kenrick, really?"

Kenrick felt the question grab just under his heart. He damned himself for not explaining it all before, the deception, the ultimate payoff. He had been reluctant to trust his own judgment of Rayna, to let feeling mix with what ought to have been the hard decisions of business.

From back along the hall, they heard voices, a door closing. "I have other people to tend to," she said. "But I'll leave you something to think about. Jean-Yves Climent told me that Sid Mathan made him an offer to pick up his latest film for U.S. release."

"Because we liked it."

"Then why is he picking it up for the studio, not this new company of yours?"

Kenrick fielded it with a glib bit of juggling that tasted bad in his mouth, every word. "It's a special kind of film, Rayna. A polished, high-quality item with a limited market. Too big a gamble for us. But I thought I'd leave the studio with something worthwhile and give Climent a boost."

Everything he told Rayna was true. It was a gift to Climent, yet Kenrick knew he had done it not for Climent's sake, but as a demonstration to Rayna of his own power.

Her eyes never left his face as he spoke.

"You're a persuasive man," she said. "But something inside me says liar."

She had started back along the hall when he caught her arm and turned her forcefully toward him.

"You're right. Not a hundred percent, but close enough. Can we talk later?"

"Talk? Sure, why not?" she tossed back. "It goes with the territory, right?"

"Don't take that way out. This is one of those times we either push things forward or lose what we've got. No staying even, not with you and me."

"And still no labels?" she said, hard, forcing him to come to her.

"You really believe words are worth a damn?"

"They would be from you."

Almost a dozen people were gathered in the lounge when Kenrick entered, Donner still to make an appearance. Near the champagne O. K. Shinn nodded a hello while, from the far corner, Dieter Furst's pale glance took him in before he turned to the shapely blonde next to him, the same girl Kenrick had seen with Donner at the Festival opening.

Rayna had joined the two young producers responsible for the official Canadian entry at the Festival, a hot team trying to cash in on the sensation their film had caused at the screening two nights before. But sensation cooled fast, and already critical acclaim was shifting to an Italian entry shown that morning to the press.

Near the bookcase, the British producer Kermit Loud gave him a small salute of hello. Just that day Loud had sold the North American distribution rights to a big-budget action-adventure film set in Africa to Allied for five million, the Festival's coup to date.

Knowing he could count on a high quality of small talk from Loud, Kenrick began toward him, only to have his arm snagged by Leo Gold. "You know what I just learned from this Johnny-come-later?" Gold said, punching a thumb toward the grinning man next to him. "Some Boston mutual fund just bought six percent of Twentieth. And I got to find out from this guy."

It was the expected conversation all right. To these people, the movie business wasn't films, but deals. For people, financing, blocks of stock. By their deals were they measured, with extra points allotted for size. Billy Wilder was right: There ought to be an Oscar for the best deal. "Hi, Teddy," the grinning man with Gold said. Lou Sulten had made a fortune building shopping centers and had bought his way into the film business two years before. He had twenty million invested in a dozen projects at various stages of production, about half of which Kenrick had been given a first look at and rejected. He was a smooth-faced, amiable man, with the smile of an unbloodied innocent. For his wife, Gladys, Cannes was turning out a dream: press luncheons, photos with Farrah, the Carradines, and Ollie Reed, his smile managing to give the impression of a loud yawn. She was a tanned, bright-faced woman with the tight shiny texture of skin that said "face-lift." As Rayna remarked, some things went with the territory.

Sulten's grin hung there, tight and mechanical, a copy of the one Nixon had practiced in the mirror. "Word is Sands is jumping EMI to form a new company," Sulten commented. "Maybe you started something."

The remark was double-edged. Sulten meant to announce that he knew, that he was *in*. Still, it was intended to put Kenrick on the defensive, to provoke some tidbit worth passing on. "You should have heard what Kenrick said when I. . . ." Self-aggrandizement, emphasis on the "I." Sulten was learning fast. "Hello, Lou." Kenrick smiled and moved on.

Near the bookcase, Kermit Loud observed Sulten with

distaste. "I hope he's still grinning when his first film has to survive in a cold, hard world."

"You'd love to see him drown, Kermit. Concern fits you like a sack."

Loud made a small cackle of delight. "You're the same brand of jade, Teddy. We should cook something up one day, we really should. I've heard what you're up to."

"When things come together, I'll be in touch," Kenrick said, and slid off toward the champagne. Loud, too, was trying to parlay his score of that day into the next one in the string. Deal while the manna was flowing.

Rayna had pulled together for Donner a roomful of heavyweights. Any one of them could package a Donner project and put his hand on the money. And they were exactly the kind of people Donner had trouble with, precisely because not one of them really gave a damn about actors. In one of his loquacious moments, Leo Gold had called Donner the perfect actor—a sack of potatoes with legs, so he could move where the director told him. It had gone around town, naturally. And Donner didn't forget.

Yes, Donner would be tested here tonight.

But, then, it might have been said about Kenrick himself.

For, as Kenrick took his first sip of champagne, he saw Rayna cross to greet a final guest. Filling the doorway, making as auspicious an entrance as any actor, was Mal Stiner.

"I want a word with you, Kenrick," Stiner said, loud enough to be heard by most of the room.

Kenrick hadn't counted out a public confrontation with Stiner, and he hadn't expected Rayna to have a hand in it.

"Let's step outside, Mal. Make a pretense of being discreet."

Near the pool, Kenrick faced him, allowing some distance. Stiner's chin jutted forward in a caricature of defiance. "What the hell are you up to?"

"Oh, come on, Mal."

"I hear you're jumping ship—forming your own studio."

"A studio head quitting to make his own pictures isn't exactly a new story, in Cannes or anywhere else."

"Yeah, but, fella, I know why. You're getting out before Don Eads finds something in that operation of yours that will bring you down."

"Anything your hatchet man finds will bring the entire studio down. And the stock of the parent company. Let's have the whole picture in proportion." Through the broad glass window, he saw Rayna cast them a glance and look away. Donner had entered the room and was moving from group to group, shaking hands, his grin quick and friendly.

It might have successfully upstaged Stiner had Mal not chosen that moment to whirl and throw his champagne glass at a wall of layered stones nearby.

"But taking Mathan, Rentzler, Archer, and Ernst Rucker leaves the studio with what? Leaves me?"

Kenrick doubted even among the rumors Stiner could have

picked up the names of the entire personnel so quickly. Conclusion: One of them had cracked under the pressure or gotten cold feet and gone to Stiner to be lured back into the fold. Which one?

"Offer them more money, that's the usual counterattack."

"If you people walk, you gut the studio. You know that."

"All I'm trying to do is buy the best possible talent I can," Kenrick said. "You'd do the same."

"And if Lehman's film turns out to be the disaster I smell, you'll have left irreparable damage, Kenrick. Irreparable."

"I wouldn't have said irreparable. You want to make films, Mal. Now is your chance."

"You're taking this damn lighthearted," Stiner said.

"I'm taking this just about the way you expected," Kenrick replied. "Now let's quit raving and go watch Donner make his pitch."

Kenrick began back toward the villa; Stiner stood his ground, calling after him.

"I've got Legal working on this. If there is any way I can sue your ass or drive you into the ground, I'll do it."

It would be a juicy item: Studio head and parent company president argue at poolside. By midnight it would have made its rounds of the meeting spots that counted.

Kenrick hoped it would circulate far and wide before the next wave of gossip nudged it from everyone's memory.

Donner's reading began well enough. A little before seven Rayna bade everyone find a chair. "Or someone's lap. Beyond this point, I am not responsible, except for the food served later. Stay if you like; go if you must. But I forbid any business to be talked under this roof tonight, word of honor from you all."

Stiner took a place directly across the room from Kenrick, a grin worn like a chip on his shoulder waiting to be challenged.

"Hear, hear," Kermit Loud said, reflecting the mood of

what otherwise appeared to be a gathering willing to be entertained. Rayna nodded toward a servant, who made a discreet circuit of the room, topping up glasses; Donner bobbed his head at the group collectively and took a position in one corner, holding a script.

Whether it was Rayna's scenario or pure accident, Freddie Harland entered the room at that moment behind Donner. He embraced him as though Donner had been missed dearly and mouthed an apology toward Rayna for being late. His glance slid past Kenrick without meeting his eyes. But Harland's presence added a weight to Donner's pitch, even before it began.

"Well now," Donner said, easing into the beginning. He held up the script. "A lot of things are said in the opening pretty fast, and without any dialogue at all. So maybe I can sort of talk through it."

He began with a description of a long master scene set at Zandvoort, site of the Dutch Grand Prix. A montage of sunrise, the crowd arriving at the track, the last-minute tuning of Formula I racing cars. "And all the while the sound is rising behind the sequence until nothing is heard but the roar of unmuffled engines, and we're looking at one car and one driver. Now the kid behind the wheel isn't a Newman or McQueen—let's say average, if anything a little bookish. He's taking instructions from an older man in team overalls, his father. And he's no Newman or McQueen either."

He might have played the veiled reference to his own part for a laugh, but Donner moved on without punching it. It was the right tack.

"The two of them have been a long time coming to this point," Donner said, "and the boy in that car—Davey Mc-Cann—making his first Grand Prix start, is everything the father never did achieve in his racing career or in life—the whole bundle."

From directly in front of Donner, Leo Gold's chirpy voice

cut like a scalpel through the mood he was trying to establish. "Nobody told me this was a racing story," Gold said from the couch. "Car stories and boat stories I don't do."

Someone cleared his throat; Harland's attention went from Donner's face to a spot high on one wall.

Donner took a noticeable breath and flashed a smile down at Gold. "Well, Leo, there are cars in this story, but it's no more about cars than *The Spirit of St. Louis* was about an airplane or *Rocky* about the fight business. It's about people and the things important to them, things that ought to be important to us all. And it can be put in the can for under five million bucks, which is the real thing you want to know, isn't it?"

It got a low rumble of laughter from everyone but Gold and Rayna; she was watching Donner fearfully.

But if Gold tested his patience, it was Donner's secret, his smile and the patient explanation convincing them all they were viewing a new Rod Donner. Except Kenrick didn't believe it.

"Car pictures I don't do," Gold said, refusing to let it go.

"Oh, Leo, shut up," chirped Gladys Sulten. She leaned over and gave him a wet kiss on the cheek. "Maybe he won't even ask you."

Her ingenuousness struck the audience, simultaneously, cracking the tension. While Gold mumbled something Kenrick missed, Donner picked up the story before anyone else could offer an opinion.

Without needing dialogue, he described the start of the race, touching upon the father in the pits, the cars, young McCann, and finally Davey McCann on the tail of the front-runner, the man on his way to becoming world champion, the Swiss driver Jon Rindt.

Donner had not yet cracked open the script, his painting of the story as carefully rehearsed as a stage performance. Moving from image to sharp image, he let each make its point in the telling. He also neatly managed to avoid any reference to the camera, describing what was seen, drawing the audience into the story, rather than making them aware of the technical difficulties an actor or director could become obsessed with.

"And then it happens," Donner said. "In a long corner, far away in the backstretch, a crash. We don't really get a good look because both the grandstand and McCann in the pits are on the opposite side of the circuit. But everyone sees the curtain of fire as one car strikes the barrier and careens down the track out of control. Coming to rest, the car erupts like a bomb. But McCann is already running. Running, closer, a blurred vision of the burning car ahead of him, its driver trapped behind the wheel. But which car? Down deep, McCann knows, just as we do. By the time he reaches the car it's too late. As a fire truck douses down the car with foam, we see the blackened figure bent over the wheel, the remains of McCann's son. And with that, we make a sharp cut to the quiet, drab inquiry room of the Dutch Racing Commission."

It was a nicely set hook, but Donner went on, layering over it a sharp change in scene that would work well on film. The author of the script had chosen the simplest tension-building devices, principally the crosscut. If, in the telling, the scenes threatened to stretch the drama too long, Donner was abridging now, the way a director might, judging his audience perfectly.

"In this inquiry room, the head of the racing board is reading the official findings of its investigation into the crash, the end of a man's life in flat, sober, official prose." In contrast with his descriptions of the opening, Donner now let his tone level out, giving an impression of even this minor character, without acting the role. "McCann is there, as is the other driver, Jon Rindt. But it's McCann we watch. While this cold fish of a Dutchman explains that the fault of the accident was held to be Davey McCann's. That he had tried to take the track away from Rindt once they had entered the turn, thus breaking one of the basic driving rules of Formula One racing. A touch of the wheels resulted in the crash and young McCann's death. The scene ends with the racing official's words—'a regrettable end to a young career, but one nonetheless due to negligence and to his own willful error.' "

Until then Donner had scarcely moved, but now he turned and began walking slowly to his left as he spoke. He held the attention of everyone, even Leo Gold.

"But you see, McCann won't accept it," Donner said. "For a reason rare enough in these times, a reason that McCann intends to stake his entire being on proving. He knows his son. He knows him as a man. He knows him as a driver. The idea that Davey McCann would make the mistake he was accused of to McCann is unthinkable, despite the testimony of one of the biggest, most respected names in the business. McCann can't accept it, and he sets out on an investigation of his own."

Donner continued the story, sometimes describing scenes, sometimes stopping to read a terse bit of dialogue, crisp verbal exchanges, as McCann cajoles, threatens, pleads, whatever tactic necessary to pry out information. A witness here, a judge in a distant tower, a bit of film from a viewer's camera, a piece of evidence that in isolation meant nothing. He follows the Grand Prix circuit from race to race, trying to reach the drivers and mechanics who might know something of value. It was clear to Kenrick that Donner had found himself a neat twist on one of the most marketable kinds of film: a simple, pure detective story. He'd projected himself naturally into a character little different from his own—a man fighting to overcome a tough, direct nature, forced to deal subtly with people for the first time in his life. The two fused perfectly, Donner and his character McCann, and Kenrick, too, found himself caught up.

Until twenty minutes into the reading, when Leo Gold

became restless. Kenrick had seen it happen before. Gold had made up his mind in the negative and now couldn't be bothered.

Donner didn't pick it up immediately. He was trying to explain, via a parenthetical side trip, the introduction of the girl who had been Davey McCann's lover. She joins McCann in his pursuit of truth, and what evolves between them is a love of a different kind, not destined to last, but sustaining to them both. It was a delicate counterpoint to the search theme, easier to establish on film with a glance or touch than by verbal description. Donner must have known the chance he was taking trying to talk it through, but maybe he had become too sure of his audience. Somewhere in it he lost Gold. When he finally saw Leo fidgeting not three feet away, Donner's concentration faltered, and Kenrick felt the audience slipping away.

"Why don't you just tell us the ending?" Gold interrupted callously. Then, thinking he would soften it, he added, "It's a nice story, Donner. Very nice."

Donner had been moving laterally, but now he spun to face the audience. Rayna must have known the look because Kenrick saw her start forward, then catch herself.

Donner's mouth opened to say something as he stepped forward until he towered above Gold.

Here it comes, Kenrick thought.

Rayna moved before Donner broke, reaching to take Leo Gold by the arm. "Come on, Leo, darling. There's a phone call for you down the hall, and if not, we'll play checkers. No one here will mind at all."

"What'd I say?" Gold said, in all innocence.

Rayna's hasty extraction of Gold brought a nervous giggle from O. K. Shinn that rang falsely, a chattering laugh like fingers across a blackboard in effect. Donner was watching the point on the couch that Gold had vacated in the manner of someone watching a man's belt buckle he is ready to attack. He can't find it again, Kenrick thought, and in about one second he's going to tell us what an execrable collection of humankind we are and offer to fight us singly or in a bunch.

But he did none of that. An instant later Donner's head went back, and he roared with laughter, looking across his audience with a grin that deepened every crevice in his face and lighted his eyes. "Well, I guess old Leo has a point," he said, smiling. "So now I'm going to tell you how the story ends."

"Bravo," Kermit Loud said very softly as Donner put down the script and turned his back to the audience for several seconds.

What possible exercise of the imagination, what thought had brought Donner back from the edge? Kenrick wondered.

When Donner faced them again, the character McCann was squarely back in place, McCann confronting the Swiss driver, Jon Rindt, in the final master scene. It's late at night outside the victory party. Rindt has just clinched the world's driving championship, the Grand Prix. The accident is months past. The scene is entirely a monologue by McCann, with Rindt listening, considering, but never saying a word. McCann presents the evidence, the pieces that together still might not be enough to convince a court of law. Slim stuff, except that McCann in his heart knows the truth. It was not Rindt who had taken the track on the corner in the race, thereby giving him the right of way, but Davey McCann. It was the new world champion who had made the error in judgment, who was responsible for the crash. McCann's speech is a request, not a threat. A plea for honor that both of them know is disappearing fast enough in the world. Honor above money. Something that was of true importance to no one but the two of them, and the honor of his dead son. But the champion says nothing.

"The short scene that follows," Donner said, "lasts five,

maybe six, seconds on the screen. Jon Rindt, the world champion, walks into the office of the commissioner of the Dutch Grand Prix. He is asked what he wants and tells them: to make a new statement regarding the crash at Zandvoort. And that's it."

Freddie Harland was thankful for the cab ride. The weather had taken a warm, steamy turn, and he had already moved plenty that day. From Lou Sulten at the Carlton out to the Hôtel du Cap, back to Leo Gold. And now, in the late afternoon, a muggy cab ride up to the villa where he was meeting Donner.

He found him sprawled nude on a chaise lounge at poolside, drinking a beer. Beads of water rippled down over his taut, muscular body, and Harland would have been more comfortable if he had covered himself with a towel. "I think we got ourselves a deal," he said, giving Donner his warmest smile. For one morning's hard work, Harland would likely make himself a bundle in six figures.

"Mix yourself a drink," Donner said, waving off toward the house. "Rayna's not here yet, and I want her to hear what you say."

"You're taking this pretty cool," Harland said peevishly.

Donner's reaction was a steady look of dislike.

A long ten minutes later Rayna Tate came out onto the pool deck, gave Freddie a coolish hello, and dropped herself into a chair near Donner. "You ought to stop advertising," she said, surveying his nakedness. "Your product, darling, isn't all that special. Here, hide yourself under_this." She dropped a square white envelope into his lap.

"What is it?"

"A dinner invitation tonight with the Festival director and your favorite actress, Siri. Be there. An order." To Harland she said, "The rumor mill is already working about our client here. It can't be as good as I've heard."

"That's the kind of deals I make, sweet, only"—he shot a glance at Donner—"I can't get this guy to listen."

Donner took another slow sip of beer, placed the bottle carefully on the deck, and folded his hands across his chest. "Okay, who went for the bait?" It wasn't the tone Harland expected, from a man about to bring off one of the coups of the Festival.

"Sulten for one," Harland said. "Or maybe his wife." He looked toward Rayna, grinning at the secret they shared. She was willing in the sack, and he was counting on a return engagement before his business with Donner was through. She understood that. "Did you know Sulten was a racing freak? Even sponsored a car at Indy?"

"Something to that effect," Rayna said casually. "I know the Sultens spent the week before the Festival at the Loew's in Monte Carlo—for the Grand Prix."

"Well, whatever," Harland said, waving it away. Donner had listened without change of expression. Rayna, trying to account for his odd silence, frowned uneasily.

"Who else?" Donner asked.

"Leo Gold."

"The contrary sonuvabitch," Rayna said.

"What about Kenrick?" Donner asked.

"What the hell you want?" Harland moaned.

"Forget about Kenrick," Rayna said.

"Oh-ho," Donner smiled. He had recognized the glow in Rayna's complexion, the fullness of her face that came from her having made love long and well. "I do believe Rayna and Kenrick danced the night away."

Well, well, Freddie Harland thought.

Rayna averted Donner's grin. "Kenrick is involved in other things," she said neutrally.

Harland said, "And an interest from someone I didn't expect. Mal Stiner."

Donner looked around. "Who?"

Rayna said, "The big, square-jawed individual who argued with Kenrick before the reading. I didn't invite him, not really. He called earlier and invited himself. Maybe he's a fan? Or maybe it's his daughter."

Harland said, "I don't know if he's buying or what. He called me, said he liked the reading, and to let him know what happened before anybody signs anything."

Behind it somewhere was Penny Stiner, Donner knew. Ten years ago, boffing anyone close to a man in power would have been standard operating procedure, obligatory, given the chance. But he didn't intend using the girl.

"Forget Stiner," Donner said. "Let's hear about Sulten and Gold."

"What it comes down to is this: If you control the property, I can deal. Actor-script, for a bunch of money up front and some other bits and pieces, including some gross after break-even."

"What about flat gross?" Rayna asked. "Gross after break-even isn't much different from net, and you know how many people see that."

"Look, in Donner's position, I'd worry about the money up front. That's the name of the game."

"And what is my position?" Donner said. "Just so we're clear."

Donner hadn't liked his phrasing, but Harland wasn't about to let some semiliterate actor intimidate him. "You want it, I'll tell you. You're not in the top twenty and never were. You've got a good story that fits you like a glove. You pulled off as slick a job of selling as I've seen in twenty years in this business. So take it for what it is: the right man in the right part at the right time. Grab the money and run."

"Ah, yes, the money," Donner said, and again Rayna looked at him, heard the peculiar tone, as though he didn't trust himself to hear about money.

"I went in with a floor at a million five," Harland said.

"Oh, Lord." Rayna sighed.

Freddie Harland smiled. "Sulten went for it, and Gold is thinking."

Rayna jumped up, kissed Donner on the forehead, and did a little dance on her way toward the house. "I'll get the champagne."

"Forget the champagne," Harland said. "I'm sick of champagne."

"Better hold off, Rayna, for a minute or two."

Donner's voice halted her in place. She came back to the two of them, her eyes riveted on Donner's face.

"I say go with Sulten," Harland advised, "and let Leo Gold hang."

It was a long moment before Donner nodded, his agreement giving Harland a flush of relief. A couple of funny moments there. "Set up a meeting with Sulten," Donner said. "And tell him it will be a long one."

"Hey, listen," Harland said. "You don't understand. We got an offer. Now we either accept or we don't. I'm through haggling money."

"Things to go over," Donner said. "A budget, some notes on cast, and a rough production schedule that can use this year's racing season. Second-unit stuff, but we'll need it."

Harland rolled his eyes, but Rayna wasn't paying any attention. Her gaze was still fixed upon Donner. "Rod, listen," Harland said, his voice rising nervously. "You been making spaghetti thrillers too long. You know, where everyone carries his own suitcase. In Hollywood we got other people paid to do this kind of work. I sold them an actor and a damn fine script. Now will you quit?"

"Yeah, well, that's just it," Donner said.

"I should have known. . . ." Rayna began a slow walk back toward the house. "That's about all, Rod, with you and me. . . ."

Donner watched her go, knowing truly it was finished between them.

"Oh, Donner," she began, but she walked more quickly then and shut the glass door behind her.

"Well, somebody'd better tell me," Harland said, "because you two may know, but I don't."

"You sold an actor," Donner said, "but it's not enough. This is my picture, and if anyone mucks it up, it's going to be me."

"I think I'm hearing you right, but I don't want to believe it."

"You've got it, Fred," Donner said, the challenge clear. "I act all right. But I also produce and direct. The whole ball of wax. You can drop it on Sulten's desk and tell him it's that or nothing."

"Get a move on, Siri girl," Remy called out, slipping Brialt's dinner invitation into a pocket. He had last worn his double-breasted tuxedo at the 1955 Academy Awards. "We have people waiting and a drive ahead of us."

From beyond the door separating their rooms he heard Siri reply, "They can damn well wait."

He sat there for a moment, a drink turning in his large hands, trying to judge her mood.

Twice during the last three days they had changed hotels. Less than an hour after arriving at the hotel in Juan-les-Pins she received a frightening call from Nicky Deane. It sent Remy out in search of someone who could deal with the man in his own fashion. He drove to Antibes to find a head cracker and found Kenrick instead. How much faith had he in Kenrick's ability to remove the threat? At some point in the past days, watching Siri's spirits hit rock bottom, he decided it wouldn't matter. He was through looking elsewhere for help. He found the hotel in the hills near St.-Paul-de-Vence, a low, sprawling complex, once a farm, surrounded by orchards and a high wall.

But Siri was scared. She saw Deane on the fringes of everything, trying to force her back to him by leaving her without alternatives. How much of it was in Siri's mind, Remy wasn't sure, but even that worked in Deane's favor. The telephone calls she put through to several agents in L.A. were unreturned or had not passed beyond the hotel telephone operator.

"You're imagining things."

"I'm telling you it's him."

He had seen one good example that Deane's threats weren't imaginary.

At the first hotel he found the photograph before Siri did, a snapshot tacked to the inside of the bathroom door. A shocker. A girl's face in close-up that might or might not have been Carole Wade. With the work done by the razor there was no way to tell.

Yet in a way totally unexpected Deane's threats were throwing her closer to Remy. He and Siri were sharing the same bed now, even if, in common terminology, they had yet to make love. Remy understood that her need to be close to him in the night might have been the desired response all right, but the reasons were cockeyed. He couldn't predict what would happen between them when she regained her mental balance. But he was resolved that this wasn't the way he intended to win Siri. His first step in shaking her back to her senses was to stop coddling the lady.

"You say you want to act again, then do it. Take the Waxler project and forget about Kenrick."

"And forget Carole Wade? That's what Nicky Deane was telling me, Hugh. Work again, and something will happen to this." She touched her face, almost a caress.

"You can't have it both ways. Besides, Kenrick thinks if you take the Waxler film, he has a way to get Deane off our backs." And if he doesn't, I do. Remy left it unsaid. "Hell, woman, you couldn't have a bigger pair of names behind a comeback film."

"With you directing."

"Forget it."

"If I can take a chance, why not you?"

"Because it's not my survival at stake."

"But you're asking me to wager everything on Teddy Kenrick."

"No," Remy said. "I'm asking you to have faith in me."

When she left him to dress, she still hadn't given him an

answer. Now, as Remy paced outside the bedroom door, he couldn't avoid the nature of his own commitment, to Siri, to himself, and prayed he would somewhere find the courage.

When the door opened, he knew she had made her decision. She wore a white dress much like the one that had been her trademark and a smile Remy had seen on film a dozen times.

"It looks like the return of Lady Ice," he remarked.

"Let's say, Siri back among the living."

Kenrick reread the printed dinner invitation from Philippe Brialt and wondered if he would survive.

The past nine days felt like a lifetime. He had always been here at Cannes. The Festival would run forever. He was no longer able to separate his mental fatigue from the physical, and now as he put on his dinner jacket, he could feel the ache of overtaxed muscles. He had pushed his mind and body beyond the point of easy recovery the previous night with Rayna.

After Donner's reading they came back to his hotel. They were wary, both knowing the power of the other to damage. "We have no time for games," Rayna said, coming to him. Later, next to her, the half-light catching the texture of her fine skin, he thought about Anne. He could no longer visualize a single time they had made love, recall the nature of the sensations they had shared.

That night, with Rayna, the past was gone. She listened without remark when he told her that the planned breakaway studio was a fat deception. "Aimed at Robert Arthur. I'm trying to draw him out because I've something to trade him. If it's played right, I take home all the marbles."

"And if it isn't?"

Kenrick replied only, "I should have told you sooner."

"Why are you telling me now?"

The answer came slowly. "Because I don't want it only for myself."

"Careful. You might slip and say something romantic."

He did. But by then, as they made love a second time, it didn't matter. They both knew.

When he met the next night with Larry Rentzler and Aron, he understood that the temptation now, with the payoff so close, was to let down. He forced a confident smile in their direction and finished knotting his black bow tie. "You're the glummest bunch of almost-winners I've ever cast my eyes upon."

"It's the word 'almost,' " Archer said wistfully.

"When this is over, I'll sleep for a week," Rentzler chimed in. "While you both are out guzzling champagne, I still have to put something on paper to satisfy Leo Gold."

"One never satisfies an ogre," Archer said. "They eat and eat and eat. . . ." He was sipping a glass of champagne, the ice bucket within easy reach.

Kenrick had met Gold late that afternoon. Leo's crabbed expression hinted that he had considered the deal to distribute the new studio's films and found things he didn't like. "But I'm going to take it. I want those films of yours so I can build a bigger organization. And I want it because if you fall apart, I am going to steal Ernst Rucker from you. Fair warning."

They agreed on a letter of intent that Rentzler would draw up and that Aron would use with the moneyman, Novotny, as another item in their trading basket.

Archer was saying, "Which leaves us short one well-known blond movie queen."

Kenrick said, "She has Waxler's proposal, and we have Hugh Remy as our advocate. Maybe tonight at Brialt's party."

"She's playing it too cool," Rentzler said, then shrugged as if it didn't matter. Odd. Kenrick marked it.

"When you have all the cards," Archer observed, "you can never play it too cool."

All the cards except the trump—Nicky Deane. Taking

Deane out of the game depended on what happened when Kenrick faced Robert Arthur, when and if. But Kenrick was drawing close.

That morning he had taken a call from a man identifying himself as Chastain. Kenrick knew the name. According to Galloway, Chastain was one of Arthur's high-powered talking chiefs. "You don't know me, Mr. Kenrick," the voice on the telephone said before Kenrick interrupted and told him to make an appointment through Gérard.

"I'm sure you understand my position."

He heard a tight clearing of a throat and the word "but" as he hung up the phone.

No surrogate Arthurs allowed. The man, face to face, or no one.

Archer checked his watch and looked up forlornly. "We're cutting it fine, very fine. I told Novotny I'd call within the hour."

"Then sit tight," Kenrick said, moving for the door.

Archer eyed the champagne bottle and held it up toward the light. It was nearly empty. "Damn," he whispered.

Rentzler rode down with Kenrick and followed him out onto the street. "Okay, Larry, get it off your chest. Before you explode."

"I figured it out. I know what you're doing, Teddy."

"I thought you might."

They headed toward the Carlton, Rentzler trying to stay abreast of him on the crowded sidewalks.

"You're jerking the rug out from under everyone. Aron, Ernst, Sid Mathan."

"People are caught in the middle all the time. They'll survive. Besides, one of our team has already defected back to Stiner. If I pull it off, you have a place. You know that."

"It doesn't matter what happens or doesn't. I'm stepping out."

Kenrick stopped and faced him. "I thought you were the lad who wanted to climb."

"Teddy, what's it worth? So you rise to the point where you can change a life with a phone call. Kenrick's definition of power, remember?"

"You don't have to buy it."

"Do you realize that on behalf of some abstract corporate power play I've lied, snooped, been your fist, and cheated on the best person in my life?" Rentzler glanced away. "Yeah, with that helpless creep Tannis," he said with disgust. "I called Tod this afternoon and confessed. He said if I wanted to get out of the city for a while, trying something on my own, he'd hang in."

"What, raise avocados?"

"Maybe. With a good person along a lot of things can work."

Kenrick envied him the simplicity of his belief.

"Your choice, Larry. It always has been."

"I finally looked around, Teddy. At the Festival, you, and I asked myself what the hell is everyone doing, building tinker toy mountains to have something to climb. You don't hear much laughter on the streets of old Cannes."

"If that's what you want to measure by."

"You're what I measured by, finally. When I took the look at your games, the deceptions, it was easy. I don't want to pass my time on earth the way you have. That's all."

≡ *Chapter 37*—The Taking

The gunman hit them at twenty minutes before eleven in the well-appointed presidential suite of the Hôtel Carlton —seven guests, Philippe Brialt and his beloved Katherine, and a waiter serving the first course of dinner.

It had already been an evening of modest surprise: the handshake between Kenrick and Rod Donner, congratulations for a deal made earlier that day between the actor and a man named Sulten; the sweeping entrance of Siri Laurence on the arm of Hugh Remy, announcing to all that she intended to make a new film, for Teddy Kenrick. The German director Gurd Frederich and his two female stars were unctuously congratulatory, but Frederich, whose film until that moment had been the topic of conversation, took insult at being upstaged and began to pout in his champagne.

While Siri told them all of finding a story that she couldn't say no to, Kenrick retreated to the bedroom, closed the door, and used the telephone.

He called his own number and told Aron Archer, "Siri played our card. Tell Novotny the first project the new company will announce is production of a Paul Waxler film starring Siri Laurence."

"That should nail it shut," Archer said.

"If he balks, offer him another quarter of a point, and tell him we'll pay it offshore."

"My, my."

Kenrick had scarcely hung up when beyond the closed door he heard the crash of breaking crockery and someone scream.

Later he would recall his first thought and regret how

wrong he was. Even as he rushed to the door, he was expecting that Donner's earlier triumphant mood had reverted to form and that he was preparing to throw somebody from the hotel suite window.

He found, instead, a white-jacketed waiter face down on the pale green carpet just inside the room, blood flowing from a rough tear in his right cheek.

Behind the waiter, back to the closed door, stood a darkly handsome young man dressed in tuxedo and black tie. The gun traversed the guests near the dining room table and stopped, aimed directly at Kenrick's chest. All too quick and melodramatic; Kenrick felt no danger at all.

Until the man held up an ugly gray hand grenade.

He pulled the pin with his teeth, spit it out, and grinned at them. Small teeth, Kenrick remembered, yellow and tobacco-stained. "Good evening," the gunman said, separating each syllable. And because, perhaps, he'd exhausted his supply of English, he said "good evening" again.

The man jabbed the pistol toward Brialt. "Have them raise their hands and move against the wall." His glance flicked to the guests. "Tell them if they do what I say, no one will be hurt. One mistake and they all die."

He emphasized the promise by holding the grenade above his head.

Brialt began to protest, trying to place the man's face.

"Tell them!" the man commanded. Brialt relayed his demand in English.

"I don't goddamn believe it," Donner said, his hands rising slowly.

Remy flexed his powerful fists once but followed suit. "I wonder if I could just promise," Siri said then sighed, "oh, hell," and raised her hands. The German director Frederich smiled nervously, certain it was all a joke. All watched the gun moving in slow, sweeping motions, except Katherine, her eyes on the gunman's face.

They had not yet shuffled to the wall when two sharp knocks of authority sounded on the hotel-room door, accompanied by a demand to open up in the name of the police.

Brialt remembered the policeman stationed at the end of the hall, a worthless precaution by the look of things.

At the sound Gaetan Rampa spun and shot once, a small dark hole appearing in the door high enough to have missed anyone beyond.

One of Frederich's actresses gave a startled cry at the gun's report, ear-numbing in the closed room. Beyond the door, silence. The policeman had gone for reinforcements.

The gunman must have reached the same conclusion, for he beckoned to Brialt with the gun.

"I want you to deliver a message to the police before they do something stupid."

"Stop this nonsense," Brialt said, outrage rising in his voice.

The barrel of the pistol slapped across his face, blinding him with pain.

"You're to listen, Monsieur Brialt. Not talk. Not think. You understand." He bent closer. "Tell me you understand."

"I understand."

Gaetan Rampa's glance took in the others, hoping the bullet fired through the door, this small demonstration of force, was accepted in the spirit he intended—a clear warning to all of them. If a moment earlier there had been disbelief, it was gone. So, it appeared, was challenge. Gaetan Rampa had won the first battle easily, but unless he moved quickly, he would lose the second. The police had to know exactly what they were facing lest they charge in under force of arms and compel him to use the grenade on the hostages and the gun on himself. That he was fully prepared to do so gave Gaetan Rampa a decisiveness that had eluded him in the days of planning, of trying to imagine what it would be like.

"Go," he told Brialt. "Tell the police I hold your guests

prisoner. Tell them how I am armed. That is important. I want them to know exactly what my weapons can do. Give me your watch."

It crossed Brialt's mind that this was all there would be. A simple robbery: watches, money, rings. Brialt picked the watch from his wrist, his fingers scarcely able to function.

Gaetan Rampa checked the time, then dropped the watch into his pocket. "You return in one hour and ten minutes—midnight. Alone. I make a request then. Each time I am given what I ask, you will receive something in return." He flicked his head toward the others. "I have many things to exchange."

"I understand."

"Tell the police I do not intend to hurt anyone, if my instructions are followed. If anyone dies, it will be their fault—your fault."

Brialt started to argue, but again the pistol raked his face. Tears flowed into his eyes with a new wave of pain.

"No questions, Monsieur Brialt. Acceptance. Yes?"

"Yes."

"When you return, you will bring three sets of handcuffs."

"Three sets of handcuffs."

"Good." His yellowed smile turned toward the others. "Now, which of you speak French?"

"I do," Katherine said, instantly catching her mistake. Brialt felt his stomach turn over in anguish.

"Well," Gaetan Rampa said, pulling up a chair and inviting the girl to sit, "I have myself an assistant. A very lovely assistant."

With Brialt gone Gaetan Rampa locked the hotel room door and stood listening for any sound beyond.

The next hour would be tricky. Too many people inside the room to control—four women and five men. Given time and a sleepless night, someone would become impatient, make him use the gun. If he could last until morning and it went well with the police, he intended, according to the plan, to reduce the number of hostages without weakening his power to bargain.

The danger was the police would act before they understood his demand. A modest demand, in their interest to accept. Who could want the bad publicity that would come with bloodshed? The press had enormous power to influence the public, and the public their politicians. Even in France the police bent to political pressure. They had discussed it often while they had planned. Make the demand modest, the pressure irresistible, and logic said they must comply. Yet Gaetan Rampa knew with a certainty born of the street that men didn't often act logically. They did things because they were hungry. Or for revenge. Or because they thought you were weak.

He looked up to find himself being watched by the actor, the one with the lined, hard face he had seen at the Palais. Donner. What do you see, ugly? Not fear. Not of an actor. The pale blonde avoided his look. So beautiful. Did she understand his power? That he could ask anything of her. To pull down the straps of her thin dress and show him her breasts. Smiling, he looked at the girl, nearly the equal of the actress in beauty. "You know what I'm thinking?" he asked.

Came the answer: "Yes, I believe I do."

In the other men, not so much fear as before. Anger. Impatience. The impatient one. That would be Kenrick. And the other tall man, older: Remy, like the cognac. He thought about telling the girl to have all the men undress. To wait naked. A humiliating thing that Maxim had used more than once as punishment when Gaetan was a child. He could no longer remember why, only the humiliation. But that, too, could make a man act. No, he would give no one a reason, not these people, not the police.

"Tell them to move farther apart," he instructed the girl. "And to face the wall."

Peter Galloway heard the police before he actually saw them. It was well after midnight, and he had been drinking his way back toward the hotel in a series of nightcaps at each of the watering spots along the Croisette. A civilized country, France, for placing its bars a reasonable walking distance of each other. He hated cities where a man couldn't do his drinking on foot.

He was crossing the road near the Festival Hall, intent on the patchwork of bright lights ahead of him—the Bar Festival still receiving customers—when he heard the rumble of a heavy vehicle, several, in fact. He peered into the darkness, only to be startled by the sound of a horn from the opposite direction.

In time he stepped back onto the curb as the gray buses slid past, nearly grinding him to powder. They turned left onto the Croisette, blue lights revolving, and stopped across the road, disgorging their contents: CRS troops in full battle uniform.

By the time he reached the Carlton the barricades were up, sealing off the entire block from outside traffic, which was sparse enough at that hour. Along the hotel driveway were a half dozen dark automobiles belonging to the local police. Instead of the usual crowds of post-Festival drinkers in the lobby, he saw a sea of blue uniforms, each neatly tailored officer carrying a submachine gun.

"Well . . ." Galloway said, and started up the driveway. His passage was blocked by a truncheon held in the extended arm of a creature that looked extraterrestrial: helmet; goggles; a thick armored vest.

Galloway eased the weapon aside with as much indignity as he dared. Not to fool with these ones. He thrust his press credentials close to the goggles, glad of the ribbons in his lapel and the scarlet, budlike rosette of the Legion of Honor. "I am of the press," he said in English, certainly able to give the man a burst of his own decaying language. He had always found outrage in a foreign language rather baffling to others.

A moment later he found himself in the colonnaded lobby of the hotel, the only man in sight without a uniform.

Inside Suite 624, facing the wall, Hugh Remy tried to view the threat as a mechanical problem, one of forces, angles, and distances, not unlike charting a course in hazardous waters. It was an exercise to occupy the brain, so that he wouldn't think about trying something stupid again; once during those first minutes he had almost gone for the kid and his gun.

Of a cooler mind now he could understand that the gunman's invasion was a last, final outrage, the straw that finally broke Remy's patience. For nearly two weeks he had given in to the will of others. He had come with Siri to Cannes, secretly smug in his role of confidant and protector. Only to discover that he was worth nothing on either count. For days he had felt bettered by forces he couldn't master— Nicky Deane, the bloody French, even manipulation by Kenrick. But here was something else again, something

270

tangible. A punk with a gun and a bomb, within arm's reach. You're a fool, Remy. An old fool, but an angry one. And then he began to separate the elements of the problem, wondering how it might be done.

Despite the gunman's melodramatic pulling of the pin on the hand grenade, Remy knew that in itself it had no effect on the weapon. A pin was a blocking device of the action arm and could be replaced by being pushed back into the slot from which it had been extracted. Release of the action arm, now held tightly in the closed grip of the gunman's hand, was another matter. It would set the chemical fuse alight, after which they might have five or six seconds before detonation. Once the action arm was released there was no stopping the explosion to follow. He'd heard it said that a hand grenade was a poor man-killer. But in the crowded room its metal fragments would wreak havoc with unprotected flesh.

Still, he found himself assessing those in the room who might be allies. One of the German actresses was young and squarely built, with close-cropped hair; she looked hard and muscular and not particularly cowed.

The American girl, Katherine, was closer to the gunman than anyone else. Several times, Remy noticed, the gunman turned his back on her to light a cigarette. But what could she do, or try to do, without help? He counted Siri out, the irony not escaping him for a moment. In this room she was in no more jeopardy than out of it exposed to Nicky Deane. The German director Frederich—a pinkish, soft man—had retreated to the farthest corner, and the waiter had prudently decided to remain on the floor, where he now looked asleep. That left Donner, Kenrick, and himself.

If it came to a fight, Donner could handle himself, but what exactly was in it for him? He had only to wait until the police reacted or the gunman got whatever it was he was after. The publicity that would eventually surround the whole business, skillfully manipulated, wouldn't do his image any harm or his forthcoming film. All Donner need do was sit tight.

Out of the corner of his eye, Remy could see Kenrick, face pressed against the wall, his expression alert. If anyone measured his life in wasted minutes, it was Kenrick. If the rumor about his breakway from the studio was true, then Kenrick was a pivotal figure, and time worth something to him. But what would Kenrick risk? His life?

And with the question Hugh Remy knew he wouldn't risk his own life either. The rage that would have been an ally in attacking the gunman was gone.

Yet, as he turned to face the wall, his eye caught Donner's and held no more than a narrow part of a second. But in that time something passed between them. Reason be damned, the look on Donner's face told him, given the opportunity, he was going to try something. It was an invitation to Remy to join the fun.

≡ *Chapter 39*—The Hour Before Midnight

Brialt again checked the time. The large clock on the wall of the *salon de bridge* continued its tricks, one moment jumping forward toward midnight, eating away the time allotted before his return, only to pause, hands motionless for what seemed an hour. Now again, it had jumped to within ten minutes of the time appointed for his return to the suite, five floors above. Commissaire Pascal had scarcely given him a word in the forty-five minutes since the policeman's arrival, black suit rumpled from the sleep he had been taking on the seat of a police bus.

As a command center the police had taken over the hotel's *salon de bridge*, a large, rectangular room one floor up from the lobby. A half dozen felt-topped tables were now pushed against one wall and stacked with communications gear, their cables snaking across the floor to the windows and looping down to the police trucks parked askew in the hotel service yard. Pascal's orders and requests for information had issued nonstop, all of it premature in Brialt's mind to finding out what, exactly, the gunman wanted.

The first to report was Commandant Haag, erect and cadaverous, his summation delivered with military precision. The streets around the hotel had been sealed off by his CRS troops, and the late-night traffic passing through Golfe Juan to the east and Mandelieu to the west was being routed away from the city.

Inside the hotel, the sixty-four rooms of the top floor were being evacuated. Police now occupied the suites on either side of Brialt's Suite 624, where the hostages were being held, and the one immediately below it on the fifth floor. Additional police, including Charpentier's SOS unit, occupied the sixth-floor hallway, the roof, and the three emergency stairwells. "A fly could not pass through without striking a blue uniform," Haag assured, but Pascal only nodded and continued his orders, plucking them from some mysterious bin in his mind, labeled "hostaging," "Carlton Hotel," "Cannes."

Order: Request the demolition unit from Fort Gazin in nearby Antibes, the command bringing a look of horror from Monsieur Besier, the hotel director.

Order: Make preparations with the hotel engineer to cut the electricity and water to the sixth floor.

Order: Have the hotel switchboard telephone each guest to remain in their rooms until further notice. "We may need to evacuate the entire hotel," Pascal warned Besier.

Brialt managed one brief phone call to the Festival president, rousing him from a sound sleep in his hotel a block away.

After the predictable exclamation of disbelief the president rallied his control. "I'll be right over."

"You are more useful where you are. I mean, by that the telephone. Pascal is mobilizing for a war."

"What can I do?"

"You have friends in the ministry. Use them. I doubt the police will bend to any pressure except from above. If we're to save those people, the reputation of the Festival, Pascal must try to avoid bloodshed, which means negotiate." To hear such concern for the Festival come forth from his own lips was a surprise. Earlier he had told himself that he cared only about the safety of Katherine, even at the sacrifice of the others.

"I'm not sure I have the influence," he heard the president say.

"You know people who do. Remind them what the Festival is to France. If it is to be destroyed by the demands of a terrorist, so be it. But don't let the Festival fail because of the single-mindedness of the police."

"I'll try."

Brialt returned to the *salon de bridge* to find Pascal delivering instructions to Charpentier, dressed now in a dark blue jump suit, crisscrossed with webbing. A heavy automatic pistol was holstered on his belt. With the neatly trimmed black beard lining his square jaw, Charpentier looked efficiently lethal.

To one side Haag watched the proceedings silently, reminding Brialt of a vulture waiting on the fringes of some grisly event for his time to come.

"Please, I go back in five minutes," Brialt said, forcing his voice calm.

Haag spoke to Pascal. "Are we, then, to negotiate with this terrorist?"

"You're not sure yet what he is," Brialt shot back.

"Perhaps a simple country bandit," Charpentier said, flashing a wolfish grin.

"Perhaps. I remembered his face. One of the performers I saw on the street."

Pascal took a notebook from his pocket, flipped back the cover, and jotted something down. Haag's look was cold; he did not take Brialt's opinion willingly.

"He didn't just wander into that room," Brialt said. "Inside, he knew exactly what he was doing."

"That doesn't mean he isn't a terrorist," Haag said.

Charpentier turned to Pascal. "The officer stationed outside the suite said the man presented an invitation, one engraved exactly like the others."

Pascal looked puzzled. "How would he have managed that?" The question was directed at Brialt.

He could answer only with a shrug. "Passes, invitations are stolen all the time, despite our security." In this case

Brialt knew it would have meant stealing from his own desk. "Maybe he bribed someone. You see, he does have a plan. And he spoke to me by name."

Charpentier dismissed it. "If he's seen a newspaper during the last two weeks, he's seen your face plenty."

"But would he have known all the others?"

Pascal was regarding him steadily. Brialt said, "When he looked around, I had the feeling he was checking off people in his mind. As though he knew who would be there. At least let's find out what he wants."

Pascal gave a curt nod of assent. "But tell him to surrender now. Before someone is hurt."

Brialt agreed but knew once inside the room, he would make no demands whatsoever. "What about the handcuffs?"

"And next he'll want weapons," Haag said.

"He has nine hostages," Brialt countered. "Surely he doesn't intend to hold nine people with three sets of handcuffs."

Haag turned angrily toward Pascal. "May I be recorded as being against any of this?"

"You may," Pascal said mildly, nodding toward Brialt to continue.

"He said he would give us something in return at each stage. He means people. We're exchanging handcuffs for hostages. Isn't that worth it?"

Without saying anything, Charpentier loosed a pair of handcuffs from his web belt and put them on the felt table-top. It was a silent vote cast in favor of Brialt.

Pascal took a long moment, seeming to have great trouble making his own decision. Finally, he sighed and asked one of his adjutants for handcuffs.

"One mistake . . ." Pascal began.

But Brialt had already taken the handcuffs and, glancing one final time at the clock on the wall, headed for the elevator.

With Pascal and Charpentier close behind, Brialt reached the fifth floor by elevator, then used the emergency stairs to the sixth. In the slightly more than one hour since he had left his suite, the top floor of the Carlton had become an armed camp. Men armed with submachine guns clustered near the top of the stairwell. In the hallway the bomb expert sat on what appeared to be a padded trash bin wrapped with heavy wire mesh, an apparatus, Brialt realized, to contain the grenade, given the chance. In the suite next to 624 were two other policemen, one listening at the wall with no more sophisticated device than a doctor's stethoscope. At their approach one of the men shook his head at Pascal.

"You're sure about going back in, Brialt? I'll report you willingly volunteered."

"No, I am not sure," Brialt retorted angrily. "Nor do I wish to be reported as a volunteer or otherwise. He has chosen me as his messenger. What choice do I have?"

"If there is trouble . . ." Pascal said, but it wasn't necessary to finish. Brialt could well imagine: policemen; guns blazing; crashing through the door to the rescue. Brialt left them, the noise along the hall falling silent as he approached the door of the suite. He knocked once and heard the gunman tell him to enter slowly.

At sight of him Katherine rose from a chair. Seated on the thick carpeting facing the wall were Kenrick, Donner, Siri, and Hugh Remy, several meters separating them. In the corner the plumpish director, Frederich, faced the wall like a child being punished. Next to him were his two girls; the waiter was still prone on the floor.

The gunman took the handcuffs from Brialt and put them on the table. "Tell me what the police are doing. Every detail."

Brialt described what he had seen. "They want you to surrender . . ."

"Of course, they want me to surrender."

". . . before something happens." He pointedly looked toward the grenade in the gunman's hand. "They think you might be a terrorist. I told them I didn't believe so."

"Yes, that's it, I'm a terrorist."

"I wouldn't joke. The word 'terrorist' makes the police crazy." The gunman considered it soberly, then shrugged and turned away. "Better if you told me what you want," Brialt said.

"Coffee," the gunman said. "Some coffee and croissants for everyone. And for me two million Swiss francs."

Near the wall Donner was trying to follow the conversation between the two men, although he understood none of what was said. He felt foolish. A grown man forced to play this kid's game. It angered him, but later he concluded, what the hell. Do nothing, sit tight, and let it all roll past. He had come into this room two hours before with things as close to being made as they had ever been in his life. He didn't intend to let a tiny bruise on his ego scupper the play of a lifetime. Sit tight. He just prayed the kid would stay away from him.

"Not so much money for so many people, do you think?" the gunman was saying.

"You weren't joking," Brialt said.

"I don't joke. When I say something, don't think I joke. Better for everyone."

Brialt made a rough calculation. Two million Swiss francs—more than five million French francs, more than a million U.S. dollars. He was struck with a sudden thought: Who paid such ransoms? Who exactly signed a check and itemized their expenditure "ransom for a hostaging"? The government? The Festival and the city of Cannes combined didn't have that kind of money. Brialt had never considered the logistics before. Had the gunman? As if in answer, the gunman put the pin back into the grenade and placed it carelessly next to the handcuffs. He took a folded slip of paper from his pocket and began to read aloud.

"When the money is ready, I will give you other instructions. I don't want the money here. I don't want cash. Understand?"

"What do you want?" Brialt no longer felt frightened. The gunman saw him as an ally, a part of his team.

"I want the money waiting in a bank. It will be sent by"—and here he paused, making sure each word was right—"by interbank transfer. You understand?"

"Yes, I think so. But I don't know how long it will take."

The gunman provided an answer. "Two days, if everyone cooperates."

"But where am I to find the money?"

"That, my friend, is not my concern. Two days. As an act of good faith I release some hostages. If my health remains good, I feel things are okay, I'll send you healthy people. *Ça va?* When the money is ready to send, I give you more instructions. Until tomorrow noon, then."

"You want me to come back at noon?"

"I just told you that."

"I don't want a misunderstanding. Any mistake because someone wasn't sure what was said."

His smile showed grainy teeth. "Very smart, Monsieur Brialt. When you leave, take him with you."

The gunman jigged his head toward the waiter. Brialt wanted to say, "No, let it be the girl," but instead he said, "How often will you let people go?"

"When it pleases me. Tell the police I will telephone when I let someone out, so they don't shoot. They want very badly to shoot, I think."

"Yes, I suppose they do."

"Then be very careful when you leave." The gunman grinned at him.

When Brialt was gone, Gaetan Rampa told the girl to tell the others what had been said.

She told them about the request for food and that he was asking a ransom for their release.

"He's about a year too early," Donner said. "I'd have to collect beer bottles to raise a bus fare." His laughter pierced the air, bringing an angry scowl to Gaetan Rampa's face.

"What does he say?" he demanded of Katherine. "Why does he laugh?"

"He is laughing because he doesn't have any money. He says he is worth nothing."

"And that makes him laugh?"

Katherine shrugged. "Americans have a strange sense of humor. Don't take his laughter personally."

"Tell him to shut up."

Katherine relayed Gaetan's command. Kenrick saw Donner start to speak and raised his voice to intercept him. "Not worth it, Rod."

"You're right. Absolutely right." Donner looked away. His neck was crimson with anger.

"At least we know," Siri said, casting a look toward Hugh Remy. "The pack of us have climbed on an auction block."

$\equiv$ *Chapter 41*—Conundrum

"Two million Swiss francs within two days."

Pascal accepted Brialt's report silently, pacing the *salon de bridge*, smoothing the lapels of his rumpled black suit. Brialt took a glass of cognac from the hotel director, Besier, downed it, and had his glass refilled. His heart was still pounding. Once he was outside the hotel room door the calm with which he had faced the gunman drained away, and he almost vomited in terror.

With the warmth of the cognac lifting his spirits, he went on to tell Pascal about the gunman's intention to release some hostages and the details of his request for the money, particularly the interbank transfer.

Nearby, Commandant Haag had assumed his de Gaulle-like posture, hands clasped behind his back.

"That's where they're beaten, this kind of scum," Haag observed. "Getting their hands on the money."

Pascal said, "Obviously he intends to transfer the money out of our reach, in some manner that lets him escape before we can close the gate. Well thought out—for a *performeur des rues*."

"He must have accomplices then," Brialt said. Haag's bland expression made his deduction sound like words from an idiot.

"Of course, others are involved. But we have him," Haag said, pointing upward, in what sounded like a vow.

Pascal circled the room, his ordinarily bland expression decidedly troubled. "Let's see what the night brings." He didn't sound hopeful at all.

Twice between 1:00 A.M. and 3:00 Pascal spoke to the director of the Sûreté in Paris by telephone. The director's voice was thick and sleep-ridden, but Pascal's report of what had happened cleared his mind quickly enough. "What action has been taken?" Pascal told him, omitting no essential detail. "You think he's a terrorist?" It was the first time the director had asked his opinion.

"No, a businessman, demanding two million Swiss francs."

Pascal thought he heard a sigh. The director said he would ring back.

Within an hour lights would be burning in the Ministry of the Interior while a dozen deskbound analysts argued lines of action consistent with government policy and the likely repercussions of each. Pascal would have preferred a good local throat slitting to an affair that touched government policy.

He remembered the roar of disapproval from the hardliners when the Austrians had given in to terrorists the previous year and their anger at the Italians' continued willingness to cough up ransom money. Any good cost accountant would have advised the government to pay, pointing to the hefty figure it would spend each day keeping the police on emergency status. Pascal had planned to argue the cost factor himself, knowing it to be a more salable argument in a bureaucrat's eye than humanitarian grounds—if he had been asked.

The director called back a little before three. He had by then talked with the minister and the minister with the president. Pascal wasn't surprised when the director said, "We're not paying."

A little before five Brialt caught up with Charpentier in the hotel lobby.

The room now looked like a staging area for an invasion. Pascal had ordered the hotel evacuated, and guests in every variety of dress from evening wear to pajamas and robes were being ushered from the hotel by men in uniform onto tan city buses. All around was the visible paraphernalia of combat. Helmets, weaponry incongruent to Brialt's eyes with the make-believe melodrama staring down at them from the film posters that lined every wall.

One look at the policemen and their guns, ready to answer his first mistake, would have convinced the gunman to give up his scheme or face the end. And anyone else's caught on the periphery.

Brialt found the black-bearded policeman near a large stainless coffee dispenser leaking darkish liquid over the hotel's marble floors. "I must know what to expect, what Pascal is planning. I have the right, Charpentier."

He thought with Charpentier's earlier support in his request for handcuffs that he had established a rapport. He was mistaken. At his request the policeman's eyes dulled with standard-issue secrecy.

"Depends on the gunman. Better if he surrendered." It was a parroting of Pascal's earlier remark.

Brialt wouldn't give up. "Surely something is likely? Some plan?"

Simultaneously they became aware of a big red-faced man nearby, peering at them through the thick lenses of heavy glasses. A florid English face, but curiously, the scarlet rosette of the Legion of Honor worn in his lapel.

Charpentier refilled his coffee cup and piloted Brialt deeper into the lobby.

"It can be played several ways. Haag's choice would be a helicopter hovering close to the window, a diversion. Then tear gas and my men given the honor of storming the room."

"Guns blazing."

"Most likely. Chances are the gunman would be taken out quickly."

"With no guarantee of the others' safety."

"I'd guarantee nothing. Only that by daylight it would be finished, things cleaned up, and a newspaper headline that a gunman had been killed in a Cannes hotel. We'd have a quick end to the business, and you a Festival scarcely the wiser."

"So much for Haag's preference. What about Pascal?"

"If he had his way—"

"What do you mean, if?"

"We're under the political eye now. I think Pascal would prefer the passive approach. The British method, if you will. Offer no direct confrontation. Let hostage and gunman alike sit and stew, learn to care about each other in their shared adversity." Charpentier gave him a wolf's grin. "Two weeks, three . . ."

"Oh, my God."

". . . but the Croisette isn't as easily managed as some dark *quartier* in Paris. Too visible."

"Why not pay the money and let the man go?"

Charpentier worked an index finger along the side of his nose, thoughtfully. "They don't intend to pay. If you tell Pascal you heard it from me, I'll deny it."

"But what choice does that leave Pascal?"

"One that has a quick ending, loses no lives, costs nothing, satisfies the public, and falls within the strictures of government policy—once they decide upon one." Charpentier made a rude noise.

"But that's impossible!"

"Not impossible," Charpentier said. "About like finding a bright orange elephant that flies backward—at the speed of sound."

The sound of the telephone pulled Rayna Tate from a deep but dream-tossed sleep.

That bastard. Now he calls. And *now* he can damn well sweat. She swung her feet out of bed to move groggily toward the insistent telephone.

There had been no arrangement between her and Kenrick to be together the previous evening. Yet, following his appearance at Brialt's dinner, she knew they would find themselves in each other's company—not really by chance, as the lyrics went. She called his hotel late and heard the phone ring to an empty room. At 2:00 A.M. she reluctantly took a Valium. Her last thought before falling off into a deep, drugged sleep was: The hell with that.

She answered the telephone, half expecting to hear Kenrick's voice and words that would wipe away the anger. Instead, there was the strident voice of Gladys Sulten, something about a shower and borrowing things to wear.

"Sorry, Gladys, try again. A bad night."

"Well, I have one to top it. Never in my life. I need a hot tub and a good stiff drink, and Lou says he could use the same, and you know he never touches it before sundown."

A buzz rising in pitch beyond the windows changed into the pulsing roar of an engine. A helicopter climbed suddenly over the ridge crest behind the villa on a course for the city. Concentric circles of color on its underbelly marked it as military.

"Gladys, where are you? What's going on?"

"That's what I've been telling you. We've been evicted.

Five o'clock this morning they evacuated the hotel. Walking around practically in our pajamas. Could we just grab a cab up?"

"Of course. But why evacuate the hotel?"

"You haven't heard? I thought the whole city was out there in the street."

"Gladys, stop talking and say something!" Irritation flooded her voice.

A wounded silence, before: "Don't be nasty, darling." Her tone was poisonous now. "We can make other arrangements, really we can."

"Of course you can, but you needn't. Come on up. The water's fine, the whiskey neat, et cetera."

Soothed, Gladys delivered her bit of information. "There's been a holdup or something. No, Lou says a kidnapping. Police all over the hotel. Apparently, there are some people being held hostage at gunpoint in one of the suites. . . ."

Rayna Tate let the telephone drop and ran for her clothing.

A little before 10:00 A.M. Brialt addressed the Festival staff, fifty people filling Durand's spacious office on the third floor of the Festival Hall. Police were at the door to keep out the mob of press.

"The first rumor I wish to dispel is that the Festival is closing down. I have already spoken to the jury, and they agree. We will continue, even if it means screening films on a hotel-room wall. I do not expect you to pretend nothing has happened. I do expect you to carry on your work."

His glance swept the room for signs of rebellion. He saw none, giving these people his silent thanks. He wouldn't have had the patience for calm debate.

"As to the business at the Carlton," he began, keeping his voice void of emotion, "a little before eleven last night, a gunman forced his way into my suite. His demand is two million Swiss francs, in return for the safety of all concerned. By accident or not, I was chosen as his spokesman and delivered his request to the police."

Poeget, the head of his press section, called out, "Who is in the room? I've heard everyone from Siri Laurence to the Niarchos brothers."

"I'm coming to that," Brialt said. "During the night he released three hostages and a waiter, in exchange for food and a large color TV set." The remark brought a short-lived snicker from the gathering. "He seems to have a plan and, for the moment, controls the situation."

"He still has five people then," Poeget said, pursuing the details with ghoulish delight.

"Yes, five. Siri Laurence and her escort, a former colleague of her husband. Rod Donner, the actor. A studio executive named Kenrick. And one of our own people. . . . Katherine." Miraculously he retained control of his voice. "Any change and you will be told, and told the truth. Until then Durand is in charge. I'm afraid I must tend to other things."

He left them with Durand and returned to his office.

But even there he was deprived of the few moments of privacy he desperately needed to resummon his courage. For, waiting by the window, watching the distant crowds gathered in front of the hotel, was his wife, Monique.

The taxi brought Rayna Tate no closer to the Hôtel Carlton than the top of the rue d'Antibes, three blocks away. There a barricade sealed off the street, and a white-gloved policeman was signaling automobile traffic onto the *rapide*, circling away around the city.

She paid the taxi driver and went on foot, taking the narrow streets that patterned the neighborhood behind the oceanfront hotels. A block from the Carlton, she came to the crowds, a wall of humanity pressed against police barriers. She skirted them, took a stairway to the narrow beach, and followed it until she reached Carlton Plage before climbing again to the Croisette.

The mob was even thicker, backed by a row of photographers, some standing on the sea wall with long telephoto lenses pointing skyward toward one corner of the hotel. She elbowed forward, only to have her progress barred by a policeman.

She spun and tried to edge past a man who had closed in behind her.

"You speak English," he said. His voice rough, East Coast American. His large, lovely eyes had a coldness in them that seemed threatening.

"I don't have time," Rayna said, but the man stayed with her.

"What are these creeps waiting for? What's going on?"

"Look, I don't know. I'm trying to find out. Some trouble in the hotel."

"Creeps," the man said, face upturned toward the hotel.

She went in the opposite direction, looking for enough space to slip through the barriers. She saw him, then, Galloway, pushing belligerently through the crowd directly toward one of the policemen. The officer saw him coming and slid the barrier aside.

She caught Galloway by the arm a yard short, in a desperate lunge, heedless of the people around her. His gray disks of eyes looked startled, then curious. "Sorry," he said. He couldn't place her.

"Tate," she said, and watched Galloway struggle with his memory.

"Ah, yes. The rain in Spain. Liza of Madras."

"Galloway, what's happened?"

"Haven't time, dear lady. Story of a bloody wasted career, and for once Galloway has all the bits."

"Is Kenrick involved?" Her chance was to keep Galloway talking, keep him from crossing through the barricades.

"Involved! Linchpin of the whole business. Delicious stuff, every bloody facet." Galloway bent forward, the smell of rancid alcohol making her stomach heave. "A financial coup under way involving who knows how many millions. And along comes this thug to bugger the whole business with his demand for a measly million. If he'd known whom to threaten, he could have stayed home and read the newspaper."

"What are you talking about? Kenrick's breakaway?"

"Something bigger's afoot. Or was. Can't happen now with Kenrick locked in up there." Galloway flapped a hand toward the hotel roof.

"Brialt's suite," she whispered. "Donner, too?"

Galloway's nod was vacant. "Donner, Siri Laurence, and a girl who works for the Festival. Began with eleven hostages about midnight and just let Hugh Remy out a half hour ago—in exchange for two rolls of adhesive tape and a large ball of string." Something made Galloway smile. "If that puzzles you, imagine the trouble it's giving the police."

"What are the police doing to get them out?"

"Read all about it," he gurgled, and swayed around toward the barrier. "Must get back before the bloodshed."

The strange lightness of the remark triggered her. "We're all a joke, aren't we, Galloway, we unfortunates born without the breeding that keeps you from really giving a damn."

Galloway whirled on her. "You don't know. Not a joke at all. An example of everything I hate in the human race. Greed and ego and stupidity. I say bloodshed because that is exactly how it will end if the police continue their game."

"Game?"

"A decision at the top. They aren't going to pay. They'll get what they can from that man up there. Promise anything, but give nothing because in their style it would be a sign of weakness. Awful." He looked away toward the hotel.

"Can't someone equate five people's lives with a sackful of money?"

"This isn't business, dear lady. It is politics."

"Galloway, take me in with you."

"You'll get in the way."

Rayna said quickly, "What if I can tell you something you don't know? Something to fit this great story of yours like a glove?"

She was talking now, without thinking, letting the words tumble out and unsure what she could tell him that he might not know. Anything to keep Galloway from escaping. "Things about Kenrick," she tried. Galloway was waiting, eyes calculating through the thick lenses.

"This breakaway of his," she said. "What if I had proof it was all a deception? A fake. A nice, first-person revelation and some good quotes."

"Deception," Galloway said, looking baffled.

"Interest you?"

"In exchange for . . . ?"

"Take me inside. I have an idea that may help those people."

Galloway made his decision and took her by the arm. "Stay close," he said. "And be brazen."

In the quiet of his office Philippe Brialt told his wife everything about himself and Katherine. In the distance, above the hotel, a helicopter hovered like some dark green dragonfly.

He spared her nothing, used none of the bland language he had spent his life hiding behind.

Brialt had always feared Monique's angers, her ingenious tactics of reprisal for even imagined slights. He was no longer afraid, not exactly. If only she would cut loose. Monique had an air of threatening calmness. "Yes, I thought it might be something like that," she said when he finished.

"If you don't let me have a divorce, we'll be together in any case." If she survives, he thought with a sudden shudder.

"She loves you madly then."

Monique had turned to the window. He couldn't see her face but had the impression she was smiling. "Katherine has shown me the terrible limits we put on feelings by words, Monique. Like trying to fence in something growing, changing each minute."

"You sound love-struck, like one of those young people who express themselves by signals and grunts."

"But perhaps communicate more honestly than we have."

"*Merde*," she said, whirling toward him. "You have a poor memory, Philippe." Her hand waved toward the door. "Go save your princess. Whisk her to your desert isle. Or is it castle? Or more simply to bed. You'll manage nicely—for a while. And I will manage better."

"Good-bye—I'm sorry."

"Sorry, *merde*. And we'll see if it's good-bye."

But Brialt felt himself unable to leave it like that, so short. Again Monique looked away. Morning sunlight caught her soft brown hair, finding the gold and reds that he had forgotten about. He felt a sudden rush of desire pour into his thighs and groin. Intellectually he told himself that mental stress often manifested itself in physical desire. But never more than this moment did he want to lose himself in the hot, yielding wetness of his wife's body. When he took a step toward her, she turned as though expecting it. She could feel his desire, as telepathic as it had once been. He knew he was going to take her there, standing if he must, against the wall or the window, he didn't care. And in the instant he reached out, a knock, hard and abrasive, sounded on his office door.

The door opened without invitation, the glance of a policeman taking in all. His announcement came in two short, breathless bursts. "Inside the hotel room . . . someone's been shot."

Speaking slowly into the telephone, Gaetan Rampa told the police he would release another hostage when they brought him some bottled water.

There were four now—Donner, Kenrick, and the two women, Siri and Katherine. According to plan, the actor Donner was next.

He hung up the telephone and pointed.

"You, ugly. Stand up."

"I bet he's talking to me," Donner said.

"I said stand up."

The girl translated.

"I like it here." Donner's grin toward the gunman was sugar-sweet.

"Oh, Christ," Siri said. She had thought about so many things here. If only they all would be set free without anything happening, she felt that one day she might look upon this business as a disguised blessing. She had come to realize that everyone was dependent, each one of them here—Donner and Kenrick no less than herself. They needed friends to help them, just as, in the past, she had needed people—Pedro, Hugh Remy, even, long ago, Nicky Deane. For too long she had fought the element of need within herself, but she understood now: It was her nature. It was normal, and it was silly to punish herself because there had always been people in her life willing to help. Just as there were people now, working somewhere, to free them.

But something in Donner's reply said he intended to spoil everything.

Thankfully the others sensed it, too. The girl Katherine said, "Please don't be stubborn. He asked the police to send us some bottled water. When they do, I think he intends to let you go."

"Why didn't he say so?" Donner said, climbing to his feet, with a grin.

Gaetan Rampa gestured to the handcuffs on the table.

"Tell him to put those on the others."

When the girl translated, Donner said, "Sure, anything he wants." It was amiable, too amiable. Kenrick felt he was watching an old Donner movie, the big, smiling stranger with the simple grin and a streak of quick violence buried about an inch deep. The gunman still gripped his pistol, but the hand grenade was on the table with the three sets of handcuffs.

Kenrick didn't know what Donner's plan was. He knew only that he had one.

"Forget it, Donner," he said across the room. "Handcuffs, no handcuffs. When the money is raised, the rest of us walk out. And you walk out now."

"I've been thinking about that," Donner replied, watching the man with the gun. Not watching, really. Measuring distance, estimating reaction time. "When I was growing up, old Merle used to make a lot of wind with his mouth. But every once in a while he'd open it, and something good would fall out despite himself."

"Forget it," Kenrick replied.

"And once I remember him saying that maybe it's the things you do when you don't have to that measure a man."

"Donner, not now, darling," Siri said.

Gaetan Rampa told the girl, "Tell them to stop talking."

"Listen to me," Kenrick said, speaking low and fast. "Save it for a Durango bar or a good drunken run along Sunset Boulevard. Think what you're blowing." He wasn't sure Donner heard him or if anyone else could guess the direction Donner's mind was working. The girl, Katherine, watched Donner, puzzled.

"Tell ugly to take the handcuffs," Gaetan Rampa said. He had sensed the odd nature of the exchange, saw the defiance on the face of the ugly one. He tried to anticipate what was coming.

The girl told him to do nothing rash, but the gunman ignored her. He walked to the table and threw one set of handcuffs to Donner, gesturing to Kenrick. "Put them on him."

"Come on, Rod," Kenrick said, turning his back to make it easy. "Clap me in irons, and get the hell out."

"You're right, Teddy," Donner said, giving a heavy, defeated sigh. "Maybe that's why you're no fun. You're always right."

He pulled Kenrick's arm behind his back. Sharp steel bit into his left wrist. But the second manacle encircled his right fist instead of his arm, leaving him to slip free at will. He heard Donner's low whisper, "Hang loose."

Right then Kenrick should have held his right hand above his head, showing Donner's error. The gunman was observing them from near the table eight, ten feet away, something withdrawn behind the eyes. The pistol was hanging loosely at his side, the hand grenade within arm's reach.

"Now her," he said, pointing to Siri. Donner started forward to get the second pair of cuffs, but the gunman picked them from the table and made a toss.

Then he reached out for the grenade, testing its weight in his hand.

"Ah, Siri girl, would that I had this pleasure years ago." Donner pulled her arms around and snapped on the cuffs. "Now who? Our little lady Katherine?"

"Tell him to turn around," Gaetan Rampa told the girl.

"What are you going to do?" she asked.

"Tell him."

"Handcuffs for me?" Donner said, wide-eyed.

But Kenrick reckoned Donner had seen it, too. Whatever fun the gunman intended to have after he put handcuffs on Donner, to do so meant giving up either the gun or the grenade. That or grow another set of hands.

Vacillating a moment, the gunman finally placed the grenade on the table. Then he thumbed back the hammer of the pistol, picked up the handcuffs, and walked toward Donner.

Donner gave Kenrick a bare flick of his eyes. Each step took the gunman farther away from the table and the grenade.

"Turn around, ugly," said Gaetan Rampa. Donner didn't appear to comprehend. "Turn around, hands behind you."

Donner followed orders. "Like this?"

Kenrick was a good ten feet to the gunman's left now and about the same distance from the table. It was too late for a change of mind. Donner had drawn him into his forthcoming attempt against his will, but to deny him his help would mean worse for them all. By his proximity Donner was accepting the gunman as his target, the gunman and the gun. The grenade on the table was Kenrick's job. He judged he might do Donner's plan one better. If he made his break an instant before the gunman reached Donner, he would draw his attention. He had seen Donner move, knew his unbelievable quickness for a big man. Kenrick was about to do something he once doubted possible. He was about to trust his life to Rod Donner.

He would think about it later. That and the thing he hadn't thought enough about: the speed of the kid with the gun.

In the Carlton elevator Brialt was conscious of his full-sized reflection in the mirror facing him. Tired, flushed with lust, looking confused and foolish. "What happened?" he asked.

The policeman who had come for him diplomatically averted his eyes. "He telephoned out and said he'd release another hostage in exchange for some bottled water. We were waiting for the hostage when we heard a scream and two shots. About three minutes later he called again and asked for you."

The elevator opened on what might have been a football club locker room. The smell of sweat and tobacco, the hall jammed with men. Brialt pushed through to where Charpentier and six men were donning armored vests under Pascal's eyes.

Pascal spoke without greeting. "I'm giving you five minutes in the room. As much as a raised voice, and these men go in. If the time passes and you don't return. . . ."

"We go in anyway," Charpentier said.

"But what am I supposed to do?"

Pascal and Charpentier exchanged a meaningful glance. "See what's happened, what he wants," Pascal said. There was a heavy silence before Pascal reached out and drew Brialt closer. "You were once military, weren't you, Philippe?"

It was the use of his given name that put Brialt on guard. *"Service obligatoire.* Nearly thirty years ago."

Pascal sighed, hesitating. In the void Charpentier spoke. "Can you use a gun?"

"I don't know. I mean, I'm not sure. Why?"

Again a glance between Pascal and Charpentier.

"Speak up," Brialt demanded.

"We have an idea," Charpentier said. "He hasn't searched you, has he? Each time you've gone back in."

"No."

"If you were to carry a gun. Perhaps you'd have a chance."

He was slow to grasp it. "You mean, shoot him. Try to kill the man."

"That's what he means," Pascal said. "You know best, Philippe. Whether you have the knowledge. More important, the will."

"But I *don't* know." He thought of Katherine and the others in the room.

Charpentier produced a small revolver. "Five shots. Nothing to think about except getting close and pulling the trigger. Middle of the chest. Better the face if you could do it."

Brialt felt his stomach contract.

"Have you ever shot a pistol before?" Charpentier asked. It might have been "ridden a bicycle" or "eaten ice cream."

"I told you. Military service. A hundred, two hundred rounds, thirty years ago."

"It's your choice," Pascal said uncomfortably. Then he turned and walked away, hands clasped behind his back.

"Never mind," Charpentier said, nodding after Pascal. "He said it was too much to ask." He cocked his own automatic and locked on the safety. "Now, if we come into the room, protect yourself. Tell the others to lie on the floor. It will be messy."

"I see," Brialt said, loathing all of them, their tricks. "I'll take the pistol."

Charpentier clipped him on the arm, grinning confidently. "Good man. Remember—the chest or the face."

As he was about to set off, Pascal held him back, studying

him intensely. "I want you to listen, Philippe. Use the pistol only if you are sure. If you do, use it quickly, without hesitation."

"And if I can't?"

"There are other ways. Tell him we're gathering the money and it will be ready in a few hours."

"But that's a lie."

"Yes, I know," Pascal said. But he shrugged and again turned away.

In not quite twelve hours the interior of the room had changed more radically than the hall outside: dirty plates; bits of food littering the floor near an upturned service carriage. Broken glasses; odors human and chemical. In one corner a large color TV set was on without sound, the flat white façade of the Carlton in clear focus, as viewed by a camera from below.

In front of the door, furniture had been stacked into a rough barricade. Let Charpentier's men crash through the door, and the barricade would slow their entrance, only a few seconds perhaps, but how long did it take to squeeze a trigger?

Using Siri as a shield, the gunman was waiting behind the door when Brialt entered. "Be quick," the man hissed, and kicked the door shut behind him.

"They said there was shooting."

"Stupid," the gunman said, pressing his weapon against the nape of Siri's neck. Her hands were cuffed behind her. She mouthed the name Donner.

He was lying behind the barricade of furniture, his right hand crudely tied to a metal radiator, his left free to caress his midsection. The fingers were crusted with blood.

Kenrick was next to him, on the floor, handcuffed. Katherine rose from Donner's side and shook her head. "I couldn't help it," she said. "I'm sorry."

"It's done," Kenrick said. His look toward Katherine was

anger-filled, and Brialt wondered what exactly had happened.

Kenrick wasn't sure himself. Not of the exact sequence, the split seconds gone wrong that had beaten their try at the kid. Kenrick had started for the grenade, the gunman with his handcuffs approaching Donner and giving Kenrick just enough blindside to be no more than a blur on the periphery of his vision. He was sure he had taken only a step when the girl screamed. God, if she had kept her mouth shut even another instant, let the kid move closer to Donner. But in the center of the room he whirled at the sound, the pistol swinging toward Kenrick. There wasn't a chance to reach the hand grenade on the table, and Kenrick had plunged forward, expecting the shot that had to follow. In that fraction of a second Donner made his move.

He must have known there was still too much space to cover between him and the kid, but he made his try and in doing so saved Kenrick from a bullet. For Kenrick had seen the pistol come up, the slash of brownish teeth in an arrogant grin, as if the gunman had proved what he had known all along: These two were no match for him, and he would punish them for the challenge.

As Donner lunged, a grunt of focused energy deep in his throat, the gunman took an agile step sidewise, spun, and shot Donner once in the stomach. He was still six feet away, coming low and fast, but the bullet must have channeled its way to something vital because the thrust went out of Donner's legs, and he dropped to one knee. He was trying to come back up, to finish what he'd begun, when the gunman shot him again.

"Tell him we need a doctor," Kenrick said to Brialt.

Brialt spoke to the gunman. He looked unsteady now for the first time, the bravado gone. Brialt could feel the pressure of the small pistol tucked in the waistband of his trousers, his jacket buttoned over it.

"We don't have much time. They'll break in if I'm not

back in several minutes. . . . We'll have to get him to a doctor."

"No doctor," Gaetan Rampa said.

"It won't help you if he dies."

"When I get the money, he gets the doctor."

"It takes time. They're gathering it."

"No doctor, and no more lies." The gunman extracted Brialt's watch from his pocket. "I give you three more hours."

"And what if three hours isn't enough?"

"I begin sending out hostages again."

Brialt wasn't sure he had heard correctly. "You'll begin sending people out?"

Gaetan Rampa drew a long knife from his pocket and snapped it open one-handed. He took a fistful of Siri's hair and sliced through it, sprinkling the endings onto the carpet. "I send people out," he repeated. "One little part at a time."

Back in the hall, Brialt reported it to Pascal. "The gun. I didn't have a chance."

It was true, they must understand.

But he saw Charpentier, farther along the corridor, turn and spit derisively onto the thick gray carpet.

"You got to be kidding," Mal Stiner said. He poured himself another tonic water and turned to ponder the ocean beyond his bungalow windows.

"About this I wouldn't kid," Rayna Tate said.

It required all her concentration to forget the level of Dante's hell she had left less than an hour before, to prevent herself from insulting the three men gathered in Mal Stiner's bungalow. "Corporate imbeciles" would be only openers.

"You want me to come up with a million Swiss francs to spring a guy who will then turn around and try to bury me?" He took a taste of his drink and let his eyes settle on the region slightly below her neck. "You're an attractive, intelligent woman, Miss Tate. I admire your appeal on Kenrick's behalf. But in terms of practical politics, it won't wash."

The other two men in the room—Lou Sulten and Aron Archer—made hums of concern, rising periodically to refill their drinks.

At the Carlton, Galloway had become an unexpected ally, hearing out her idea of trying to raise the ransom money from people with a financial interest in the hostages. "It's a better chance than trying to convince some French bureaucrat in Paris by telephone to reach into the treasury." They had found a willing advocate in Philippe Brialt.

"It's not just for Kenrick," she explained, trying to keep her voice calm. "There's still no guarantee the French police will accept the idea. Brialt thinks they may if they can avoid making it look like the government appeasing a gunman."

"I wouldn't have imagined doublethink difficult for a

bureaucrat," Archer said. He was sipping vodka over ice, his third since she had arrived.

"Hell, Mal," Lou Sulten croaked, "look at the gamble I'm taking. Putting up six hundred thou to spring maybe a corpse."

Sulten's callous reference to Donner made her teeth come together, biting off the words "cock . . . sucker." Sulten saw putting up half the ransom money as nothing more than a way to insure a deal. She wouldn't let herself think of Brialt's description of the hotel suite, of Donner on the floor, powerless to help himself. The probability that he had brought it upon himself only made her pain more acute.

Stiner studied her, one hand touching an iron gray sideburn. She knew that look. "Aaron, how long to get that kind of money transferred from New York to this Geneva bank?"

"Normally a half day to arrange on our side, with a value date—the time when they can collect—forty-eight hours from the date of the transaction. Say, three days in all." He cocked a suspicious eyebrow toward Lou Sulten.

Sulten's hands went up in defense. "Anybody starts asking where my half of the money is coming from, forget it, the deal's off."

It confirmed Archer's private opinion. Sulten had cash squirreled away offshore the U.S. government didn't know about. He had gone for the Donner project because the foreign settings allowed him to use offshore money to make the film, while taking credits and profits clean and pure at home. Sulten hadn't been giving Donner any gifts.

"There's your answer," Stiner said to Rayna. "Three days."

"I said, normally," Archer added emphatically. "I can likely arrange to have funds available by bank opening tomorrow. Provided I get a couple of calls through. I happen to know somebody who would love to have some dollars available—"

Stiner interrupted. "I don't need a lesson in international banking. . . ."

"Then give me an authorization and two hours on the phone." Archer's warning came to Rayna. "And make sure your instructions are right."

"Your decision, Mal," Sulten said.

Stiner probed at his squarish jaw, a picture of a man with mental cogs turning.

Rayna said, "If it helps your decision, I'll tell you one thing. Turn away from this, and I'll make sure everyone you do business with knows what happened in this room today. If anyone dies because Mal Stiner didn't think it was worth six hundred thousand dollars, you may still do the business. But people will know you stink."

"You have a nice, clear way of putting things, Miss Tate." He took a pause, brows rumpled. Then he looked at Aron Archer and said, "Go!"

"What a marvelous piece of theater," Aron Archer said, exactly forty minutes and two telephone calls later. He reached for his glass. He and Stiner were alone now. He had just made the initial moves that would transfer six hundred thousand dollars, plus or minus, from the parent company's corporate account to a merchant bank in Rhode Island. Simultaneously a private bank in Zurich was arranging a courier delivery of a million Swiss francs to a branch of the United Bank of Switzerland in Geneva.

Stiner laughed, coarsely and derisively. There had been a low point that morning, when he learned that Kenrick was sequestered at gunpoint, caught up in something beyond the control of either of them.

"You didn't really think I'd let Kenrick stew, given a way out?"

"You made a good show."

"What was I supposed to do, volunteer? Sulten and that Tate girl both know Kenrick is out to sink the studio and make me look like a jerk. Hell, man, I need Kenrick out and in business. Kenrick's success is very important to me."

"Yes, I know," Archer said, his voice heavy with fatigue. He went to the bar and filled his glass with vodka, not bothering with the ice. "Cheers," he said, and took a draft that he hoped would float him up awhile longer. A trying business, living with a foot in each camp. He wasn't sure whether his indecision to go with Kenrick or remain loyal to Mal Stiner made him a double agent or a triple one. Archer's belief that one should never make a decision before being forced into it was taking its toll on his nerves. "What some people do for money," he said aloud, but Stiner had already stepped out onto the terrace.

"Tell him we'll have the money in time," Pascal told Brialt. "Get his exact instructions for the transfer."

The turnabout on the part of the police came late afternoon the second day. The reasons were abundant enough to alter anyone's hard-line position, yet there was something in the nature of Pascal's change of mind which hadn't set right with Brialt. Earlier he had described the conditions inside the hotel suite, told the police about the furniture barricade and the gunman's decision to hold the seriously wounded Donner until he received the money. Charpentier's opinion added additional weight. "No matter how fast we went in. A twitch of the finger"—Charpentier's thumb and forefinger snapped the air—"and we've lost someone else."

By telephone the mayor added his own burden to Pascal's load.

"We've received the first convention cancellations," he berated. "Do you realize that a half dozen European capitals are watching this dreadful business on direct television?"

"I'm sure the city looks lovely in color," Pascal said, and assured the mayor the affair would be finished within a day.

Following the offer to provide the ransom money brought by the Tate woman there had been a series of private meetings among Pascal, Commandant Haag, and Charpentier. The open telephone lines to the Ministry of the Interior were in constant use now, but it was the other call that put the cap on Pascal's decision.   ✦

A little before three in the afternoon one of the telephone operators in the *salon de bridge* sat bolt upright, flapping his hand toward Pascal. "The palace."

The call lasted not quite four minutes. During that time Pascal said, "Yes, Mr. President," three times, made one remark to the effect that there was risk in everything, and just before he hung up said, "I understand, Mr. President."

For a long moment Pascal sat motionless. Then he rose, speaking to Brialt in a voice thick with fatigue. "Tell him everything is ready."

Eleven minutes before the end of the gunman's deadline Brialt had gone again to the suite on the sixth floor, this time without the revolver. He returned five minutes later with the instructions for the bank transfer of the money.

There were four of them now, analyzing the request, aided by a director of the Banque Nationale de Paris in Cannes named Dejoux. The banker drew a meaningless diagram on a sheet of yellow paper as he spoke.

"Nothing extraordinary about the transaction, even the amount."

"He knows about banking then?" Pascal frowned and made another note in his book.

"Not banking, exactly," Dejoux corrected. "The procedures —what can and cannot be done."

Brialt found the whole thing incredible. "But won't the fact that someone is going to walk out with more than a million and a half dollars after identifying himself by nothing more than a French banknote with a particular serial number make the Swiss suspicious?"

Dejoux shook his head. "If the procedure is followed correctly, no one would consider a challenge. Upon what grounds? There is nothing in the transaction itself any different from thousands that occur daily. Even the amount of money in volume is only about so-by-so." He carved a space in the air with his hands about the size of a small suitcase.

"We'll notify the Swiss police and request surveillance without action," Pascal said.

"Why not have this accomplice arrested after he makes his phone call?" Haag said.

"No action," Pascal repeated. "Suppose he calls first to make a plane reservation and the Swiss police move in. We're not dealing with fools. They've thought of something else. Some small wrinkle. Without the call to our man we're in a worse position than we are now."

Brialt could well imagine an only slightly delayed blood-bath, with the hostages' release so close. The vision was clear before him of Donner graying and more exhausted with each hour that passed. The look in Katherine's eyes pleaded with him to hurry.

Pascal added, "I care little about what happens in Switzerland as long as our man upstairs receives his call. He must believe all is well."

It was Monday again in Cannes.

Despite "the business at the Carlton," as it was called by those it inconvenienced, the Festival rolled on toward closing. Films were screened; the jury met; deals were made.

On the tennis courts of the Hôtel Montfleury a Canadian financier named Koch sealed an agreement with an Israeli producer to underwrite production of a German authored best seller with a cast of Americans and directed by an expatriate Czech. It would be the deal of the Festival. Yet owing to scarcity of available telephone lines, Koch was unable to call either his principals in Ottawa or his wife in New York with the good news. Koch damned the Festival, drank a bottle of beer alone in his hotel room, and went to bed early.

Across town, a forty-eight-year-old Greek director named Spiradakis, suffering what the French would call a crisis of boredom, picked up a young girl lounging against the fender of a parked car on the rue de Latour Maubourg and a little after five in the afternoon, in a small airless apartment, suffered a myocardial infarction while the girl squirmed beneath him. By the time the ambulance pushed through the stagnant traffic, the Greek was dead. The driver cursed the Festival, but what could one do?

In the late-afternoon heat the locals pulled their chairs beneath the shade of the palms along the Croisette to watch the promenade drifting toward the Carlton. They had never seen bigger crowds in Cannes, they complained, nor could they remember a heat wave so fierce in May. With perfect equanimity, both were blamed on the Festival.

And everyone waited.

Earlier, toward dawn, inside the hotel suite, Kenrick had seen Donner stir and look in his direction.

Kenrick had managed a few hours of shallow, drifting sleep. From where he lay now, hands cuffed and pinched behind his back, he had watched the sliver of sky in the space between two curtains, seen it turn from black to deep, soft blue. The gunman had drawn the curtains when earlier a spotlight blinked on below, illuminating the room in a hard carbon brilliance that made their faces look like the ocher-painted masks of savages.

Kenrick could see him now, facing them in a chair, heavy-lidded. The pistol was in his lap. His composure had fallen apart since the shooting. Twice between noon and Brialt's final visit he had pulled the grenade pin and let it drop to the floor. He would laugh then, knowing the metallic sound sent a jolt of fear through all of them, and replace the pin, only to repeat the process a few minutes later. Once he went to the window and looked down upon the crowd, giving them the doubled-up fist rammed home in the air.

From below, the crowd cheered.

Katherine said something rapidly in French that made him pale and take a step to one side.

"What did you say?"

"Not to be a fool. There is probably someone out there watching, ready to kill him."

"Let him find out on his own," Donner managed.

Siri caught the thinness of Donner's voice. The two small bullet holes in Donner's abdomen belied the damage inside. Kenrick had been trying to remember enough anatomy to calculate what they might have hit. Pancreas? Liver? Hour by hour both he and Siri had witnessed Donner's decline.

But Donner was awake now, whispering his name.

At the sound the gunman's eyes snapped open, but he said nothing.

"Easy, Rod. Another few hours we'll be out of here."

"A good try, Kenrick. Hell, man, that's half the fun."

"Stop."

"Can't. Been thinking crazy things." In the half-light Donner's feverish grin gave a wicked gleam to his eyes. "Remember when Gold nearly broke me at the reading?"

"Never forget it."

"You know what bailed it out? Me realizing I cared more about that film than any of you. To me it wasn't just a deal. So I tried to remember the funniest thing I'd seen in my life, and you know what I came up with? The look on your face that night I punched you in the eye. Like how could anyone dare?"

Kenrick had to smile. He could well believe the turning points in a man's life were often so small they passed by without recognition. At least Donner had seen his time, the moment when he was going to win or lose, and maybe that was the hardest part.

"I pulled it off, didn't I?"

"You're damn right."

"About Rayna. . . ." He shut his eyes, and Kenrick moved closer, wanting to help him hang on. He had nothing to use but his presence. A moment later, eyes still shut, Donner began to smile.

"Hello, Mal. I wish I could say a pleasant surprise."

Exhaustion had finally extracted its toll from Rayna Tate, and she collapsed on the couch in the early evening. A knock on the door awakened her, and when she checked her watch, she found it was only ten in the evening. Mal Stiner waited on the porch. Even dazed by sleep, she recognized the look, part booze and part the midnight's hornies.

She didn't invite him in.

"I thought I'd drop by," Stiner said, "for a visit."

"A visit."

"A bit of unfinished business to do with the ransom."

"I hope you kept the cab. It's hell getting off this mountain."

"I think we understand each other, perfectly. I've heard you're understanding."

"About what, exactly?"

"That you do your job, cost a great deal, and know enough to add something that a lot of people who sign checks can't say no to."

"You mean I'm a good piece of ass."

"Better than good, it is said."

She supposed it was a smile. "Do I have to slam the door on your prick?"

"Oh, come on, Rayna."

"It's not Rayna. Not to you."

"Look, be nice. And I'll be nice to you and Kenrick. I can still put the stop button on the money. Or maybe the slow button. Hell, we might have some fun."

"Fun. You'd use a lever like that just to get yourself laid."

"Whatever it takes," he said jovially. He didn't appear bothered by the admission. "Well now."

She stood aside and let him step in.

"How about a drink?" Mal Stiner said. "Sort of get to be friends."

Rayna thought it would be easy. But it wasn't.

So clean, thought Maxim Rampa. Such a wonderfully clean city.

He took in a breath of fresh, crisp air and forced himself again to look across the traffic-glutted rue du Rhône. Even the bank looked clean, an exterior of glass, bright blue paneling, and shiny aluminum.

He stopped on the corner for almost a minute, unable to will himself to traverse the intersection. The suitcase in his hand, of good quality, was small and empty but felt heavy.

The pains were starting again, radiating from deep in his bowels to every extremity of his body. Maxim Rampa knew he was a sick man, sick enough to die unless something were done; prison would put him in a coffin. He thought of pretty women, the blonde he had seen in Cannes, and prayed to his *Bon Dieu*, "Not yet."

He looked away at the sight of a white-helmeted policeman approaching from the far corner. The policeman passed him by without even a look. But you could never tell. Everyone around him might be police, waiting to spring their trap until they were certain who had come for the money. He thought about finding a café, settling the fear and deep pains with something to drink.

But Gaetan's words rang in his mind: "Follow the instructions, Maxim. Step by step. And nothing to drink." He had already broken the commandment on the long train ride from Nice to Dijon. He had finished a second liter on the connection to Geneva. He always drank on trains. Trains bored him, and a bottle of wine helped pass the time. But the instructions were simple enough for a child. He had arrived in Geneva early the previous evening and found the small hotel on the edge of the old part of the city. Modern and clean like the city, on the fourth floor of an office building, but too expensive. But then so was the new suit of clothing Gaetan bought for him in Cannes. It had taken less than an hour that morning to find a suitcase the exact dimensions written in his instructions. Large enough to hold four thousand five-hundred-franc notes, even if they were old and doubled in bulk. The girl had considered everything. He left the vinyl suitcase filled with clothing that reeked of tobacco in a *poubelle* on the lakefront, with pleasure. He owned nothing in this world now except a new suit of clothing and a small, expensive suitcase, quite empty.

Follow the instructions, Maxim.

He stepped from the curb and crossed to the bank.

Inside, he stopped, marveling; it was just as it had been described to him. A gray-uniformed bank porter surveyed him over the top of his podiumlike desk, a practiced eye taking in the cut of his clothing, the luggage in his hand. To his left sat a woman behind a desk, the sign saying "Information, Renseignements, Auskunft," From this second on, he mustn't hesitate; once the act had begun, you always pressed forward. Maxim Rampa gave the woman behind the desk a courtly *bonjour* and let the sentence roll from his tongue exactly as he had practiced it, still not sure of its exact meaning: "I wish to speak with someone, please, about funds being held here at my disposition."

She made a telephone call, repeated his words exactly, then nodded to the bank porter. "Take this gentleman through to Hibert." She didn't ask his name.

The pale, bespectacled man awaiting him greeted him in stiff, formal French, then grew silent. The room was furnished like the sitting room of a small flat, without a desk, paintings on the walls that looked very expensive to Maxim Rampa. The man folded his hands.

Only a servant, Maxim, remember that. *You* are the client.

"What may we help you with?"

"Two million francs."

Feeling foolish, Maxim Rampa unpinned the hundred-franc note from the lining of his vest, carefully unfolded it, and smoothed the bill before the man.

In his heart, he lacked the faith that the numbers on a single hundred-franc note would bring forth anything but a loud laugh.

The man didn't laugh. He looked at both sides of the bill, rose, and told Maxim to come along. They went to a second room, smaller, paneled in wood, with a large table in the center and four chairs.

"If you'll wait," the man said. Taking Maxim's precious one hundred-franc note, the man left him alone. Immediately a new fear clawed at his already-tormented insides. No wonder they hadn't needed policemen on the street. He had delivered himself into a room no larger than a cell.

The sound of the door's opening made the blood drain from his face. The man had returned. With him was a bank porter carrying a large wooden tray, which he placed in the center of the table.

Maxim Rampa found himself looking at the neat stack of pinkish banknotes.

"Two million francs, Swiss, five-hundred-franc denominations," the banker said without inflection. "And one hundred francs, French." He added Maxim's bill to the stack. Maxim felt himself smile. It was going to be all right.

"You will count?" the man asked.

Maxim Rampa declined. "You count," he told the banker. "And I watch."

Four hours later from the *stazione centrale* in the town of Varese, on the Italian side of Lake Como, he telephoned the Hôtel Carlton in Cannes. The number with the five-digit prefix was the last instruction on his list.

After that Maxim took a very long walk along a treelined boulevard, looking at the girls.

"Yes, he'll take a hostage," Pascal told Brialt, scowling. "Without a hostage, he has nothing to keep us frightened."

Brialt's fingertips rested against his throbbing temples. Ten minutes after the gunman received the long-distance phone call for which they had all been waiting, he issued his final demand: a car to be parked near the emergency exit at the northwest corner of the hotel building within half an hour.

"Smart," Pascal said. "It will be growing dark. One street, a turn, another street, and he is out of the city."

"But where then?"

"A change of cars. Once, twice. Perhaps the mountains or

to lose himself in Nice. And when he thinks he is safe, he lets the hostage go. Or perhaps not." Pascal nodded grimly. "That will be his plan."

Wrong, Brialt thought moments later.

The gunman didn't take a hostage. He took two.

The man named François arrived early afternoon, driving a black Renault 12. Charpentier met him in the parking lot across from the gray *commissariat central.* To Charpentier's eye he appeared neither old nor young, his forties somewhere, with a round, softish stomach. His dark beard wanted for a shave, and Charpentier guessed that he had been brought in by aircraft. But he asked no questions of François.

As they drove toward the Carlton, François wasted no time, making his demands in a ragged *pied-noir* accent. It fitted. There were former French Algerians peppered throughout the heavy-handed branches of the SDECE and the closets the ministry kept for such occasions. "Does Brialt know what you intend?" Charpentier had earlier put it to Pascal.

"No one knows, and no one will know."

François was saying, "I'll need a large-scale map showing the routes out of the city. Then we'll look at the *quartier* near the hotel. He won't give us much time, this type. He knows with time, we make plans." By the time the gunman called down for his car François appeared to have all the possibilities covered.

"He'll be coming out here," he said, a thick finger stabbing at the plan of the hotel. The building was E-shaped with its middle member gone. In the space was a service yard, the hotel laundry, the business office, and a storage area. There were three flights of emergency stairs, one winding down behind the elevators, one in either wing. The stairs in the north wing were eight meters from the entrance to

Suite 624. "He won't expose himself much," François said, tracing the gunman's probable route of escape. "Out the suite to the stairs, this exit, and into the car. Come on," he ordered. "Not much time."

Charpentier followed him across the service yard. "Remember the hostages," he reminded François.

The caution made François smile. "Why do you think I'm going to this trouble?"

"It will be dark."

"It won't matter."

Charpentier watched while François climbed into the Renault rounded up for the gunman's escape. Three times François sped away from the hotel's rear exit and made the hard right into the narrow street that led directly away from the Croisette. It was without traffic; police barriers sealed off the entire *quartier*. The street ended at the wall of a small hotel. There the gunman would have two choices: a sharp, hairpin left that turned along a narrow street back toward the Festival Hall—deeper into the city. Or an easy right that put him only blocks away from two of the major routes, out and beyond.

Each time François piloted the small car along the street faster, needing to apply the brakes at the corner. A final time they walked the route together. Charpentier could hear François's anxious breathing, sharp, dry intakes of air. "Put a parked car there," François instructed, indicating a place short of the corner, "to crowd him in."

Near the entrance to the Carlton garage, François scanned the wall across the narrow street and the thick stand of orange and pepper trees in the yard beyond. "He can't make the corner without slowing. The car will lug down about there, and here he'll need to shift—right-handed, the hand with the gun."

He took another moment to look into the darkness of the yard, then along the street in both directions. Satisfied, he told Charpentier, "That's it." A finger pointed into the darkness. "I'll shoot from there."

Five minutes before his exit time the gunman unexpectedly called for Brialt. He wanted him in the suite.

"You'd better hurry," Pascal said, relaying the request. Brialt had been waiting near the window of the *salon de bridge*, watching Charpentier and another man dressed in black near the small Renault, parked in the service yard, that would carry the gunman away.

"But what can he want?"

"Obviously something we didn't anticipate." Pascal touched his shoulder with unexpected gentleness. "You've done well, Brialt. A bit longer."

Again Brialt took the elevator to his own private version of hell.

"What was I talking about?" Donner asked.

"Nothing, Rod. You hadn't said anything."

"About Rayna. I'd started to say. . . ."

Kenrick studied the drawn face gray with shock. The suite was in semidarkness, one wall splashed orange from the setting sun. During the past hours Donner had shouted names in his fitful sleep—Lehman, someone called Merle, Kenrick himself. It had been twelve, fourteen hours since Donner had spoken about Rayna.

Siri glanced at Kenrick, then away.

"That's right, you were talking about Rayna."

"Can't figure what she sees in you."

"Damned if I can tell."

"Wait till she knows you like the rest of us do. You and I finally going to have something in common, Kenrick, because she'll drop you quicker than me." He smiled at the thought.

"She told me you left *her*."

"Not true. I wouldn't have been that stupid. If I . . ."
he began, but let it drop. A moment later he said, "What
a goddamn limp-prick way to go." He touched one of the
bullet holes. "Funny, it doesn't trouble me anymore. Nothing from here down."

"Easy, Rod."

"Don't screw up, Kenrick. With Rayna. Take a chance."
Kenrick wondered if he could.

"My last words on the subject. Now what was I talking . . . ?"

His mouth tried to finish. But the jaw hung there, the
life slipped from behind his eyes, and he was gone.

Entering the suite from the brightly lighted corridor,
Brialt had a few seconds of blindness. As his eyes adjusted,
he found it all as before: the stacked furniture, the rubble,
but something he couldn't comprehend. The gunman appeared to be binding Katherine with the adhesive tape Brialt
had brought earlier. Then he saw it: the ugly gray metal
of the hand grenade wrapped tightly against her upper arm.

"He's full of tricks," Siri said. She was on her feet near
the door, hands cuffed in front of her. The conclusion made
Brialt ill: The gunman was taking both women.

"What do you want?" Brialt asked. "We've given you
everything."

Katherine spoke up. "I asked for you. I promised I
wouldn't struggle if he'd let you come up."

"Do you know what he intends?" Brialt questioned in
English. The gunman appeared not to care.

"He'll keep us until he's out of the city—until he's safe.
He says we won't be harmed." Katherine looked down at
the ugly metal weapon, for the gunman's purposes, now part
of her body. "Philippe, will it be all right? Have the police
done everything he asked?"

"There's a car waiting. I've seen it."

"No tricks. I think he might hurt us then."

Brialt shook his head. "No tricks."

"We'll be all right. Don't worry."

"Enough," the gunman said, pulling the pistol from his belt.

"Take *me*," Brialt pleaded suddenly. "In place of them."

"I don't want you."

He turned Katherine roughly and pushed her toward the door. He drew Siri next to him, rested the gun against her neck, and spoke to Brialt. "You first. Tell them we're ready."

Brialt opened the door, wincing at the bright lights. "They're coming out."

"Good-bye," the gunman said in halting English. And then, as with his greeting three days before, he said "good-bye" a second time.

Brialt watched them cross to the stairs in unison, as in some children's game, the gunman in the middle, the women on either side. Then they were gone, the door of the emergency exit swinging shut behind them.

Immediately from along the hall came voices, somebody using a telephone. Two armed men ran toward him.

Exhausted and drained, he couldn't bring himself to watch their departure. "Where's the doctor?" he shouted angrily, and started for the phone.

"Too late," Kenrick said. "He's dead."

≡ *Chapter 47*—Axe Rouge

Gaetan Rampa pushed the women through the double doors into the hotel service yard.

The yard was poorly lighted, hard bare bulbs reflecting from police helmets—two dozen, three dozen. He couldn't count them all, but he wasn't frightened. More police, less police, what did it matter as long as he held the women? Rotating Katherine by the arm, he showed them the hand grenade taped to her upper arm. Then he nudged Siri with the pistol.

The car was pointing toward the gates and the street beyond. He pushed Siri into the rear seat and ducked in behind the girl Katherine, making her crawl across the seat. He didn't want to be taken from above. "Next to me," he told the girl, with a thick, lecherous grin. "I want to be able to reach you." She looked away.

The car started with the first twist of the key. Good. If they were going to play tricks, he expected it here, with the automobile.

He eased out past the gates and turned right, away from the Croisette. In the rearview mirror he saw the barricades behind them, all behind them. Ahead, the street was clear. A parked car at the far corner, but no one. Gaetan Rampa felt suddenly free and trod down upon the accelerator. The small car leaped forward.

In the rear seat Siri let her head sink onto her chest.

Gaetan glanced at the girl, still facing away. She doesn't trust herself, not yet. But yes, he saw her triumphant grin. Approaching the corner, he swung wide of the parked car and braked enough to take the corner without losing too much speed. As he reached for the gear lever to downshift, the girl's hand touched his, a touch unseen by anyone, but clear in its meaning: Together they had done it.

He began to laugh at the thought. All those police, the rich, beautiful people. All of them fooled. His mouth opened to laugh, but it was no longer a mouth. Part of a lip, a few grainy teeth set in shattered bone as the entire side of Gaetan Rampa's dark, handsome face exploded in an audible puff. Eyes snapping open as something shook the automobile, Siri saw his body slide sidewise, head mostly gone, as the car veered out of control. Before the crash of impact she began to scream.

Charpentier witnessed it from the darkened entrance of the Carlton garage. "Done," he breathed. François had known his business sure enough. With a single, well-placed bullet he delivered to Pascal his bright orange elephant.

A moment before, Charpentier had taken the radio call direct from Pascal. "Two hostages, the gunman driving."

Charpentier waved into the darkness of the yard across the street and received François's low whistle of readiness.

In fewer than twenty seconds the car reached them. Approaching the corner, it slowed, the engine changing pitch as the driver downshifted. At that instant came the sharp crack from François's weapon—a long, bull-barreled rifle, small caliber, mounting a cyclops light beaming infrared. Charpentier saw the driver's head whip from impact, the windshield frost with cracks. The car continued its turn, grating noisily along one wall of the garage, then rolled to a stop thirty yards along the street. Above the sound of the engine whining out of control, he heard someone screaming inside the car.

Charpentier began to run.

He reached the car, pistol drawn, and pulled open the driver's door, wincing at the wash of human debris spattering the interior. He would testify later, at the closed police hearing, that the dome light was on, illuminating the interior of the vehicle sufficiently to see what followed, without mistake. Nor had it been an accident on his part or the girl's.

He reached in and turned off the ignition, the Laurence woman's scream resolving itself in a stunted, nauseated cry. Neither woman appeared hit, although, considering the mess, it was hard to tell. He extended his hand to the girl in the front seat, cowering against the far door. Her eyes were fixed on the gunman's body. She said the name "Gaetan," then said it again. Before Charpentier fully understood, she looked up at him. The rest would remain in his memory a long time, lips drawing back in a hideous grin, her index finger probing the weapon taped against her upper body. She said a word, one word he could pronounce phonetically but didn't understand. "Pig," she whispered, followed by the chirp of metal against metal as she jerked the pin from the hand grenade.

≡ *Chapter 48*—Aftermath

Galloway felt light-headed, for once with good reason. He had worked through the night finishing the story about the business at the Carlton—fifteen hundred words for the *Guardian.* He was out of shape for that sort of thing.

It had been midnight when the press corps jammed into the Grill Room of the Carlton to hear a prepared statement read by a smallish man in a dark, rumpled suit.

Chef de District Auguste Pascal felt himself duty-bound to dispatch this final bit of business in what he viewed privately as a thoroughly dishonorable affair.

Pascal waited uncomfortably until the assemblage quieted. He began by telling them the gunman had been positively identified: "Gaetan Rampa, age twenty-seven, birthplace St.-Girons, profession. . . ." There followed the recorded details of his life which the French police could have assembled on short notice for any citizen. It was the final comment that made Galloway sit up: "Motive unknown."

Bloody devils, thought Galloway.

The policeman went on to reveal that the woman who had died in the crash with the gunman was an American, Katherine Todd Mackey, age twenty-six, birthplace Brentwood, California. "An accomplice," Pascal said, causing a wave of sound through the room as reporters checked to make sure they had the name right.

Galloway sourly put quotes around the words "automobile crash." He had already done his legwork on that respect and had uncovered an eyewitness. A Madame Régine Vazot, aged sixty-six, resident of a small apartment building on the rue du Canada, twenty meters from the site of the so-called crash. She told Galloway that before the car crash she heard a gunshot and that the automobile caught fire only after an explosion. He might have discounted her precise observations about the nature and sequence of what she had heard and seen, if not for something else he learned. Madame Vazot was the widow of a former colonel in the Second REP and had lived in Algeria during the civil war. Weaponry and the sound of *plastique* were no strangers.

Galloway also put the note "To Query" next to the girl's name. He didn't doubt her involvement. But how? The birthplace Brentwood, a rather posh suburb of Los Angeles. Echoes of Patty Hearst? Rich girl involved with low types, etc.? He'd take whatever hook he could get. The police were revealing nothing more than a photo received from the Sûreté in Paris, after the fact, Pascal was careful to emphasize. Two men in tuxedos on a Paris street corner, *performeurs des rues*, with a lovely blond girl collecting throw money from the crowd. A bushy-haired reporter from the L.A. *Times* pointed to the photo and asked the obvious question. "Who's the other guy?"

"Brother of the deceased," Pascal said. He gave the illusion of being direct, wanting to help, on *their* side. And for that Galloway was all the more distrustful.

"Was he involved?" the reporter asked.

"We're making inquiries," the policeman answered. The transparent phrase meant they thought so but hadn't proved it.

Galloway rose, his voice booming from the back of the room. "What happened to the money?"

Around him the voices dropped, until the room was silent. Pascal sought him out in the crowd. "The gunman and his accomplice, and I emphasize again, whom we thought at the time was a hostage, were allowed to depart after careful negotiations. No money was involved."

"I heard two million Swiss," Galloway pursued.

"It is not the policy of the French government to pay extortion money. You heard incorrectly."

Galloway let it go. He knew how the police were handling it—cover-up. It was enough for a story. He had Rayna Tate's account of gathering the money from private sources, whether the police denied it or not. But what had become of the cash? *Query.* Most of the reporters would be filing stories around the hook of Rod Donner—true-life hero?—or Siri Laurence—will she ever act again? Myths would be built or augmented that evening, giving Galloway a queasy feeling about his chosen profession.

By the time he telephoned in his fifteen hundred words he was ready to focus on the real story, of which the hostaging was only a part. He still didn't have the final pieces, and the man who could provide them was missing. Kenrick. Presumably he had gone to ground and wasn't due to surface until four o'clock that afternoon. A blue mimeoed bulletin waiting in his mailbox at the Festival Hall press club announced a Kenrick press conference to be held at the Palais Miramar. He would answer questions about the siege but also make an important announcement.

Galloway went out the side door of the Festival Hall, intending to reward himself for a night's work well done. Doubting he could get a drink on the Croisette that time of the morning, he turned, by instinct, in the direction of the railway station. They were places you could always count on.

Walking rapidly, he began mentally resifting the evidence.

If the important announcement Kenrick was to make later that afternoon concerned, as everyone expected, formation of a new studio, then Galloway had been misled by Rayna Tate—her assurance that the planned breakaway was a deception. Or had she been lied to by Kenrick? If she was correct, what was Kenrick's reason for a feint, this rather grand deception that included a number of commitments being gossiped around the Festival? It all was related somehow: Kenrick's deception, true or false; the rumor the studio was being shopped around for sale; the financier Arthur's presence on the fringe of things.

Galloway rounded a corner, peering at the checkerboard of objects ahead: The beginning of the rush hour, a glut of vehicles engulfing the Côte as surely as Paris, London, or New York. He skittered across the street ahead of a wave of *mobylettes* and gunning engines and continued walking.

To make better sense of the evidence, he tried rearranging things in sequence of time. One, Stiner seen talking to Munson in London. Reasonable conclusion: Munson wants into the film business via a buy of the studio, Stiner his chosen spearhead. Two, a week later Kenrick is laying groundwork for a breakaway company that will hurt both studio and parent company. Three, Arthur arrives in Cannes *before* it all falls together. And four, the joker, Kenrick doesn't really intend breaking away at all.

In Galloway's mind the key was not so much in the events, but in Kenrick's intention. What was Kenrick after? Answer that, and the rest would come clear. "Looking too hard," he said aloud.

Galloway heard the klaxon horn almost at his shoulder and supposed that lost in himself, he had done it again. Careless man. Have to pay bloody attention. But in that instant he made the mental jump from Kenrick's motives to exactly what Kenrick intended, all of it becoming wonderfully clear. "I've got it," Galloway said, but as he reached for his notebook, the world exploded. From deep within his body he felt a sharp, expanding pressure that sent his arms and legs whirling in one direction and his mind in another.

For the barest slice of time his thoughts remained clearer than he ever remembered them, his perceptions sharp enough to reason even while sensing the feeling of motion. Then the current stopped, the source crushed by several tons of gray iron, and Peter Galloway's lights went out.

≡ *Chapter 49*—Exit

Rayna Tate saw Galloway dead in the street, as she later described it to Kenrick, like some broken pelican tossed upon a beach.

She was on her way to meet Kenrick after the police and a doctor were finished with him. A crowd gathered at the side of a busy intersection reminded her of something from childhood she hadn't thought of in years: the beggars who would come out to Juhu beach in the early morning to create magnificent sculptures of sand. Grand palaces, beautiful princesses, and the erotic ones intricately portraying the act of love.

She pushed through the crowd to find Galloway lying in a slick of purplish blood.

A policeman bent over the body in a pantomime of giving air, while two others gathered shattered spectacles, notebook, some coins, and one shoe all sent flying by the impact. Nearby was a gray police bus.

"Came down the hill like a bullet," a man told her in English, "and that clown steps right off the curb in front of it. Did you notice? No skid marks. Didn't even have time to hit the brakes."

She fled then, hot tears welling in her eyes. It had settled over her, layer upon layer. The inanities of the Festival, the dealing and casual coupling that drained her spirit. Then Donner's meaningless death, and Galloway the final accretion. They weren't tears of sorrow. Rayna Tate was angry.

When she told Kenrick about Galloway, he took it silently, circling his hotel room, touching things, straightening papers, only to straighten them again. Then he had a shower, ordered breakfast, and began to dress.

When he took the telephone call from Aron Archer, she felt mentally dismissed.

"Novotny is still in," Archer said breathlessly. "Don't try to guess how it would have broken if the Siri business had happened twenty-four hours sooner. He has people committed up to their eyeballs and is no doubt already counting his commission. The press conference is at four. You ready?"

"I will be. And you?"

"What an odd question. Of course, old chum. A thousand percent."

Kenrick put down the phone to find Rayna's expression full of something he couldn't read.

"Say it." He stepped to take her in his arms, but she moved away.

"I've made up my mind about you and me."

"That sounds like a girl walking out."

"You nearly sold me. Many a good lady has been drawn in by that all-American dream of helping some powerful, wonderful man reach his so-called destiny."

"Rayna, Arthur hasn't gone for it, and he has exactly five hours left to bite."

"But he will. You know it. He'll come around, and you'll win. Even though, back inside yourself, you know it won't be enough. Oh, hell!"

"Go on." He watched her, motionless.

"I'm guessing, but I think this goal of yours is a thing you fixed on when your wife died, to keep alive. I saw something just now when I told you about Galloway. I thought it bounced right off you, but it was just the opposite. This way you have of focusing on the small tasks, taking care of each moment to keep from thinking about something that hurts." He accepted it with a reluctant nod. "It's a nice survival device, Kenrick, blinders like that. It may even help you get this payoff of yours. But your winning isn't enough. Not for me."

"What would be enough?"

"To try something of substance. Something together. I'm not going to settle for the featured supporting role in the film about Teddy Kenrick's life."

"You're asking me to walk away from the payoff of a lifetime."

"Am I? Look, I've already talked to a lawyer and to Lou Sulten."

"Sulten?"

Her almond-shaped eyes were dancing with life now, and she rose suddenly, moving around the room as she spoke. "Lou doesn't want to hear anything about Donner or his script, and we could pick it up on a cheap option."

It took a moment to sink in. "You're mad."

"Why not? If you and I couldn't turn Donner's script into a damn fine film, who could? Are you telling me that between us we don't have enough talent and push to match a Paul Waxler?"

"I've been the guy the Waxlers go to." It had the tone of a discovery.

"So welcome to the trenches. You know what Donner once said to me. There is only one part of this business worth a shit. Making movies. Really making them. He said the rest of you guys might as well be dealing in soybean futures. I want to make that film, Kenrick."

"For Donner?"

"For myself. I still owe him. And I want it for us."

"Now you're sounding like Galloway. Old-fashioned honor and people of good intent."

"Maybe Galloway was worth listening to, plum in the mouth and all."

He was about to say "maybe" when the telephone began an insistent buzz.

For a moment Kenrick let it ring, Rayna watching him carefully. The small things always betrayed the noble speeches—an unguarded look, a move away from your lover's touch. Kenrick crossed the room, snatched up the phone, and heard a thin, reedy voice say, "Kenrick?" It wasn't a voice he recognized.

"Yes, it's Kenrick."

"Kenrick, this is Arthur. I think it's about time we meet."

The scenario as written.

"Kenrick, you hear me?"

"When and where?" He listened to Arthur's instructions and said, "I'll be there."

"We should have talked sooner," Arthur said, "but no matter."

"None at all."

When he hung up the telephone and turned to face Rayna, the door to the hall was ajar. Her exit had been silent, and Kenrick could feel the emptiness of the room.

Many times that week Hugh Remy walked up the long hill to the small Anglo-American hospital in Cannes. He must have looked like an odd bird to the policeman guarding the entrance, a tall figure pacing the hospital grounds long hours before he could gather the courage to enter. Expert on every hummock of the land nearby, uninvited adviser to the workmen patching the wall of flat stones that ran to the edge of the ravine. And each day after he made his rounds, calculating, he would visit Siri.

"You're acting like a man with nothing better to do," she chided through the bandages.

The use of her senses was returning slowly. Smell first, she thought. Or was it taste? A taste. Harsh, chemical, and the feeling that a hot iron had been run down her throat. "Quite normal after an anesthetic," the doctor explained. His accent was English, and she imagined him tall and very proper.

Her last clear recollection was the terrible few seconds in the automobile before the explosion. The driver's shattered head, the blood. Then the bearded man reaching in even as she had heard that peculiar metallic pop and smelled acrid smoke as the weapon attached to the girl hissed itself alive. How was she to know the man was trying to help? She fought him. Then the explosion.

Later, the odor of chemicals, alcohol, hospital smells, and yes, something else, heavy and familiar. But the doctor's hands had been there, touching, soothing, his voice saying that it was all right.

The darkness had been the mystery until her hands found her own face and touched the thick bandages encircling her head. A tiny slit for the nose, a bigger one for her mouth. For the rest she might have been caressing a bundle of rags. Except that beneath the bandages there was pain.

"Hugh, the girl in the car. What happened?"

"The grenade exploded before you could get out."

"And the girl . . . a pretty girl."

"It's over, Siri."

He was wrong. She wanted to scream, but Hugh Remy's hands closed over her own, big, strong hands, not at all like the doctor's, which she could tell even when he didn't speak. Remy's were calloused and scarred and scratched. He spoke out of the darkness.

"I've had a specialist flown in. English with a lot of letters behind the name, and you're gonna love that. Broomwitch. Mr. Broomwitch."

"Don't be diplomatic, Hugh. It's not your style."

"Okay. . . ." He hesitated, then said, "Broomwitch has taken eight bits of metal out of your face and scalp. Thank a cop named Charpentier there weren't more."

Remy had watched the last change of bandages, unwilling to believe the surgeon's summation that it looked worse than it was. Jagged scars across bloated purple mounds of flesh, her eyes swollen shut. A rough line of stitches crowned her forehead where a shard of hot metal had nearly taken her scalp. Her head was shaved.

The reconstruction and skin grafting would come later. Already the small office of the surgeon Broomwitch, one of the best, they said, looked like a memorial to Siri's career. Publicity stills and newspaper photos were pinned across an entire wall, while X rays of her face covered a second. "I saw *Lady Ice* four times," he admitted, with all the naïve awe of a teenaged fan. He was a lean man with a woolly red beard, too young for his awesome reputation in Remy's eye. "Sometimes we even manage to improve upon nature," he said.

But Remy remembered Monty Clift's face after the automobile accident, what the ever-so-slight alterations looked like on film. Every feature the same, but not quite, and the accumulation of small changes had been enough. Remy didn't know what Siri would look like when the operations were finished. Beautiful, he guessed, if the determination in Broomwitch's voice meant anything. Remy doubted her face would ever work the same magic with the camera again.

He hoped he was wrong.

"You're in for a rough year," he told her.

She accepted it, silently, then changed the subject and asked him to describe the hospital.

"Small, in some pretty hills behind Cannes. English nursing sisters."

"Are there trees?"

"Yes, a big elm in the courtyard and olive trees, one just outside your window."

"And flowers?"

"Not yet. A hard winter. One of the sisters told me they're planting new ones."

"He was here. I thought I'd dreamed it, the gardenias. Nicky was here."

"No, Siri."

"He was," she said. "It's not over, I know it." When Remy tried to take her hands again, she pulled them away.

The helicopter was waiting on the asphalt pad next to the Palm Beach Casino. A man in a dark business suit greeted Kenrick, his hand extending reluctantly. "I'm Chastain."

"Yes," Kenrick said. "We talked once on the phone."

Three minutes later they were airborne and crossing above the apartment blocks and hothouses that marked Antibes, following the coast eastward. They hadn't quite reached Monte Carlo when the pilot banked sharply and dropped them down onto a large triangular lawn ringed with palms. In the center was a large white villa, old and grand, built by the wealth of another era, one before income taxes and the SEC. If, in his freewheeling style, Arthur was a relic of the past, he had chosen his habitat well.

Climbing from the helicopter, Kenrick saw a man in shirt sleeves walk onto the veranda to observe his approach. Closer he recognized the full head of pure white hair.

"Welcome, Kenrick. I knew you'd show up here sooner or later." It was a reedier voice than on the telephone, old womanish and petulant.

Hiking his bagging trousers up around a trim waist, Arthur led him to a large room with white walls and a small cupola looking out upon dark green foliage and a cobalt blue swimming pool. "A drink, Kenrick?" Arthur asked, but something in his tone made it clear he didn't approve. When Kenrick declined, Chastain, who had waited to serve him, exited without a word or look. Kenrick watched him go, wondering what he did for fun, only to turn and discover Arthur watching *him*. Close-set, neutral eyes, without much color or expression. That one glimpse years before hadn't shown the eyes.

"Sit anywhere. Don't value desks much."

What do you value, old man, besides robot yes-men and money in large sums? Through the window in the garden he could see two children playing, twin girls about six or seven, dressed identically. Nearby was a pale dark-haired woman, young and very lovely. Arthur caught his interest but made no remark.

"We'd have talked sooner if I'd reckoned on you being such a pain in the neck. You healthy after that business at the Carlton?"

"Well enough." The images were buried but shallow. He forced himself to concentrate on Arthur, this moment.

The white-haired financier sat facing him in a hard straight-backed chair. He looked ill at ease, unable to enjoy the room's comfort. "You know why I've asked you here?"

"I think so."

"I'm not sure you do." Kenrick only nodded, while Arthur flicked at a cowlick invading his vision. "I've followed your career. I know you're ambitious as hell, on the climb, and, as the magazines say, a private person. I wouldn't think anybody with your obvious brains would enjoy being made a fool of."

"You wouldn't," Kenrick said. "Why should I?"

"Stiner is playing you for an idiot. You've been so busy scheming you haven't seen his trap."

So that was to be the tactic: Make it a contest between him and Stiner, with Robert Arthur in the role of interested spectator.

"Perhaps," Kenrick offered.

Something passed behind Arthur's dead brown eyes, there and gone. "You're involved in something too big for you to recognize. Stiner can't see it either, dazzled as he is by that Cockney rogue Munson. Munson is using Stiner as his wedge into films. Enticements, I'm sure—salary, stock options, a few of those glittery trinkets you Hollywood people show off with."

"More control in running the studio. That's Stiner's nerve, not trinkets."

Arthur reflected a moment. "Possible," he admitted, grudgingly, but was more careful when he spoke. "To aid Munson, all Stiner need do is pick away at stockholder confidence in the studio's worth. The obvious strategy is discredit the man most responsible for the studio's success. You, Kenrick. He's been out to stampede you. By forming this breakaway company of yours, you play right into Stiner and Munson's hands."

And out of your own.

"I know," Kenrick said. The dead brown eyes flashed to life, then dulled. Arthur took his time studying Kenrick and then made a quiet *ah* of comprehension.

Kenrick added, "As you said, it's a more complicated game than Stiner realizes. Complicated and bigger."

"Not so big," Arthur said lightly. "The studio is inconsequential in itself. The gross of the entire parent company doesn't put it among the *Fortune* Five Hundred. There isn't a studio in the business as big as Schlitz or Oscar Mayer. I could tell you where the studio fits in the scheme of things— my scheme of things—but it's hardly worth the time."

He was good, Kenrick gave him that. A wary old fighter, in trouble, but covering and dancing away. Arthur didn't say it was a game of peanuts, but his implication was clear. Kenrick wouldn't let himself be drawn in. His presence in this room was clear evidence to the contrary.

"Then I'll tell *you* where the studio fits," Kenrick said, "and we'll make it worth the time."

For a bare instant Arthur looked startled, but just as quickly the emotion was dealt with and hidden away. He bade Kenrick to continue.

"I don't know all of it . . ."

"Bold of you to admit."

". . . but I know there is something beyond your unloading of studio stock. Another step, and probably another after that."

"The assumption that I wish to sell my stock is dangerous enough, given the implications."

"I don't think anyone understands what comes next except you. Not your mouthpiece out there, no one but yourself. You've sold companies you control to other companies you control so far back through a web of umbrella organizations, it takes time and a good detective to figure out how. Or more precisely why, the exact nature of the big payday. I don't know how many companies you have a piece of. Or who you've allied yourself with, here and there, to get what you want."

That was the payoff, the last phrase. He watched to see if the implication would take. Arthur's expression was unchanged, unfathomable. Not even a twitch, the bastard.

"And thus you believe I am about to sell off my share of the studio."

"History," Kenrick said. It was Galloway's lesson. Galloway with his pyramids and theories and a moral stance that ran counter to everything Arthur was. If indeed Kenrick was on the verge of selling himself to the devil, it was a conscious sale, uncoerced, and he would remember in hell to thank the devil for the opportunity.

"Four years ago you and your organization bought fifteen percent of the studio's parent company for two dollars a share. That much is public record. How much else you control through cousins, front men, trusts, and proxies I can't guess, beyond plenty."

Arthur graced him with a scant nod.

"As of yesterday's closing that same stock was trading at twenty-six a share and moving up on the prospect of the highest projected profits in company history and the belief that next year's films will top that. You picked a good time to get out, Arthur. The right point in the crest, the right week even. But a little too late."

For the first time Arthur looked doubtful. Kenrick had the old man off-balance and kept going.

"Now, if nothing happens to the stock before you take your next step, you'll return about thirteen times on your original investment, which beats hell out of a savings and loan. But if the stock dives—"

Arthur cut in. "Which it will. If you pull out with this breakaway company of yours."

"And the world gets a look at Pedro Lehman's film," Kenrick put in.

He remembered the people who had helped him reach this room, Anne, Larry Rentzler. None of them would have wanted what he had come here for, been willing to do what he had intended. He thought of the alternative held out by Rayna, the changes in himself it would demand. Donner couldn't or wouldn't change, and it had killed him.

Arthur rose from his chair and, hiking up his trousers, walked to the window. The children were still playing in the garden. One of the little girls waved. It went unnoticed. "All right, I made a mistake. You knew about Stiner's intention to stampede you all along. Used the threat of the breakaway to get my attention." He turned to look at Kenrick. "Which means that you and I, being reasonable men, might find a solution."

"We have until a press conference at four."

"Be civilized, man! I know when I've been maneuvered into a seller's market. Let's find out if the price is worth it."

"You'd know better than I. With the breakout aborted and one other stunt, it's likely, barring an oil price rise or a sneeze from the President, that the stock will keep trading high until you've made your move. In cash, that's worth a profit to you of forty, maybe fifty million dollars. That's if taking a profit now is your ultimate aim."

"I'm waiting for your price. More money? Control?"

"I came here prepared to ask for one thing. Into your

organization, not the way Stiner was or Chastain is. The chance someday to sit where you are now."

A harsh croak came from deep within Arthur's throat, an attempt to laugh with an apparatus gone to rust. "With what you have to bargain?"

"I calculate it's worth it down the line. To you and the people you're involved with."

"Dammit, man, you keep coming back to these other people."

It was Galloway's logic again. "Because too many things can only be explained by the presence of another someone." Arthur's head shook, denying it. But Kenrick pushed ahead, intending to leave Arthur with not a straw of reasoning to hide behind. "One example, Arthur. The people who had the other half of Cayman Bay Enterprises."

"Yes, there was another party involved, so. . . ."

"Something you once told a reporter named Galloway about dealing every day with pimps and hustlers and con men. As you said yourself, that's business. I know who the people are."

Arthur came back to his chair, lowered himself into it, and thought for several minutes before speaking. "Worthless information, Kenrick, without proof."

"Fine. I take my new company out and let the studio sink, with Lehman's film driving it down. Watch the parent company stock go with it."

Arthur was silent a full minute. There was something else in the brown eyes now. Hatred, fear, Kenrick couldn't tell.

"You say you have a price. If I choose to accept, how do I know you can deliver?"

"It would take the two of us." The words felt suddenly alien in Kenrick's mouth.

"Go on."

"At the press conference this afternoon, instead of announcing the formation of the new company, as everyone is expecting, I squelch it. Call it a rumor, and reaffirm my allegiance to the studio and the most ambitious production schedule in our history. That's the easy part."

It was a distant, arid smile. "You've planned it this way all along, haven't you? The breakaway, the feelers out for big money, those people you've been gathering. A deception."

"That's right, Arthur. A dirty little game that ought to make you feel right at home."

"You won't be a popular man."

"I never have been," Kenrick said. "But I don't mind nailing Stiner to the wall long enough for you to move."

"But if the Lehman film is the disaster you hint? I've seen what happens to a studio stock with a *Doolittle* or *Lucky Lady*."

"We smother it in the can."

"I don't understand."

"You understand all right. Destroy it."

Arthur weighed something in his mind, but not for long. "I thought there were multiple negatives, surely abundant prints." It was Arthur's sort of question, a concern with practical matters, absent of any postures about right and wrong. If their voices carried to the grave, Galloway was swiveling in his coffin.

Kenrick said, "There's a stage in processing when a film is vulnerable. The final negative in one-of-a-kind form. Studios sweat through that time, and so does the lab. The insurance companies make a lot of money on a few days' coverage, which they earn in the risk. Lehman's film is there now."

"Yes, but how do we do it?" He punctuated the point with an index finger jabbing his thigh.

"Lab fires happen. Everyone will weep; the studio will write it off. The funny thing is Pedro Lehman's reputation won't suffer in the slightest."

"Can you arrange such a thing?"

"No, but you can."

It wasn't the place he expected Arthur to balk. He wouldn't have if he could simply have paid someone money. Arthur saw that by admitting, through his contacts, he might indeed be able to arrange a lab fire, he was telling Kenrick that his assumption of well-hidden connections with the hierarchy of the mob was true, giving him his proof and a longer lever. Kenrick intended to take the final chance of denial away from Arthur.

"I have a story for you. About myself and cards and dice and some things that not so long ago helped me get through the day. It's not a time I'm proud of."

Arthur didn't quite meet his eyes. "I'm aware of your former entertainments."

It was a small admission, perhaps intended to reaffirm to Kenrick the breadth of Arthur's knowledge and power. But for Kenrick it was the final confirmation. He wanted to smile but instead matched the man across from him, let his face give away nothing.

"Once, when I found I was a bad gambler or a foolish one, I cheated. Now, maybe I was set up. To this day I don't know. But I was caught."

Arthur was silent, his thoughts closed off again.

"But instead of broken knuckles or something more subtle, I was let off and sent home."

"One should accept good luck gracefully."

"Except it didn't fit. I'd given a man the power, via a videotape of me caught in the act, to squeeze me dry. But no demands came, nothing. Not until later."

He saw the question in Arthur's face but held up a hand, forestalling him. "It took awhile, but I finally decided that Nicky Deane didn't have the authority I thought he had. That he'd gone to someone else and was told to keep off. Now, why was I so valuable, Arthur? And then I realized it wasn't me. It was the studio and its continued success."

"An interesting conclusion," Arthur said dryly, still trying to discount Kenrick's logic. But it was a listless effort, the final sidewise moves of a chess king trying to avoid check.

"Interesting when I found out later that Nicky Deane once worked for the same people you were associated with in Cayman Bay. Somewhere, up past Nicky Deane in the pecking order, was someone else. Someone you deal with. Let's call him Pluto. I guarantee he can arrange all sorts of things. If it's worth it to him."

It was several minutes before Arthur rose slowly and without a word left the room. Twenty minutes later he returned and again sat facing Kenrick.

"Suppose it could be done—this lab fire?"

"Then tell Pluto I want the tape."

"So I would imagine."

"I'll give you something in exchange. Deane used the tape to blackmail me into taking on the Lehman film. For a long time that didn't fit either. Why would you and Pluto, with everything riding on the studio's climb, force me into taking the Lehman film, then try to sink it?"

"Sink it!"

"I didn't understand until I learned here in Cannes about Deane and Siri Laurence, Deane's interest in the lady going a long way back. Until he was cut out by Pedro Lehman, Deane took a nice slow path to revenge. He set out to ruin Lehman financially, humiliate him as he felt he'd once been humiliated, I suppose. Even if it meant going against the interest of the people he worked for."

Kenrick thought again of Jackie Bolinas, the mobster turned film producer, who died in a motel room for stepping beyond his Mafia brief. He wondered if twenty-four hours from now some mob executioner would climb on a plane for a similar appointment with Nicky Deane or whether it would be a transfer to some organization Siberia. He didn't give a damn.

"You tell that to your friend on the other end of the telephone and see if it's worth a videotape."

Waiting on the veranda, both men were silent while the engine of the helicopter coughed to life. The prop began gathering speed until the sound threatened any further exchange. Arthur raised his voice to make sure he was heard. There was something alive in the old man's brown eyes for the first time. More than a share of men went against their natural inclination in the name of commerce and profit. Kenrick was one of them, he knew now. But not Arthur. He had enjoyed every minute. "A game nicely played, Kenrick. When you're ready to come aboard, we'll haggle out the details."

Arthur extended his hand to seal their agreement.

In the hard clarity of the moment Kenrick recognized the time for what it was: the point that had faced Donner the night of his reading. The time when you took the thing of value you had finally uncovered in yourself and ran with it or hid it away forever.

Arthur was offering him a million-dollar handshake. More for Arthur. A million times forty or twice forty. Maybe Arthur could do it without him, patching here, staving up until he could get out from under. He would try. Kenrick had given him the blueprint.

But the quick paleness beneath Arthur's complexion, as he waited, hand still outstretched, signaled that Arthur didn't think so. He sensed it: He was about to lose.

When Kenrick knew exactly what would follow, its simplicity amused him. When he began to smile, Arthur looked at him curiously, as though he were more than a little mad. When the smile turned into laughter, Kenrick's head tilting upward toward the bright, clear sky, Arthur's voice rose in frustrated rage.

"Don't be a fool, Kenrick. It's here for you, a handshake away, everything you want."

"Arthur, you have nothing I want," Kenrick said, the words feeling clean and right as he spoke them. "Not a damn thing on this earth."

* * *

With the Festival ending, Hugh Remy made a final hike up the long hill to the Anglo-American hospital. His first stop as usual was the young surgeon Broomwitch, who assured him that Siri's progress was exactly as he intended. "You needn't trouble yourself here much longer," the doctor told him.

The room was in semidarkness when Remy pulled a chair close to Siri's bed. He could feel the slow thump of his heart, and he had nearly fortified this visit with a stop at a friendly bar.

Siri stirred from a shallow sleep and said the name Gerold.

"It's Hugh, Siri."

"You sound different. Has something happened?"

"Nothing for the worse." Keep going, Remy boy. He cleared his throat and began, "But I could benefit from a little advice."

"Since when?"

"Since some people asked me to take a crack at directing. Sent me a script of the film Donner wanted to make, along with his production notes and a rough budget. Some careful work."

"Hugh, you must do it. Who had the good sense?"

"Kenrick and a lady named Tate."

"Kenrick wanting to produce. I'd laugh if I could. The last I heard he was on his way to head a new studio."

"That's the way everyone heard it until his press conference a few days back. He was expected to announce this breakaway of his. He announced a new company all right. One to make Donner's picture with this Rayna Tate. The word is he's stepped on a lot of the wrong feet, but I tell you Kenrick is doing a lot of smiling these days. Downright mystifying."

"Wait until they go looking for money."

"They have it. From the Shinn brothers and a German named Dieter Furst. Watching Kenrick and the Tate girl talk about the picture sort of makes you think they'll make a good one."

"They will with you along. You must do it, Hugh."

"Well now, that depends." Don't stop now, Remy told himself. "Siri, I've been talking to Broomwitch. . . ."

"Gerold?"

"You're due for a break before the next operation, and well, summer is coming on. I found a boat, not any measure of the *Pelican*, mind you, but right for coasting along the Med, down to Portofino, Corsica. Broken a couple of commandments, I guess. Getting myself involved with boats made of wood . . . and actresses."

She withdrew her hands gently from his.

"It won't work, Hugh."

"It might, dammit! Get you out of this cell into some air where you can think. Let me teach you to sail, show you what it's like out there on the water. Pedro, Nicky Deane, that life is gone, I promise."

"Hugh, did I kill him? Am I responsible for Pedro's death?" The directness of it caught Remy off guard.

"I think Pedro let his car go over for what in his mind was a good reason. But it wasn't you."

"I lied, Hugh. With Nicky Deane, the time we met in Palm Springs. We ended up in bed because I thought it would be enough. In the hotel suite when we were being held hostage, I went over it again and again. He made photographs, something to use against Pedro, I know he did."

"He tried, Siri. A week or so before Pedro gave up, Deane sent him photos, I guess to destroy the last thing Pedro had left. I snagged 'em first and burned them."

"So you knew all along."

"I know what I'm chancing, Siri. With the both of us."

She was silent a moment, choosing her words. "Gerold said when he finishes, within a year, I'll be ready to work again."

It took a long moment for Remy to face squarely the change in Siri and add it to the special something in the surgeon's voice when he spoke of the operations he intended to perform. He couldn't hold it against her. She always gave the men she chose, and needed, a thing in return. Nicky Deane, Pedro, himself during the brief weeks of the Festival, when she had counted upon him. And in exchange she had forced Remy toward seeing the possibilities in himself beyond the limits he had settled for.

"I'm sorry, Hugh."

He left her then and had reached the hospital courtyard before he decided he was through running hangdog and tail dragging.

He retraced his steps and had neared the door to Siri's room when inside he heard the voice of the surgeon Broomwitch speaking rapidly but too softly for Remy to understand. He could hear only Siri's voice in reply, full of hope and happiness as it reached him in the quiet of the hospital corridor. "Yes, darling, yes," she said. "It will be wonderful."

After that, Remy went down the hill to Cannes, found himself a comfortable working-class bar, and bought himself a whiskey long overdue.

≡ *Chapter 52*—An Ending

The Festival was over. Even as Brialt removed the final items from his desk, he caught sight of James Bond's handsome face on the roof of the Carlton restaurant, a block away, being dismantled panel by panel.

Below on the Croisette, posters and announcements littered the street, scattering the names of the famous and the unknown without favor. The crowds were gone, by all appearances, swallowed by the sea. Inside the Festival Hall temporary walls were falling to what in effect was a crew of wreckers. Everywhere the veneer of luxury given the hall by plush draperies, furniture, and rich wooden paneling was being carted off to storage to await another occasion. The thick red carpet was gone from the foyer, as was the sign over the entrance announcing "Festival du Film."

The one that replaced it gave Brialt reason to frown. In fewer than thirty-six hours the Festival Hall would be the site of a builders' convention.

By an act of will he and his staff had salvaged the Festival's final days. The hostaging, Katherine's part in it, the entire sordid business were more harshly stamped in his mind than the public's. Charpentier struck the heart of it when he observed, what the public hadn't seen they would forget. In Brialt's opinion, they found little real difference between one kind of spectacle and another.

The previous evening the prime minister's wife had flown in from Paris to preside over the Festival's closing gala. The press termed it *"une brillante soirée de cloture"*—kind but decidedly inexact. Twenty-four hours earlier they had been informed that the Lehman film scheduled to premiere that evening had been destroyed in a lab fire in Los Angeles. At the last second they airfreighted in a replacement, the new Billy Wilder picture, generously applauded by the final night's audience.

The president, wooden-faced as ever, assisted in handing out the awards with a dazzling list of international guest stars, who forgot lines, missed marks, and appeared to a nation of television viewers thoroughly confused. The Palme d'Or for best film went to a beautifully photographed Italian epic; the awards for best male and female performances to an American actor and French actress, a balancing that left national prides intact.

He attended the ceremonies with his wife, Monique, dutifully at his side. To her credit she spared Brialt the obvious point of attack: the foolish self-deception of a middle-aged man over a younger woman and the way he had been manipulated to aid the criminals. They were to spend a week or two on Corsica, and doubtless, in some sequestered hotel room they would have their battle. What would be the outcome, he didn't know. What was ahead in another regard was clear, as he told the press that final day.

In the crowded press hall, he let his gaze pass over the faces, his affection for these people unexpectedly strong. More than the police, the press could have killed the Festival but had not. He raised his hand for silence and said, "The date of next year's Festival is the sixteenth of May. I hope to see you all with us again."

A reporter called out the question he knew would come. "There's a rumor you're resigning."

Brialt answered carefully, avoiding the pat phrases that would have sufficed. "I think everyone has a time when he questions the worth of what he is doing. Or doesn't it happen among the press?" They rewarded him with polite laughter. "I'd reached that point, I admit. But I can tell you I am not resigning. I intend to serve this Festival as long as I am able.

We need festivals. Festivals, games, places where people can join together. Here, for two weeks each year, as Cocteau once observed, we have a political no-man's-land, a microcosm of what the world might be if we could, all of us, reach each other directly and speak the same language. We can let no one, criminal, terrorist, government, or the law, prevent our coming together. For if we as individuals give in, those presences will rule. If for no other reason, I declare let there be festivals. Let there be this Festival, grander, more glamorous, bizarre, or however outrageous—but let it exist."

The remarks were printed in that morning's *Nice-Matin* under the headline "Brialt's Declaration of War."

Yet it wasn't the article that caught his attention, but the lifeless face staring up from the newspaper's fourth page. A photograph of an unidentified man found in a shallow ravine near the Anglo-American hospital in Cannes. The police were theorizing that the murder was related to the mob violence flaring along the Riviera, since the man had been stripped of identification and died of a brutally crushed windpipe and neck.

Brialt shook his head. Another death, this one thankfully unrelated to the Festival. A life wasted certainly, for there was purpose in the face. And even glazed by death, the man had the most beautiful, feminine eyes.